Finding
My Muse
in 1968

Also by DH Parsons

Life Ain't Nothin' but a Slow Jazz Dance
Summer, 1966

Not Exactly what I was Expecting:
Fall 1966–Spring 1967

1967 San Francisco:
My Romance With the Summer of Love

Shades of the Past…Shadows of the Future:
Fall 1967

Eat Yoga!

Book of Din

The Diary of Mary Bliss Parsons
Volume 1: The Strong Weet Society

Volume 2: The Lost Revelation

Volume 3: Beyond Infinite Healing

Finding
My Muse
in 1968

by

DH Parsons

Finding My Muse in 1968

Disclaimer

This story is an impressionistic account of people and
events in the life of the author as recorded by him
in 1968. The names of the participants, and certain
specifics of some of the events have been altered for
the preservation of anonymity and exercise of artistic
license. The work is based on journal entries from
the time, and as such, accurately depicts the life and
aspirations of the author.

ISBN: 978-1-948553-22-3
Library of Congress Control Number: 2024911012

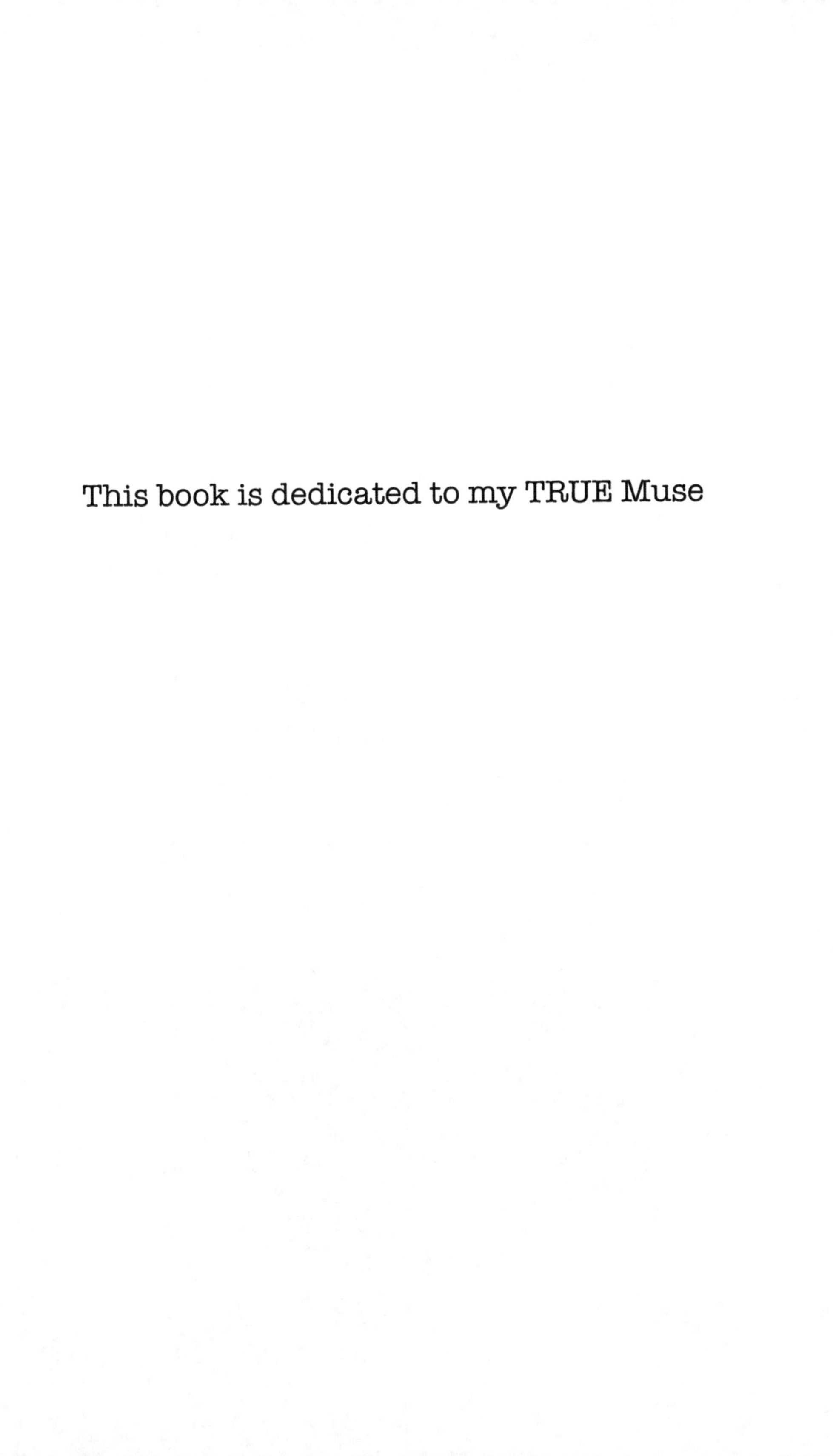

This book is dedicated to my TRUE Muse

A Note from the Author

1968 was a year marked by change, turmoil, and growth on a global scale. Whole societies around the world were awakening to new realities, new identities, and new responsibilities. It was a time of great hope, great possibilities and great uncertainty.

As individuals at that time, many of us stood at the cusp between adolescence and adulthood. The coming changes in the world at large influenced our response to the individual physical, mental, and emotional changes we each experience as we begin to explore adult life. For me, historically and personally, it was a magical period that will never come again.

I began keeping a personal journal sometime around 1966, and continue to do so to the present, making entries almost daily. The Muse spans the events of several months during which my existence coalesced from the vague whims and desires of post adolescence into confident self-awareness as a young man and as an artist. Although taken from the pages of my journal, it is not an autobiography or a memoir; it is a retelling of the interaction between myself and those closest to me at that time—a small group including artists, musicians, and professors; each one being friend, companion, and mentor to myself and to the others.

Names have been changed, and events have been altered for the usual reasons, but for the most part, the experiences in this book are related as recorded in my journal.

It's about 1968. It's about fellowship, and Art, and the Art Spirit. It's about finding one's passion. It's about love found, and love lost, and lost love. It's about dreams, and aspirations, and inspiration. What a time it was.

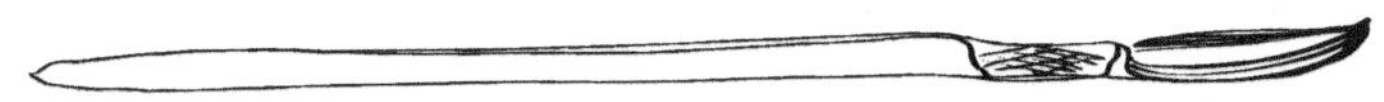

Day 1

My home is a single bed, a clothes closet, a small desk and a sink, all of which occupy the northeast corner of a two-car garage that has been partitioned off to create the tiny apartment I now occupy. I pay only $100 a month because I don't have a kitchen and because the living area is so small, but mainly because it's in my parent's garage. That helps.

The smallness of this room has little effect on me. The only thing that's important is that it's all my own — a virgin room never before lived in. Two of the walls aren't even painted yet, so I've taken the liberty to interrupt their bareness by tacking up black and white photographs of dead artists. A picture of Picasso when he had a beard stares down at me as I write these pages. I use that picture as a dartboard. Pablo has two green darts stuck in his lower lip and a yellow one in his right ear. No disrespect meant to Pablo.

My favorite piece of furniture is my desk which I have anointed with personal necessities: art books, stacks of poetry, hot-plate and coffee pot, tobacco, pipe, and a stack of history books that review the lives of philosophers and artists from the beginning of time to the present. These possessions are all that I am — at least for now. They're my personality, my romance and a piece of whatever future there might be for me.

My desk, along with its contents, represents the script of my life. If I could bundle up its contents and bind it all together, the result would be a journal unto itself, and I would never have to write another word. It would be the honest ramblings of a man who has been created completely out of the lives and experiences of other men who have come before him, placing themselves in his path in an effort to force *him* to copy *them*. Bad copy?

I do as others have done and add little of my own creativity to the world. Even the thoughts that form in my mind today were formed years before in other minds, borrowed from the minds that came before them, and carried to the grave by previous minds under the illusion that they had made an innovative contribution to society. They believed that they had succeeded in manufacturing something out of nothing. Rocks out of air. Buicks out of mountains.

I spend most of my days in this room, with the exception of those that I work at the factory. Three days a week I clean the string filter system at the nearby lemon products factory. My job consists of scrapping large hunks of lemon pulp from the gigantic string-sieve devices that separate the lemon's juice from the lemon itself. If the string filters become clogged, the entire system backs up and the juice of thousands upon thousands of lemons overflows onto the factory's floor.

Since my job is entirely manual labor, I have plenty of time on my hands to think of other things. Mostly I think of what I'll do when I get off work. Where I might go. Who I might meet. I try to think of anything other than the string filters and of the miasma of concentrated lemon juice and oil accumulated over the years and coating every exposed inch of every piece of machinery in the factory.

Like everyone else, I'd rather not have to work for some fat, bossy, boss man, but the job pays the rent, feeds me well, and keeps me comfy-cozy in art supplies. Artist canvas isn't cheap, but I have to have it. Sometimes it doubles as a warm blanket when I come home too tired to sort out the realities of my apartment.

Today was another day at the factory, and it was a total disaster. I fell down the last couple of steps on a stairway and twisted my ankle. I didn't break anything, but the foreman insisted I report the accident to the main office so I could get an x-ray. Company policy. As I limped toward the office I heard a voice behind me.

"Damn! Who the hell is he?"

"I don't know," came the sharp reply. "Some damned newcomer! One of them damned college kids!"

Then the first voice again, "Well, that damned newcomer just broke our 210-day safety record!"

Newcomer! I've worked at that stupid plant for several summers and I'm still only an unknown face in the crowd of good-ole-boy regulars. I don't fit in. They don't even know my first name. It's always, "Hey you!" or "Big bad string filter man! Over here!" The only one that calls me DH is the secretary who hands out the Friday paychecks. To everyone else I'm just some dumb college kid, ignored until needed for something that will benefit somebody's laziness. Admittedly, I have little in common with these men who spend their entire lives feeding on the rough victuals of factory work, country music, and pressed-meat sandwiches. They desire only to do their jobs, tinker with and talk about their cars, watch television, bed their women, and look forward to a time of retirement when they can collect inadequate pension checks and die much too early from the hard effects of factory life—too much alcohol and too many cheap, non-filtered cigarettes. Their dreams are simple. Their fantasies are contained within the slick pages of the wrinkled men's magazines they brag about stealing from barbershops. They have been trained to think only in terms of women, heavy boots, and gear oil, and their gutter language reflects the inner workings of their souls.

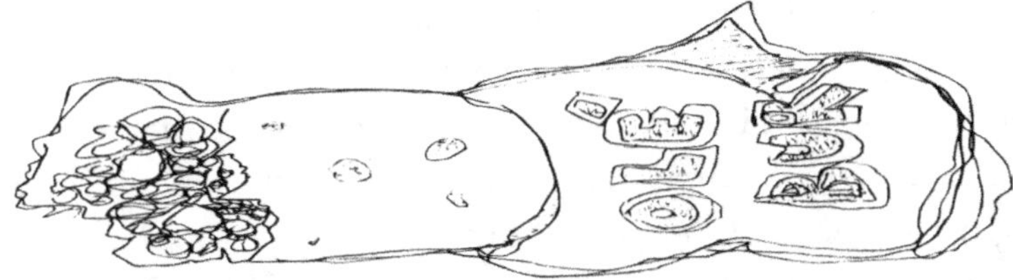

My own dreams rise from somewhere in the middle of Paris in the late nineteenth century. My fantasies are wrapped in the soft, warm arms of beautiful French courtesans, attending famous literary salons with notorious American expatriates, and the consumption of large quantities of Bordeaux in the company of famous writers, painters, and philosophers. Why the heck not? I just don't belong in a lemon factory, eating egg and bean burritos at two o'clock in the morning, and swinging around from station to station via the overhead water pipes. Doing this and that little task. This and that little diversion. Putting aside the exercise of creative thought for at least an eight-hour shift. No comfort for the brain. Mind dead for eight hours straight. No way out. No escape. Not much future.

Since I'm too poor to travel to the South Pacific like Gauguin or Stevenson, I've decided to enroll for another semester at the local community college, Riverside City College—RCC to those of us who love being there. That's another thing I do to keep busy, hang out at the college. I don't study hard. Sometimes I don't study at all. And I never really think seriously about finishing a degree. I just like being around the other artsy hanger-outers that mill around the art and philosophy departments. It's something to do. It doesn't cost much, and the women are attractive—especially outdoors at night under the artificial campus lights.

Later That Evening

I got bored at home, so I drove over to RCC. I'm now sitting in the outdoor cafeteria area. The brethren of my art group call it "The Pit," or "The Concrete Womb," or similar appellations, but most often just "The Pit." It's located at the bottom of a never-ending flight of massive, Greek-styled stairs that take a tall man two strides to cover one step. It is the gathering place for anybody who isn't anybody—the semi-starved art-bums who do nothing all day but guzzle coffee, smoke pipes and ogle women as they climb the stairs rising up out of the Concrete Womb.

It was in The Pit thast semester that I met Frank Reed; the big, fantastic artist that I had seen walking around campus in faded blue jeans and matching jacket, looking as if he owned the world, because he knew that we knew that he had an art show somewhere in Europe. And he was right. We were all impressed with his swagger. We were impressed with everything about him, I more than anyone. I knew there was something more to this man than even what he was attempting to portray. I knew there was a depth to him and that he had the *Kunstwollen*—the driving force of the Art Spirit—hanging like a halo around his head.

Maybe Frank does own the world, or at least a bigger piece of it than I do. He does have this sort of world-owning way of walking; a slow stroll that gets him from one classroom to the next and then down into The Pit, where he transforms the ordinary act of sipping coffee into an exotic, artistic ceremony.

Most of the time, Frank carries an olive drab pack slung over his shoulder. He was in the Marines for a time, and served a few months in Korea during The Conflict. He said that at that time the only things he carried in his backpack were a couple of pairs of dry socks and a "tin or two of English tobacco." Today, here in The Pit, his pack is overflowing with all the latest art journals which he has, no doubt, memorized from cover to cover.

As I write these words, Frank is sitting across the table from me puffing warm grey clouds from his pipe. The tobacco is an English blend, heavy with Latakia. The smoke drifts around The Pit, the intense aroma turning heads at even the farthest tables as if the Pope, himself, was holding audience in this magical place, and the Latakia is the incense for the Mass.

Frank bears a strong resemblance to Mark Twain, and it was difficult for me to take him seriously at first. But I'm growing to respect the incredible volume of information and knowledge he has sucked into his black hole of a mind. He always has a verbal comeback or a tidbit or a quip for any problem or question or topic that might be discussed. His knowledge of art history seems infinite. He knows all the big boy philosophers, and can recite their names in alphabetical order. He knows the chemical compositions of pottery glazes, oil paint and molten bronze. He can distinguish between the various Chinese dynasties by reciting specific details about each one's contribution to the world of art.

Frank Reed's mind is a steel trap set for art-stuff trivia, and his mannerisms more reminiscent of those of a noble Spanish Don than of a Southern California artist.

I'm watching Frank now as he attempts to load his pipe and wave his hands through the air at the same time. He speaks with his hands, sometimes so expressively that you have to be on guard for fear of being hit in the eye. He's conversing with a small group of artists who are on a break between classes, me included. Mostly to me. For some reason Frank has zeroed in on me for a friend. This is a good thing. I don't have a clue where this friendship will lead either of us, but I do know that I will learn much from this man.

Day 2

It's Thursday, and I was called to the factory for a while this afternoon. I don't know why they called me in. The work was unusually light, so my mind began to drift from one thought to another, to anything but factory thoughts. Sometimes the steady hum of the machinery can be soothing, other times, almost majestic like a Dvořák symphony. Symphony Number Nine In E Minor *From The New Factory*, by Me. Sights and sounds of the string filters, the steam lines, the sulphur dioxide gas leaks, and the coughing men; all so soothing in a way because of the familiarity. Because I work here, I suppose. And I relate to those noises and those fumes. A home away from home. Miserable wretched retching home away from home. Lemons upon lemons to smell, and to turn the color of my skin to a yellow-dirt hue. Thoughts of other things — anything — creeping in, filtering through the string filters and into my head. And I'm a single, young guy, so yeah, thoughts of "love" try to push their way in, but they just can't seem to break the lemon barrier.

But who cares about the thoughts of love. This factory has taught me that such a concept can never truly be defined or experienced. It should never even be thought of. I supposed that for so long it was my duty to think about love because I'm a lonely man, and who else but lonely men will think of such things?

Gasping now. Gasping out thick, sickening factory air. But the factory is right. The factory is always right, at this point in my life. Because there is a definition for "factory." It can be defined and, therefore, it exists. All things that can be defined exist. Frank taught me that. All things that exist can be defined, but there has never been an adequate definition for the concept of love. Definitions for love don't work — like a factory worker works or like a dictionary works.

So, I am *factory-fied*. This factory is a part of me. More than rotting fruit, smoke, and moving parts. A mistress. Am I just a factory worker who is trying to be in love with his mistress "the factory," or am I going crazy? I hate this place.

Day 3

I was awakened at 8:00 a.m. this morning, Friday, by Frank, who was on his way to Los Angeles. It seems some big time gallery is interested in his work and wants to see more of it. There's also an exhibit at the L. A. County Museum Of Art (LACMA) he wants me to see with him. I think he gets a kick out of his status with me, master to apprentice, so to speak. But that doesn't bother me.

I told him I'd go with him. The LACMA show is a large exhibit by some guy named Soutine. Never heard of him before, but I'm always open to seeing other artists works. It should be a fun thing.

Two Hours Later

I'm now sitting on a bench in front of a Chaim Soutine landscape at the LACMA. I'm listening to Frank as he lectures me on the subtle nuances of Soutine's technique. And, of course, Frank knows every nuance.

Soutine was a Russian Jew who left Russia because of his great desire to paint. I can't help wanting to identify with him. He felt the romantic pull of Paris, and even though I'm not a Jew and I'm just a tiny bit Russian, I've felt the same pull. Like now. I wish I were in Paris right now, at some sleazy rendezvous in some deep dark cavern of a nightclub, sitting at a bar next to a hard, older woman with cigarette breath and bad makeup. There would be a line of dancing girls straight out of a Toulouse-Lautrec painting, and there would be a really bad American jazz band playing somewhere in the background. The hard older woman would turn to me and invite me up to her room, but I probably wouldn't go for fear of getting mugged. Such is the way my mind works.

Frank has his own art show coming up in October. His mind is occupied with thoughts of his new gallery contract. He's also thinking of the words that flow majestically smooth from his mouth, about the precise way he moves his body when he speaks, and about his appearance—for his show, he's going to wear a three-piece corduroy suit that he said he bought two summers ago in Spain. He has one hand in his pocket and his other hand is gracefully waving about in the air. Everything Frank does is graceful. From the way he sits, to the way his hands move to illustrate every word that he says. Like the conductor of the New York Philharmonic. The effect is hypnotic. I am spellbound.

I had never heard of Soutine before Frank gave me his hundred-dollar lecture on the man. I was genuinely interested in the exhibit because Soutine seemed to epitomize all of the stories—all of the tall tales—that I've ever heard about romantic artists. He was poor. He was a bit insane, at least in the eyes of others. I suppose that was due in part to the excitement he generated within his own mind. He acted out that excitement. He painted from his emotions, and he died an early ulcerous death. A hero among art heroes. A giant, stereotypical, never fulfilled, love-starved, paint-covered maniac, but a complete and undeniable hero. A lonely man. And that seems to be the main quality that makes a great artist great—loneliness. Maybe there's hope for me yet.

Back in Riverside

It's Friday evening, and we're back in town now, at Frank's house, "The Castle," as he likes to call it. I'm reclining in the corner of the living room on the mattress that Frank and his wife, Maxine, use as a couch. I'm writing in this journal while Frank works on a painting in the adjoining room. The entire house has become Frank's studio. I think just about every room serves a different artistic purpose, with the exception of Frank and Maxine's bedroom and the kid's bedrooms. They have two sons, Jules and Mike. Both appear to be bright boys, but Jules seems to be the most like his father, while Mike is a bit more reserved. I'm sure both will do well one day. To have Frank for a father and Maxine for a mother pretty much guarantees success. Maybe not like the world sees success, but perhaps success of a deeper nature.

Over the months I've watched Frank's paintings and drawings grow in size and in number, like a creativity virus, taking over every available space, nook, cranny and corner of his house. When a new space opens up, the virus attacks and eliminates it. I once told Frank that he'd better slow down in his production, at least until he hit the big time, so he could afford a larger place to live. He laughed *The Laugh* that only he could laugh, and replied simply, "Hogwash!"

It's eight p.m. and the boys are off somewhere playing a game. I can hear them growling and making noises like chickens, "Cluck, Cluck". *The Laugh* from Jules sounds just like his dad. The boys stay pretty much out of the way of their father's wild path. I think he might even intimidate them a bit. But I know it's just the way he is and the kids go along with it. It's part of his role; part of who he is.

Maxine is lying on the floor in front of me. I think she's reading a European fashion magazine because the cover is written in French. I've always thought of Maxine as a beautiful woman. She was lovely when I first met her and she is lovely in this quick moment in time. I've learned to expect loveliness from her. It's the one thing that remains constant, and dependable for this little world that I live in. The factory isn't lovely. My apartment isn't lovely. Trees are lovely, rainbows are lovely, and Maxine is lovely. Those large liquid eyes …

"Are you keeping a diary?" Maxine asks as I fumble around on the mattress.

"How did you know?"

"When you turned your page over I saw the word "Friday" written at the top. What's it for?"

"Just something to do." I'm so incredibly shy when she speaks directly to me. She always speaks with a smile that illuminates her diamond-edged, exploding eyes, and I can't look directly back at her.

"Maxine," Frank's voice booms from the other room. "You got some coffee on?"

I'm living in a dream world, I guess. I so painfully desire to find just the right woman to be a part of me. I suppose it's a cultural thing. All of my art friends have girlfriends and I'm the odd man out. Because of that, I'd welcome meeting a girl tonight — any girl walking down a market aisle. I've never really had a real, steady girlfriend, only shadows that came and went before I got to know them. Blank faced women that never meant anything to me. Girls in pink slips. A girl with a blue towel. I can't see their faces now. I can't remember their conversations. Even the first girl I dated in high school, short, fat Catherine. I took her out because she was short and fat and because I was short and fat too at that time. The pretty girls wouldn't go out with me — the blond ones that had to wear bras. Catherine didn't need a bra, so I was able to take her to a school dance where all of the girls sat around staring at the boys or danced with each other. And the boys stood around because they were too afraid to ask the girls to dance. I danced one dance with Catherine, aware of the budding little chest bumps that she tried so desperately to make me aware of. I took her home early and, upon her suggestion, kissed her goodnight. I think she fell in love with me at that moment, but I never dated her again because she almost had a mustache.

Maxine's returning with Frank's coffee, and Frank is yelling from his studio/dining room, "DH! Get your fanny in here!" There's excitement in his voice. He's finished another painting.

"Ain't that a beauty!" he almost screams before I can get to him. "That's REAL ORT!" *The Laugh.*

The painting is a large one. It fills up at least half of the room's dominant wall. It seems far too vacant, too minimal, to be one of Frank's more recent works. The background is painted entirely a deep dark black. The foreground is a rather simple creation of seemingly random-placed flesh colored lines. The design almost looks like a Rorschach representation of a large bird mirroring itself from one side of the canvas to the other. But it's beautiful.

"It's really nice Frank," I say, sputtering out the words.

"Look at that color," he explodes, "The way the pink vibrates on top of the black!"

I don't know what to say. The painting is, indeed, rather exciting, and Frank is just being himself—enthusiastic and filled with that Kunstwollen stuff.

"I'm not just cranking these things out!" Frank is serious now. "These things have deep meaning. Everybody knows that in order for an artist to make it these days, his paintings have to have theories behind them." He rolled the word out into three exaggerated syllables: thee-oh-rees.

"What's the theory behind this one, Frank?" I ask carefully, having ingested a goodly amount of wine.

Frank Laughs. "The theory is that it really doesn't have a theory. But since it looks like it should have a theory, and since those nobodies down there at the gallery already go gaga over my work, I'll sell this thing before the sun goes down!"

Confidence, that's what Frank has. That's one thing I guess I don't have. Maybe that's the major thing that sets him apart from me. He has confidence. And BRAVADO! I love that word. Frank has it.

As usual, Frank is right. He's had much more experience with the galleries than I have, but I've had enough to know how the business works. It's all about money and name recognition. Robert Rauschenberg, one of the leading artists of our time, has been living off his name for a long time now. (I think Frank knows him personally.) All Bobby Boy has to do is spill coffee on a piece of old cardboard, put his signature on it, and the galleries will snap it up. It has nothing to do with art or reality in any way, it's the fame of the name that brings in the money. It's all nonsense, and Frank knows this. I know this! But there is a wagon-load of young artists out there who are all Rauschenberg clones, wanting to do what he does, wanting to make the money he makes. This is obvious to Frank and me, but Frank is so bluntly honest about it. That's one of the things I admire about him. He has the guts to come right out and tell it like it is. I don't think his brain will allow him to be shaped and shifted by the whims of mere culture. He has a one-track mind, and that track always leads to his ability to understand the moment, and to use it to his best advantage. Perhaps that's truly where his brilliance lies. He can move into any crowd, anywhere, and take it over in a minute — captivate it — simply because he knows how to read every emotion in the room.

"I've got so much good luck," Frank mused. "You know, DH, there ain't nothing bad in this world! You just have to hang around long enough, meet the right people, and make them come to depend on you. Then you can sit back and watch everything come flyin' your way."

At first I'm thinking this is some more of Frank's bravado stuff, but at second thought, no — it's honesty. He truly believes this because it really is true.

"All good luck! Then you kick back and do anything you want and sign your name to it." Frank is warming to his theme. "The gallery thinks you're good because they think they made you good! Talent has nothing to do with it any more. They buy you and they own you. They support you. They talked you up at the right kinds of parties and they know that if you look bad, they look bad, so they keep on lining up at the door with dollar-stuffed fists. They'll keep buying your work no matter what it looks like, and they'll talk themselves into believing it's good, whether it is or not. That's why there's so much bad art out there! That's why it's hard for real artists with the real Art Spirit to ever break through the manufactured nonsense. These guys will even make those theories up for you, if you can't come up with them on your own. It's just a circus."

Frank is right. A gallery exhibits only those artists who pay the rent. Frank Reed has made it to that level, but it's been a claw and kick fight all the way. We've had a talk or two about that.

I'm writing all of this while Frank is doing his thing in the studio room. Maxine has fallen asleep on the floor here in the living room. I don't blame her for sleeping. Most of the chitchat that goes back and forth between Frank and me is nonsense fed by the wine, but I'm having the time of my life here. I'm with people that are so much more than what this world commonly produces; one in a makeshift studio painting a painting, and one asleep on the floor in front of me.

I enjoy watching humans. This morning at the museum I enjoyed watching a girl as she glided around the museum hallways, studying the paintings intently, like a fresh little art-girl who had never seen such wonders before, her eyes, taking in every detail as the eyes of the paintings stared back at her. The girl was an absolute delight. No matter what she did, she was a pleasure to watch. In the museum cafeteria I happened to catch her eating some sort of messy sandwich. She let just a little bit of mayonnaise drip out of the corner of her mouth, and I thought how exquisite she looks with the mayonnaise resting there just below her bottom lip. I felt that the entire universe zeroed in on her at that specific moment in time, and I know that the center of the universe lay somewhere within that solitary drop of mayo.

When ever there's an action or movement that's very close to me, and that action catches my eye, I realize that I'm witnessing something that has never before happened anywhere throughout all history. I know that this one particular action takes place only at this one specific spot in time, never again to be repeated. Nowhere else on this globe, or on any other, will mayonnaise drip from a beautiful girl's lip in just the same way that it did from hers.

And then she vanished. I couldn't find the Mayonnaise Girl anywhere! Maybe she's a Muse. Could it be that she's the Muse responsible for my own desire to paint? Could it be she didn't really exist? I mean, not in this dimension. Maybe she popped in for a moment just to let me see what she looks like. And maybe that mayonnaise drip was all a part of the plan just to catch my eye. Heck, I don't know how this art stuff works. Who does? I guess if I did I'd be a millionaire like Rauschenberg, or any of the other art guys that are actually making a living off their stuff. Frank just might be "one of those" one day. I hope so. I know he has the stuff, and I know he has it to the max — especially the one quality that most of the other artists seem to be lacking. He has the Art Spirit. He's a romantic like my buddy Van Gogh, and like me. Frank feels his art from the inside out, and sometimes he can't control what he does or says or thinks, because he has a Muse, too. And let's face it; a Muse is a kind of sickness to have, really. It's like the proverbial monkey on your back. But it's real, and Frank and I both have one. And I don't think they have anything to do with ancient Greek history. No tall Greek women in togas! It's a genetic thing, some sort of brain burp we inherit at birth from an ancestor who had the same burp. Frank's a Norwegian by ancestry, so his burp has that kind of accent. I'm primarily French, Great Britain, Irish, and German, with some Welsh and Italian tossed in the mix, so my burp comes mainly with lutefisk and Guinness. I wonder if the Mayonnaise Girl looks like one of those cute little Celtic dancers when she goes back to her dimension? Wow, I just remembered, did she have reddish hair? I think she did! That's the only confirmation I need! She has to be my Muse.

A yell from Frank in the other room pulls my attention away from my journal writing.

There he goes again. "Look at this, DH!"

"I'll bring my wine," I yell back.

As I enter the studio, I'm confronted by a painting of the face of a woman—I think it's a woman—that looks like she's kind of melting all over the place in yellow, red, and pink. It is exquisite. Frank is beaming like a kid at Christmas.

"You like it!" He doesn't ask, he commands.

"Yeah. I like it." There is no other answer. Every piece of art that Frank turns out is good.

You know, I've thought a lot about who are the most influential artists in my life, and here's the truth: I think Soutine will be a huge influence on my work now that I've seen him. Van Gogh has always been an influence, but only his wild spirit and not that my painting style mimics his. What I'd like to say right now is that I wish Frank could be a big influence in my work as well, but it's just impossible. Anyone can copy Van Gogh. Soutine is a bit harder. But Frank Reed is impossible! When I first began to hang around Frank I attempted to mimic his style. It just can't be done. That's what separates a great artist from a simple wannabe. I know Frank's got all the art business junk spinning in his head at a hundred miles an hour every minute of every day, and I know he wants to make it big and sell his work for bunches of cash, but I also know he's a consistent artist with an incredible talent, the likes of which the art world has never seen. Yes, other painters have influenced him, but he always breaks away from that. He has something deep inside of him that forces itself out onto his canvas. It's his Muse! But his Muse keeps him honest at his work, and she makes him create and be truly original, and that's what sets him apart from all the little Mall Show artists out there, and all the little college kids who think they're born again Picassos or whatever.

Frank's pontificating again—something about Gauguin on a boat in summer. Where does he get this stuff? He's memorized the entire universe. He stores everything up. He knows everything. I know I sound like some little kid worshiping a big time artist, but that's not it. Frank really does know.

I think it's his nose. That's why he knows so much. He sucks it up through his nose. His nostrils are two sizes too big. He breathes more air than I do and he's ten years older so he's sucked up three times as much air as I have and for ten years longer. Does this make any sense? It does to me. Irish guys have smaller noses than Norwegians I guess, but since I'm part Norwegian there is still hope for me.

"Are you going to start another painting tonight?" asks Maxine. She's awake now, and a bit groggy.

"Not tonight," Frank replies. "I think I'll finish this little bit of wine and go to bed." Then he gets all smiles and excited. "Big day mañana, Pardner!" he says, turning to me.

"Oh?" I ask.

"Yeah. I gotta go back to LA. The gallery wants to see more stuff."

"Cool," I reply.

And that's pretty much the end of this night. Frank is kind of like the Pope. When he says it's over, it's over. Or was that Yogi Berra? But I'll bet when the Pope says it's over, he trumps Yogi.

Day 9: Thursday Morning

Home. Ran out of money. No money for food. I tore the mold off a hunk of Italian bread that I've been saving for who knows how long, and ate the bread. My cheese was too far gone. It used to be a two-pound block of Canadian Black Diamond. I think it's supposed to be some kind of white cheddar but I'm not sure. What I do know is that it's really good and it goes great with wine. But my wine is spoiled, too. It's a burgundy that I'd left the cap off for a day or two. Horrible memories are coming through here. The last time I drank a bottle of bad burgundy, I was unable to straighten up for a week. It bent me over double. Bad stuff. C'est la vie — I'm only 19, so I shouldn't be drinking this stuff anyway, but many of my older friends bring it when they visit, so, what's an artist to do?

I'm alone in my room. It's quiet except for a dog barking in the distance. There are too many dogs too close to where my window opens up to the outside world. It makes sleeping difficult.

My desk seems a bit trashy today. The books are open to where I left them last Friday night, and there are ashes from pipe tobacco smeared on the pages of one of the books and a tiny cinder has left a brown charred circle three pages deep. One of the pages reads: "Eugene Delacroix" but the first "E" and half of the "u" in Eugene are burned away. "Delacroix … famous for his celestial lighting effects." What the heck are celestial lighting effects? "Notice how the suns rays burst through the clouds to illuminate the principle figure's face." That must be what it means.

Rossetti! Here's a photograph of Christina Rossetti. What an exotic looking woman. Pretty. Only two of her poems are in this book. Both are about death and romance. Since I'm a bit fascinated by both death and romance, I'm enchanted by Christina's poetry. Her lovers always seem to win through the act of dying. In life they are tormented. In death they are victorious. Always. Death is always portrayed in poetry as the ultimate romantic statement. What kind of deal is that?

I painted my first painting of the Mayonnaise Girl today—my Muse. I painted her leaning on a garbage can. I don't know why. I guess it's because at the museum she was sitting next to a garbage can and it seemed to fit. Nothing else seems to fit in this world any more, but that did. And I've manufactured a darned good likeness! I hung the portrait on the wall at the end of my bed so I can open my eyes to her pretty face every morning.

I've named my Muse, Ann. I don't know why. That name just came to me in the night. Literally. Last night I had a dream and golden letters that looked like ANN appeared on a black background. I just felt inside that it was the Mayo Muse attempting to contact me. Of course I would rather have her appear to me right here in my room, but that never seems to happen except in the movies. There must be some sort of rule about that from dimension to dimension. Regardless, Ann is more and more in my thoughts, and I'm even seeing her clearly in my mind in the daytime too. Hallucinating. She's in the skies painted by Dali, popping out of the clouds, frightening me, and at the same time bidding me to come to her. I've read the Greek myth of Pygmalion a dozen times, and now I'm praying daily that my painting of the Mayo Muse comes to life, and all of the sketches I've made of her—all of them at once, dozens of colors and blacks and whites—choke me and take away the pain of not knowing who this Muse is. Kill me Ann! I'm even starting to write love poems to her. Christina Rossetti where are you? And I'm dying anyway. I'm diseased by you Ann. I'm drinking too much cheap wine and letting this pathetic body of mine run its course too quick and too soon. My room has become a shrine to you sweet Ann. A temple. A church. I've become some sort of romantic priest who lights incense and candles to his Goddess. Kissing holy books of poetry and offering sacrifices of prayers and half finished paintings to my Saint Ann, who is radiant and fathomless. Infinite. Pure. Innocent. Mischievous and spirited and impossible to look at.

Day 10: Friday Night

Another Friday night, and Jack is here at my place. He's brought me five gallons of Red Mountain. He told me I should store some of it in my closet for a rainy day. Jack is a special friend; I drink wine with him, and he likes to suffer with me because I'm single and he's not.

"To suffer is the height of joy!" he told me. "To be single is to enjoy the freedom of time. When you put time and joy and suffering together, it always makes for a good party! And married men have none of the above. Their wives won't let them."

I can talk to Jack about my Muse. Because we're both just a little bit loony, he and I can enjoy the depression of the conversation.

The first time I ever saw Jack he was standing by a shade tree at the college. He was holding a Mexican Delicado cigarette, which was lit but never inhaled. He liked to hold a lit cigarette simply for the effect he thought it had on the girls because he looked a lot like a young Marlon Brando. I wanted to know him, and I felt I could trust him. Fast forward two years later and we're friends who share the deep thoughts of our shallow existence in a superficial society and who have no credibility with that society because all we ever do is drink wine and make art all night.

"Art and women can't be separated," Jack is telling me now. "Therefore, if a man is to be an artist—a true artist—he must also be a womanist. Not a womanizer! Womanizer doesn't rhyme with artist! If a man wishes to make art his life, he must also make women his life, and not necessarily in that order."

Jack knows as well as I do that the women who would have us at this time in our careers, which is to say no careers, wouldn't be worth having. "Prodigal Part-Time Hussies," Jack calls them. Like the ones hanging around the Stage One Theater downtown. The Stage One shows the latest European art films as they come out of LA. Jack and I have spent many a night there, but most of the movies are a bit predictable for my taste, and so "hip, in and groovy," that many of them are down right corny. But, in this town, it's another thing to do to kill time.

Jack is holding up a piece of soiled notebook paper. "Here's the answer to all our problems!" he declares.

"I didn't know we had any."

"Look around you, DH, we don't have any women. If we don't have any women, we got us at least one serious problem!"

The paper he's holding is some sort of hand drawn street map that was given to him by an old girlfriend who said it would get us to the "hottest little red-light district in LA." Jack told me his ex-girlfriend could be trusted because she was a "wanton woman" and wanton women can always be trusted if you get to know them on a personal basis.

But I was apprehensive about soiled notebook paper maps to red-light districts, and evenings with women who never took the time to know a man's first name. I didn't want to go. My mind was racing through foreign movie scenes with dimly lit rooms and gaudy flowered wallpaper and crooked brass beds; pale-thin-diseased women who reeked of cheap perfume and layers of cigarette smoke. I could see myself going in and never coming out. Fear. But in the end Jack talked me into driving the two of us over to LA. in my VW. I told him I wasn't really interested in red-light districts, but it would be a good thing to get out of Riverside for a few hours. Maybe we could guzzle a pot or two of dark coffee at Tiny Naylor's in the middle of our adventure.

Two Hours Later

We are parked on a dimly lit street in Beverly Hills. Jack made me pull over "so I can at least look at this map." But fears of sick, wanton women and murderous pimps were all in vain. The map is inaccurate, and the only red lights we see are the occasional taillights of a passing Mercedes. We seem to be on the edge of Beverly Hills. A very inaccurate map, I would say.

"Isn't that Dean Martin's house over there?" I ask.

"Oops."
"We've been here before Jack. This isn't a red light district."
"I thought that gated driveway looked familiar."
"Dean Martin! I love that guy," I said.

Day 11: Saturday Morning

Jack is driving my Volkswagen. I love that word—it sounds so very German. We're on our way back to Riverside now. We didn't sleep last night. Drove around a little bit looking for the end of the rainbow, then parked again by the beach to watch the sun come up. We stopped at Tiny Naylor's on Wilshire Boulevard; it was too early for the art museum. While sipping some strong coffee, Jack finally asked me what I was writing in my notebook.

"I'm keeping a journal," I replied.

"I tried that once. It lasted about two weeks."

"You're too nervous to keep a journal," I said.

"Just be careful not to be too honest with it."

"If it isn't honest, why bother?" I asked.

"Because you want somebody to read the stupid thing!" Jack replied. "The whole point of a journal is the secret hope that somebody will pick it up one day and read it. That's the subconscious desire of anyone who takes the time to bleed their guts out, on the pages of some boring, personal diary. I mean, if you don't want it to be read, why write it down! Why not just go lock yourself up in a closet and talk to yourself?"

I love the way Jack turns things over in his head, even though sometimes I have no idea what he is saying. But this time I knew he was right. I've often toyed with the idea of letting Jack "accidentally" stumble upon my journal some night when we'd been imbibing a bit too much. I guess I really do want him to read it, even though he already knows most of the story. But even from Jack there are a lot of things I've kept hidden.

I grasp for something to say. "I don't want to repeat my life."

"But a man can't be anything more than the sum total of all his experiences," Jack responds. "The way he dresses. The way he thinks. The car he drives. The way he writes in a journal. It's all been done before anyway."

He sounds just like Frank.

"And that's my point," I snap back. "I don't want to do what I've already done before. I don't want to repeat what others have done. I don't want to be a look-alike."

"What do you want? You're an artist! The look-alikes don't know one end of a brush from the other."

"What good is that," I reply, still full of angst. "What good is it to sit around all day on your butt painting flowers and trees and pretty girls? Maybe I should just be a teacher."

"With all of those gorgeous girlie-students runnin' around?" He laughs.

"For cryin' out loud, Jack, I'm serious. What the heck are we doing with ourselves? We're not selling paintings. We're just occupying space."

"So what? Is it that important to sell what we paint?"

"Well … if we sell paintings we don't have to work for other people. And it makes some sort of statement about the validity of our profession."

"What if nobody buys them?"

"That just means they don't like 'em."

"Or understand them," he added wryly.

"That's a cliché. Paintings don't have to be understood to be enjoyed."

Paintings, decorator items, pretty pictures on a wall. Bright greasy colors smeared on an old rag, as Frank would say. Looks good over the couch. Or a recorded image of Aunt Martha's face preserved for time and all eternity in the hallway next to a coat rack and a potted plant.

Saturday Evening

I'm sitting on the floor in Jack's apartment, which is bigger than mine because he lives with his girlfriend, Lisa, who has a steady job as a secretary. Jack drives a truck for a bakery and makes a good enough wage to share the rent with Lisa and to keep him supplied with what he calls the "three necessities of life as we know them to be on the planet earth: women, wine and art supplies." Spaghetti comes in at a close forth.

Jack is looking for a piece of wax or clay to make a sculpture. He's throwing books and pillows around the room, breaking pottery that he knocks off the bookcases because he's too drunk to be coordinated. I don't think I've ever seen Jack coordinated.

"Catch!" he yells.

He throws me a piece of clay. I feel the texture of the water and the dust slam into my hands. THE WATER AND THE DUST. On my fingers. The clay is alive. A part of the original creation. Something from out of nothing. Not even air. As close as I can come to true creativity. Touching raw earth. Mud. Admiring that which was created by Whoever or Whatever created artists.

"What do you think about a naked woman sitting in a straight-backed chair?" Jack asks out of nowhere.

"If you've got her hidden away around here somewhere, bring her out."

"I mean a life-sized bronze sculpture with all the trimmings."

"Sounds expensive."

"Yeah, but what a project! Think about it. The smooth cold metal skin of the most beautiful woman in the world. Closed eyes. Pouting mouth. Long muscular legs like you see on those exercise shows on TV. I could place her right in the middle of the room and I could tiptoe around her all day long and spill wine on her and tickle her tummy with a feather duster if I wanted to. Man, what an inspiration!"

Day 12: Sunday at Noon

I've just gotten out of bed to plug in the coffee pot. My eyes are open but they aren't doing what eyes are supposed to do. I didn't come home as early as I thought I would last night. Jack wasn't as drunk as I thought he was, but he was getting crazy, so I wanted to get out of there. Just as I started to open the door to leave, he began to jump up and down on the furniture yelling something like, "The night is young! Long live the night!" And his girlfriend, Lisa, came out of the bedroom and ordered us both to "Get the hell out."

When the night air hit our faces out in the alley—because Jack's door opens into an alley—it brought us back to some sense of awareness that we were still human beings and that we could still form words and guttural sounds with our mouths. We could also place one foot in front of the other in a rather primordial attempt to give the appearance of walking. I was even capable of driving, so I took Jack with me to a local coffee shop where we ran into a friend who told us about a party up on Palm Tree Hill. Not being very sound of mind at the time, we never even considered that not only is Palm Tree Hill one of the wealthiest areas in town, and that any party held on Palm Tree Hill was sure to be a rather formal affair, but the likes of Jack and I would never be invited to such a party. We only considered the fact that it was still relatively early in the evening for us and there was a wide world of women somewhere out there to conquer. And, yep, we were still able to bring another glass of wine all the way up from anyone's table to our awaiting mouths. So, we weaved our way back to the VW, and unintentionally began to play Russian roulette with the other cars on the highway, as we drove ourselves to a party we were not invited to.

The party was given in a Roman-styled mansion with scores of rooms connected by hallways that went off in several directions, and a kitchen that appeared to us as being wall-to-wall Jamaican rum. Since we were basically uninvited, Jack and I decided that the best thing for us to do was to sneak in through the back door, grab a couple of whatever there was to drink, and try to slip into the main body of the party as nonchalantly as possible.

The plan worked beautifully until I discovered that mixing red wine and Jamaican rum was not a good idea. I didn't make it all the way to any one of the seven bathrooms before throwing up on one of the sofas in the living room.

It was the first time I'd ever thrown up in public. I wanted to leave, but Jack kept muttering something under his breath like, "I'm hungry for the flesh of a passion-starved woman …" He was asking every girl at the party to kiss him.

The girls were all perfection on the outside. Young sorority type women with flawless Breck Girl faces, and perfect blonde hair falling down over perfect pink shoulders. "They look like a bunch of bloody bridesmaids!" Jack mumbled a bit incoherently to one of the male counterparts who luckily didn't understand what he said.

Jack was in heaven. He watched as the girls sipped slowly at their drinks while holding little crackers in their hands but never taking a bite. The way they sat down, primly, knees together, their short, blue, sorority girl dresses inching up toward the top of their legs …

It was all too much for Jack. The good times ended abruptly for us both when he "accidentally" spilled a glass of rum onto the lap of one of the young blue-blooded ladies, and then proceeded to dry it off slowly with his shirt that he had ceremoniously ripped off his body, à la Errol Flynn.

But what he had intended as gallant gesture was not interpreted that way by the girl, who screamed loudly and started to run away from him. Her boyfriend then appeared out of nowhere with several other big bruiser, blue-blazered fraternity boys, who proceeded to chase us through the house as we hurdled over chairs and tables and bolted through numerous doors to find our way to the car.

As we pulled out of the driveway and sped off down the hill, I was reminded of the scene from the old black-and-white Frankenstein movie, where all of the town's people go crazy, running up and down the streets and the mountains carrying torches and clubs trying to get at the "monster," because that was exactly what was happening with us. We were the "monster," and about a zillion torch-carrying frat boys were coming at us like a lynch mob. As I careened down the driveway, we could hear the ungodly wailing of a dozen or more blue-dressed hens cackling and crying and carrying on. It was a freak show; a soap opera gone bad. We were lucky to be alive!

But that's not the end of the story. I had jumped into the car, but Jack didn't quite make it all the way, so he made an incredible, though not very graceful leap, up onto the rear bumper, clinging to the back of the car as I sped away, hoping against hope that he wouldn't fall off and be killed on the highway.

We outran the frats, and at the bottom of the hill I pulled to a rather abrupt stop. In the rear view mirror I saw Jack hurtle forward, to reappear on the front hood.

"You okay?"

"Wow!" he gasped. "That was fun. Like a ride at Disneyland!"

I broke down laughing.

Day 13: Monday

Riverside City College bought one of my paintings today in a purchase-prize exhibition, "Old Man With Flowers." Not a very creative title, but that's what the painting was about. The face of the old man looked like Picasso's face. I thought about painting Frank's face in there just to do him the honor, but it didn't work. The problem was that the canvas was too small — 18 inches by 24 inches — and Frank's head just didn't look right. Picasso was pretty much bald, so his head took up less space. Frank has this incredible hair that makes a statement all by itself and fills up a whole hunk of canvas. So Picasso won out on this deal. But one day I will paint Frank's portrait.

Anyway, one of the professors told me that my painting was one of the most sensitive paintings the college has ever purchased. I tried to get him to elaborate on what he meant, but that was a mistake. He started giving me an art history lecture and I couldn't get him to shut up. I never did find out what he meant by the word "sensitive." He just kept rambling and ended up talking mostly about himself.

I also entered some other paintings and a small sculpture cast in lead. The little sculpture brought me a second place ribbon and twenty-five dollars. I was told that it was the first lead-cast sculpture to ever be exhibited by Riverside City College. Frank was there at the exhibit. When he saw that I'd picked up second place he patted me on the back and said, "Good job, DH! But you have to get beyond this stuff. You can't live on twenty-five bucks a shot." As usual, he is right. I'm just glad that he didn't notice that I had molded the face on the sculpture into the likeness of Maxine.

Day 14: Tuesday

I saw Bill Mitchkelly today. Bill is one of the finest men I know at this time in my life. Everyone needs a Bill Mitchkelly. Everyone needs a stable, honest, hard-working, down-to-earth figure in their life. Bill is mine. He's the ceramics and sculpture teacher at the college, but he's really more than that. He's become a good friend to me.

Bill is a fragile looking man, with pale white skin, bushy black eyebrows, and the kindest looking face anyone could ever hope to encounter. A Jimmy Stewart kind of guy who gave up smoking cigarettes several years ago but still shoves an occasional piece of chalk into his mouth as a substitute out of habit.

I remember the night we had a raku party at the college. Everyone was there, even Frank. And, come to think of it—Holy cow, my Muse was there, the Mayo Girl, I'm sure of it. Ann, I know I saw her—it's just now hitting me—she was there! I was standing very close to the raku kiln, which was very, very hot. It was dark outside and we were all drinking wine. As I looked over to the left, toward the bougainvillea that covered the wall, I saw a face. It was her! I just saw the face and nothing else, glowing softly out of the darkness at the edge of the party. She was eating some popcorn that we had cooked up over the kiln earlier, and ... Yes! I saw a small drip of saliva coming out of her mouth, glistening in the moonlight. Her spit was in the same place as the mayo back at the museum! But that isn't the weird part. The weird part is that she made the same gesture with the spit that she did with the mayo. Then she looked right at me and winked.

It was Ann! How strange is all of this? Who is this girl flipping in and out of dimensions at will? I think I'm starting to memorize her features now. Her hair is a deep reddish brown, put up in some sort of fashion in the back, maybe even a ponytail. Her hazel eyes. And those lips! Lips that only Dante Gabrielle Rossetti could paint. Something out of the 1800s.

That's it! That's why I know this is my Muse. She just doesn't fit into this current time or setting. She stands out like a lovely sore thumb. Always in the shadows, always alone, always something dripping from that precious lip. And always making the same gesture to wipe it off. She is magic! But of what kind?

But back to Bill Mitchkelly; that night really belonged to him. Bill talked art, he demonstrated art, and he made art. Every piece of raku pottery that came out of the kiln was perfect. Every piece was beautiful. And while so many of us were struggling to get the technique up to even its basic lower level of competence, most of us failed miserably. But Bill created one masterpiece after another. Even Frank was quiet and respectful as he watched Bill work his magic.

Earlier today Bill and I had chitchatted in The Pit for a while. Bill looked squarely into my eyes and said, "You know, DH, I think you're really going to amount to something one of these days." But this afternoon as I remember back to the raku party and my sighting of Ann, I have to wonder if I ever will. In order to be able to "amount to something" in this world, a person needs to be able to focus on a dream for the future. My dreams appear to be not of the future, but of some other dimension or an altered state of reality. How can a man ever amount to anything if the things he dreams about don't exist?

Day 15: Wednesday Evening

Red bench … green trees … palms … rising up in the almost night sky. The scene reminds me of the night I arrived by train into the state of California from my childhood home in Oklahoma back in 1958. Just before the trip I had been rushed to the hospital, sick as a dog with double pneumonia. In fact, while I was lying in a hospital bed going in and out of consciousness with a fever of 103, I apparently died for a while, before the doctors were able to stabilize my temperature.

After I rejoined the living, I remembered seeing an incredibly bright light, an angel, and a saint. Later my mother told me that much of that time I was in the hospital I was not aware of being there. During my "out times" I talked to a woman who was not there. To this day I have the memory of the woman I thought I met in my hospital room. She had red hair and a pretty voice that sounded like Glenda the Good Witch from the Wizard Of Oz. My Mother told me that no such woman was ever there in the room with me, but she did hear me talking to a woman who was not there.

I was still sick beyond sick when my family rolled into the San Bernardino train station back in 1958. My dad, who was and still is (believe it or not) a rocket scientist—actually, more of an aeronautics engineer—had come to California earlier and bought a house for the rest of us in a little village called Mira Loma. It was because I was so sick that my mother brought my brother, Jim, and me along later on the train. The doctor would not release me.

I was seated on my mother's lap in the observation car, wrapped up in a blanket when the train rolled into San Berdoo at dusk. I saw the palm trees silhouetted against the twilit California sky, and man-oh-man I was in Heaven. To be honest, I suppose I really was near Heaven because I still couldn't breathe very well after the pneumonia. Every breath I took was labored, but when I saw those palm trees it took away what breath I had left. What a site that was! I was a little kid rollin' into a real life City of Oz. The Kansas Kid! That would be me because, like Dorothy, I was born in Kansas, and I expected to see Dorothy and her puppy, Toto, dropping down out of a whirlwind at any moment.

But they didn't, and I just slid silently into San Bernardino. As we got off the train a lady came over, smiled at me, pinched my sick little cheek, and said, "Poor little boy." Then she turned away and walked over to a bunch of people who were waiting for her, and cameras were flashing. When she got to where all the cameras were, she looked back at me and blew me a kiss. My mother told me later that it was Lucille Ball. I didn't have any idea who that was at the time, but when she told me I Love Lucy! I was thrilled! The sick kid with his momma and brother, experiencing Hollywood-type stuff for the first time. Talk about a dream!

Back to real life. Who would have thought at the time that I would grow up to know Frank Reed? I'd rather know him than all the movie stars in Hollywood. Well, maybe not all of the movie stars.

Who would have known then that I would become an artist myself? I had no idea what I wanted to do with my life. I was just a little kid. Who I will meet along the way to the future, and what friendships will result from those meetings? Even now, I'm not sure I have what could be called "friends." I'm too young to have true friends—I think those come with age. But a few beings in this world do stand out from the others as I write this journal entry. Number one, of course, would be Frank. Not because he and I are really close, in that we hang together all the time, because we aren't and we don't, but because he always includes me in at least a part of his busy life. Whenever he has an art show in Riverside, I always get an invite. He doesn't have to do that. I'm just a nothing kind of nobody in his world, but Frank treats me as if I were someone special.

In the end, who knows? I'm not sure how anything is going to turn out. Frank is, indeed, something special, but I'm not sure what he will do with his life and I'm not sure what I will do with mine. I am convinced that we are equals in many respects, and I don't discount the possibility that Frank and I will go in different directions as time passes. Maybe we'll both "amount to something," as Bill Mitchkelly says. It's a good thought. I like it.

Day 16: Thursday Morning

Back in The Pit at the college. Brilliant white clouds blind me as they puff up into giant popcorn thingies over my head. I am fascinated by their simple reflections in my tea. There goes a duck! The duck changes into the profile of a woman; I like that better than the duck. The woman becomes a buffalo. That's interesting. The buffalo changes into something that looks a bit like the USS Enterprise from *Star Trek*.

The Pit people are coming out of the shade and are forcing themselves into my brain. How alive they appear to me. The activity and the conversation. The colors and the clothing. The movement. I'd forgotten about these folks for a while — the thirty odd people sitting at tables all around me — and now I can hear their heartbeats. I can see the luminous dials on their wristwatches that aren't lit up. The women are cold and happy, and the men are sucking cigarettes. Living coffee. Living books. Breathing. The breathing of the people is in synch with the billowing clouds.

I have very few memories of myself as a child in Kansas. I left there when I was around a year and half old, so what kid that age would have any memories at all? But believe it or not, I do have a couple of memories — the clouds, the wheat fields. I swear I remember those sights. I have only a few family photographs of those times, and in most of them I'm just a toddler in some sort of toddler swing contraption that doesn't look very comfortable. But I must have been happy because there's a smile on my face in every photo.

In all those photos my mother took of me, there were big billowing clouds up in the sky. I believe now that I used to stare up at those clouds for hours when I was allowed to. I believe I felt I was looking through the clouds into the deep space beyond. My father once told me that I was no Earthly good because my head was always somewhere "out there." He would point up at the night sky when he said it. "If you want to grow up and be somebody, DH, you're gonna have to pull your head down out of the clouds. Either that, or become a spaceman and leave them all behind."

Back in Kansas, while my mother was in labor with my little baby body, she had several rather serious complications and needed a blood transfusion. The only folks in town who responded to her needs were a family of people from the Italian community there in Winfield. Their name started with a "B" and it took a little trouble to find out what the name of the family was, but when I did, it didn't mean much to me, until I mentioned the name to Jack.

"You gotta be kidding!" he told me. "That's a very prominent American Mafia family! It might not be a good idea to write that name in that little book of yours, DH."

Jack told me that everybody in America would recognize the name. "You've got their blood flowing in your veins! Technically, you're a part of their family now!"

The point being, that I have some rather notorious Italian blood flowing through my veins, but I love it. And when I tell people this blond, hazel eyed, pale pink boy is Italian, they just can't wrap their heads around it. But it's true, and at this point in my young life I don't know much about my extended Irish/French family roots, and very little about my Italian sort-of-family. I would be delighted if any of them would accept me into the fold. Even the notorious ones.

Hmm … I wonder if they ski in Sicily.

Day 17: Friday Morning

Frank awakened me at seven this morning on his way to the art school at Claremont College. He's been invited to take some sort of a test to determine whether or not he will be granted a four-year degree in Fine Arts two years early. Even though Frank looks old enough to pass for forty, he's only thirty-three. But he has the idea that his age combined with his European travels and all of his other worldly experiences should be credentials enough for some sort of college degree. Seems logical to me, and apparently the college feels the same way. If he passes the battery of tests they have prepared for him, he will automatically be granted a Bachelor of Arts degree. That would mean it's only a matter of time before some college or university offers Frank a teaching position with their painting department, and that would be the smartest thing they ever did.

It has nothing to do with Frank's personality and how incredibly verbose he can be at times. It has to do with the fact that he's talented at what he does. What the heck is a BA? What the heck is a teaching job? It's just the right thing to do in order to recognize Frank for being what he is: an artist in league with all the other great artists who have ever lived. He has it all. There is nothing missing. I once sat across a café table from Frank while he ate a piece of apple pie and sipped on a cup of coffee that never seemed to run out because the waitresses were so entranced by him. I will never forget what he said to me as he ate that pie.

"DH, everything can be labeled art. Absolutely every thing is considered a form of art. This pie is art and your shirt is art. Toasters are art. But what makes every one of these common things special is the spirit of the artist who designed them. Is he real or is he a fake? Is he a maniac or is he a saint? If an artist doesn't live his art—I mean truly live it—then whatever product he produces, toaster or painting, just isn't art." That makes sense.

Then he said something that really surprised me, "Art is running out. There aren't too many real artists out there any more. Van Gogh may have been the last. Not just because of his paintings but also because of WHO HE WAS.

"He was a genius, but only a few, in predictable circles, recognize that. The world just thinks he painted purty pictures! Ha! He had a spirit. I have that too, and I ain't braggin' about it even though I should. And oh yeah, I think you do too, DH. You know, I have a lot of art friends, but you're the only one I feel like I can let my hair down with. I may be brutally honest about a lot of things to just about everybody I meet, but I tell you things I don't tell anyone else. And I'm not so sure why I do that! Ha! You ain't that special!" Then he added, "Just slap me when I do that."

Day 18: Saturday

The Claremont trip was relatively uneventful. I spent most of my time waiting in various places around the campus waiting for Frank to rush in and out of six or seven different offices. He was trying to tie up any loose ends that might hang in the way of the awarding of his degree.

The highlight of my day was the dozens of little gardens hidden all over the college campus. It was actually rather pleasant just sitting around doing nothing in a locale other than my room back in Riverside. Before the day was over I had nursed down several cups of coffee, filled a sketchpad with drawings of the incredible foliage that surrounded me wherever I sat, and taken particular note of the bevy of beautiful women parading by me during their class breaks, every one of them ignoring my existence.

Speed forward to real time. Now I find myself back in my room, alone. I appear to have caught some sort of virus or bacteria or whatever. I feel like the walls are pressing in on my outer flesh, making me feel heavier than usual, and more sensitive to the presence of sounds outside my window, and to the lack of sounds within my room. It might just be the can of beer I drank that I opened three days ago and left sitting in the fridge. It tasted kind of strange.

I can't get Frank out of my mind. He's a kick in the pants. Even though I spent most of the day at Claremont by myself, interacting with him between his sessions was fun. Watching him run around in and out of the buildings like an excited child made me laugh more than a few times. Frank always makes me laugh. Although he has the greatest sense of humor I have ever experienced in another person, he can be very serious at times. But his outlook on life is accurate and he makes fun of it more than he worries about it. That Laugh of his—I must have heard it a hundred times at Claremont. Even though he was facing a stressful situation he was able to have fun with it.

"Man, DH, these guys don't have a clue," he exclaimed between a couple of meetings yesterday. "I don't need their lowbrow degree. I have more knowledge from my life experiences than half the people on this staff."

I have no doubt that he was right. I don't know that many brilliant college professors myself. I do know they profess to be brilliant but they really aren't. Most have a one-track mind, and it leads to and from their own ego. Maybe that's why they're called "professors," because they profess to be something they aren't. I know I'm generalizing here, and there are tons of decent professors out there, but I've met only about a half pound of them in my circle.

Once during the morning, he came out of one office, sat down next to me, grabbed my coffee cup, drank it all down in one gulp, and wiped his mouth.

"HAAAAAHHHHHHH. Thanks, I needed that!" Then he was off to the next office.

That was fun. That made me laugh. That's the real Frank, his character, and there is more to him than meets the eye. He deserves every one of the accolades he is given.

If anyone was ever a dedicated and determined artist, it's Frank. I think the reason is simply because he's always known he has the talent. I think from birth, Frank probably knew he was something different and more special than all the rest of the human clones walking around out there. He was right. Frank is different. He is special. I've known about 247,923 people in my life and several are artists, and I have never known anyone like Frank Reed. That has to be because he's not like anybody else. Whether or not he ever makes it to the big time, like all the other famous dudes running around out there, is totally irrelevant. Van Gogh never made it either. But now look at poor Vincent! There isn't a person on earth who doesn't know his name. That may be Frank's fate. I don't know. I hope he does make it big one day—really big—then he can pay me back for that cup of coffee.

I took a nap this afternoon, and I had one of those really

lucid dreams of Ann, the Spirit Creature that won't let me go. It may have been my fever—or my confusion. Dreams don't really mean much, any way. They seem to be a hodgepodge of bits and pieces of still pictures of experiences happening in the course of a complex and varied lifetime. They never make sense. Giant faces. Falling off buildings. Flying over boulders. Spiders. Or some combination of all of the above. They just don't make sense.

I spent the day flat on my back with this cold or the flu or whatever it is, planning several sculptures of Ann in between dreams. One will be a woodcarving. One cast in bronze. One made entirely of plaster. That one will be the quickest and the cheapest. I just wish Ann would materialize in front of me like Galatea in Pygmalion. Come to life and … I don't know what I'd do if she did. My legs are becoming weak and shaky from the mere thought of that happening … but …

Later That Night

I was feeling better this afternoon, so in a rare burst of bravado I called Jack and asked him if he wanted to accompany me on a short trip. He just said he'd be right over. He didn't even ask me where we were going. Jack is always ready for an adventure, and within the hour we were off heading for Venice Beach.

On the way, we decided to detour over to Sunset Strip just for the sake of something to do. It was early and I was trying to bolster up the courage to do something I had never done before, and I wasn't sure what that was really. I just wanted to live dangerously, at least as dangerously as I will let myself in this little world of mine.

Somewhere along the Strip, Jack mentioned that he was hungry so we made our way to a little place where we had eaten several times before, the Israeli Café. It's run entirely by a group of young women who came to America from Israel only five years ago. The woman who owns the place has worked very hard to make it all work here in the Big City. She had an uncle who had been killed in one of the many Israeli-Palestinian-whatever skirmishes that go on over there 24 hours a day every day of the year. The uncle was a highly regarded army colonel or commander, and since his niece had also made some sort of a name for herself in one of the border raids as an IDF soldier he wanted her to have everything he owned when he died. Even though her uncle didn't have a dime to leave her, he did gift her something she valued far more—his highly determined spirit and imagination. She remembered him telling her "You got a lot of me in you, Little One. When I die you're going to inherit all the rest." She certainly did.

As we approached the cafe we noticed a couple of rather large, thuggish men watching us. Sure enough, as we got nearer, they confronted us and tried to take our wallets. I felt sorry for them because I know Jack. If there was one thing Jack doesn't liked, it's taking orders from anyone for any reason.

A few years ago, Jack enlisted in the Army in an effort to avoid what he saw as the inevitability of being drafted. He figured that if he enlisted he would have more input as to what the Army could do with his talents during the conflict that was, and still is, exploding beyond all reason in a little country called Vietnam. His strategy worked. Jack was stationed at an army base in Georgia where he spent a lot time supposedly preparing and repairing helicopters for combat. However, during that time he also received advanced training in stealth and infiltration, hand-to-hand combat, and survival skills. At some point the army decided to push him out of a helicopter into the jungles of Vietnam along with some other guys, to work behind the lines. To make a long story short, Jack can take care of himself regardless of how big the other guy is, how many there are, or even if they are armed.

When the thugs demanded Jack's wallet from him, Jack's reflexes took over. Before they knew what was happening, they were both unconscious and tied up with their own belts. After Jack removed their wallets, he left a note for the LAPD: "Sorry. Didn't want to bother you with such a trivial thing." One of the wallets contained over three hundred dollars in tens and twenties.

"It makes you wonder what those guys needed our money for,"

I said to Jack.

"How do you think they got all this?" he asked.

"Gotta be drug money," I said.

Jack grinned. "Well shoot," he said, "Budweiser's a drug, ain't it?"

"You bet."

"Then we're gonna use this money for the purpose it was originally intended."

Inside the restaurant Jack and I guzzled Budweiser and dunked pita bread in a garbanzo bean dip called humus. Our waitress, the owner, recognized us immediately, and appeared genuinely happy to see us again. Jack and I were both fond of giving large tips to attractive waitresses, and this one was no exception. Her name was Reshka—she of the long, black hair. Jet black, and so shiny that it reflected the light from the candles on the restaurant tables. Every time she leaned over to refill our espresso cups, our conversation came to a halt while we watched in awe as her large bosom overflowed the undone buttons at the top of her shirt. Like lava flowing slowly from the upper rim of a volcano. We knew she did it on purpose.

When she turned to walk away from our table, Jack said, "I don't think I've ever seen anything quite like that."

"Me neither," I agreed.

The atmosphere of the Israeli Café was so inviting that Jack and I hung around until the last candle had been snuffed out. Rheska sat with us in the dim quiet. We listened with interest and increasing respect as she told us about her experiences in the Israeli army, about her family back in Israel, about her brothers and one sister who were still in the army. She told us the details of how she and her friends had struggled at first to get the restaurant going. Their English was rudimentary, and that was a bigger problem than money.

We left the restaurant after midnight. I suggested to Jack that we forget about Venice Beach and hit the road for home. We could pick up a gallon of Red Mountain burgundy along the way, and stay up all night trying to capture Reshka's incredible whatever on canvas. He liked that idea.

Day 20: Monday

Monday, Monday
So good to me
Blah, blah
Blah, blah, blah

I hate to write what I am about to write. I tried to fight it.

I think I saw Ann, the Muse again.

I think I think I think.

When Jack and I got back to Riverside, I found a written message pinned to the door of my room. Frank had written the following:

> *Where are you when I need you? Got a great idea for some graphite works and I want to bounce them off of you. You're the only one I trust for this. Keep it to yourself. This could be big!*

Frank called first thing this morning and told me to meet him at the Royal Scot restaurant so that we could talk about his new discovery. Of course I dropped everything I was doing and I drove over to meet him.

The Royal Scot is a rather ordinary little coffee shop downtown. What atmosphere it has is generated by the clientele — many of them local artists — and the staff, rather than by the building and the decor. We go there all the time for the coffee and the waitresses. There's one waitress, Norma, who looks like she fell out of a movie from the 1950s. She wears her hair up in a bun, and has a gorgeous face. She looks like a famous actress, but I'm not sure which one. All the artists are in love with her. One day while she was serving Jack and me coffee, Norma lifted her shirt up very quickly and showed us what she was made of. We sat there stunned, like two rabbits caught in the beam of a flashlight. We didn't know what do or say. I suppose that's the problem with being young and reasonably inexperienced with women. When they do some something like that right front of you, you sit there looking stupid, and then they wiggle away before you know what happened. That's exactly what Norma did. She wiggled away laughing.

Frank came in shortly after I got there. He had a little red notepad with him. I asked him what it was for and he told me he was writing poetry. We found a booth, and he showed me one of his poems. It was actually very good. He had written it in a form of non-rhyming prose, where each word put on the paper had a deep meaning in relation to the entire poem.

He pulled the page out of his note pad and handed it to me. "Poetry ain't got much life left in it. It's kind of like painting. But this is yours. I wrote it for you."

It read:

You have your Muse
I have tea
Tis an honor you confided in me
about
Ann so
I confide in you about my
Tea leaves
Not as pretty as Ann
Not as intelligent as DH Parsons
but real good tea
In the end though
Ann wins

He signed the poem, "Peace to my great friend, DH Parsons, from his great friend, Frank Reed."

"I don't know what to say, Frank."

"You can tell me it's a really terrible poem, DH." *The Laugh.*

"But …"

"It ain't a serious poem! I scribbled it down out there in the parking lot before I came in." Again, *The Laugh.*

"I thought it was a bit …"

"Corny?"

"Well … maybe a bit."

Just after those words left my mouth, I saw her. It was Ann! I knew it was her. She was sitting at a table not twenty feet from us, wearing a green t-shirt and Levis. I think. My head went a bit blurry. I was trying to concentrate on the conversation I was having with Frank, but I kept looking over at her and she kept looking over at me.

Frank finally asked, "What the heck you lookin' at boy?"

"It's Ann," I managed to whisper.

Frank turned to look. "Where? I don't see any Ann. She's a brunette right?"

I followed his gaze, ready to tell him that no, she is a redhead, but Ann was gone.

"DH?"

"Yeah."

"You okay, Buddy?" He was grinning like a Cheshire cat. "Thought I'd lost you there. What's the deal with this Muse of yours? It's like you're seein' spooks or something."

"Sorry, Frank. I just keep seeing her in the oddest places. Maybe she is a spook."

"She's gotta be a POWERFUL spook to make you go ga-ga like that. Are you sure this ain't some wacko broad stalking you?"

"I'm not a movie star. Don't know why I'd have stalker. Especially such a pretty one."

"You ain't no celebrity, but you ain't a bad lookin' dude. Maybe you turned the head of some chick in one of your art classes."

"I doubt it. I don't think that's it. You know, even at night when I go to bed and I start to dream, I think she comes to me. I saw her name written on a wall in a dream once."

"Now that's spooky."

"Not really. I woke up the next morning entranced by the dream — maybe literally."

"So she's a looker huh? You told me she was a brunette but that's it."

"She has brown hair with a kind of red tint to it that she always wears in a ponytail. Her eyes are hazel, I think. She looks young, and every time I see her she winks at me and then disappears."

"Maybe you need some professional help, DH," Frank said, grinning, but then he gave me a sideways look, like he thought maybe I really am crazy.

"I think I'd know if I was loony. Maybe its just coincidence. Maybe I just see a girl in a crowd here and there who reminds me of Ann. And maybe when I go to sleep I see her because I've been thinking about her all day."

"You gotta stop thinking about her so much."

"That's not easy. I'm not sure I want to."

"Well, the next time you see her, tell me quicker 'cause I want to see her too," Frank laughed.

The entire conversation was so silly that even I had to laugh about it. But the "sightings" of Ann were and are very real. I really do see her, and I don't have a clue why.

I change the subject. "We're not here to talk about my Muse. What's the deal with this graphite stuff?"

"Well, DH, it's a layer thing, done with a pencil. You can buy big graphite sticks and cover a lot of ground quickly, but I want to use a single pencil and do it all the slow way. I want to draw several drawings on top of each other in graphite, and then fill in all the blank spaces with more graphite. I'll start out with a few smaller ones and see if the gallery people like it, then I'll make some larger ones, like eight feet by four, and I'll frame them under glass. I actually got this idea from you after you showed me that graphite drawing of the little British girl you did."

"It sounds expensive. The glass and framing would—"

"But quality in art is THE most important thing. We got billions of those mall show grannies runnin' around making all that stuff they call Ort, and they have their paintings and drawings framed in frames they must have found in the trash—all covered with stains and beat up. You can't present art like that! But even when you go into galleries you find the same thing. Some guy does a pencil drawing and he accidentally smears graphite into an inappropriate section of his drawing, or worse, he gets it on his matting, and he displays the work anyway! I'd never show garbage like that! The major galleries won't take it. These guys will be stuck in shopping mall displays for the rest of their lives. But the tons of crap they turn out pollutes the image of all artists everywhere."

"I agree with that. And I think you need to do everything and anything you can in order to get your work out there."

"Oh, I will! Whatever it takes." He had a somewhat demonic glint in his eye.

"Frank, can I ask you a question? Are you in this business because of your Art Spirit, or because of the money?"

"MONEY, HA! It has to be the money. Whatta ya want to do? You wanta starve yourself at some job pushing around burgers and fries all day?" *The Laugh.*

"But there's more to it than that isn't there? I know you too well."

"Yeah … if you say so." Again, *The Laugh.* "Nah, you're right. It isn't the money, it's the experience. Think about it! What better life is there? Painting and drawing and living on emotions all day. You wanta be a ditch digger?"

"You're a piece of work, Frank Reed."

"Everybody's a piece of work. That's why the whole world is nothing more than a great big canvas with a trillion colors on it. The world is a piece of work. But don't you love it?"

"Most of the time," I answer.

"Most of the time? You got a problem with the world?"

"Just parts of it. Mainly the people parts."

"Here's my theory: 95% of the people on this planet are stupid. Five percent are trying to understand what life's all about. And out of that five percent there are only TWO — ME AND YOU — who know what the heck is going on!" More of *The Laugh*.

"I'm not so sure I know what's going on any more," I say, more to myself than to Frank. "The future looks a bit bleak to me."

"What's bleak about it? We got some wars going on, and we got some dim-witted politicians running the show. But so what? That stuff's been going on for years! I'll tell you where the hope is, it's in art, REAL ART, not ORT art. Try fighting those friggin' Congs with a paintbrush! It ain't gonna happen. If everybody, even the Vietcong, painted paintings and became Van Goghs for the 20th century, we wouldn't have any wars or hatred or whatever, and art stores would make a fortune!"

"So, back to the graphite things. Did you like the little girl drawing I did in pencil layers?"

"Loved it! I think it's one of the best thing's you've done."

"I think it's Ann."

Frank rolls his eyes. "Back to the Ann thing."

"Seriously, there's no other explanation for it. These drawings haunt me just like this girl does."

"Paint, DH. Paint her. Paint a hundred paintings of her. The paint keeps the dream alive, but it also kills the pain."

Frank is right. He's always right. The man has a brain the size of a football field. Everything he says makes sense to me. Ancient wisdom, of sorts, in a modern package.

Late That Evening

The Ann thing is starting to bother me. She's become an Icon. What's really happening? Does she physically exist, or am I making it all up in my head. Maybe Frank is right. Maybe I need a psychiatrist. But, what if she really is—real? What if she's some sort of immortal specter popping in and out of this dimension at will? But why would she choose me? How can a finite man share an emotion with an infinite Being such as she must be? To even make the attempt is to court disaster—or suffer pain deep inside. Kierkegaard once wrote that in order for a man to become truly happy he must first go through a certain period of suffering. The Catholics call it the "Dark Night Of The Soul", as described by St. John of the Cross and Thomas Merton in his book, *The Ascent To Truth*. Everyone has to go through some sort of physical and emotional trial in order to get to "somewhere" spiritually.

I think love is spiritual. It just has to be. It can't be rooted in the mundane stuff of this world. If that's the case, then I shall one day be due for infinite happiness in direct proportion to my current suffering over these apparitions of Ann—the mental anguish, the emotional instability, the lost sleep!

I am in total conflict with myself. I haven't the words or the thoughts to define my feelings for this creature, Ann, whose appearances are without my invitation and beyond my control. It's all so incredibly illogical—beyond belief—and rather than allowing the emotion to run its course, to die within me, I continue to dwell on her. I continue to study the portrait I painted of her, down to the minutest details of the features of her face. I try to merge any memories I have of her smile with the mouth I have given her in my painting, to render the true sparkling light that is found in her eyes in the eyes I've placed on the canvas. But with every thought of her, my own despair and anguish intensifies, as if I want to believe that Kierkegaard had actually been right, and that somehow all of this magnificent suffering would one day soon result in some joyous union between myself, and the Ultimate Goddess of The Other Realm—Ann.

As a result, even though it's late, I find myself seated back in The Pit at RCC. Home away from home. Depressed. Watching the people go by. Something, perhaps everything, weighs me down.

The reality of watching the reflections of the private, concealed lives of the people that are etched clearly upon their faces, weighs me down. The people increase my suffering. The weight. The common man is gathering in, around, and by The Pit. The Pit of Suffering. Blah, blah people for the masses—amassed.

Alienated. Breeding indifference and disgust to those around me. The people. The weather is somber, with a sky of dark pthalo blue and grey. But for me, my own self-pity seems glorified in the Stygian melancholy. My own existence seems to be just one step above the natural depression that surrounds me. I am thrilled as I watch the massive clouds above me playing at dark war with one another. Is God up there somewhere? Behind the clouds? Or is Odin there, producing this spectacular display just for the sake of making a point, of giving me notice that my own little self-centered essence is meaningless, and it doesn't count in the scope and magnitude of this universe, and perhaps a trillion others.

Something is missing from my total makeup. I feel a void, a hollowness that even my poetry or my painting can't touch. A void crying out through the rain that is beginning to fall, and the mist, and through the sun and the brights and the colors, through the darks and the lights at the same time. There's a double world inside of me. The one that looks out over nighttime tables and over the benches of The Pit, the one that the people are free to study at their leisure, is the facade. The other, the double, the lookalike, is the reality. Where the double lives is the true abode of the reality of me. The ultimate truth that mixes with the cold air, and the rain makes me drunk on something even stronger than wine.

The irony is that The Pit is still an old friend. I cherish my visits here. I cherish the warmth it affords even on cold winter days. I trust it for what it has always given to me. I lay myself bare to it in trust—vulnerable. Never feeling fear or concern for retaliation or harm. Affection. Solitude. Sanctuary.

And here comes Frank. Total surprise!

"What the heck you doin' here?" he asks.

"Just passing time."

"You aren't studying are you? You never study, do you?"

"Not much. I'm writing in my journal. Why are you here so late?"

"I had this phone call from a gallery in LA. It ticked me off so I came down here to have a cup of java and cool my heels."

"They rejected your work?" I asked.

"No! It was all a money thing."

"They didn't come up with the right price?"

"Nah, I don't have a right price. But they wanted to take a ton of percents out of my work! The jerks. I do all the work and they drive a few nails in the wall to hang my paintings on and they want to take 40% of the profit! What's the deal with that?"

"It doesn't seem right," I agreed.

I'd never thought about it before, but all these galleries do is hammer nails into walls, and hang paintings, and make bazillions of bucks, while the artists do all the work. It doesn't make sense. Frank's right, it's a scam.

"It may be the way the market works, but I don't work that way."

"So what do you do now? Not show?"

"Are you kidding? I just find better galleries! There ain't no way I'm going to play by their rules. They need to play by mine. And this isn't an ego thing. It's what's right! What right do they have to take all that money from me! Who do they think they are, the federal government?"

Like a cheerleader, I inject "Don't let 'em get away with it, Big Daddy."

"Ha! You've called me that before! That was a movie wasn't it?"

"*Cat On A Hot Tin Roof.*"

"So how do I fit into that equation?"

You just do, Frank. You just do." I smiled.

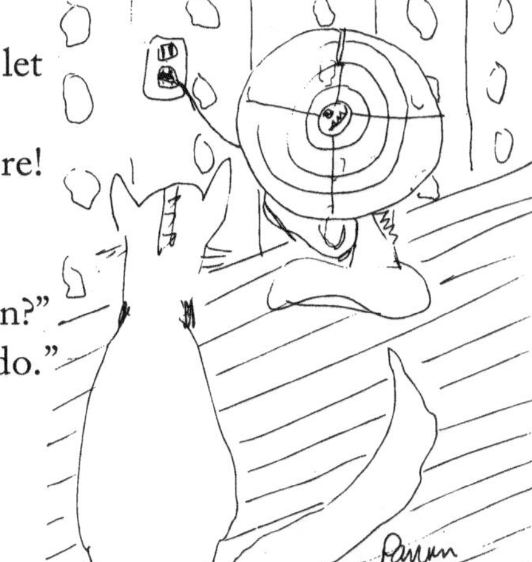

Day 21: Tuesday

Here's the deal: Real or not, I'm going to do a sculpture of Ann. I have to because she beckons to me. I don't think I've ever used that word before, "beckons." But she does. She beckons to me. In fact, I'm going to sculpt her in plaster. This is where my journal gets a little weird. I've been crying that Ann should appear to me like Galatea did to Pygmalion. Well, she did! I wrote the following down right after waking up from a nap. The weird thing is that during my nap I was dreaming that I was writing, so I'm not really sure if I wrote the following excerpt after the nap, or during the nap:

When Ann first "arrived" she was wearing a bright red, low cut, clingy-thin-silky dress that rippled with her slightest movement. She made a motion with her arms, the simple sweep of crossing her arms downward to grasp the waist of her dress then to pull it up over her shoulders and her head like a gentle stream flowing upward. I stood captivated—motionless—a priest in prayer before his Celestial Deity. Watching as this apparition's golden arms tossed her dress lightly onto the floor beside her. Then she seated herself softly upon the virtual stool that wasn't really there. It's the story of Pygmalion in reverse. In my dream my beautiful maiden Galatea sat there upon the stool, and I stood beside her—Pygmalion attempting to reproduce that which was already the totality of perfection. My perfect Goddess was already a reality—I think—but there was no need to go through the motions, to make the feeble attempt to bring my dream to life. And now my project seems absurd.

But I've already started the sculpture at this writing, and I continue to stretch and form the wire and the wood into some sort of shape to act as an armature for the sculpture. I realize now it can never be what I originally intended for it to be. I continue to force myself to concentrate on the sculpture instead of the Being. It's much easier when I don't start thinking of that smile of hers that may or may not exist. If she truly does exist somewhere, she must have no idea how the wetness of her teeth makes me feel.

In my dream, Ann saw me writing in my journal. She asked me if I was making some sketches of her. I lied, knowing that it was impossible for me to properly compose myself for a long enough period of time to justify even the slightest attempt to produce her likeness on paper. I told her that I was making some quick line sketches of her to help me with the flow of the sculpture. She was delighted and told me that she wanted to see the sketches when they were finished. And here comes the really strange part—keep in mind this is a dream—I remember thinking: *so now I'm forced to punctuate my writing with quick, nervous impressions of Ann tossing her hair—what color is that again? Chestnut? What the heck is chestnut? Why was that word in my mind? Her hair is perfectly straight, and so iridescent, inner-lit like a rainbow, but what color—a deep reddish brown.*

In the dream Ann said, "I've got to take a stretch." Then she stepped down from the stool that did not exist and raised her hands high in the air in a long, exaggerated stretch.

"Oh that feels good," she cooed with her eyes closed. "How long have I been sitting there?"

"I have no idea," I told her.

"How is your armature coming?"

"Not too bad," I lie. "It still needs a lot of work."

At this, Ann, the fictitious creature of delight, smiled at me. Awake or asleep, I've never known a girl so beautiful. It's like she's in a tiny stationary bubble and the entire universe is revolving around her. Like she is both aware and unaware of her surroundings at the same time. Like she has no concern for what may happen next. Like it just doesn't matter. Everything will be carried on by the strength of the beauty of her smile and that alone. Nothing else is important. Nothing else is necessary for sustaining life on this planet, in the entire cosmos, or in this room.

Maybe she's a Faerie. I think I've seen those in my garden. I do believe in faeries! I do! I do! I do believe Ann just might be one because of the way she keeps doing whatever it is that she does. I know this isn't all in my mind. I know I'm not crazy. I see these things. I just don't know where they come from. Maybe I'm Psychic. My mother is psychic. My Aunt Mealie was psychic — in fact, my aunt was the talk of the town. People either stayed away from her, or they went to her for advice. Kind of a double standard, but I guess I understand. People are strange. They've always been strange. What they don't believe in they seem to fear, and that leaves a whole lot of stuff out of the mix. Because there are so many wonderful things out there that are unbelievable, but they are not to be feared. Like Faeries for instance. How wonderful is the concept of the Faerie world?

I can't help but think of one of the lines from my favorite movie, *The Night of the Iguana* by Tennessee Williams, starring my favorite actor, Richard Burton. The line comes up in a scene on a bus while Richard Burton, in the character of the Reverend T. Lawrence Shannon, is being forced to listen to a bunch of church ladies who are on a tour of Mexico. One of the ladies — who will later attempt to destroy the Reverend Shannon's reputation because she thinks he's playing around with a young girl on the tour — begins to lead the entire bus load of church ladies in a song or two. It's a bizarre scene and very funny. The camera zooms in on Richard Burton, an incredible actor with an incredible voice, sitting at the front of the bus. In response to the forced gaiety, he simply rolls his eyes as  he delivers that famous one-word line, "Fantastic." It's a hoot! He goes on to explain that we live in the realm of the fantastic, which brings me back to Faeries and Ann, and even Frank. Fantastic!

If anyone lives in the realm of the fantastic, it has to be Frank Reed. He truly is bigger than life, so some of his life has to come from someplace else — maybe from where Ann resides. I know he is but a mere mortal, and I believe that if I were to talk to Maxine of the Big Eyes, she could tell me that Frank has his flaws. But it's the way he presents himself, flaws or not. He knows how to "strut and fret his hour upon the stage" as Shakespeare once said about another powerful man. But he does it so naturally that you know that it really is him and not that much of an act. OK, maybe a little bit of acting. But I believe Frank is kind of like Alexander The Great. He's great for a reason, and the reason is that he believes in himself. He BELIEVES in himself. It's that kind of attitude that just might bring him to serious greatness. How many famous people do we know who sat around all day not believing in themselves? All of the giants, all of the great artists had one universal trait about them: they had the belief that they were something special. Something different from the common man or woman.

Belief is an inner drive and it's a drive that Frank has. I can see it in everything he does or says. I can see it in the way he struts around the college campus with his little entourage of groupies. I can see it in the way he moves those graceful hands in the air while he talks. But more than that, I can see it in his eyes. Those great eyes that could be like railroad beacons if they wanted to be. I read in art books all the time about how hypnotic Picasso's dark eyes are, but they don't hold a candle to the majesty that pours out of the eyes of Frank Reed. To be honest, I think Picasso is indeed one of the greatest artists to ever walk the face of the earth. In fact, I think that art and artists have gone down hill since him. Except for Frank! If the word ever gets out about Frank Reed, Picasso just might be dethroned.

… and my phone is ringing.

Day 22: Wednesday Evening

Just as in the dream, I've begun a sculpture of Ann. I've spent the last two hours trying to smooth out the plaster that I roughly threw onto the armature. What was once a dream is now becoming a reality. I actually like the way it looks so far. Even though it's a bit rough I've smoothed things out and it's taking shape. It's becoming something.

At one point in the dream, Ann was wearing a black leotard, so I painted that area of her plaster likeness with black paint. Finally, I placed around her sweet, plaster neck a yellow paisley tie that I had bought in Haight-Ashbury, in San Francisco last year. I swear, that as I brought the tie close to her, I could smell perfume. It was lovely, smelling of pink roses on a spring day. I kissed the tie gently after I put it on her.

I've named her statue, "Ann Of The Darkness." It seems an appropriate title for such an otherworldly representation of my Muse. But I can only stand back and stare at the faceless head. I can't seem to capture her facial features without her being here.

She would be here in my head if Frank hadn't called me to tell me about some new shade of red paint that someone has just developed. He was very excited about it. Apparently it's just the right shade of red for a new painting he has planned that he will call, "Red Storm." Always good to hear from Frank, but this time he zapped my daydreaming session with Ann. I forgive him. I would have done the same thing.

Midnight

I had to escape my room and from my statue of Ann. I'm standing just outside of my apartment in the front driveway where I park my Volkswagen. I'm leaning on my car, staring up at the deep night sky. I'm here to think. I look out into space, and my gaze just keeps going, farther and farther. My vision never stops. It never runs into a brick wall or a tree or a building. It just keeps on flying. I'm seeing the nothingness of the space that represents the distance between me, and the end of eternity, and I'm wondering which star Ann might have come from.

Maybe it's me that came from another star. Maybe I'm the one that's out of place. Maybe I don't belong. The night air is cold, and it makes me feel much older than I am. It causes me to feel the lines and wrinkles of age forming on my face. The dryness of skin. I feel tired. Weary. Bitter. Bitter at what? Just bitter. And frightened. Frightened at the thought that has slipped quickly in and out of my mind. The thought that I just might be going insane. Maybe those theories about Van Gogh are true. Maybe he sucked up too much lead-based paint and that's what triggered his early demise. I might have the same problem. I paint with several brushes at a time, and I always hold at least one in my mouth. Some of that lead and other exotic metals have to be getting into my brain. Maybe that explains everything. Maybe I need to be committed.

Speaking of insanity, between my wild trips to LA and my encounters at the local college, I'm not without women companions. I've been meeting many women lately. Paula, who comes over to my apartment every once on a while and poses for me while I scrawl pencil sketches on cheap newsprint. Her posing is only an excuse that she uses to be with me. She thinks that she's in love with me and she doesn't miss an opportunity to tell me that. The only problem is that a woman has to be more than just a body for me to fall in love with. She not only has to own a mind, but she has to display it upon occasion. Paula has never displayed much mind to me.

Loretta, a student at RCC, likes to hang out in The Pit and drink coffee with me and the other art guys. But all she can talk about is rock music. She's in love with the Rolling Stones and yaps about them on and on. I get bored after being at the same table with her for more than five minutes.

Gloria, a pretty blonde divorcée who goes topless out on the ranch she won in her divorce agreement, is into some sort of back-to-the-land lifestyle. All she likes to talk about is canning beans and raising goats. Her mind isn't as vacant as some of the other women I know, but behind her back all of the men at RCC ogle and stalk her, and can talk only about her breasts. It seems that they have made up a game called, "Gloria Sightings." Every Saturday they park in the trees near her house and try to catch her in the yard with her shirt off. Gloria apparently knows about it and doesn't care. She seems to enjoy the attention. Knowing that about her makes me uncomfortable to be with her, and I usually leave The Pit when she comes around.

Cathy is a young blond, who claims to be a professional dancer. She is totally naive— clueless actually—but she has a nice smile and a good heart. I don't mind being around her because she just doesn't seem very with-it. Not into TV, not into politics. She just likes being with me and doing nothing. She lets me work on my paintings without bothering me. But, then again, the mind thing. Cathy's mind is not very developed at this time in her life.

There has to be more than this. One day I will no doubt meet the woman of my dreams, and she will have a mind.

Day 24: Friday Night

Friday nights are so non-climactic for me. But that's what this is, another Friday night. I'm sitting on a bench by a wall above The Pit and it's a clear, peaceful night with the light of the full moon illuminating the entire quadrangle. I can see each individual leaf on every giant oak tree. It's also cold and the dew on the grass sparkles in the silver moonlight, making me think of Christmas somehow. The lights from the classroom windows peering through the trees look like the lights on Christmas trees.

The steps leading down into The Pit are wet and slick, reflecting the moonlight, giving the impression of rectangular lakes or puddles. The benches in The Pit are dry, but they have been freshly painted and they, too, are enhanced by the bright moonlight as if it were mid-day.

I remember so many Christmas times with my family. But the one that stands out the most was when we lived in Tulsa, Oklahoma, when I was about seven. My family hardly had enough money to buy food. My brother, Jim, and I both had allergies, so we could not have a real Christmas tree. What we were able to buy was this really simple, silver metal Christmas tree, about four feet high. We hung it with green and red balls, and had one of those colored light wheels to shine on it. We sat that thing in the corner of the living room next to the TV, and as plain as it was, at that time in our lives, it was the most beautiful sight in the world. You know, when you're a kid it doesn't make much difference if your family has a million dollars in the bank, or if they just wing it from week to week on a small paycheck. Everything that hits your eyes is magic. Especially holidays. Christmas to me and Jim was truly a magical time. I don't know how Jim feels about it now, but on Christmas Eve back then, I fully expected Santa Claus to land on our roof, and somehow get into our house. We didn't have a chimney, but the next morning, sure as shootin', we'd get up and there would be a pile of toys under that silver tree.

I don't know how my parents did it on the income they had back then, but there were always lots of presents. Jim and I would run to the tree, all wide-eyed and excited in our pajamas with bears or whatever plastered on them and we'd grab those presents and rip them open as fast as we could. It would be all over in a minute. The presents would all be laid bare. The wrapping paper would be scattered across the room, and Christmas would be over. But that tree in the corner by the TV continued to captivate me until my mother took it down on New Years Day.

That was the same year my dad brought home a piece of plastic you could stick on the front of your black and white TV to make it look like a color TV. It was the lamest thing in the world. It was blue at the top, green in the middle and brown at the bottom—as if every show on TV was a landscape. We used the plastic screen for about three days, but when *Gun Smoke* came on Sunday night and Marshall Dillon had a green head, we took it off.

There are very few classes on Friday night, so the Quad and The Pit are virtually deserted. I've only seen three people since I arrived over a half hour ago. I stopped on the way here to buy a Jack-in-the-Box burger and some fries because I was hungry, and also because they're great burgers. One of my favorite things to do is sit in front of the TV and watch Bewitched on the tube, while eating Jack-in-the-Box burgers. Who knows what that "special sauce" is made out of, but with dill pickles it tastes pretty good.

And who is this? I can see a girl coming this way. I can barely make her out, but it's probably Cathy, because Cathy spends most of her Friday nights in The Pit reading romance novels.

Whoever she is, she's walking very slowly through the evening mist, like an apparition stepping out of a storm-enshrouded seascape that Turner might have painted. Devil or saint, walking only in straight lines, there is no word for the way she appears. There is no word for the color her face in this unreal scene the night has created for her. She is stunning. I wonder if she knows it. She looks familiar, but it can't be any of the girls I know. None of them walk like that. None of them can float a foot above the ground.

It's her, I know it! I can see her reaching up and wiping the corner of her mouth! My Muse. It has to be. And she's looking right at me!

She's stopping. She's just standing there on the seventh step up. The starlight is twinkling in her eyes. And she's smiling at me! She's … no. No! She's turning around and walking back the other way. Ann, don't go!

As Ann turned to leave, I decided I would not let her get away this time. I quickly got up from my table and started running toward the steps. I got about twenty feet when I slipped in a puddle and fell down hard into the water. When I looked up to see where Ann was, she wasn't. She had disappeared into the night.

A Bit Later the Same Night

I got home this evening and Frank called to tell me he was coming over. About 15 minutes later, I heard his motorcycle out in the driveway.

We had a nice chitchat for about half an hour. It seemed like he had a troubled mind and just wanted to talk to someone. He was distraught about a lot of things. On some things he swore me to secrecy, and I will honor that. But the main things he talked about were his sons, Jules and Mike. He said over and over again something to the effect of, "These guys are part of me. I love them both, but that Jules is a piece of work. He's got so much of me in him it scares me. I hope he doesn't become an artist. I don't want either one of them to become artists. They have to do their own thing. I'm not sure what Mike's gonna do, but I think Jules is gonna explode into some sort of odd whatever. I don't understand him."

"I like Jules too," I replied. "Mike seems to be the quiet one and Jules … well, he really is like you, Frank."

"Are you writing this down in that notepad of yours!"

"Whatta you think?"

"You jerk." Out comes Frank's great guffaw. "One of these days you're gonna publish a book outta this aren't you?"

"Who knows?"

"Nonsense. Every time I see you, you're writing about something. You've got that goofy journal in your hands 24 hours a day."

"To tell you the truth Frank, I don't know why I do it. It just seems to be in the blood or something."

"You must be related to Walter Cronkite. Maybe he's an uncle your mama didn't tell you about."

"I doubt it. I just have this urge to record things. I record lots of things. Everything I see and everywhere I go."

"And everything I tell you?" He sounded worried.

"Everything you tell me, except what you tell me between you and me. I never write that stuff."

"Better not." He waggles a no-no signal with his finger.

"But you haven't really told me much that would be a problem for this journal. Nothing earth shattering that the world would be destroyed by."

"What, I didn't tell you about the time I slept with Marilyn Monroe!"

"Yeah … blah, blah, blah."

Frank responds with *The Laugh*, and then tells me he needs to leave so he can get back to work.

So that's the way it's going to be. Frank leaves. He and his bike rumble off into the distance. The night gets quiet again, and all I have left to do is hit the hay and hope against hope that I will dream. Of Ann?

Day 25: Saturday Morning

I didn't dream about Ann last night. I drank too much wine. I thought the wine might make it easier to connect with her, but it didn't. It made it worse.

I did have a confrontation with Cathy, the Go-Go dancer. Just after Frank left last night I heard a gentle rap on my door, and there she was. She was wearing an abbreviated tank top thing, and a pair of cutoff blue jeans that were cut off way too much. She had tears in her eyes.

"My cat died!" She dissolved into sobbing convulsions.

I tried to comfort her as best as I could. I really wasn't in the mood because it was so late, but she just went on and on and on, refusing to leave until I'd given her two or three glasses of wine. But she still didn't want to leave. She told me she wanted to spend the night. She didn't want to go back home because she was so depressed.

We ended up sitting on the bed reading magazines. All the while I kept thinking of Ann. Ann at the museum. Ann at the raku party. Ann in The Pit. I had this half-clothed, pretty girl sitting next to me on my bed, and all I could think about was Ann. Every time I looked at her I saw Ann's face superimposed on hers. It wasn't that I was trying to do that. It was something supernatural happening in my mind. Cathy was squirming around and doing just about everything she could to make me more "interested" in her, but I kept seeing …my Muse … her face.

Cathy finally left around 3 am. I know I had offended her a little, but she was nice about it. All she said was, "Well, I guess I'll go." And that was that. Out the door she wiggled.

I think I must be really sick in the head. I'm going to call Dr. Connery tomorrow. I'm so tired. I'm so sleepy. I have to get some rest. You know, I don't have too many stresses in my life. I'm not old enough to have that many stresses. But all of these calls and visits late at night are taking their toll on me. I need to take a nap, do something. Rest.

Day 26: Sunday

Finally! I laid down on the couch about an hour ago for a bit, just to rest my mind and, I was sound asleep before I knew it. In my head while I was asleep I heard a phone ring. I saw myself picking up the phone. It was Ann. I swear. This is the most incredible dream I have ever had. It was so lucid. I was right there in it, and aware of everything.

Ann asked me to meet her at the park across from the Parent Navel Orange Tree. I'm not sure how these supernatural things work, but in an instant I was there! I was at the park.

From the edge of the park I could see Ann sitting on the grass under a giant tree, cross-legged, wearing what she almost always wears when I see her in my dreams or sightings: a blue cotton work-shirt, and a pair of green army fatigue pants.

I could tell when I approached her that her thoughts had taken her off somewhere else. Her eyes were closed and she had a smile on her lips that told me she was in some other realm. There were no other people around, just her under that tree, all alone in a large park that should have been filled with active humans doing the things that humans always do in parks.

She looked so exposed, so very real in an unreal sort of way. Soft and hard at the same time. Warm and cold. The sky surrounding Ann and her tree was several shades of blue, punctuated by a few grey clouds. As I stood staring, Ann and the tree became silhouettes in front of the sky—a perfect composition—surrounded by an entire galaxy that had now somehow diminished in importance within the universe. All eternity in every direction speeding out and away from Ann, becoming nothing more than a colorful blur of light; a sort of natural or supernatural masterpiece created by Ann's simple agreement to participate in it. I felt out of place, like I was observing something sacred, fit only for priests and seers.

The air was a bit chilly and I could see the lovely mist of Ann's breath rising up into the leaves of the sacramental tree above.

I watched as the mist floated slowly upward, as if it had no desire to leave her immaculate mouth. I was spellbound. I wanted to become a part of the mist. I wanted to dissolve my body and join my molecules with the molecules of Ann's breath and reside in the bliss of … of what? Of Ann. Of whomever she is and wherever she's from. It would be enough to be imprisoned within any part of her.

But what if I actually touched this creature? What if the mortal man and the Muse came into contact with each other in a physical way? What if the molecules of my body really did mix with hers? Would there be some sort of cataclysmic explosion? Like the meeting of matter and anti-matter? Would it destroy this little world called Earth?

In my dream, I began walking toward Ann. I came to a complete stop a few feet away from her, when she finally saw me. As she turned her head I noticed that it looked like she'd been crying! Can an apparition cry? The sun's rays were reflected, shot back out into space, by tears that balanced delicately on the rims of her eyes.

"DH?" She spoke so softly, but it was the only sound in the afternoon air, so it was as if she had shouted. As if a choir of a thousand angels had sung a million words compressed into a single second of time.

"Ann?" The holy name. The name that has haunted me for so many sleepless nights. I forced the unspeakable name from my lips. It, too, whispered out over the distance between us to find a sweet refuge in her ear.

Ann rose from the hallowed ground beneath her; ground that would never be the same again. I couldn't feel my steps as I moved toward her. My legs didn't belong to me any more. I could only sense within me that Ann was growing larger, like Alice in Wonderland, very slowly, so I knew I was walking toward her. Then, of a sudden, all movement stopped and I could feel the warmth of the blood flowing through her veins. I was no longer cold.

"DH?" She watched me watching her.

Can anything be said about the ambrosial fragrance of an

enchantress? Ann smelled freshly of meadow flowers; of natural perfume from some deep part of her.

"Are you well?" she asked me.

Remember, this is a dream I'm having!

"I …" I had no words.

"Come and sit by the tree. You look so pale," came a tender voice like the tinkling of flower petals striking the air.

I was dizzy as I sat on the ground beneath the tree. I followed the hot coals that were her eyes as she sat—floated—down beside me. I closed my own eyes for a moment, almost hoping that she would disappear. But when I opened them I was still imprisoned by her Divine Presence.

"Thank you for coming to my dream, D." More soft tears gathered on her lashes. Why did she call me D?

"Ann?"

"That is my name."

"Why are you crying?"

"I am crying because you haven't noticed me."

"What! I've seen you everywhere I go, even in these dreams. This really is a dream isn't it?"

"It is a dream."

And she disappeared just as quickly as she had appeared. My dream Muse—Poof! The dream was over.

Sunday Evening

I've spent several hours in my apartment tonight, resting but not sleeping. The phone has rung a dozen times but I could only bring myself to answer it once. It was a young girl selling magazine subscriptions. I mumbled something incoherent and a bit hostile. She hung up on me, as well she should have, but I was angry at her calling me so late. I went back to bed. I don't remember hanging up the phone.

I've only been up for two hours now, and I'm attempting to create some sort of sculpture out of an old orange tree log I found at the side of the road yesterday. Of course, it's intended to represent Ann, but the work is so slow and I've run into a small complication with the definition of her back. The only way I could work it out was to diminish the overall proportions of the entire carving. I'm learning that wood is very easy to take off a log but impossible to put back on.

It's good to work in wood again. It's good to experience the reality of the three dimensions. I've been painting on canvas for so long that I've forgotten how heavy a carving mallet can be, or how good it feels to pound it down hard upon the chisel and watch the wood splinters fly around the room in all directions. I've forgotten how beautiful the wood grain looks when it's revealed with every cut of the chisel.

While I carve, I contemplate on what I've read about the German Expressionists of the 1940s. About all of the anguish and torment they seemed to create for themselves. Real or imagined, the results of their personal torture produced magnificent works of art. I want to put that same emotion into my own work. I want to feel the same depression they felt and I want to apply it to the wood. I also want to caress Ann as I caress this golden log.

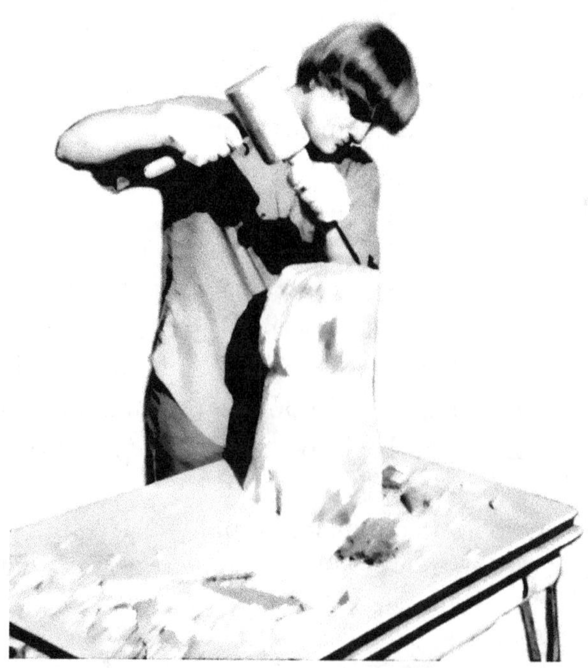

Day 32: at Frank's Place

It's Saturday morning. I love Saturday mornings. I was out shopping when Frank pulled up beside my car on his motorcycle. I couldn't believe my ears but he actually asked me to come over to The Castle and teach him how to do a lead-cast sculpture. What an honor! So here I am sitting in my usual spot on the mattress-cum-couch in the corner of the Reeds' front room. I've been supervising Frank in the process of doing a lead cast. The mold is out of the oven, the lead has been poured in, and the whole thing has cooled enough to handle. Frank is now trying to break off the investment.

I don't often enter Frank's main studio room to watch him work. It's not that he doesn't want me in there, but I just don't feel comfortable being there. I don't want to disturb him as he creates. I love to watch him working though. He's so intense, as he should be. So motivated. But he isn't careless like me. I'm a sloppy kind of artist. I jump into every painting with a wild abandon—brushes in my hands, one in my teeth, and three or four in my pockets, arms flying all around. Paint dripping and slopping down on the floor, on my shoes, ruining just about everything inside my little studio. I had a wasp in my room a few weeks ago and it actually ran from me! I don't blame her. It must have been quite a sight. The mad artist—Dr. Frankenstein making another monster, or perhaps more of a Mr. Hyde.

Frank is meticulous in everything he does, and that's really the way it should be. Each brush stroke is applied to a specific area at just the right slant. Every color is mixed perfectly to exactly what he wants it to be. Everything is perfect when he applies it, and everything is perfect when his work is completed, or he won't show it. It's just who Frank is. But that's what elevates him above the competition.

"Let me know if I make too much noise in here," he yells from across the room. "I'd hate to screw up your train of thought."

"My writing keeps my hands busy when I'm not painting."

"A work of art unto itself, huh?"

"Yeah. Maybe some day I *will* write a book about all this stuff."

"You'd better spell my name right!" And he laughs *The Laugh*.

"Who says you'll even be in the book?"

Frank smiles wickedly in my direction and says something like "you weasel" in a laughing, gravelly voice while throwing a used-up tube of paint in my direction. He misses me by a mile. We both giggle like school kids.

I love to watch Frank's face. It doesn't matter what he's doing, his face is like a Walt Disney production, animated all the time like a piece of clay that shifts and changes with every emotion he feels. His laugh though, that's the best of all. I feel like I'm back in the womb when Frank laughs. I know that's an odd thing to say, but you just have to hear it — *The Laugh*.

Ten Minutes Later

I'm watching as Frank's sculpture appears out of the mold. The bright metallic nose and one hard-edged eye of the face of a woman have become visible. I can tell — feel — that this cast will be perfect, as he continues to gently chip away at the formless lump of plaster, revealing the life-sized mask within. She is very pretty. I wanted to touch the hot lead of her face, but that would be a big mistake without the heavy leather gloves that Frank has been wearing.

"Look at that, Buddy boy!" he cries. "Man! It's gonna be perfect. Guess you ain't such a bad teacher!"

It wasn't difficult to teach Frank the lead-casting process. One of the things I have always admired him for is his ability to comprehend quickly and to master anything he attempts. After just a few minutes of my rather simplistic instruction, Frank attacked his project without hesitation. He molded and formed the brown sculptor's wax into the exact, and I mean EXACT, shape he wanted. He carefully applied the gas vents and the pouring gate. With even greater care he flicked the wet mixture of plaster and sand to form the investment — that is, the mold — into every crevice of his mask.

Frank did everything with the utmost precision and delicacy. "It's what separates the true artist from any body's old Aunt Maisey," he said earlier, as the lead that would be poured into the mold melted in a coffee can on top of the kitchen stove.

At this moment while he is brushing away the final flakes and crumbs of the investment, Frank reminds me of myself. I feel just the way he does when I watch a successful part of my own soul take shape on the white surface of a bare canvas or emerge from a plaster mold. I can sense his elation. I can see the sweat from the excitement beading up on his forehead, just as I feel it beading up on my own. Art is a drug.

"Look at this!" he yells.

I stand beside him, looking past the awkward pouring gate, and the vents that have now been transformed into solid metal, past the bits of plaster that still cling to the mask.

"As soon as I cut off these vents a new baby will be born into this savage world! Just a snip of the old umbilical cord!" *The Laugh.* "A flawless child of beauty."

"Wow." I mutter, uncreatively. Not just to fulfill expectation, but because it's true.

"It's only the first, the start of many to come." Frank's voice is soft now, trance-like as he fingers his new "child."

"It's magnificent," I say. And I really mean it.

"What was nothing has become a something. I've worked a shapeless ball of wax into what we see here before us." In spite of his words, his manner is humble. I've never heard him speak like that before.

It's times like this that deepen my appreciation and respect for Frank. He is a constant surprise. At one moment he is the puffed-up, self-centered, egomaniacal genius that every artist in the world wants—no, HAS—to be and the next moment, in the flicker of a thought, he becomes a child.

"Here," he says softly, handing me the mask. "Touch it. Tell me what you feel."

"It's warm," I reply.

"What do you really feel, DH?" He sits on the edge of his stool, eyes wild. But Frank is never dangerous when he's doing art. He's challenging me in some way, and I can almost feel his heart pounding in his chest.

"I feel what you feel, Frank. A new creation. Where there was once air, now there is life."

"Exactly, you patronizing son of a gun!"

We are like two little boys in the kitchen baking a cake. He continues with wild abandon, "Holy bones of Beardsley, DH. This is a Genesis moment! An eye-opener! And you and I are right here for the whole thing."

Day 36: Wednesday

I saw Jack today. I love that guy. He was sitting in the quad at RCC playing with a ball of twine.

"Hey, Jack. What are you doing with the string?"

"If I braid this properly, I can make a hammock. It should be able to hold several hundred pounds," he explained.

I laughed. "Are you planning on gaining weight?"

"It'll hold a bronze sculpture. My dream lady. Stark naked. All laid out for me in my hammock." He saw my puzzlement and continued. "I'm making the hammock first 'cuz I can't afford the bronze. If I fiddle around with the hammock long enough, the urge to make the sculpture will pass, and I'll save money not buyin' the bronze. And I'll have a nice hammock."

Such is the mind of Jack.

Jack is an incredible man. He never sleeps. He's always thinking about art He sees art in terms of the details of the processes of making art—how hot the bronze has to be before it melts; what powdered pigments have to be mixed together with what types of oils to produce what kinds of colors; what different glazes, when fired at different temperatures, on different mixtures of clay, produce what colors. That's Jack.

After a few minutes, it was easy to see that he was so preoccupied with his string that a shared conversation would be impossible. So I took my leave wondering if Jack even saw me go.

Day 37: Thursday

Bob, a potter friend of mine, called me this morning. It seems that his sister, April, has some sort of crush on me, and is demanding that he set her up with me. My first thought was, that's all I need. I've never given April any notice—I don't even recall what she looks like. But after further consideration, a date with a totally unknown entity might have possibilities. I'll give it a shot.

I'll take her to see the Soutine exhibit, which is still showing at LACMA. This will give me a second opportunity to study those magnificent paintings, and the prospect of female company adds to the attraction.

I picked April up at her home at 8:30 AM. It turns out that she is quite blonde and quite attractive. She is at least two inches taller than me. She has a lovely face and a nice lean, long body. There was very little conversation during the hour-long trip to the Museum. She just sat there on the seat beside me all the way to LA. Maybe she was nervous. I have to admit, I was a bit nervous myself. Like most people, she had never heard of Soutine, so I tried to give her a brief run down of his painful and difficult life. She seemed moderately impressed, but added little comment in return except, "Wow," and "Oh really." It was with great relief that we finally arrived at LACMA, and walked into the actual exhibit.

The day was a disaster. I had borrowed a suit to wear from a friend. It was a sharp looking suit but the pants were so baggy, that I had to constantly readjust them, using my belt to bunch them up around my waist. That left the folds of cloth to flop around below as we walked through the galleries. I was constantly checking my crotch to make sure everything stayed in place. I couldn't help but worry about what April must be thinking.

You know what was really going on though? It was Frank! It didn't take me long to realize that I was trying to do for April what he had done for me, during my first tour of the Soutine exhibit. I remembered watching Frank at some of his own one-man shows.

He always dressed sharp, and looked like the king of the world. I borrowed the suit I was wearing so that I could impress April, as if I'm made of the same stuff as Frank—the same swagger, self-awareness, knowledge, whatever. Like the suit, it didn't fit.

The day went from bad to worse. Apparently April had been blessed from an early age with a bladder control problem, and right in the middle of our museum visit, her dam, so to speak, let loose with a fury. April excused herself quickly and didn't leave too much of a trickle trail to the restroom, but she saw that I had already seen.

We drove back to Riverside in total silence, both of us acutely aware of the fact that we would probably never date each other again.

Day 42: Tuesday Morning

This morning I began a new painting. I am determined to harness my technique; to put something down on the canvas that will be totally of my own design, my own personal style. Frank tells me I have to stop copying other dead artists; that I need to do my own thing from the heart and from the gut. "That's when it comes alive."

It's difficult to be innovative with painting these days. It's hard not to copy someone else's style, even when I lock myself away in my own studio without the visual aid or influence of museums, books or photos. I may paint for hours and think I've come up with something that's uniquely my own, only to step back from it to find bad copies of Van Gogh, or Matisse, or Derain, staring back at me.

Today I think I've finally done it. In fact, I think it's the finest painting I have ever begun, and it may be finished, as it's very strong just the way it is. I call it, La Petite Parisienne. When I began the painting I had in mind to depict my spotless Ann, my Muse, in a regal pose: a profile, with a single breast exposed; a representation of a more worldly Ann. What she might look like if she ever became mortal. Lipstick and rouged cheeks—much more make-up than Ann would ever use. Her body draped in blue-grey cloth; the same color scheme as the sky the day I had the vision of her in the park. But as the painting progressed, it began to take on its own personality. It began to direct itself. The result is a strange mixture of features that resemble every vision of Ann I have ever had. Her hair—auburn, red brown, whatever color—and those lovely eyes that I can't seem to get out of my head. I see those eyes everywhere I go. But the coloration of her skin! The golden, yellow-brownish, pinkish, flesh tones of the skin are what I'm most proud of. I've produced a color that I had thought to be impossible to mix in earthly pigments—the color of Ann's beatified, incorruptible flesh. I'll let the painting stand just as it is for a few days, before I attempt to do more, if any, work on it.

Tuesday Afternoon

It's 1:30 in the afternoon. Frank called earlier today and asked me to meet him at the RCC sculpture lab. He's begun the process of immortalizing something or other in bronze. Not content with a mere leaden mask, Frank has a full three-dimensional head-study with hair, neck, and partial shoulders. The wax has already been invested and is being baked out in the giant gas kiln at the college. He will be ready to pour in the molten bronze by two p.m. Bill Mitchkelly will be there to help him with the kiln work, but he also asked if I could help him with the pouring process.

"You seem to know what you're doing, Big D," he told me over the phone. "Not that old Bill doesn't know what he's doing. It's just good to have an extra pair of hands around for something this important. I trust you DH."

I'm now standing in the sculpture yard at the college. Bill is here. Bob is here. Bob's sister, April, is lurking in the shadows over by the kiln looking shy and apologetic. I'm here, but the only person who really matters, Ann, is here, too. I saw her. I saw her over near where April is standing. She had that grin on her face, and that outfit she always wears, and most importantly, she wiped the corner of her mouth with her hand and winked at me. Then I blinked and she was gone. I'm getting used to that now, even though I don't want to.

Frank had been standing in front of the kiln, lecturing and bragging about all of the paintings, drawings, prints, sculptures, and artful constructions he's working on. He has every right to brag. He's currently in the process of a wood sculpture, a wood block print, several clay pieces, dozens of drawings, and the bronze head that he will be casting in just a few minutes.

He's moved to one side, and is now in the midst of a friendly argument with Bill about semi-contemporary big-time artists like Picasso, Dali and a some new artist named Hockney that Frank tells me I look like. They do this all the time, so I can never tell if either one of them is serious, but they always end well.

"The man's a saint!" Frank is saying of Picasso.

"He's one of the most insensitive jerks to walk the face of the earth," cries Bill.

"You can't just look at his personality, Bill! You gotta take the man as a whole. Look at all the art he's put out in his lifetime. Nobody else in the world does art like that. He doesn't sit on his butt all day, burnin' his life away at some Podunk college in Surf City, USA!"

"You just like him because you identify with him!"

"What the hell is that supposed to mean?"

"It doesn't mean anything in the scope of all things, Mr. Frank Reed. You can be Picasso if you want to be." Bill flashes his smile that kind of looks like he should be a farmer somewhere out plowing fields.

Frank responds with *The Laugh* — that slow, rolling guttural thing he does that defies physics — and pats Bill on the back. Bill shakes his head, and Frank yells, "Forget about Ort, where's the booze?"

Another round in the never-ending Frank and Bill, argument discussion, art-talk thing. No one ever wins. No one ever loses. They both just get tired of playing the game, so it's time to quit.

The sculpture yard is teeming with activity. Bob and I have prepared the bronze ingots that are presently cooking away inside the furnace. Bill is seeing to the kiln, getting ready to pull out the investment mold at the exact moment the bronze is completely melted. It's important that the mold is still red hot when the molten metal is poured into it, or it's possible that the entire thing will blow up. That would be a disaster.

As usual, Frank is directing traffic. "Turn that gas jet up! You got that sand spread out so we can put the mold down into it? Hey! This bronze is getting ready to boil over here!"

I like and admire them both, but I think Bill might be just a little jealous of Frank's talent. Maybe that's why they clash so much. Bill knows that Frank really does know his stuff, and that he's a top quality artist in every way; it shows in his work. In fact, today Frank seems to know more about what's going on than Bill. That's no insult to Bill. I believe it has more to do with Frank's Art Spirit than with his talent. Even Bill has mentioned to me on occasion that Frank is a force to be reckoned with, so there may be both jealousy and respect here.

Tragedy a Little While Later

It's 3:05 p.m. The high spirits of the afternoon have turned somber. Frank had miscalculated the thickness of the investment needed to contain the weight of the bronze and had made it too thin. The bottom of the mold gave way as the bronze was poured in, and molten metal spilled and splattered on the ground around us. Fortunately, no one was hurt, thanks to quick reflexes and steel-toed boots. With a rueful smile, he shook his head in resignation, muttering, "Pisser of a party, huh boys?" He turned to us, thanked us graciously for helping him out. Then he said, "Mea Culpa, partners. Mea Culpa," and walked off into the sunset.

One of Frank's many admirable qualities is that he's able to admit when he's done something wrong. He knew immediately when the bottom fell out of the investment that he'd blown it, and in true form he didn't make excuses, or try to blame it on anybody else. He took full responsibility. I think that has to be one of the primary qualities of a great artist. That's what they do. An artist won't make it to the top by making excuses about his work—blaming the paint mix, or the time of day, or the quality of the canvas, anything to deny the truth that his work is simply a piece of junk. Frank never does that. It would have been very easy for him to try and place the blame with Bill for maybe not having the kiln hot enough to cure the investment. In fact, he could have done that and gotten away with it because it's a real possibility. But he didn't. He took the sword.

Day 45: Friday

I quit my job at the lemon factory today. I've only put in a few days there over the past several weeks. Apparently the weather has damaged the lemon crop beyond any hope of salvage and there just isn't much to do around the old plant. I don't mind. I'm tired of hearing about the boring lives of the boring men I've been working with. I'm tired of the stickiness and the stench of the lemon pulp that works it's way into every thread of clothing I wear when I go to work. I will never miss scraping the string filters, and I will be ecstatic if I'm never forced to listen to country music again. One guy has a tape player he plays all day, every day. Loud. And only one tape! Sometimes, while trying to sleep at home after a long day with the lemons, all I could do was lie there and listen to his country western thing running in my head like a Hindu mantra.

I do have to eat, though. I currently have only twelve dollars to my name, so I took another job working for a local politician who's attempting to secure a seat in congress. He's a stereotypical, over-weight, whatever kind of politician. These guys all look alike! He pays me $1.80 per hour to write short, cliché radio blurbs about how sincere he is. I also deliver a variety of campaign items — buttons, posters, leaflets, et cetera — to locales throughout the county. I really don't know if I want this man to be elected to any office in the county, but I do want him to pay my salary. I suppose that makes me no better than he is, but I won't lose sleep over that.

I saw Frank tonight. I can't believe it. The man is a genius. In just two days, he has managed to create a wax model identical to the one he lost in the disastrous attempt earlier this week. Only this time, he will pay a professional foundry to cast it. "It's not that I can't do it myself," he explained, "I just don't have the time. And if I did have the time, I wouldn't want to blow it again." *The Laugh*.

Day 47: Sunday Night

I'm home, and Frank's here at my little pad. He arrived about five minutes ago with a large brown bag containing two gallons of wine that I've never heard of—Casa de Something-or-Other. I've never seen him this impatient or restless He is currently tearing up my apartment in search of a glass or a cup to drink out of. He's about to destroy the contents of my desk. "Over there on the shelf," I direct.

"I need a drink." He's found a large glass.

He sits down on the end of my bed, pulls one of the wine bottles out of the bag, fills the glass, and drinks it down in one swallow. He pours another, and repeats the process. He just sits for several minutes, guzzling wine and staring into the space around him. Staring at my paintings. Staring at my bookshelves. Staring at the piles of plaster on the floor in the corner that were left over from my unfinished sculpture of Ann.

"You got some darn good paintings out there leaning up in your garage, DH. I never knew you were that talented. Why are you hiding all that stuff away?"

"I have nothing to hide." For some reason I choke on those words.

"Some of those canvases look just like Soutine walked in there and painted on 'em."

"That's the problem. You took me to that show, and I was so influenced by him, that my stuff now looks sort of like his. But I'll get over it."

"No! Don't get over anything, DH It really is good stuff. And it ain't pure Soutine. That's a good thing. You have a lot of DH in it too. All you have to do is slowly remove the Soutine and add more DH. Then you've got your style!"

"Frank, you seem agitated. What's the deal here?" I ask cautiously.

"So now you're a psychic? I can't hide anything from you."

"I guess I might be. My mother is. But you're all fidgety and I don't see you like this very often. And you never drink like that. You like your wine, but you aren't a raving drunk."

"Ha! Maybe I should be!" He takes another gulp of wine. "I've got this show coming up soon here in Riverside. I don't know why I'm nervous about it, but I am. I'm going to take some chances with this one. I'm gonna pull out all the stops."

"What the heck are you talking about? What do you mean by 'all the stops'?"

"I'm gonna do this up right. I'm going to price my paintings the way I want to price them, and I'm going to arrive in style, like a Hollywood production. But I'm still kind of concerned about it.

"Give me some more info, Frank. What do you mean by the 'prices' thing, and the 'Hollywood' thing?"

"I'm going to price my paintings as if I were the greatest artist alive — lots of big bucks. But some of the smallest paintings are going to be the most valuable. I may put up a six-foot canvas for five bucks, and an 18x24, for $3,000! I don't know any other artist doing that!"

"I don't either."

"The point is," he continued, "that art is art! If Picasso can step in cement in Cordoba, Spain, and have the mayor pay him for the sidewalk, then that's the definition of art!"

Frank is referring to the story he once told me about how Picasso stepped in the wet cement of a freshly laid sidewalk as he was coming out of a shop in Cordoba, Spain. Instead of citing him for damaging public property, the mayor asked him to sign the sidewalk, and then paid Picasso a few thousand dollars for his having stepped into it! It pays to be king.

"The point is that if I paint a canvas 2 inches by 2 inches, it's still a painting by me! It's the name and the talent. It's always the name and the talent. It doesn't make any difference if the painting is ten feet tall or two inches. It is a creation of the artist. Are you getting this, DH?"

"I am. And I agree with you on this one. If the world deems you to be a great artist, then anything you make is great art, and priceless in a way."

"Ha! Not priceless! I have a price for everything!" *The Laugh*. "But you're right. Great is great, and anything else is mall show crap. Pay up or shut up."

"What about the Hollywood thing?" I'm almost afraid to ask.

"Style, DH, style. I'm gonna pull up in old Harvey."

Harvey is his 1935 Ford Touring Deluxe Sedan.

"I'm gonna step out of that car and walk into the gallery, wearing the gold corduroy suit I bought in Spain. I'm gonna turn some heads. But that's all a part of the game. It ain't ego. It's called showbiz. And that's what art really is, showbiz. Heeeeeeeeeeere's Johnny!" *The Laugh*.

I know he's right. It is all about the show.

Day 52: The Next Friday Night

Jack and I drove to LA tonight. We found a place to park about a block away from the Israeli Cafe. As we walked up the street, we were joined by two girls who began chatting with us. They weren't too bad to look at. One had kind of dishwater-blond hair, and the other was darker, a brunette. The brunette had a gap between her front teeth, and a couple of tattoos, and both of them smelled just a little like marijuana. But Jack and I didn't care. They had pretty faces so we decided to take them to dinner at the Israeli Cafe.

I've been coming to the Israeli Cafe for a long time now, and Reshka, who is the owner and the main waitress, once told me, "Watch out for the girls that hang around outside. This neighborhood is notorious for hookers."

"Why would I even care when I have someone as beautiful as you in here?" I replied, seriously.

She laughed. Her uncle, Moshe, gave me an icy glare.

Moshe is really a nice guy, but he has quite a history. He's a compact man with the muscles of a prizefighter. I guess that comes from his military training. He's a tough dude—looks like a Mafia strong man. Looks like he ought to have a baseball bat in one hand, and a pile of cash in the other. But he's really a sweet guy when you get to know him. He's been wounded in action more times than he can remember, and he has at least one scar to prove it, running the whole length of his nose. His only problem is that he drinks too much. Reshka doesn't know what to do with him. He's kin. He's a war hero. But he also fouls up everything in the restaurant because he doesn't pay attention. This café is a pretty popular place, and just two weeks ago, when a major bigwig politician from Israel walked in with his entourage, Moshe was so drunk he didn't know what he was doing. Reshka had to have her bouncers take Moshe into one of the back rooms and lock him up until the politician left.

Reshka is one tough Tessie. She has to be six feet tall, and has the strength and stamina to go with it. In Israel, the women as well as the men are required to do a year or two of military service. She must have done well during her stint in the army. The thought of Reshka carrying a gun kind of frightens me and turns me on at the same time. In spite of her tough exterior and impressive physique, she has the sweetest disposition anyone could ask for. I mean that. Reshka is a kind and compassionate person. One night I told her about how my little Chihuahua puppy, Skeeter, got hit by a car the first week I had him. Tears spilled from her eyes and she hugged me in sympathy. I think I fell in love. As she hugged me, and pressed her chest against me, nothing else in the world mattered. Russia could have dropped an A-bomb on LA, and I wouldn't have even felt it.

Her brother, Dieter, was killed in combat not long ago during his time in the IDF. When he died, I sent a dozen roses to Israel to be placed on his grave. Reshka was deeply moved by my gesture. She told me that was the sweetest thing any one had ever done. Because Dieter had died a hero, the Prime Minister of Israel sent one of MY roses back to Reshka, with a letter the PM personally signed, and that's what bonded us together. After that, anything I ordered was on the house.

"Good to see you, DH," said Reshka when she returned. "What can I bring you this evening?"

"Good to see you too, Reshka. Bring us an order of humus and pita bread, and Jack and I will have some of that special lamb stuff we had last time. Girls, what would you like?"

The blonde, still looking at her menu and not finding anything she recognized asked, "Can we get a couple of cheeseburgers?"

Reshka gave me a look that made it clear that she doubted my sanity, or at least my judgment. To the girls she said, "This is a Jewish restaurant. We don't serve cheeseburgers."

The blonde looked puzzled, but the brunette said simply, "Just hold the cheese then," without missing a beat in her rapid staccato gum chewing. Reshka gave me an icy look, and I gave her a wink. She left without writing down our order.

She came back in a few minutes with our food, The girls examined their sandwiches doubtfully—grilled meat patties inside pita bread, garnished with tomatoes and cucumbers.

"What is this?" asked the brunette.

"Grilled lamb inside pita," Reshka replied.

The blonde looked stricken. "I can't eat that! Little baby lambs are too cute to eat."

That was it for Reshka. She looked at me with narrowed eyes, made a slicing motion with her finger across her throat, and walked away.

"Well," I said flatly, "I guess I'm not as hungry as I thought I was.

"Me neither," said Jack.

Jack and I ushered the two bodies out of the cafe, Reshka, herself holding the door for us on our way out. I thought she was really angry with me for having brought the girls in, but she pinched my butt as I went out the door, and gave me a sly grin, so I think everything's okay with her.

There was a small nightclub about a block from the café, so Jack and I decided to take the girls there for some drinks. Jack was hoping all the way that we might get some sort of "experience" out of them. I wasn't so sure it was worth it.

When we got settled in, the girls both decided it was time to dance. "Oh great," I thought to myself, because I'm not a dancer. When I finally got up enough courage to hit the dance floor, my brunette with the tattoos took the lead. My efforts to keep up with her must have made me look like I was on LSD. While we were dancing she kept kissing my neck, which wasn't too bad. After a little while, she surprised me, whispering into my ear, "Isn't it time we go somewhere private?"

"But Jack and I don't have a place to take you," I whispered back.

She replied, "We have an apartment a block from here."

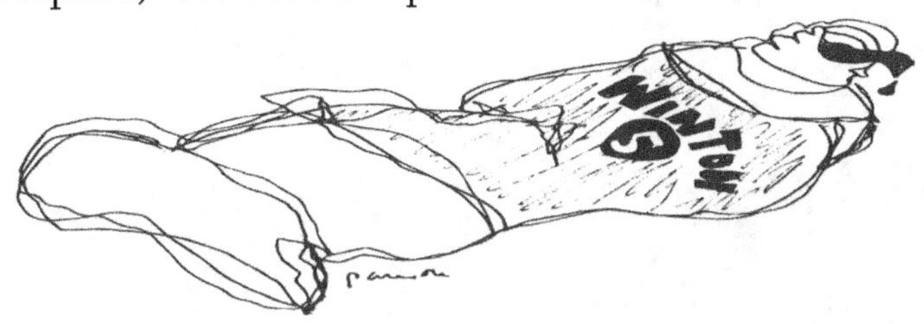

Day 53: Saturday Morning

It's 6 am and I'm very tired. I've been up all night talking with Rena—the brunette. I'm sitting here in a chair at her desk, writing in my journal while Rena is asleep on her bed. Jack and I went with the girls to their house, which was only a short walk from the nightclub. It was a dump. There was trash overflowing in the kitchen, record albums all over the floor, panties and bras all over the place, and a rather nasty looking cat with a limp that apparently spent most of its life peeing on things and shredding the couch. Not a good first impression.

Each girl has her own bedroom, so Jack went into one, and I went into the other. Jack isn't awake yet, so I don't know what his room is like, but my Rena's bedroom is immaculate. What a surprise! I mean this place is something! The rest of the apartment is a mess, but her bedroom, spotless.

I really have very little experience when it comes to girls, so even though Rena and I never did anything last night but talk, I assumed all along that she and Betty—the blonde—were "ladies of the evening". Along about 3 a.m. I asked Rena how much I was going to have to pay her.

"Pay me! What are you talkin' about? Pay me for what?"

"It's just that you've been so nice to me, and I know that even though all we did was talk, I still monopolized one of your evenings. It isn't fair to you that you lost money tonight because of me."

At that Rena's face turned red. She started to say something but she was having trouble getting the words out.

"Wait a minute," she said, "you think I'm a hooker?"

I didn't know what to say. From the tone of her voice it seems that Jack and I made a bad call on this. Then she started to laugh.

Long story short, I was quickly informed that Rena and Betty both attend classes at UCLA. Betty is a cheerleader there, and she's majoring in biology. Rena is a singer in some sort of something she called a corral, and has won several state scholarships in music.

But it all worked out pretty well. Rena thought it was funny that we thought they were hookers, and we both wondered how Jack had fared next door with Betty. Did he make the same mistake I made? We wouldn't know until they came out, and we certainly weren't going to go in and ask them. We might interrupt something.

6:30 am

Jack and Betty came out a while ago. Jack had made the same mistake; only he got slapped for it. But Betty was very forgiving and they ended up sleeping together the rest of the night.

After a nice little breakfast prepared by the girls, Jack and I decided to hightail it back to Riverside. And that's exactly what we did. We told the girls that we had both had a good time, and we promised to visit them again. And I think we just might do that. As we were leaving, Rena smiled and said, "Don't forget me."

So, we're on our way back to Riverside now. Jack is driving and he's asking me the same question that Frank always asks, "You still writing in that journal thing?" "Yep" I tell him. "One day I might make a book out of it." But I doubt to myself that will ever happen. Who would want to read about the lives of a bunch of wise guys growing up in the 1960s?

Jack is whistling something from The Doors — *Come on baby, light my fire...* I'm so beat I almost feel like nodding off. But we're almost home, so I'll write a little more.

Guess I'll write some more about Reshka. I really think she has some feelings for me. I'm trying to think of some movie actress to compare her to, so if anybody ever reads this journal, they can get a mental picture of her beauty. Let me think — there isn't an actress today who looks like her, but I did see a photo once of a woman named Berthe Morisot who was an Impressionist artist back in the 1800s. She hung around with Manet and Cezanne and Pissarro and the boys, and she was a real looker. I guess that's about as close as I can come to putting a face to Reshka. She looks a lot like Berthe.

I think Berthe and Manet actually may have been lovers, but

I'm not sure. The only thing I'm sure of is that Berthe's paintings are better than Manet's! She was a brilliant painter.

Reshka is brilliant as well. She's a graduate of Harvard, with a law degree under her belt. But when she was given the opportunity to start up the Israeli Café, she made the choice to follow her heart rather than her head. Her dad, Maurice, was supportive of her decision, and proud of her courage and independence, but he didn't have any money to put into the business. Every dime he got from his soldiering career back in Israel went to buy booze and bad shirts. Maurice wears the gaudiest shirts on the planet, most of them Hawaiian, with palm trees and hula girls, and the like. That's kind of weird to me, this Jewish war hero with about three million IDF medals, dressing in Hawaiian shirts.

Since her father didn't have the resources to help, Reshka came up with a brilliant plan. She recruited a group of Israeli women living in LA, and they pooled everything they could scrape together into a big pile to buy and refurbish a beat up warehouse downtown. The rest is history. The Israeli Cafe is one of the most popular restaurants in LA. Most of the women who helped Reshka get it going are very friendly and very pretty. The only one I don't like is the one who supervises the kitchen staff. She's a tank. Once when Reshka took me back through the kitchen on the way to the bathroom where she would kiss me, old Gilda swatted my butt, and gave me a look and a growl, that I've never heard coming out of a human woman before. For some reason she hates me. I don't know what it is but I have my theories. I think Gilda's a manly girl, if you know what I mean, and she has a crush on Reshka. But who wouldn't, so I understand where she's coming from.

Saturday Night

I'm sitting in the fifth row on the right side of the Stage One Theater here in Riverside. Jack and I got home not too long ago, and I decided to go see a flick. When I looked at the movie section in the newspaper, I was excited to see that *The Stranger* was playing.

The Stranger was originally a book written by Albert Camus, the existentialist philosopher. I think I've read it about ten times, and Frank and I have had many discussions about it.

"Existentialism! Ha! What a crock of crap that is! Much ado about nothing—literally," Frank told me once. "Who do these guys think they are, telling us how the world works? And who gives a flyin' rat's patoot any way?" *The Laugh.*

As usual, he was right. I don't see much point in sitting around philosophizing on questions that can't be answered because the questions don't have any answers. That's what existentialism is all about, but *The Stranger* was a good read, and I am enjoying this movie.

The reason I can write sitting here in the theater is that the film reel broke about fifty minutes into the drama. Some projectionist with glasses and short hair came out a few minutes ago. He said his name was JJ, and he was trying to splice the film. He did give us all free popcorn, "for your inconvenience," and that's the main thing any way. I come to the theatre mainly for the popcorn. I love that stuff.

I'm just looking around at the people in this room. Old JJ has turned the lights up a bit while he splices his reel. There are only about thirty or so people in here, and some of them look pretty seedy. I know one guy that's sitting about three rows in front of me, because I saw him when he went back to get his free popcorn. He's a professor at the University of California, Riverside. Teaches botany. I know him because one time when I was parked at the mall, this guy pulls up in a pickup filled with all kinds of plant things in the back, and when he opened his door he put a dint in my VW. Hmmmm—I think The Doors were playing on my radio then, too. He was really sorry. He offered me a handshake, and his home phone number, but he looked kind of weird and I thought it was kind of odd—the entire conversation. It seemed almost like he was coming on to me. Maybe he's gay or whatever. That ain't no big deal to me, those guys make their own thing, for better or worse, but I like girls.

Every once in a while, here in the theater, the botany guy looks over his shoulder at me and smiles. He knows I'm here. He's recognized me, too. And I'm sort of thinking I'd better sneak out of here after the lights go out again. He's making me nervous.

Day 54: Sunday Morning

I made it through the movie without a hitch. The Professor started choking on a piece of popcorn and had to leave the building. He didn't come back.

Got a call this morning from Frank who wants me to meet him at the Royal Scot in about 15 minutes. I'm really beat after the weekend I've had, and the late night watching of *The Stranger* affected me in some way; I'm not sure how. Those things are tough for me to figure out at my age, and I don't have the time to waste on it right now. So I'm off to The Scot.

Twenty Minutes Later

OK, I'm here at the Royal Scot, and Frank isn't. Norma is at the counter polishing glasses, looking over at me every ten seconds or so, and winking. I give her a wink as I see Frank come sauntering in. He's such a kick. He always wears his Levis suit and a blue work shirt. You can see him coming anywhere and anytime. Nobody dresses like this guy; nobody looks like this guy. Nobody on Earth.

"DH, the show opens Friday night!"

"What show?" I ask.

"The one we talked about earlier. It's going to be at the Mission Inn Gallery and I'm gonna make a killing."

"How do you know that?" I ask.

"Because of a phone call or two. Before the show even opens, I've already sold two paintings."

"Good grief, that's great!" I am genuinely enthusiastic.

"Where the heck is Norma? I want some coffee," She's standing right behind him.

"Right here Mr. Big Time. You want the usual?"

"No Honey"— *The Laugh* as he turns to face her —"I ain't got the time. Just bring me some coffee."

Norma walks away with a smile and a shake of her head, but not before giving me another wink.

"She's got some body, huh, DH?"

"She does." I agree.

"You know, you're a lonely pathetic single son of a gun. Why don't you go after that stuff?"

"I'm attracted to her, but I'm also attracted to a lot of girls."

"Well what are you waiting for?" he laughs.

"I guess I'm waiting for the perfect girl."

"Fat chance. The perfect girl doesn't exist. I haven't been married to Maxine long enough to be an expert on the subject, but I know she ain't perfect, and neither am I. We just grow together. We both have our ups and downs but we always come back. Me, more downs than her." He sips the coffee Norma puts in front of him.

"Thanks Norma. Got some cream?"

"Not for you," she replies. She turns and winks at me, squeezes her left breast and walks away.

"I told you she likes you, DH! Go for it!"

"I'm working on it."

"Work, shmirk! Ask her out!"

"We're already kind of friends, Frank."

"Ooooo … what does that mean?"

"I'm not sure I want to tell you about that."

"Come on! I'm like the Pope! You can tell me anything!"

"Norma and I do things when we can—most of the time here at the restaurant. We've kissed."

"Holy cripe, DH. You kiss? What are you, a moron? You could probably marry that girl." *The Laugh.*

"I'm not sure I want to marry Norma. She's attractive on the outside, but I want to marry a woman that has …

"A brain!" Again, *The Laugh,* and Norma is standing right behind him ready to refill his coffee.

"So I don't have a brain, huh, Mr. Arteest!" She is livid.

"Sorry darling," he says, throwing me a grin and a wink, "Didn't know you were standing there." To Norma, he says "Say honey I gotta talk to you. NOW."

Without further words, Frank gets up. Taking Norma by the arm, he leads her back toward the kitchen. *What is he doing?*

They pass through the swinging door into the kitchen. I can hear Frank talking to someone back there, but I can't make out the words,but ... Hang on ... There's a big guy wearing a chef's hat and waving a meat cleaver. He's yelling and coming this way! What's going on?

A Little Bit Later

OK, I admit it was funny, but I'm going to get Frank for this. Here's what happened:

The cook, a big Italian guy, came barreling through the kitchen doors with a cleaver in his meaty hand and fire in his eyes, shouting a stream of Italian sprinkled with a little English. The only thing I could understand was "You bettah be rite wit Norma," delivered with a flourish of the cleaver as he headed right for me.

I began to suspect that the situation was not serious as I could see Frank over by the kitchen door trying hard not to laugh, but I don't think Norma was so sure. She came running after the chef. When she got to him she grabbed his cleaver arm, and brought it behind his back like she was a cop or something.

"Carlo!" she screamed. Everyone in the restaurant was watching, waiting to see what would happen next. It was like something out of the six o'clock news.

"Carlo! What are you doin'!" she screamed again.

Frank can't hold back any longer, he is in stitches back by the kitchen. Even though my life appears to be threatened by this crazy chef the size of a gorilla, I can't help but smile; I know this has all been choreographed by that wizard, Frank Reed. Still, the chef did look serious. He did have that cleaver up there, and it did look like it had some sort of animal blood on it. And Norma—geez—I thought she was going to bring this guy to the ground!

Then it all came out. Carlo the chef started cracking up. Norma started cracking up. And Frank, in tears from laughing, came back to the table and sat down.

The mood lightened and smiles appeared as the customers relaxed, laughing at the impromptu farce staged at my expense. One of the cooks in the back had called the police and the beat cop came in to check out the story that the head chef was going to kill me. But Frank pulled him aside, charmed him a bit, and that was the end of the story. The cop left. Then Norma whispered in my ear "Meet me in the bathroom."

Norma took me into the bathroom and apologized to me profusely. I was right; Frank had set it all up and the cook, Carlo, who's some sort of Mafia goon, played along with the joke. He scared me a bit, but during the scene, every time I looked over at Frank, I got the impression that all was well.

Norma filled in the details. Carlo, who is her uncle, is pretty much hard-core Mafia. In fact, from what Norma tells me, he's what they call a "made" man, meaning that he's been involved in killing at least one guy. He looks the part, too. Huge dude with big biceps.

Norma was worried that I might be mad at her for what Frank had set up.

"Don't worry, he does that to me all the time. I expect things like that from him."

Her expression changed and she said softly, "You know, he's got a point. What do you feel about me?"

That took me off balance. What do I feel about Norma? I really don't know! She's nice enough, no doubt, and I've had a lot of "conversations" with her in this bathroom, but—and don't get me wrong—she's beautiful, like Marilyn Monroe with brunette hair. But I'm just not sure she's for me. And there's Reshka. There's also this confusion inside of me that tells me to hold back. Hold back. I don't know where that's coming from, unless the psychic link Frank asked about really is a factor here. But I can't help feeling that Norma is not the one. There's somebody else out there. I mean, I'm just a kid compared to the rest of the world. I'm only 19. I don't want to commit right now.

Add to all of the above the fact that I'm sure I saw my Muse, Ann, sitting at a table not too far from me, just before the fracas started. I was going to take a better look when old Carlo started coming at me with the cleaver, and I got sidetracked. But it had to be her! She was eating a burger, and the split second my eyes met hers, I noticed a drop of something running down from her lip. She smiled and winked. It had to be her.

In the Park With Frank

I couldn't finish writing at the Royal Scot because I got involved in that conversation with Norma. But Frank and I are now sitting quietly in the park and I want to finish relating what Norma started with me. Frank is lying on the grass with his head leaning against a tree. I think he might even be sleeping. He looks like Rip Van Winkle lying there with a toothpick in his mouth. He's got my LA Dodgers baseball cap pulled down over his eyes. Wish I had a camera.

But the Norma thing; when she asked me what I felt about her, I genuinely didn't know how to respond. I just stood there silently like a bad imitation of Gary Cooper from High Noon.

Why do women always do that? If a guy doesn't come right back with the answer they want to hear, they always throw that line in. I'm bettin' that line is written down somewhere on a cave wall from the days of the Stone Age.

"Norma! No! I mean, no, you're wrong," I told her. "And yes, I do have feelings for you. But I'm not sure how to answer you right now. We've never even been on a date, never gone to the beach, never done anything together."

"But you do have feelings?"

"Of course I do. And they're pretty strong. But we're both still pretty young, and we have long lives ahead of us, and it's tough to make a decision right now."

"But other people do."

"I know they do, and sometimes they regret it for the rest of their lives."

She got icy. "So you would regret marrying somebody like me. A mere waitress just ain't good enough for you?"

"Norma …" I took her face in my hands and said gently, "You aren't a mere waitress to me. I'm just an art student at a tiny little college in the middle of nowhere USA. I'm even mere-er than a waitress."

That struck her funny and she began to laugh. She was crying and laughing at the same time. I told her that was also funny. We ended up hugging and she gave me a kiss, then I told her I needed to leave. I knew Frank wasn't finished talking to me about his art show opening, and he would either be gone when I came out of the bathroom, or he'd be fidgeting at the table.

I was half right. He was fidgeting by the door.

Back to the present. Here we sit in Itchicoo Park. Just kidding. It's the same park where Ann and I met in that dream.

"Don't you ever get tired of writing in that thing? You have to have arthritis in your fingers by now." Frank is not asleep. "I swear, you really are related to Walter Cronkite. Except you ain't that ugly yet,"

"Nope. No journalism for me. But I would like to be an author. One day …"

"So are you coming to my show?" I knew he wasn't finished with that topic.

"Wild horses couldn't keep me away, Frank." I meant it.

"It's at seven p.m. I'm gonna arrive fashionably late of course. But not too late cause I don't want anybody leaving before I get there. I want to make some cash!" *The Laugh*.

"In Harvey, huh?" I mentioned before that Harvey is Frank's car. A 1935 Ford Touring Deluxe Sedan, and it's a real head turner. A while back I had told him that I name all my cars. After noticing that his license plate frame read, "Harvey Motors," I told him he ought to name his car, Harvey. At first he thought that was silly, but he did that guttural laugh and said, "Harvey, huh? Ha! Okay Parsons. You got it. From here on old Harvey and I are a team."

"I'm gonna drive on up in Harvey, my new best friend, exactly fifteen minutes late. Maxine and I are gonna be decked out like Christmas trees, and we're gonna strut into that gallery and take it by storm. How bout you bein' an usher/parker guy for me?"

"Maybe you'd better get there early so you can get a good parking spot."

"That's all covered. The gallery's gonna tape off a spot right out front. Nothin' too good for old Harvey."

"You have all your paintings framed and ready?" I ask.

"Oh yeah. Most of them are already at the gallery. It's gonna be quite a show. I've got some good stuff in there, DH."

"Anything I've seen already?"

"I think you saw a couple at the house. That little one I was working on about a month ago. You were there in the afternoon while I put the finishing touches on it."

"You mean the one with the pinks and yellows? The girl with the paint running down?"

"Yep. It's gonna be there, and I think I'm going to put a whopper of a price on her, just to make that point I talked to you about before."

I remember Frank telling me once that he had a patron who collected his work on a regular basis. I think that's a smart idea. One of these days his work will be worth some big money, and if someone were to buy several pieces right now at today's prices, in 20 years they could make a fortune. I wish I could buy one of his paintings, but I don't have that kind of cash. I guarantee I would never sell it if I had one.

That reminds me of the time when I visited LA County Museum for a show they had of the artists of the 1800s. The paintings were mostly Impressionists, and although Van Gogh was not an Impressionist, he and a few other borderline expressionistic kind of guys were included in the show. I have always loved Van Gogh, and on that particular day while I was staring at one of the Van Gogh paintings—and I swear this is true—a small chip of paint popped off the canvas and fell to the floor right next to my left shoe.

Now, I would frequently touch the paintings in the museum. In fact, I got caught once doing that to a Cezanne, and almost got thrown out by a guard who looked like he ought to be handing out cash at a bank, and not working as a security guard. I could have taken that guy! But when that Van Gogh chip fell to the floor, I had nothing to do with it. I never touched that painting. So I calmly reached down, acting like I was tying my shoe, cause I knew everything was on camera there, and I picked up that little chip. I carried it around the museum with me for the rest of the day. When I left the building and got back to my car, I ripped a small piece of paper from one of the pages of a college book I had sitting on the seat. I put that little Van Gogh chip inside that paper, and stuck it in my wallet. I still have it. I could never afford to own a real Van Gogh painting, but I have a part of one. I have piece of him.

"So come on over for a while tonight. We'll drink some wine and talk about the show," Frank says, getting us back on track. "You can bring one of your weird friends with you if you want. That Jack guy ain't too bad, or what's that little black haired thing called? The one trying to grow a mustache."

I laugh. "That's Manny. We're all trying to grow mustaches, but I guess we weren't blessed with your hairy genes."

"That thing on Manny's lip just doesn't look natural." He laughs. "But he's a good kid. Bring him along."

Sunday Evening

It's Sunday evening, and Manny and I arrived at the Reed Castle at about 7 p.m. Frank's motorcycle, his car, Harvey, and Maxine's little VW are in the driveway. I add my VW to the line up. It will be good to see Maxine again. I love talking to her. She has those big wild eyes that go all over the place when she speaks, but she always has a smile on her face. I love to watch those eyes. Hypnotic.

Manny and I are sitting on the couch in the living room of the Castle. I tried to get Jack to come with us, but he said he was incapacitated, and couldn't do it. I heard some odd sounds in the background while we were on the phone, but I didn't go there with him.

So Manny and I are here, Maxine is in the kitchen, and Jules and Mike are running around like they always do. Mike just knocked something over in the studio area that made a really big bang, but Frank goes on working, yelling out the side of his mouth, "Slow down!" And I hear Maxine echo the same words from the kitchen. I think she's making some salsa.

Manny is sitting here drinking wine, a bit confused by the whole thing. He whispered to me when we first sat down that he's a bit intimidated by Frank, and I think he's a little shy about being here tonight. So I just told him, "Relax and enjoy the wine and the mood. These are the neatest people on the planet, and I guarantee that before the evening is over, you'll have some fun."

Manny rolled his eyes and said, "This guy scares me."

I laughed and said, "What are you talking about?"

"I don't know what I mean. He's just scary. He has a lot of personal power. I don't think he's a bad guy, but personal power always scares me."

"He does have power, but don't let him scare you. He's a big teddy bear. And Maxine is the sweetest person around, and just as smart as he is. In fact, I'm more intimidated by her than by Frank."

"Why's that?" Manny asks.

"Lots of reasons. First of all it's those eyes of hers — like something out of Greek mythology. The eyes of Athena maybe."

"I noticed that!"

"But it's more the way she talks and the way she thinks. She's way out there. Like she belongs about fifty years in the future. But that ain't a bad thing. Trust me, you'll see what I mean if you hang around the Reeds long enough."

All the while, Frank is in the studio making art. It's what he does, and when he isn't making it, he's thinking about it. He's working on a wood sculpture right now. I think it must be a portrait of his Muse. He also turned out a silkscreen print of Maxine recently.

Both pieces are exquisite. I mean really exquisite. This guy gives me the same feeling that I get at the museum when I'm looking at a Van Gogh or a Soutine. I know I am in the presence of something more than just ego. I'm in the presence of a great artist. Just as people used to sit in the smoke-filled bars in Paris back in the 1800s, sipping their absinthe, totally unaware that Manet and Morisot and Pissarro were siting at the next table. The world went on around them, but they were living a moment that would eventually become history. That's how I feel about being here. Every time I come to the Reed's home, I feel I am living a moment in history; that one day Frank will be bigger than life, and I will have been a part of it in my own small way. But if he never makes it that far, I will still love him and Maxine, and those two boys that are now sitting on the floor in front of me playing with their toes.

I brought my tape recorder with me tonight. When Frank gets tired of working on his art, maybe he will come in here and chit chat with us, and we can tape it "for time and all posterior" as Frank says.

An Hour Later

Manny is a bit more relaxed. Maxine has brought out food and some more wine. Frank is sitting in his chair in the corner gesticulating with both his voice and his hands, and laughing like crazy. We're all laughing. We're making a very Dadaistic—as Frank calls it—recording of a bunch of nonsense. I see Jules over there by the wall watching. I have to wonder what's inside his head as he takes it all in. Jules is only five years old but he's observing everything, like he wants to be a part of it, but knows he can't. I have no idea where Mike is, but he's missing out.

Of course we've all had a bit of wine. I don't have a clue what the wine is—something purple, maybe a Cabernet. I brought over a gallon of Red Mountain burgundy, but we went through that pretty fast, and this stuff of Frank and Maxine's tastes a whole lot better, so it must be something Maxine bought. I can't afford anything but Red Mountain at a couple of bucks a gallon.

It does the job and it doesn't taste too bad.

We're in the process of satirizing just about everyone on Earth, from presidents to TV hosts. No one is safe, not even the "Mahareesheeeee Mishmash Yogi," as Frank calls him. "What a phony old bag of wind! Anybody who believes in that TM guy is a piece of limp skin hanging from the bone." *The Laugh*.

"But they can all levitate." Manny has the courage to say.

"Manny, that ain't levitation," Frank expounds. "It's camera tricks. These guys just flop up and down on cushions. Real levitation means you STAY UP IN THE FRIGGIN' AIR! Ha! Floating and flopping are two different things."

I visited a Transcendental Meditation meeting once. Even I almost fell for the sales pitch they gave. It was very attractive and well polished, but when they asked me to bring a white flower and a whole bunch of cash before they would tell me the secret mantra I would use for the rest of my life, I saw the real scam. At the meeting, this one guy up front talked about levitation, and he proceeded to demonstrate how it's done. It was the kookiest thing I've ever seen! Frank is right. This guy sat in a lotus position, and then he started pushing his knees into the pillow in order to bounce up and down. He was exerting a tremendous amount of effort. Sweat was forming on his forehead, and he was getting off the ground, I have to give him that, but he didn't stay up in the air, he always came back down on his butt rather quickly. His butt cheeks must have been bruised at the end of the meeting. It was ludicrous. Levitation is when a person rises slowly off the ground and stays up there for a while, like Frank says, floating, and I don't really believe anyone has ever really truly done that.

Our subject shifts from gurus to famous artists, with Frank, of course, taking the lead role in this play. He is becoming every artist that he slams, and it's hilarious.

"The famous Jacques Lip-shits! (Jacques Lipschitz) One of the greatest sculptors to ever live! But he's a dandy!" *The Laugh*.

"Sue Tan! The swarthy skinned lady who thought she was a man, so she became a painter, and smeared colored grease on an old table cloth, and the world called it ORT!" *The Laugh*. He was talking about Chaim Soutine.

"Salva Door Dolly! He runs a Buick dealership doesn't he?" *The Laugh*. "What's with that ugly broad he was married to anyway? That Gala babe—ain't that a bathroom tissue?"

"Mikey Angelo! Here's the story on this guy. He was hooked up with the Mafia. Used to be a bouncer! Never ever made a piece of Ort in his life! He hired his goombahs to do it for him. If we could ever figure out who those guys were, man, that would be a story! But it's too late for 'em to get any cash out of the deal. There's a statute of limitations ruling on art cash." *The Laugh*.

"Man-Zoo, here we go again! (Manzù, of course) Great artist, but he spent some spare time working at the zoo. Trained the elephants. His real name was just "Man" but that didn't get any press so he added the "Zoo" to it, and overnight the guy became rich and famous. It's all in the name! Just goes to show you what marketing can do!" *The Laugh*. "Think I'll change my name to Frank Seed, then I can market my Ort better! If that doesn't work I can open a feed store." *The Laugh*, again.

Of course, all of the above information about these artists is inaccurate and untrue, and virtually nothing we recorded will make any sense at all if we ever listen to the recording. It's all just the musings of a few people who have ingested a whole lot of whatever, having a good time.

We ended the night by singing Frank's favorite country western song, "I've Got Tears in My Ears From Lyin' On My Back Crying Over You (Blues Baby)." The last two words were added by us—it just never seemed complete without them.

Day 56: Tuesday

I went to my pottery class today and ended up having a long talk with Bill Mitchkelly out on the porch. The porch of the pottery house is really nice. You can make pots for an hour or two inside and then come out onto the porch and watch the squirrels jump around in the yard. If it's a stormy day you can listen to the thunder, and hear the rain falling softly on the porch roof. Those are my favorite pottery porch days. I love the rain.

Bill was deep into his favorite subject, the personalities of various artists. Among the topics we discussed was Bill's favorite, The Picasso Fraud. It's an old argument, perhaps even a cliché at this point in time, but I went along with him. It seems—so they say—that Picasso hides his greatest works away in his studio, and sells substandard work to the public. Possible, I guess. Pablo is a kind of bizarre little man, but he's always been at the cutting edge of the art world with great success. It looks like anything he produces can be sold for a phenomenal price. I'm not so sure that's bad. So many of his paintings have been deemed masterpieces, including Guernica. What a brilliant work that is. I have always loved this guy. I believe he is perhaps the greatest artist now living, and it has nothing to do with his popularity. It has to do with his talent and his mind. I once saw a short blurb on TV about Picasso, during which he created ten works in about three minutes! I couldn't believe it. And if he is keeping his good stuff packed away while selling only the bad stuff, I'm not sure I can tell the difference. It all looks good to me. As Frank would say, "Good marketing technique."

Bill went on to talk about what he called Dali's "pseudosity." I'm not sure if that's even a word, but he uses it to express his opinion that Salvador Dali is too much of a showman, and that his showmanship is merely a front and a cover for bad painting. My opinion on this one? Granted the man is a clown, but good grief, he can paint! His paintings are perfect. I know there is very little of the personal statement or the emotion in Dali's painting—it's pretty much formula painting — but his technique is flawless, and we have to give him that.

It's hard not to love Bill though. I don't agree with him about most of his art talk, but he's one of the sweetest men on earth. I'm going to be doing a couple of bronze sculptures soon and I didn't have the money to buy the bronze, so Bill bought the bronze for me. Tell me that ain't sweet.

I'll be using some old gates and vents from Papaleo's foundry in Orange County. Good bronze. $10 worth. So today I created my wax figures: a man and a woman. The woman is more sensual than the man. The man is a bit lumpy. But these aren't meant to be masterpieces. Just a trial run for something better later on — maybe even a full sized figure.

It only took me about an hour to create the wax figures. Now I'm trying to put the flick, or first coat, investment on them, before the final investment coat goes on tomorrow. When one does a flick investment, one dips his hand in prepared Plaster of Paris, mixed with a few other ingredients, and he then literally flicks the messy plaster goo onto the wax. And he flicks it good baby! So that it forces the flying goo to go deep into every crevice of the wax sculpture, in order to pick up every detail in the mold.

After the flick investment goes on, then the artist just starts piling plaster on it in the shape of an oval mold. The flick part is the most important. If you don't do it right, the entire work is compromised. If you do a good job, then you set the mold aside for a few days to dry thoroughly. You have to be careful that it really is dry. If it isn't, the intense heat of the kiln when you're melting out the wax figure inside, could cause it to explode if there are moisture pockets inside the mold. The same is true for when you pour in the molten bronze. The mold had better be dry or BOOM.

Day 59: Frank's Show

It's the big night here at the Mission Inn Gallery! It isn't a very big gallery, but it's classy on the inside, and Frank's work is stunning.

Frank did exactly what he said he would do. He drove up in Harvey just a little bit late, parked the car in front of the gallery—I made sure that his parking space was reserved—and Frank and Maxine got out looking like more than a million bucks. Frank looked like he should have been running the world in that Spanish suit. And Maxine was magnificent, which is easy for her. She'd be gorgeous in a potato sack.

The two of them walked through the front door of the gallery like they were royalty. Everyone got out of their way. The waters parted, and the show was on.

Now I'm sitting on a folding chair back in a corner of the gallery, watching everything as it unfolds, and of course taking notes about it. To me, Frank is fascinating to watch as he does what he does whenever he gets into any public venue. He seems magnified tonight in his gestures and mannerisms; I suppose that is because this gallery show represents the bigger part of who he is. At any rate, he's in seventh heaven, once again strutting and fretting his hour upon the stage, hopping from this person to the next, a glass of wine in one hand and the other flourishing with exuberance, as the words flow from his mouth. The man is a magician. He shakes a hand here, winks to a woman there, and *The Laugh* is everywhere evident, like an earthquake or a sonic boom, it resounds in the atmosphere of the gallery and the public is pleased. The public is enamored by the power that Frank exudes from every pore. At this one small moment in time, if Frank were to choose to run for president of the United States, he would win hands down. No one, absolutely no one, would vote for the other guy (whoever that might be.) But Frank isn't that stupid. He would never be a politician. He'd have to come down several rungs on the intellectual ladder to do that, and that ain't gonna happen.

I'm barely able to pick up the conversation. Too many people talking all at once, and of course, *The Laugh*, echoing around the gallery every so often. But here's a smattering of what Frank is saying, as he sweeps around the floor like a dancer gone mad:

You like that one, huh? Yeah, it's one of my favorites too. I hate to part with it, but I guarantee it will be sold before the evening is over.

That's a fairly new piece. Most of these are new. But I did that one just a few weeks ago. The paint's barely dry. But I love it. I think it might already be sold. I have this patron … blah, blah, blah.

What a master.

As the evening goes on, I'm having way too much wine, and so is everybody else. Maybe even Frank; I can't tell. But he's doing a good job, and I have no doubt he will sell most of the work here, if not all of it.

It's really warm in here, and a lot of people have taken their jackets off, but not Frank. He looks too good in that Spanish suit and he knows it. The suit has become a part of the production. A living exhibit in and of itself, and Frank isn't even breaking a sweat.

Frank is looking over at me now kind of quizzically, motioning to me with his free hand. He wants me to come over there. I'll catch up on the journal after I see what he wants.

45 Minutes Later

I left my comfy chair and followed the motion of Frank's hand. I don't know why I didn't see her before; I guess she had been standing behind Frank when he waved at me. But when I got close to Frank I saw Norma standing there. Without me knowing it, Frank had invited her to the show, and she had come. I know there had to be ulterior motives. He's setting me up again. Then I saw Chef Carlo and I wondered if he had a cleaver under his coat. But the goombah looked pretty good, all decked out in a shiny suit that seemed to be about thirty years old, and two sizes too small. I swear, Carlo's biceps were about to split the seams of that thing. Frank grabbed me by the arm and pulled me over to the wall.

"Listen DH. That chick is hot for you, and Carlo's just here for the hell of it. This ain't no joke. I *inn-vah-ted* both of them," stringing the word out for effect. "But don't get all pissy on me. She's going to enjoy the paintings, drink a little wine, and who knows, maybe romance will blossom." *The Laugh.*

"You know the experience I had when I took April to the Soutine exhibit," I remind him.

"Yeah, yeah," he said, brushing it off with one elegant movement of the wine glass hand, not spilling a drop. "But DH, this ain't April. She was kind of an odd duck. You know what I mean? And you're wearing a suit that fits your butt tonight!" *The Laugh.* "So go for it! What have you got to lose?"

Carlo, who was standing about five feet away, winks at me and nods his head as if to give his imprimatur to the whole idea. I see him mouthing the words, "She loves you," but I ignore him, looking over at the table where the booze is. There's Norma, looking coy and absolutely gorgeous in a low cut, light blue dress.

"You jerk," I say to Frank. "What are you supposed to be, an artist or a match maker?"

He laughs *The Laugh* again, and gives me a nudge in Norma's direction. "Will you just get your bachelor butt over there, and don't you ever tell Maxine I set this all up for you."

"Why not?" I ask.

"I have my reasons."

I suppose I'll never know the reason, but it doesn't matter. To make a long story short, I did go over to talk to Norma. Of course Carlo followed me, but I wasn't afraid of him any more. When I told him to take a hike, he winked at me and walked over to look at some of Frank's paintings. He was attempting to act like he knew what he was looking at, but out of the corner of my eye I could see him watching me.

"Hi Norma," I said. She really did look good.

"Hi DH. This is really nice stuff. I never knew Frank was this talented. This is the first time he's ever invited me to one of his shows." She smiled demurely.

"Frank is pretty good alright." I glanced over at Frank, sending him an eye dagger or two. He just smiled me off.

"Absolutely," Norma said.

It was all just small talk for about ten minutes. But Norma and I both had had a few glasses of the bubbly, so eventually …

"You look lovely tonight, Norma," I blurted out.

"You think so?" Her eyes widened.

"I know so."

"Can we go outside for a bit and get some fresh air?" she asks.

"Sure."

We left by the front door and just started walking. We walked all around the block, all around the Mission Inn, and then down the mall. We ended up sitting under a tree in the mall, when Norma decided it was time for us to kiss.

Thirty Minutes Later

I'm back in the gallery and things are slowing down a bit. A lot of the people have gone. Frank whispered in my ear that he had "sold a bunch." And life on planet Earth goes on. "Where's Norma?" he added.

"I sent her home."

Frank looked at me kind of strange and said, "You should have taken her home with you, Bud! What's the matter with you?"

"I don't know Frank. I just don't know."

Frank shakes his head, and Maxine comes over our way. Frank tries to change the subject by saying, "Thanks for your help tonight, DH. I sure appreciate it." He winks at me, and I take off for home.

Day 60: Saturday Morning

I'm sitting on the front porch of the ceramics house at RCC. Bill Mitchkelly is in the back yard tending to some stuff. The bronze for my two figures has been poured, and I've already cleaned the gates and vents off of them. The casting was fairly successful except for a couple of blowholes in the necks of the figures. I called Frank, and he told me that the problem was probably a result of the temperature of the bronze. The melting point of bronze is around 1800 degrees, and the best temperature for pouring is around 2100 degrees. Our highest temperature before pouring was only 1900 degrees, so we just got impatient. But it could be anything, or a number of things, that caused the holes. If the gas escapes too fast during the pouring, that can cause problems, or the investment might not have been dry all the way through, although it should have been. I think Frank's theory is the right one. If the metal is too cool, then the bronze will cool too quickly. The gases will form bubbles inside the investment instead of escaping through the vents, and holes will result.

We were just impatient. But still, I'm pleased. The holes can be repaired, but I prefer to leave them as they are. And hey! I got a check from my politician boss today for $29.42. Don't know what I'll do with such an enormous amount of cash, but I'll think of something. Ha! I know what I'll do with it. I haven't gone to the beach in a long time. I think I might drive down to Laguna or Capistrano. The best Italian restaurant in the world is near Capistrano Beach—La Strada. Geez Louise, the clam linguine they serve is out of this world! I'll have dinner there first, then head to Laguna, sit on the beach, and watch the sun go down. I'll take a gallon of wine and this journal with me, and I'll just write some whatever while I'm there.

9:15 p.m. On the Beach at Laguna

I don't know what's gonna come out of my head tonight, writing wise, but who cares. I'm sitting on the sands of Laguna Beach, and I don't think much else matters. I can't believe how beautiful this spot is, and it's made even more beautiful, because there aren't very many people here.

The sun's gone down, and the tidewater is glowing a bright green — some kind of algae thing going on, or so I heard on the news earlier. There's a full moon, or nearly full, up over there, on my right, and the whole ocean is brightly lit. My journal pages are a bright white in the moonlight. I also have a candle in a used up wine bottle I found on the beach.

The dinner at La Strada was out of this world. The food was good and a really pretty waitress started to talk with me — what's the deal with waitresses and me? She was a looker. Had deep, genuine black hair that was kind of cut off short in the back, a little above shoulder length. A Celtic beauty maybe? Or Italian? I think she said she was born in the Midwest somewhere, and now she was living half the year here in SoCal, and the other half in a place called, Clinton, Missouri. She did have a sort of an accent, but it was cute on her.

I told her I was an artist and that I was headed over to Laguna to write poetry on the beach. She said she'd join me after she got off work. I doubt that she will though because it was just a passing conversation, and passing conversations seldom yield much.

If anyone is ever reading this, I'm telling you, it's beautiful tonight! I've been on this beach a thousand times in my life, even more than a thousand, and I've never seen a night like this before.

The only thing that fouls it up is a group of hippies several yards to the left of me. They have a small bonfire going, and they're all dancing around, slowly undulating with the leaping flames, I guess. It's disturbing my silent retreat here at my favorite spot in the world. I have to admit though, a couple of the girls over there doing the undulating stuff look pretty interesting. One is naked from the waist up. Why do they have to do that? How am I going to concentrate with that going on during my writing?

I'm trying to get into the minds of those people. The males are having such a good time being drunk and playing guitars, and the females are all looking like they're doing screen tests to be go-go dancers on Laugh-In. In reality, they're probably just showing off for the males. It's so corny. This is the part I just don't get about humans: this silliness. Yeah, the girls have breasts and all that. I get it. But the crazy dance undulations they're doing; I'm sorry, it just looks silly. The guys seem to enjoy it though, but they look pretty stupid too. One guy is even playing bongos. Give me a break. Forget *Laugh-In*, I think they're all auditioning for a Frankie Avalon movie.

Twenty Minutes Later

I'm starting to get hungry again. I wish had some Mexican food, but all I brought with me is a pack of weenies. A few minutes ago, I got the crazy idea to take them and head over to that hippie bonfire. I thought I might roast two or three of them and bring them back here to my spot before they notice anything. Suddenly, a shadowy figure approaches me from the left as I'm starting to walk over there, scaring the heck outta me.

A voice from the shadow calls out, "Brother!"

I've had a few sips of Red Mountain, and now I hear this word coming out of nowhere, sort of.

"Brother," it repeats itself, "do you want to dance in our light?"

"What light is that?" Now I see the shadow as a solid figure.

"Our simple bonfire that we have built for world peace, brother."

Finally, I see the face coming out of the darkness of the beach night, catching the light of the big fire. I start to get mixed feelings about this scenario. *Numero uno*, it's a bit unnerving, *numero two-o*, this guy's face kind of looks like what I imagine Che Guevara might have looked like, only this guy isn't carrying a gun, he's holding a beat up guitar. He punctuates every line of his speech with an extravagant strum on the guitar strings and a goofy grin on his face.

"Brother," he says gently, touching his hand to my shoulder. I recoil like a rattlesnake. "I saw you over here watching our ceremony, and I felt you should be a part of us." His face is plain spooky. "You know," he continues, "there is one of ours who wishes to be a friend of yours."

"Pardon me, Che, but I haven't got a clue as to what the heck you're talking about," I tell him. "I just saw your bonfire, and I've got this pack of weenies here, and I was gonna ask you if I could put 'em on a stick and roast 'em. I wanted to bring Mexican food but ..."

"Sweet Brother, you may borrow our fire, but the lady is still interested in talking to you. I'm sure I don't know why. It's the policy of our group not to solicit those from the other side."

I ask him what he means by that. I always thought the other side is where you go when you die.

"No, my dear brother. The other side is merely our way of speaking about those who are not of our way."

That was it for me. I told the bozo, "Number one, I ain't your brother, number two, I just want to fry my stupid weenies in that fire over there, and number three, I think you're a really distorted example of some genetic project that went way over the top. Leave me alone. I want to write some poetry now. I'll just eat my weenies cold."

"But what about the girl?" Che asked, looking terribly maligned.

"Send her back to the mother ship, buddy, 'cause I've got things to do."

And that was the end of that, I thought. The bizarre creature merged back into the silhouetteville of his bonfire and I came back over here where my candle was still burning.

So now what? I'm sitting yoga style on the blanket that I brought with me, and it's really gotten dark. I can see the cult bonfire glowing in the distance. They're still dancing. I'm going to write a poem or two, I think. The candle and the moon will help me, but I'm not sure what will come out of my head tonight.

I have my little battery-operated radio—Donovan is singing "Jennifer Juniper," and all that. I have some Bic pens, and my black cardboard-covered journal. I do wish the mother ship would turn down the noise.

> *1948*
> *good year for wine*
> *bad year for blind dates*
> *women didn't exist for me then*
> *neither did philosophy ... I was a baby*
> *war torn fields of Kansas*
> *cow wars*
> *wheat wars*
> *drought wars*
> *no visions back then of college degrees*
> *or girls*
> *at least 'til I was seven weeks old —*
> *there was this one baby sitter ...*
> *had some good lookin' gypsy woman*
> *a lady with shiny fake jewelry*
> *kiss me on the forehead once*
> *and I liked it*
> *daily bread*
> *and a tree house that came later*
> *and prairie dust*
> *made me pragmatic*
> *even though I couldn't walk yet*

Soooooo ... there's my first poem of the night. Not much to write home about, but it's a part of me — from somewhere in here.

Pardon the interruption — some chick is walking over toward me from the hippie party. Great, now what?

Holy moley! It's the waitress from la Strada. I don't believe it. What the ...? Is she a part of that hippie ritual? I don't even know her name. Hang on here ...

Day 61: Sunday Afternoon

I was simply going to write poetry all night, but I got sidetracked by the waitress from La Strada. I could see the sand grains dropping off her naked feet as she walked toward me. The light from the giant bonfire hit behind the grains at just the right angle, making them look like tiny diamonds. She was carrying her sandals in one hand and a bottle of wine in the other. Like I needed more wine.

She plopped herself down on the sand about three inches from me and started drinking from her wine bottle. I held my breath. I thought I was going to have this dead drunk chick on my hands, but I discovered as the evening wore on that she could hold it better than anyone I'd ever known before.

"So where's your poem Mr. Artist?" She smiled and reached for my journal. I grabbed her hand in mid flight and smiled back at her. "Hang on," I said. "If you want, I'll read it to you." I never let anyone touch my journal. How did she know about the poem?

I read her the poem, but I couldn't keep my eyes off her; something about the moonlight on her shoulder-length black hair that was such a shiny black it reflected the moon. She was wearing a yellow bikini, but I couldn't keep my eyes off her smile. She told me her name is …

"Slim."

"Slim?" I said. "How odd is that?"

"Where you from Mr. Artist?"

"Kansas," I replied.

"So, name yourself."

"What do you mean?" I asked.

"Slim is my nickname, and you think it's odd. You need to have a nickname so we can be on equal footing."

"Okay … uhh … how 'bout, 'Winfield'. That's where I was born, and can I just say something here?"

"Go for it, Winfield."

"I'm sorry, but I think you are one of the prettiest women I have ever seen. Period. End of story, and no more compliments.”

“Wow. It must be the bikini.”.

“No, it’s just you. I wanted to tell you that at the restaurant.”

“What about me is so special to you, Winfield?”

“I can’t put my finger on it, Slim. Everything I guess, and I don’t even know you. Mainly your face, I think. That smile. Those eyes. When you look at me your eyes seem to draw me into you.” Then I got stupid and muttered under my breath, “I wonder if you’re the one?”

“The one what? Are you crazy?” She looked taken aback by my words.

“Never mind Slim, I’m not sure I know. I just know that something is terribly right, or something is terribly wrong about this night. Maybe it’s just the wine.”

“Write some more poetry, DH.”

I look at her, a bit confused. “How do you know my name? I don’t recall telling you back at the restaurant. In fact, I kept thinking all the way here that we had forgotten to exchange names, even when I invited you to come to the beach as I was leaving La Strada.”

“Some girl told me back at the restaurant. I think she said her name was Ann.”

“My god! Was she alive?”

She backs away from me a little. “What are you talking about?”

“I’m sorry Slim. I’ve had this apparition following me around for a long time. I call her my Muse.”

“You mean like a ghost? Like a spook haunting you?” Her look tells me that she is assessing my sanity.

“Yes. Just like a spook. And I don’t know what to do about it. I’m not sure I even want to …”

“You aren’t sure you want to do anything about it, huh?”

“I’m not kidding. Was she alive? What did she look like?” I have to ask.

“I … guess she was … I think she had brown hair in a pony tail, with … I don’t know. I don’t remember. I’m just a waitress. She ordered a super large burger, and I remember her eating the whole thing. Oh yeah, she was kind of sloppy. Some of the secret sauce started dripping out the corner of her mouth."

"I knew it!" I jump up, kicking sand all over Slim and everything else I'd brought with me.

"Are you crazy or what?"

"I'm not crazy," I say loudly. "It's my Muse, this girl, Ann, that haunts me."

"You need to see a doctor, DH." She starts to get up.

"Oh yeah? So, how again did you get my name?"

"Got a point there." She settles back down. "But listen, you're kind of spacing out on this Muse thing, aren't you?"

"I guess, but it's all so confusing. All I wanted to do was lay on the beach and write poetry and not even think about Ann any more, and she seems to have followed me all the way down here."

"So, she's a past lover?" Slim asks.

"No, just a dream, I think."

"Well, how's this for a dream, DH?"

The Morning After the Night Before

I'm not sure how to describe what went on last night, or for how long it went on. After that last question … Well, you get the picture.

"Just trying to take your mind off things," she said, at last. At least I think that's what she said. "Let's mess around a little, and then I'll let you write me a poem. I'll bet I can get rid of that Muse of yours."

We messed around. Then I wrote her a poem:

> *The older women haunt me*
> *Inside and out and*
> *Are*
> *Softer warmer deeper*
> *Hollowed out and pillowy*
> *And ready with warm lips*
> *Used lips*

Lips with college degrees
Older women
Know how to breathe warm wet air
And
To writhe
When completely still
Breathe when dead and
Smile earthly smiles
With soft breasts
And
Experienced thighs

"So you think I'm and older woman?" she asked me after I read it to her.

"Well, you are aren't you?" I asked carefully.

"Just how old are you, DH?"

"I'm nineteen. How old are you?"

"Good grief! I'm old enough to be your … older sister. Crimeny! You're a kid! But …"

Then she took my hand.

"I don't care how old you are, DH, I'm not that much older than you." She paused for a moment. "I guess I could be your mother, but I would have had to have you at an early age."

"Slim, how old are you?"

"I'm forty DH. I'm sorry …"

"Sorry about what?"

"That I'm forty and you're only 19, I guess. I'm twice your age."

"So?"

"So, I'm an old lady to you!"

"But you're a nice old lady. What's age any way?"

"Age is old, DH. Age is old."

"Age can be old and age can be young, or age can be in between. In the end what does it matter, Slim? Here's a poem just for you:

Roses are red
Violets are blue
Elephants are grey and
I think I really like you.

"You do?" she asked.

"Of course I do," I answer sincerely. But here's your real poem, Slim." And I recited it for her:

the soft ocean breeze touches
me
in a sad lament
crying out this night
in the darkness that is the beach
all that it
is
"touch me if you can!"
the spirit of the sea cries out and I would caress the soft
cheek of the wind
of
the breath of this Selkie I have just met.—
Untouchable
Sweet flesh.
Enchantress wind.

"DH, that's lovely. Nobody's ever written me a poem before." Her eyes were wet.

"Why are you crying?" I asked.

"I don't know. Maybe it's just the sea air, and the candle, and the wine," she said.

"You are lovely in the candle light."

"Thanks," she said, wiping the tears from her eyes, "but I gotta go now. The others over there are gonna want me to come back."

"What's the deal with those guys? One character came over here and I almost decked him."

"That would be Bella."

"Bella! Like Lugosi?"

"No, like Silverstein. He's some guy that left New York a couple of years ago, and got hooked up with the group a few weeks ago. He's kind of a pain in the butt."

"You bet he is," I agreed. " But what the heck are you doing hanging with those creeps?"

"I don't know. I'm not really hanging with them. They came into the restaurant one day about two months ago. I guess about twelve of them. I started talking to this one girl, who was pretty nice, and she invited me to this wingding tonight. To be honest I think it's pretty silly. I just wanted to eat barbecue. Then I found out they're vegetarians."

"Ha! So you aren't a UFO kook!"

She giggles. "No, I'm just me. I'm a silly little waitress who doesn't know what to do with her life. But when you came into the restaurant, I was … attracted to you."

"And what was it that attracted you to me?"

"Lot's of things really. The fact that you came into the restaurant all alone is one thing. Most people don't. Your beach-blond hair was a big draw to me. That black book you were carrying looked like a mystery, and I'm a woman, I simply had to find out what was in it." She grinned.

"This is my journal. I write everything in here." I held it up in both hands. "My whole life experience, just as it happens day to day. Everything. For better or worse."

"Wow. I never thought of doing such a thing, but I can see where that would be very valuable. Then you could look back on all your mistakes and try to correct them, and all the good times, and try to repeat them."

"That's one thought, but more than that, I kind of look at it as a sort of chronicle of an age. One day many years from now, I'll read this journal, and it will bring back all the memories of this time and of this beach, and a million other things."

"And me?"

"And you," I tell her.

She paused. "And that Muse you told me about earlier?" she asks, rolling eyes just a little bit.

"Yeah …" I tried to find the words. "For some reason I just know she has to be written in my journal. That's the biggest mystery I've ever experienced. There is no way to explain any of it, but I feel there is something very important about my little Muse."

"Okay, Winfield, whatever you say, but I have to go now. I think the party is over at the bonfire and I'll miss my ride."

"Okay Slim. I wish you could stay." And I really did.

"Me too. I wrote my number down on a piece of paper before I walked over here. Will you call me sometime?" She handed me the paper.

"Yes, I will."

"Maybe the next time you come to La Strada, we can meet up and go off somewhere to write a poem together." She smiled.

"I'd like that. Maybe next week sometime." I smiled back.

"I'd love that." She lingered on the word "love."

Back to Real Time again

Last night, Slim handed me the paper with her phone number and walked away into the light of the bonfire.

Earlier this afternoon, I tried calling Slim at the number she had given me. A male voice answered and I asked to speak with her. He told me he was her brother, and that Slim had been killed in a car accident on her way home last night.

I just hung up the phone. I didn't even say goodbye. I didn't get the brother's name. I don't even know what to write here. I don't know what my feelings are—were—for her. She was so beautiful, and I sensed that she was more than just a body walking around, unlike all the other bodies out there. She had a spirit about her.

Day 64: Wednesday

Frank called me this morning. I was still feeling pretty distraught, and I guess he could read it in my voice.

"DH? You don't sound like the DH I know," he said. "You okay?"

"A friend of mine was just killed."

"Man. That's tough, DH. I'm really sorry."

"It's okay."

"No. No it isn't. How about you meet me over at the Royal Scot for some coffee and chit-chat?"

"I don't know."

"I don't give a hoot if you know or not!" *The Laugh.* "I'll be there in twenty minutes."

"Okay," I agree, reluctantly. I'm not too enthusiastic about seeing anyone right now, but if it has to be someone, Frank would be the only one.

Thirty Minutes Later

Frank got here first on his motorcycle. My VW bug is fairly slow, so I usually arrive everywhere after everybody else. We're sitting at a table near the window, and Norma is treading lightly 'cause she knows something's wrong. We're being pretty quiet, more so than usual. I don't think Frank really knows what to say to me about Slim's death and, quite frankly, I don't know what to say to him. I'm not even sure how I feel about it. I hardly knew her, yet, I sensed there was something about her. But I have to admit, over the past day or two, a little birdie, something in my head, has been telling me that Slim wasn't the one either—the one I am meant to be with—that the one is still out there somewhere. Maybe in the near future. But still …

Frank breaks the silence. "DH …" he pauses, looking down at his cup of coffee. "You know, life is tough. None of us knows what the heck is going on half the time, and we haven't got a clue about what's gonna happen next. I could get on that bike out there, and start riding back to the house, and some fat, cigar smoking trucker could plow through a red light, and end my art career forever!" *The Laugh*.

"Frank, I'm not sure what I feel about this whole thing, but thanks for being concerned for me."

"That's what friends do, DH. So, you gonna be okay with this?"

"I think so. Slim was just a friend. I hardly knew her."

"Pretty, huh?" He smiles.

"Yes, she was. But she was more than just pretty. I think she was just … special. That's all."

"That's enough."

"But thanks for caring."

"I do care." He smiled again. "There aren't a lot of people I care about, but you're one of them."

"And why is that, Frank?"

"Good question. I think it's mainly because you aren't a gallery owner!" *The Laugh*.

"That's the only reason?"

"Of course not. It's because I can let my hair down when I'm with you. I can say what I really feel. You can't do that with gallery owners, or even family sometimes. Everybody needs somebody to just flake out with."

"Well, that's a pretty big responsibility for me, to be that kind of flake for you." And we both laugh.

"No kidding, DH. You're a straight-up guy, honest. And not a bad painter, but I'll never admit that in public!" *The Laugh*, again.

"I've been working on some new paintings, Frank. Why don't you come over and see them sometime?"

"You mean come over to your garage?" He smiles.

"I can't help it that I live in a garage. I can't afford anything else right now."

"Don't sell yourself short, DH! It's the height of romanticism for an artist to live in a garage. Maybe that even makes you a better artist than me!"

"I don't think so, Frank."

"You know, we've talked about the Art Spirit before, DH, and I honestly believe you have it every bit as much as I do. You're a little shaky around the edges about settling into your technique, but that spirit's inside you. I guarantee it!"

"How can you guarantee something like that?"

"Because I let you hang around with me!" A major Laugh.

"I guess that's a compliment."

"The best I can do." Again, *The Laugh*.

I do take it as a compliment from this wizard of color and oil. He's never said anything like this to me before. But he might just be saying it because of the death of Slim and how that has affected me.

"Hey Bud, you got any wine in that garage of yours?"

"I have some Red Mountain."

"That awful stuff! I guess it'll have to do. Let's get out of here and go to your place. We can look at some of your new paintings, and I'll criticize them for you, no charge!" He smiles.

"Okay. That would be kind of a kick. I love for my work to be criticized." We both laugh again.

Forty Minutes Later

I don't have much space in this garage apartment. It's not even fair to call it an apartment; it's just a room. A tiny, little room I call "The Hole." My grandfather built it for me a couple of years ago because my brother, Jim, and I each wanted our own room. We had been sharing a large bedroom upstairs in our parent's house. I mentioned earlier that the garage I live in belongs to my parents, and that I pay them $100 a month rent, not because they need the money — which they don't — but because it's right. My stepfather, Wayne, is an aerospace engineer, and my mother, Norma, is the secretary for the head honcho at the Sunkist Lemon processing plant in Corona, so money isn't really an issue with them. We have a very nice house here in Mira Loma, but Jim needs his space, and I need mine, so Granddad built this little one room apartment thingie for me. I named it after a Toulouse-Lautrec painting that mentions "The Hole" as some sort of cabaret or nightclub.

I have only one chair in the room and it's in front of my makeshift plywood desk. Frank is sitting there right now. I'm sitting on the bed. We just got here a few minutes ago and …

"You'd make it a whole lot easier to chitchat if you stopped writing in that thing," he says.

"I can talk and write at the same time. I just feel this journal is something I have to do."

"Well, can you write and move things at the same time? Bring out those paintings you're working on. I want to see what the great romantic garage painter has done recently." He smiles and sips Red Mountain from one of the two cups I own.

"Hang on, let me just set the stage first."

"Set the stage for what?"

"For these paintings I'm about to show you."

The Laugh. "Set what silly stage! Just show me the paintings! Don't ever explain your talent, DH! Let the paintings speak for themselves."

I know he's right. He always is. So I walk out the door into the main part of the garage, and bring back two of the seven paintings I completed over the past few weeks. One is a self-portrait, and the other is a small portrait of my Muse, Ann. I hold the first up to Frank's critical gaze.

"Hmmm." He pulls both sides of his mouth down. "Not bad. But why are you wearing a tie?"

"I have no idea. I just thought it would look good with the green sport coat."

"And the bright yellow background?"

"It both harmonizes and clashes with the green at the same time."

"I hate to say this, DH, but this painting ain't half bad. I can see a lot of Soutine influence in it though."

"I agree. I think that show you took me to really had an effect on my work."

"But you gotta watch that. It's okay to sorta be influenced by another artist, but at some point, if you want to make it big, you have to leave that all behind you and paint your own heart."

I already knew that while I was painting the painting.

"But I'm just getting started in this art thing, Frank. I'm sort of experimenting as I go along. We've talked about this before. I don't really have a style yet."

"I know that, Bud,"—he's been calling me that a lot lately—"but you're still young! I'm an old man and you're only 19! You have eons to get your style together. Just don't work too hard at it. Let it grow out of you naturally. If that Art Sprit is in you, there ain't no way you can hold it back."

"I know. You're right, Frank."

"I'm always right!" *The Laugh*. "What's that other painting you have over there with the front turned discreetly against the door? What are you hiding from old Frank?"

"Hang on."

I had changed my mind about showing this one to Frank, but there is no way to get out of it, now that he has seen it. I place the painting of Ann in front of the closet door so Frank can get a good view of it.

"Wow! Now that's a painting! Who in the world is she?"

"Ann."

"Ann ... Ann ... ?"

"My Muse. The girl that keeps appearing to me day and night wherever I am."

"Oh yeah, The Muse girl. I just didn't remember her name. Good grief, DH, that's a hot painting. And it doesn't look like Soutine! You may be onto something with this one. You got any others you've done since you turned this baby out?"

"Yep."

"Where are they?'

"You really want to see more?"

"You got any more wine?"

"Yep."

"Then I really want to see some more of your paintings." *The Laugh*.

I go back out to the garage and find a painting I finished a few weeks ago. I don't know what Frank will think of it, but I think it's exquisite — my "La Petite Parisienne." I feel this might be the painting that represents a breakthrough for me, from the more traditional to the experimental. There's a finesse to the woman's face that I had not been able to accomplish in past paintings, and the overall color and design is quite harmonious. Many problems were solved with this painting, and I'm very pleased with it. But what will Frank say? He's never really been my critic before. He's not seen much of my work. Usually I go over to his Castle and watch him work and view his paintings.

I have to say that I appreciate Frank for coming over here today. He's done two things for me. He's placed a personal value on my painting abilities, and he's made the death of Slim a much more gentle passing. I will never forget him for that. The look in his eyes back at the Royal Scot when he asked me if I was "gonna be okay about this?" I saw a tear form in his left eye. He knew I was hurting, and somehow he hooked into that hurt. As that tear came down I saw his embarrassment, so I turned to fake a cough, and give him a chance to wipe it away.

"This just keeps getting better!" Frank says as I place "La Petite Parisienne" in front of the closet. "DH, this is exquisite. This could be hanging in any gallery in any town in any country. I had no idea you were painting this kind of stuff."

"You need to come over more often," I say, grinning.

"Now, mind you, it ain't the quality of my stuff! But it ain't half bad." Then more seriously, "These are really good, DH. I advise you to keep on keepin' on. If you carry this out long enough, you just might find that style you're looking for. In the mean time, one more cup of wine and I'm outta here."

I fill Frank's cup and I notice the expression on his face, almost sad, and I ask him "What's wrong, Frank?"

"I'm worried about you DH. You sure you're okay with this Slim thing? I mean your friend just died, and we're drinking wine and talking about Ort. That's gotta be tough on you, and I'm not sure I want to leave you just yet."

I heard the quiver in Frank's voice as he spoke those last words to me … and I lost it. The vision of Slim and the night on the beach near the bonfire came into my mind and I felt the tears welling up in my eyes, and I just couldn't control myself. Frank saw what was happening. He moved smoothly from the chair to the bed and sat beside me. He wrapped his arms around me and he rocked me back and forth like I was a little kid.

"I'm so sorry DH. I'm so sorry."

The death of Slim has taken more out of me than I would ever admit in public. There was a connection there. I have no idea what it all means, but there was also a clarification of some sort, and it's made me think hard about life and death, and about how fragile we are. There was a demonstration at the University at Berkeley yesterday. I watched it on TV. Kids running around acting crazy and stupid. Why is it always kids? Why aren't there ever any adults at these protests? I used to be at least halfway concerned about politics, and several other semi-relevant concerns of this contemporary culture, but as I watched the vacant faces of those robotic, almost soulless protesters during that newscast, Slim's beautiful face kept coming to my mind. As a result, I didn't care if this world, and all of its infantile foolishness, was blown into a zillion pieces. I could only think of how vital and how wonderful Slim was that night. And then in one moment of time she was gone from this dimension. Dead. Her single life had been worth far more than all of the dirty, angry humans I saw in that TV newscast.

"DH," Frank spoke, "I'm gonna hang around here for a while. I'm not gonna leave you till this has all passed. How 'bout we send out for some pizza and drink some more wine. You got any Coltrane tapes? Cause I ain't goin' nowhere."

After Frank Leaves

I do have a Coltrane tape that I never play. For some reason I don't care to listen to music much any more. But I put it in my player, and Frank and I just sat there listening to the tape, talking small talk. I felt kind of embarrassed because of my emotion over the Slim thing, but Frank didn't bring it up again. I showed him several other paintings. He was amused by some of them, but mostly supportive of others.

When Frank left I made him swear never to tell a soul about my little breakdown. He crossed his heart and smiled and said, "No way Bud. No way." He smiled again and hugged me close to him.

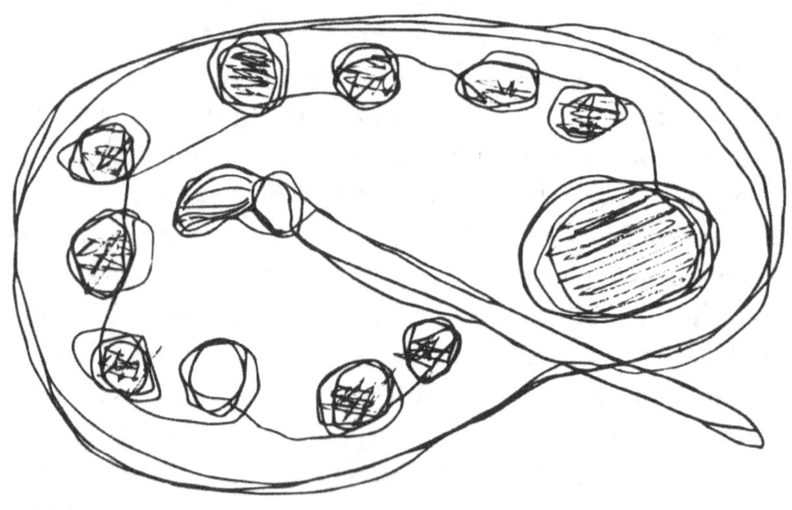

Day 65: The Next Day

Artists are insane, and women are beautiful, and that's the reason artists are insane. A simple and accurate formula.

I'm in The Hole, and I need to quickly relate this day's events before I'm interrupted. I've started a painting of a girl who has recently caught my eye. Her name is Donna. I think she's just a year or two younger than me and she's an art student at RCC. I seem to be running into her a lot these days. This morning when I went to my ceramics class there she was. She's primarily a painter, but she was at a potter's wheel spinning out one of the sweetest vases I'd ever seen.

Donna has short blonde hair, a pair of riveting blue eyes and nice lips. I suppose that's what I'm attracted to the most—her lips. While she was working at the wheel, I noticed that once in a while, whenever she gives it a kick, she pinches her lips up like she's kissing something. I don't know why that fascinates me.

When I walked into the class, Donna looked up at me and smiled.

"Hi! You're DH, right?"

"Yes … I am," I stuttered. I always stutter when I speak to a girl for the first time.

"Mitchkelly told me about you." She didn't stutter. In fact, she was incredibly calm and almost bubbly. She was radiant.

"Bill Mitchkelly?"

"Who else?"

"I guess that was a stupid question, I don't believe there is another Mitchkelly on this planet, huh?"

"Not like our Mitchkelly." She smiled, still forming her vase.

"So what did he say about me?"

"Got a dollar?"

"What?"

"Give me a dollar and I'll tell you what he said." She smiled up at me, never missing a kick.

"Okay. I'll give you five dollars if you tell me everything—even the bad parts."

"Ha Ha! I don't want your money. I was just teasing."

"I think I knew that. At least I hope so."

"Mitchkelly told me that he thinks you have some serious talent and he hopes you do something with it. That's all," she said.

"He did?"

"You sound surprised!"

"I am! I can't make a proper pot if it meant saving the whole planet."

"He wasn't talking about pottery, DH. He was talking about painting."

When she made that statement I was a bit confused because Bill is a ceramics teacher. But then I remembered one day I had him over to The Hole, and he insisted on seeing some of my paintings. I showed him a bunch of stuff, old and new, and he just stood there with his hand caressing his chin, and his eyes all bunched up in an almost worried look. All of a sudden he blurted out that famous line of his, "You think you'll ever amount to anything, DH?" And I knew that was his way of telling me he liked my paintings. But this statement by Donna was like a lightning bolt out of the blue. I have the highest respect for Bill Mitchkelly. What an honor for him to say such a thing about me.

"Exactly what did he tell you?" I asked.

"He said that the painting you sold to RCC, the 'Old Man With Flowers,' is one of the best paintings he's ever seen. He said he was very surprised a young guy like you could turn out something like that. He said it had the quality of a master painter."

"Wow." It was all I could say.

"So, you like my vase?"

"Oh … yes … I love your vase. How long have you been doing this?" I felt the need to change the subject.

"This is only my first year. I'm really a waitress, but I want to do something special with my life. I'm not sure if this is it or not."

Can you believe it? Another waitress! What's with this?

"I just like making things out of clay. It seems to come naturally to me."

"Well, you seem to be pretty good at it. I have to admit that's one of the nicest vases I've seen turned out in this class."

"Thanks. So what kind of paintings do you do?"

"Whatever comes to my head, I stick it on a canvas. I really like Expressionist landscapes, so I try to use bold colors and big brush strokes, but I also like the Impressionists, so I pile on lots of light. Here lately though, I seem to be gravitating toward portraits."

"Who are you painting?"

"Just people I know."

"Well you know me now," she said, glowing. "Will you paint me?"

"I guess so. In fact ... I would love to paint you." I stutter again. "Do you have any photos I can use?"

"Can't I just pose for you? I don't have a problem with that. The painting teacher here at RCC uses me for nude modeling all the time. Pays me $7.00 an hour. But I wouldn't charge you." She smiles.

Was this girl wanting me to paint her in the nude?

"Okay ... yes ... you can pose for me."

This Evening in the Hole

And that's the position I find myself in now. Donna will be here in about five minutes, and I haven't a clue as to what the evening will bring. She doesn't know it, but I've already started a painting of her. It's a portrait of just her head. I'm not going to make any assumptions that she wants to be painted in the nude. In fact, I'm betting she wants something really simple like a portrait. I hear a car pulling up right now.

Three Hours Later

Oh boy, what a time. I didn't dare bring out my journal and do the writing thing because I didn't want to spook her. But I paid very close attention to the details of the evening and I'm going to try to write them down just as I experienced them.

When Donna got here, I went out to the driveway to greet her. She had driven here in a Lincoln Continental! Who would have figured? My first thought was, where the heck does a waitress get that kind of car?

She told me that her father owns a car dealership in downtown Riverside, and he lets her borrow any car off the lot, any time she wants. He even pays for her gas. I guess her Pop is pretty well off, and she stands to inherit a bunch of bucks when he kicks. Donna didn't seem to have a problem telling me everything about her life, and all the time she was rattling on I was thinking to myself, "Hmmm … it might be a good idea for me to try to see more of this girl."

I couldn't help feeling just a bit embarrassed about bringing this wealthy girl into my little garage apartment, but she seemed to love it.

"Wow, this is amazing!" Donna said as she entered The Hole.

"Well, that's not a word I would use for it," I replied.

"It's an artist's garret," she smiled, "and you are the artist! Just like Van Gogh!"

"You like Van Gogh?" I asked.

"I'm taking a lot of art history classes and I just love them," she explained. "Van Gogh is my favorite artist ever."

"He's my favorite too, followed closely now by Soutine."

"Chaim! I've been in love with Soutine ever since I saw his exhibit at LACMA."

"You're kidding! I saw that exhibit twice!"

"Then we have something in common, don't we?" She smiled as she began to explore my little room.

"Look at all these art books. You need a bigger place, DH."

"I can't afford it, Donna. I wish I could have a bigger place, but for now this will have to do."

"Here's a program from the Soutine show!" she exclaimed. "Come over here and sit on the bed and go through this with me."

We flipped through the pages very slowly. I kept watching her hands — the hands that had formed those vases. They were so delicate.

"I think you have the prettiest hands I have ever seen, Donna," I blurted out. What a dolt.

"My hands?"

"Yeah, I watched you making those vases of yours and …"

"And?"

"You're so gentle with them. Your hands are so long and slender."

Donna just looked up at me. Grabbing my face in those delicate hands she pulled my face to hers and kissed me.

I was dumbfounded.

"Do you have anything to drink, DH?"

"Just cheap wine. You're probably used to better stuff."

"Bring it out."

"It's Red Mountain."

"Never heard of it, but wine is wine to me," she replied. "Do you still want to paint me?"

"What? Of course I do."

I took her hand and we walked out of The Hole and into the garage. My parents have been kind enough to park the family cars out in the driveway to allow me to use the garage space for my main studio. Our driveway is quite long, as the family property covers about three acres, so there's plenty of parking room. It might be a different story if we lived somewhere that had blizzards, and we had to dig our cars out of snow drifts every morning.

I sat Donna on a stool at the end of the garage, and fed her wine while I drew several sketches. She asked me if I wanted her to remove her clothes and I told her I thought it best if I did a few clothed painting sessions before tackling that project. She looked a bit disappointed, but the evening yielded two very nice paintings, and she was very happy with them.

Later on, just before Donna got into her Lincoln to leave, she told me she had a very good time, and gave me her phone number. I'll call her—you bet I will. I had a good time too, and she's easy to be with, but I'm not sure about one thing. Is she The One? If not, who is?

The phone rings.

"Get over here, DH." It's Jack. "I have three gallons of wine and about five pounds of sculptor's wax! I want to do some lead sculpts, can you make it?"

Of course I can make it. It isn't that late. I love the times I have with Jack. We always do simple things together, and it's okay to do simple things once in a while, and tonight sounds fun. We haven't done lead sculptures for quite some time. I'm going to call Frank and see if he wants to join us.

Thirty Minutes Later at Jack's House

I called Frank and asked if he could meet us at Jack's. He was game for it, so now Frank, Jack, and I are sitting here on Jack's couch talking about art and philosophy, and making up dumb poetry. As I write these words, I have to wonder if this journal will ever mean anything to the world. As Bill Mitchkelly often queries, "… think you'll ever amount to anything?" I'm not sure any of us will. But the three of us do what we do at this time in our lives, ever hanging to the dreams we all have of becoming "someone." It's a fifty-fifty proposition right now, considering nearly all young adults of this era are pressured by the culture to drink too much, cuss too much, and get involved in situations that older, wiser people, would never even dream of. This present time is chaotic and unbridled, but I am counting on the future — maybe too much — to bring some sanity and stability to this world. I'm just not sure it's possible. Evolution? I don't buy it any more. If humanity is evolving, why is it not exhibiting a more perfect, sensible, specimen of human? It seems the truth of the matter is that people are getting weaker, and worse as time goes by, not stronger and better.

Jack says he's hungry and wants to make some spaghetti, so Frank and I walk into the kitchen to watch Jack do his thing. It seems like an off-the-wall type thing to do at this moment, but it isn't. This is just Jack being Jack. I've had his spaghetti before, and it will be well worth the time we take to make it happen.

"I've got mushrooms and hamburger and oregano and … some anchovies! Let's do this!"

Jack brings out a couple of large pots, one for the pasta and one for the sauce. There is no way in the world I will be able to follow him in my journal. He's throwing things in the sauce pot at light speed. He put the hamburger in first, then the mushrooms, and a whole bunch of herbs and spices. "This is the real thing!" he yells with glee.

Frank, being Frank, quietly asks him, "Just exactly what is it that sets this apart as the real thing?"

I laugh to myself. Frank is so sarcastic and so suave in the delivery of his sarcasm, but somehow it is not obnoxious coming from him, as it would be from most other people.

But Jack didn't catch the sarcasm. He's gone into lengthy explanations and justifications of exactly what the heck he is doing with our dinner, with scientific principles and formulas for every little move he makes. It's actually starting to make some sort of sense.

"Let's just get on with the pasta, puhleeeese," Frank implores. He gives me a sidelong glance, indicating his opinion of Jack's sanity.

I don't think Frank likes Jack, but I'm not really sure why. Jack is a brilliant artist, no doubt about it. His drawings are the most amazing, exquisite things I have ever seen. He does have an incredibly strong personality, and I think that's what rubs Frank wrong. It's a personality conflict. Both of these guys are heavy in that department, but Jack is impulsive, often taking action before he thinks. On the other hand, everything Frank does is carefully planned and executed, hence the tension. But as the spaghetti is coming together, and the wine is flowing, there are no fisticuffs, and all seems to be going well on planet Jack.

Frank walks over to the stove and says, "I'll cook the pasta. DH is gonna be worthless at this. Heaven knows, he can't write in that journal and stir pasta at the same time." *The Laugh.*

"Go for it," Jack says.

Frank, being Frank again, is as elegant with his pasta maneuvers as he is with his paintings. I've written this before, but I need to mention it again, I love watching this guy's hands. He's like a ballet dancer. I don't know if he plans it or not, but every wave of his hand is so graceful, that nothing else in any room gets any notice. Even Jack is entranced by the hands of Frank Reed.

I grab a spoon and dip into Jack's simmering sauce pot.

"Man, this sauce is good!" I exclaim.

Frank is still wondering how I can eat and write in my journal at the same time.

"How'd you do that—write and eat at the same time?"

Jack chimes in, "That's what he does! He's a numbskull journalist! But that journal of his ain't gonna go nowhere, because it's all about art. Art don't sell, and it don't do squat."

"What do you mean by that?" Frank asks. Jack has finally caught Frank's interest.

"I mean," Jack continues, "that art is just what it is. It's wine and canvas and color. That's all it is. It doesn't make any difference what a painter paints or what a writer writes about art. Life goes on."

"That's a rather simplistic way of looking at it, Jack," replies Frank, smiling calmly.

"Think about it, Frank. Pick up any magazine. How many artists do you see? The answer is zippo! Nada. Zilch. Everything is about Hollywood and politics and whatever. The only time you see an article on an artist is after he dies. When Picasso dies, I guarantee he'll get a big write up because he's famous, but the next day, probably nothing. When Liz Taylor dies, holy crapola! Wait till you see what the papers print. There'll be reams of superficial nonsense and sentimental baloney, and the articles will go on for weeks, maybe months. Every TV station will run Lizzie movies, and her old interviews for weeks."

Jack may be right on this.

"It's always been that way, Jack," Frank says. "That's the rule! If you want to be a famous artist you have to die, and dyin' don't necessarily get the artist anything, look at Van Gogh. But that doesn't negate the work of any artist. He just can't paint any more when he's dead!" *The Laugh.*

"I see what Jack is saying, Frank," adding my own two cents. "Art is so demeaned in our society. At least fine art. I have a problem with calling Hollywood 'Art'. Art to me is painting and sculpture and maybe pottery. I don't know. It's such a loose term. I do know that art goes beyond mere entertainment. Hollywood is about entertainment. Actors act. Art goes deeper than that. It penetrates to a deeper level in a human soul."

"Our resident philosopher speaks." Frank smiles and gives me an affirmative nod.

"Every time any actor takes a leak they call it art!" says Jack, shaking his head.

"But is or isn't acting an art form of a sort?" Frank asks.

"Of course it is," Jack replies. "But not everyone is an actor. There's a lot of junk on the silver screen these days, and just because some man or woman has made a few movies, they think their junk is special."

"I can buy that," Frank says. "So let's see some of your work, Jack."

"It's all over the place!" Jack says loudly. "Sculptures on the bookcase, a painting on that wall, about twenty pots here in the kitchen. There's a stack of paintings behind the couch, and three or four portfolios of sketches under the couch."

"But what are you trying to do? Are you a potter first or a painter?"

"I'm pretty much anything I want to be, but my first love is sculpture. If I had my way I'd buy a foundry and turn out big bronze pieces day and night."

"Ha! You're talking lots of money there, big guy."

"I know it. But I love to work with molten metal and investments."

"I do too," I add. "Especially at night over at RCC. There's something kind of magical about that."

"You're the perfect romantic artist, DH," Frank says. "But it ain't about the purty night sky or the ohm-bee-ance, it's about the ORT! It's about the final product and the money it will bring in.

As usual, he's right—at least in the contemporary, commercial aspect of making art. Unfortunately, I fly with my emotions more than I do with the practicality of the business world. I've never been good with that. I can't even balance my checkbook.

Jack announces that the spaghetti is ready.

"I'll leave it on the stove and we can piece on it all night," he explains. "Lets go make some art."

"What have you got in mind, Jack?" I ask.

"I don't care. Anything. We can do a lead cast or a painting. What do you think, Frank?"

"Whatever." Frank looks a bit bored. "You got some more of that cheap vino?"

I grab the jug and pour Frank another glass of wine. He smiles and rolls his eyes again in Jack's direction. So I make a suggestion.

"Hey, if we're gonna make art, why don't we do a group thing. Like one large piece of canvas and the three of us doing our own individual styles. We can divide the canvas into three equal sections, and each take a section, or we can just mingle our styles together all over the place. Either way is okay with me. But we do have to come up with a theme."

"How 'bout war?" Jack asks.

"I don't think so," counters Frank.

"How about just a simple landscape?" I suggest. "We can put cows and fences and whatever in it if we want. Do you have a large canvas, Jack?"

"I have at least 20 feet."

"I think about 6 feet would be fine," I suggest.

So, Jack goes and gets his canvas roll. We cut off about six feet and tack it up on his dining room wall.

"What's the Other Half gonna say when she sees this?" Frank asks.

"It doesn't much matter," Jack says, and we just leave it at that.

Frank and I both know Jack and Lisa are having problems, but they're still planning on getting married soon. I don't get that. I like them both, but they have such opposite personalities. Jack is the loose-goose artist, and Lisa is a hard-core businesswoman, who has very little patience with such trivial things as art and artists. I know Lisa will not like coming home to a bunch of wine soaked artists, spilled spaghetti all over her carpet, and an oil painting thumb-tacked to her wall. I'm having second thoughts about this whole thing. It just doesn't feel good.

But here we go anyway. It's pretty much not my call, and since Frank is considered the master, we let him go first. He begins to draw a magnificent farm scene that takes me by surprise. It kind of looks like Grandma Moses, in a way, but a bit more technical. Jack moves in and applies the first layers of color and shadows. They're saving me for last. Frank says, "You're the wild man of color, DH, and color is the cherry on top of every painting." I suppose that both of those observations are fairly accurate.

Jack is painting a bunch of different blues here and there; even one of the cows is blue. When he puts down his brush to get another glass of wine, I pick it up and do my thing. I begin to add the color I love to play with—lots and lots of color, but I do change the blue cow to brown before Jack gets back. Frank heaves a deep sigh of relief.

Frank is now drawing little farm animals all over the canvas, and I begin to think that we're all getting just a little silly. Jack blurts out, "We need some women!"

"You mean mingling with the cows on the painting?" Frank asks with a roll of his eyes.

"I think Jack means real women for the here and now, Frank." But I know Jack doesn't even know any women other than Lisa.

"Man oh man," Jack says. "I guess I need one of those little black address books."

"DH," says Frank, "How 'bout Norma? You got her number?"

"You think I'm going to invite her to come over here to be accosted by you two lunatics? No way."

"We wouldn't accost her," Jack says. "We'd let you do that. It would just be nice to have some female air in the room."

I'm not sure I totally trust these guys, but I'll make the call. Hopefully she won't answer the phone.

Norma did answer the call, and she was delighted to be invited over. Great. She's on her way. She said something about being down at the mall all day and now her evening was free. She was bored.

"Fantastic! I'll be right over!" she cried gleefully from the other end of the line. I gave her the best directions I could, considering I'm not sure where she lives exactly, but it's somewhere close and she ought to be here very soon.

"She's on her way."

"She got any friends?" Jack asks.

"I asked her that, and she said she'd try to find one or two," I answered. "But you guys had better leave Norma to me. You start hitting on her and this party is over."

Frank does *The Laugh*, and Jack just keeps on painting. Wonderful. He's painting that cow blue again.

Three Hours Later

I couldn't write in the journal because there was just too much going on. I'll try to bring it up to date here. Norma arrived with one other girl who looked like she fell out of a sci-fi movie. She was very thin, and very white, and had really short blond hair, and bright red lips. She also had a sweet puffy nose that was cute in an odd sort of way, and she was wearing the shortest pair of white shorts I've ever seen. Her butt cheeks were hanging out in the back a tad bit.

"We're gonna let her paint a lot tonight, Bud," Frank whispered to me with a wink, anticipating the view we would have while she was facing the canvas to paint.

Norma introduced her friend as Gigi. She told us that Gigi had mentioned to her that she was a bartender at a club downtown. Just looking at her I could believe that. But man, I have to admit she really is something. I gave her a glass of wine and asked her if she'd like to do some painting.

"I'll give it a shot!" Gigi said, her front teeth gleaming. "What do you want me to do?" She stood there with her hands on her hips like a little kid.

"Just try to stay inside the lines," Frank said sarcastically. Then under his breath, "This oughta be good."

"So, I can just fill things in the way I want?" Gigi grinned at me.

"You can honey," Jack said.

"Just draw, Gigi," I tell her. "Forget these other bozos are here, just draw."

Then we all got the surprise of our lives. This little pixie knew how to paint! I couldn't believe it. Frank was standing straight, paying close attention. I could tell by his face he was impressed. Jack just … well … sat on the couch drinking wine. Norma was next to me on the other couch and she had a big smile on her face.

"I forgot to tell you, Gigi has been painting for years," Norma said. "That's why I brought her tonight. She's an art major at UCR."

The Laugh exploded from Frank. "A ringer! Who'd a thunk it!"

"Who painted that cow blue?" Gigi asked.

"I did," Jack replied.

"Cool. I like that." Frank and I both rolled our eyes. Norma laughed.

"Blue is Gigi's favorite color," Norma said.

Tonight Norma was the goddess out of every Mythology ever recorded. She looked like she was dressed for some sort of formal thing, not a painting party. She was wearing a short black dress, very low cut, black high heels and black nylons. I could feel the heat of her sitting that close to me on the couch. She kept looking over at me and staring—just staring with a smile on her face. Her hair looked beautiful, too. At the restaurant she always had her hair done up in a bun type thing, but tonight it was loose and flowing.

"Is there somewhere I can talk to you alone, DH?" Norma asked.

"I guess we can find a place. Hang on."

I asked Jack if Norma and I could go into his bedroom to talk for a bit. I told him she seemed to be a bit depressed. He said, "No Prob." So I took her hand, and while Frank was painting on the farm scene, Norma and I slipped away into Jack's bedroom. We sat on the bed.

"Is something wrong, Norma?" I asked.

"Yes. DH. Something is terribly wrong."

"You haven't kissed me in days," she said, and she placed her mouth on mine and kissed me."

"What's going on here?" The indignant voice from the living room penetrated the closed bedroom door. Lisa was home

Norma and I got off the bed, adjusted our clothing and walked out into the living room. I saw Frank slipping out the door quietly like a cat burglar. Jack stood in a kind of drunken stupor, a paint-brush in one hand, and a glass of wine in the other, facing down the wrath of Lisa.

"What are you doing?" Lisa screamed. "You'll get paint all over the walls!"

She was right. I knew this was going to happen.

"And who are these bimbos?" She was talking about Norma and Gigi. The little sci-fi girl strode over to her, got right up in her face, and said, "I don't know what you mean by 'bimbo,' but you're gamblin' with your front teeth."

But Lisa wasn't having any of it. She threw us all out. I tried to apologize to her, but she had gone after Jack and didn't hear a word I said. Norma, Gigi and I slipped out the door, and headed for our cars.

"Man," Gigi said, "that chick has some serious problems."

"I think so," I replied.

"Bummer. I wanted to make an evening of this," Norma said.

"Can't we do something else together?"

"You got a place Artist Man?" Gigi asked, cocking her head to the side in an odd kind of way.

"It ain't the Ritz. Just a little room in a garage." I was honest.

"Forget the Ritz, it ain't nothin', let's go to your place," Gigi demanded. "But you better have something to drink."

"I got at least two gallons of Red Mountain wine hangin' around," I offered.

"That ought to get me through an evening," Gigi smiled.

I looked at Gigi and asked, "Are you really a bartender?"

"Heck no. That's just my cover." She smiled and looked at Norma. Norma puzzled, looked at me and shrugged her shoulders.

Then Gigi leads the way.

Thirty Minutes Later at the Hole

Ha! We get to my place and there's Frank, sitting on his motorcycle looking like he hopped out of a Brando movie.

" 'Bout time you got here," he says, coming to meet us as we get out of our cars. "I knew that bat would throw you guys out. At least you brought the girls. Probably saved their lives. God help poor Jack." *The Laugh*. Thank heaven my parents are away tonight.

"Who was that crazy woman, DH?" Frank asks. "There were bolts of fire comin' out of her eyes!"

"She was a dog," Gigi says. "Jack seemed like such a nice guy, a little weird, but he ain't compatible with that Lisa thing."

"Let's take this party into The Hole," I suggest.

"What hole?" asks Gigi.

"You'll see." I lead them in through the breezeway entrance, then through the side garage door, across the garage, past the double sink, then into The Hole.

I don't think I've ever had four people here in The Hole at the same time. This is going to be a trick. Frank gets the chair by the desk as usual; that's like his throne. I guess I have to sit on the bed with these two girls. Gigi smells nice. She's wearing something that smells like orange blossoms. Then I remember my parents have some folding chairs out in the garage.

I bring in a couple of chairs, but the girls don't want to sit on them. They like the bed. So here we sit, like three old hens on a roost, and Frank is sitting back in that swivel chair with a big grin on his face, nodding his head as if to say "We got us an evening here Bud!"

Maybe, but I know he won't have anything to do with these girls. He's got Maxine back at the Castle.

I have a Beatles tape playing in my little recorder, and Gigi is swaying and moving to the music. I have to admit, she really is attractive in a different sort of way. An exciting sort of way. Norma is sitting tight next to me, like we're already married. I'm not sure that's a bad thing, but I'm also not sure it's the right thing. I can feel the heat from her thighs radiating into mine.

Strawberry fields forever … blah, blah, blah …

Frank starts the conversation. "We gotta do more than just sit here. We were gonna do some Ort over at Jacks, why can't we do it here?"

"What do you have in mind?" I ask.

"This is a tiny room, but we can put some paper down here on the floor, and do some drawing," he explains. "I'm kind of interested in what this Gigi chick can produce."

Gigi turns to Frank and gives him the evil eye, her shoulders hunched up oddly in the back.

"Hey," Frank says, "That was a compliment!"

"Sounds like a put down to me." She glares at him.

"You don't like men?" Frank asks.

"I love men. I love them everywhere I go." She turns to wink at me. "But I don't want to be dismissed as just another dumb, human broad."

"Let me tell you this Gigi," Frank pauses to emphasize the serious nature of his comment, "when you were painting over at Jack's place a little while ago, I wasn't thinking about all that gender, feminist crap. You're one heck of a painter! Similar to Berthe Morisot."

"So, what the heck is that?" Gigi asks. There is a glint of steel in her eye.

"Not a what, a who," Frank explains. "One of the greatest artists who ever walked the face of this naughty little world. She was also kinda sweet on Manet back in the 1800s."

That's the second reference to Berthe in my journal in recent weeks. How strange is that?

"So that's a compliment?"

"That's a BIG compliment!" *The Laugh.*

"Gigi," I explain, "Berthe Morisot was perhaps the greatest woman Impressionist next to Mary Cassatt. To be honest, I think her work was even better than Mary's."

"I know Cassatt," Gigi says. "I did a paper on her. But I've never heard of this other woman."

"She isn't that well known," I tell her. "Check her out. She's wonderful. I think I'm in love with her." I smile. Norma doesn't see my joke, and slaps me softly while sending daggers at me through her eyes.

Then Gigi says, "Did she look like me?"

"Not a bit," I reply. "She had dark hair and dark, deep eyes."

"Which do you prefer?" she asks, stabbing me with her own eyes.

This is one powerful little being, this Gigi. I don't know how to answer her. Dark haired Norma is sitting next to me, and blonde Gigi is in front of the bed swaying to the Beatles. Frank is laying out paper to draw on, pretending to ignore the whole exchange.

Norma leaves to go to the bathroom. Frank says he left his pipe in a pouch on his motorcycle, and he goes out to get it. I'm left alone with Gigi. Great. I hope Frank gets back before Norma.

"You like me?" Gigi asks with a quizzical expression on her face that makes her look oddly alien.

I don't know what to say. She is drop-dead gorgeous, and the most unusual girl I've ever encountered.

"Of course I like you," I stammer. It's hard for me to look at her and I'm not sure why.

"How do you like me?" She smiles impishly. "This side?" She stands before me, undulating to the music. "Or this side?" She turns around and dances toward me with that tiny little butt of hers leading the way.

"I think I like this side better," I stammer again.

"What's the deal with you and Norma?" She grins like a ten-year-old girl. "She's no artist, just a cute body walkin' around. Why do you hang with her?"

"I thought you were her friend." I say, wondering when Norma is going to pop in through the door.

"Till I met you. I'm everybody's friend till I meet the real thing. Norma ain't real. She's got so many facades, her own ghost doesn't even know who she is."

"Hang on. You mean to tell me that out of the three guys you met tonight, I'm the one that appeals to you? You don't know a thing about me."

"Jack's a mess. He's tied down to that tornado tomato he wants to marry. Frank seems to be pretty well grounded and in love with his wife, or at least he's putting on a cool show tonight."

"So, this is a numbers thing? I come in third?"

"Of course not!" she says with frustration. "I like you because, well, I like you. I don't need any other reason." Suddenly changing her tone, she asks, "Can you dance?" "I took ballet for a couple of years." I'm nervous. She's really got me off balance.

"I took ballet too. Will you ballet with me, right now?" She grabs my hand and pulls me up to her.

Just then Frank walks in. And Norma walks in. And this little white Vixen from outer space is glued to the front of me like gum on the underside of a table. Frank rolls his eyes and smiles knowingly, but Norma's face turns dark as a thunder cloud. I expect to see lightning bolts shoot from her eyes. Instead, she heads for the door. Gone. Just like that. Frank breaks out with *The Laugh*.

"C'est la vie. Now what do you do?" he says. "The big one got away, DH, but you caught the little cutie."

This was all a misunderstanding. If Norma is that hair-triggered in a relationship conflict, she would be very tough to live with. I really like Gigi. There's something about her that just clicks with me, and she's a painter! She's wandering around in The Hole right now, picking up books, smiling at me.

Coming close, she whispers in my ear, "Get rid of Frank." But Frank is already heading for the door.

"Adios, Bud, you've earned this." Again, with the knowing look. "And she might be the keeper, so don't throw her back in the water too quick."

I knew he was referring to Slim when he said I had earned this. His statement gave me mixed feelings, but I know he meant well by it. He was talking about me being such a wreck because of the death of Slim. But Gigi … I don't know what planet Gigi comes from, but there is something about her that I connect with. She has a mystery buried inside her that I don't get yet, but I'm willing to go along for the ride.

"So, Mr. Artist. Why don't you and I do some art together?"

"You mean real art?"

"Yeah, we can go to bed later." She's so abrupt about everything. "I think you and I could do some drawing together and it would look terrific."

"I'm game," I say, and I didn't stutter for the first time in a long time.

She's looking though the papers strewn about on the floor. "That Frank guy drew some really good stuff here while we were arguing, but I think we ought to do our own thing. Make it personal. Just us."

"Okay, that's a good idea. Hey! I just remembered I've got a roll of butcher paper in the closet, hang on." I get it out. "We can start at one end of the roll, and roll it out as we go. What do you want to draw? You got a theme?"

"How 'bout the universe? Outer space, planets, and science fiction." She gleams in anticipation of the project.

I knew it! She is something out of a sci-fi movie. And I laugh.

"What are you laughing at?" That cool, defensive glare of hers comes back.

"I'm laughing because when I first saw you walk through Jack's door, I thought to myself, 'That's a doll! A living doll. But she looks like she came right off a sci-fi movie set.'"

Gigi's face bunches up into an angry scowl. Uh-oh, I've really put my foot in it. Then she bursts out with a laugh. "Ha! That's a compliment to me! If you only knew."

"Thank Heaven for that," I say. And she laughs again.

"So let's draw some aliens, and the planet Mars, and the moon, and we can interweave some paisley color patterns in between. You got any Buffalo Springfield?" Gigi, this surprising, fairy-like little creature, asks me.

"Let's just do that, little pixie," as I get up to fetch my Buffalo Springfield tape.

"What did you call me?" She seems caught off guard, and her eyes have grown misty.

"Little pixie. I'm sorry if that offended you. I wasn't thinking. I didn't mean anything by it."

"No. No … my dad used to call me that all the time. He died just a couple of weeks ago." She wipes her eyes and turns her head away like she doesn't want me to see her doing it.

"I'm sorry Gigi. I didn't mean —"

"I know you didn't. It's okay. It was a good death. He was killed over in South East Asia somewhere trying to rescue some marines that got caught in a firefight out in the jungle. My dad was a chopper pilot," She says so proudly, puffing up that little chest of hers. "A good one too! But while he was trying to land his chopper down in the trees, some stinkin' Cong hit his chopper blade with a bazooka or something from the ground. It sent the chopper spinning out of control, and he crashed along with seven other guys on board."

"It's tough to lose your dad." I don't know what else to say.

"Hey, we got even. Thirty minutes after my dad went down, the whole Marine Corps flew in there, and blasted everything in sight!"

The tears are streaming down her face, and she's shaking like a leaf.

"Gigi—"

"Call me Pixie. Just for now." She sits beside me on the bed and I do the same thing with her that Frank did with me. I hold her in my arms and I rock her like a baby.

"You don't seem to be the warring type, Pixie," I whisper in her ear.

"I'm a military brat. My dad, my dad's dad, my dad's dad's dad …"

"Holy cow. Goes a long way back, huh?"

"But you're right. I hate war. That was always the biggest contention between me and my father. He was a highly decorated colonel with a whole lot of colonel friends, and they would always come over to our house for barbecue. I hated it. It was always war talk. Then I joined the Students for a Democratic Society."

"You're kidding! The SDS! I was in that for a while! But I got out of it because I'm not that good at being in the public light."

"That's where I've seen you!"

"What are you talking about?"

"At Orator's Rock, RCC!"

"That would be me. I made a few short speeches there."

"You're famous! DH! You're that guy!"

"I was that guy. But I had some serious problems, or should I say complications, with that Orator's Rock thing."

"What?"

"My dad's in aerospace. He's connected with a bunch of government stuff, and when I started giving SDS speeches, apparently, the 'big guys at the top' began an investigation."

"Of your dad?" she asks, rolling her big eyes, and bringing her right hand up to wipe her puffy nose.

"Of my dad—and me. Of course they couldn't find anything on me. I'm just a kid. Just a speeding ticket or two. They couldn't find anything on my dad either, but they gave him hell. So I stopped the speech thing and concentrated on my art."

"Those jerks! Did you quit making speeches completely?"

"I had to, Pixie, he's my dad. He would have lost his job if I hadn't.

Besides my speeches weren't all that hot, and the demonstrations got taken over by outside factions that don't really care about peace. They want to harm America, and I don't want that. The only demonstrators left out there now are just a bunch of young punks who don't have a clue what it's all about. Some of them are even on a payroll. I met some not too long ago, and I don't know how to put it, but they had an evil glow about them that I didn't like."

Total silence from Gigi. I've seen that look on her a couple of times tonight—a kind of distant stare in her eyes. I don't have a clue what it means, but I think she's already gone on to another topic in her mind.

"Are we going to draw or what?" I ask, pulling her back to the here and now.

"How 'bout if I draw a tattoo somewhere on your body?" she asks brightly.

"Maybe later." Placing my face within one inch of hers, I say, "But now I want to see what you got, little Pixie alien artist Gigi."

She pulls up her shirt and says proudly, "This is what I've got." But in a flash the shirt comes back down. "You ready to paint now?"

Two Hours Later

I can't believe it! This thing is beautiful, and I hate to admit that Gigi has done most of the drawing. She's placed swirling suns and constellations and zodiac symbols all over the place, and one drawing of the full moon—earth's moon—is exquisite. All I did was draw in the black space behind her work. She really is a gifted artist.

What the heck is that noise? I hear a motor outside. My parents aren't due home till tomorrow. Oh boy, if they came home early, I'm dead!

Now there's a quiet knock on the door. It's Frank.

"Frank!"

"Sorry guys," he says, "but you gotta help me. I'm bored to tears. I drove home, and Maxine and the kids weren't there. I tried to drink some coffee, but we started this night off by making art, and

I guess I need to continue making art. I can't start art and not finish art! Am I interrupting anything?"

Gigi gives him an icy glare, but quickly puts on a little smile as I say, "No! We're just making a drawing."

Frank looks down at what we've done. "I like that!" he says, genuinely impressed. "You didn't do this DH! It has to be this El Chicko Greco Gigi here!" *The Laugh*. By now Gigi is sort of getting used to Frank's way of doing things. "Hey! I didn't say CHICK!" He laughs again, and Gigi sort of smiles, but her arm is around me and she squeezes my butt hard as she forces the corners of her mouth to rise upward.

"So," Gigi says coldly, "you like it, Mister Reed?"

This should be interesting. I think I have two steamrollers coming together and they are about to crash. This might be the end of the universe, the collision of matter and antimatter.

"You don't have to call me Mister."

"What do I call you then?"

"How 'bout Frank?" he says with a smirk.

"So, Frank, I know you don't like me. You asked me to try to paint within the lines back at Jack's, but you can just stuff it for bein' a jerk!" She cocks her head in the peculiar way she has.

Frank laughs *The Laugh*. If I were to place money on this one, I'd put it on him. I'm not sure Gigi can handle this guy.

Frank laughs again. "You're a firebrand aren't you?" Turning to me he says, "Bud, I think you might have a winner here with this little midget!"

"Midget my butt! Look at that half-baked mustache on your face MISTER Reed! Who do you think you are anyway? You got nothin' on me! Where've you been? What have you done with your life that's so stinkin' hot?"

"You got one fine temper little girl," Frank says.

"I ain't your little girl," she fires back.

"Thank God for that!" *The Laugh*.

Then Frank begins to weave his special magic. I'm glad he does, because I'm getting uncomfortable with the prattle going back and forth. The Hole is way too small for a fistfight.

"DH, where's your wine?"

"Gigi," he continues as I pour him a cup, "I apologize profusely for any insensitivity I may have displayed toward you, but you're just so darned cute when you're mad, that I have to keep you like that all the time."

Gigi turns to me and says, "What's with this guy?"

I smile and say, "Don't blame me. It's just Frank, being Frank." Frank laughs at that, and gets a tiny smile out of Gigi.

"I'm a mean old sucker aren't I?" Frank tries to look menacing.

"Get lost," she says, smiling. "I'm picking up on your game. You're a pompous jerk, but it's all for show isn't it?"

"Maybe. That's what art is all about, honey."

"Jerk! Calling me 'honey'. But I got your game now. So, show me what you can do on this butcher paper. But don't touch me, I'm his." Gigi looks at me and gets fiery again. I think I have a new girlfriend.

Two Hours Later

It's been a long night. Frank left about ten minutes ago, but not before helping Gigi and me make a four foot long, butcher paper masterpiece. What a team the three of us make. I'm not sure I can describe what we drew. It was Frank's brilliant idea to do everything in pencil lead. No color. Then Gigi said, "Let's do a drawing of the Goddess Athena!" It was an odd suggestion, but I liked the idea, and so did Frank, so we started off on it.

I now have this four foot tall Athena drawing, each of us making fairly equal contributions to the project. Frank drew the outline form, Gigi filled in the face, and all I did was cover the rest of the paper with graphite. But what a night. Frank and Gigi are now at least getting along. I can tell he really respects her talent, and from the several side-glances she gave me, I can tell she thinks he's okay. But they still don't quite trust each other.

Gigi is lying on my bed. The minute Frank left, she took off her clothes and stretched out on her side so her backside is turned toward me.

"Come lay down," she says softly.

It's really late. Actually early—like 4 a.m. I'm a mess of thoughts and images. My mind is spinning. This Gigi creature is taking over pretty quick, but I think I like it. There's something about her.

I have a poem running around in my head and I have to write it down.

"Hang on, Pixie. I have to write down one more thing."

Wave of emotion
Comes and goes
Rises and falls
Hits hard
Can't pick it up and remake it
Close your eyes
Close your eyes
Turn away from reality
Don't witness true life
Live in solitude
Live in disappointment
Live with a secret no man can bare
No tears
No understanding
Too many islands unto themselves
No pity
No one pities any more
Short on love
Short on compassion
Incomplete
Best laid plans
True feelings go unsaid

I'm writing this while sitting in a folding chair next to my bed where Gigi, on her back now, is lying half asleep.

"DH?" Gigi says dreamily.

"Right here."

"I'm really drunk."

"I know you are Gigi."

"I can't drive home," she states matter-of-factly.

"You don't have to. Just stay there. Sleep it off and I'll see that you get home tomorrow."

"But I wanted you to have fun with me."

"It's okay. I'm fine with just looking at you."

"If I go to sleep you can go ahead and do me. Do anything you want. I won't care."

"If it's okay with you, I might just sit here all night watching you, nothing more."

But she's already asleep.

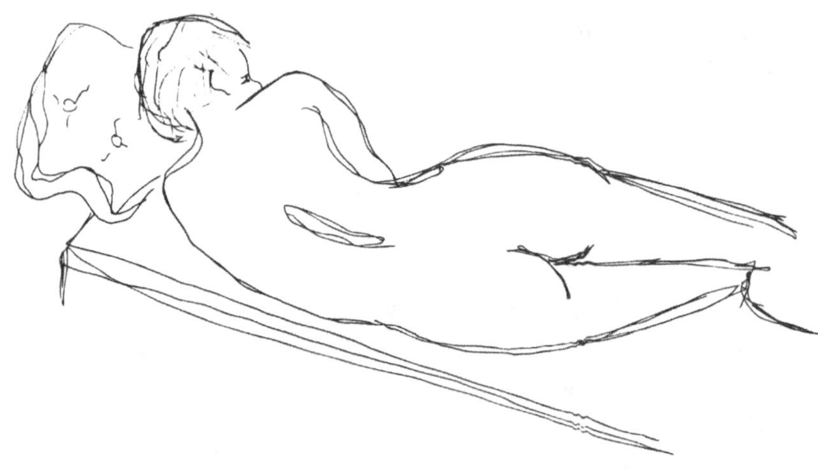

Day 66: Noon Friday

I'm sitting in the chair at my desk and I'm looking at Gigi lying there on the bed. I've been here all morning.

"DH?"

"Gigi?"

"What time is it?"

"Almost noon."

"I gotta get out of here!"

"What's the rush?"

"I have a job interview at 1 o'clock!"

"What job?" I ask her, a bit perplexed.

"At a bar downtown. They're gonna pay me eight bucks an hour."

"Gigi …"

"What? What's the matter?" She comes over and touches my hand.

"Do you really have to work at a bar?"

"You don't like bars?"

"I don't," I reply.

"Good, I don't really like 'em either. But I like you. In fact, I think I'm already in love with you, but I have to make a living." She smiles oddly, but then she turns away as if she's hiding something.

What's that noise? Good grief! All of a sudden it sounds like there's a squadron of helicopters going over my house. I hope some murderer isn't on the loose out there.

"I heard those things last night! All night! I wonder what's going on?" I stand up and start to go outside.

"Don't worry about noises, Love." Gigi glances down at the floor. "Just relax, those choppers must be doing something important."

"But Gigi …"

"DH, I don't know what to do. I know I'm in love with you, but I have to eat and my mother's ticked off at me already." She sounds like she's trying to change the subject.

"I'm sorry your mother is mad at you."

"You don't know the half of it. When my daddy died mother got all of his military pension. But what you don't know is my mother is …"

"Let me guess—The Queen of England?"

"My mother's father was a very well known artist. Very good. Not like a New York abstract thing, a good portrait painter. He painted just about everybody who was anybody, from celebrities to politicians. When he died, he left my mother millions."

"You're kidding!" I'm stunned.

"I'm not kidding. My mother keeps wanting to chart the course of my life. She hates it that I want to be a painter. But that doesn't matter, my mother is out of the country right now."

"I don't know what to say, Gigi."

"Ha! You thought I was just some little fluffy college bimbo, huh?"

"I never thought of you as that, but you do keep surprising me."

"So … now you know I've got all this money behind me …"

"Money doesn't mean anything. The only important thing is the you that you're hiding somewhere down in here." I touch my heart.

"I'm not hiding anything DH Parsons! I'm just me."

"So? What's the deal?"

"What gives you the right to tell me I'm hiding something inside?" Gigi shouts. Then she confronts me like a gladiator. I want to smile, but I don't dare.

"Calm down, Gigi. Calm down."

"I get so sick of people telling me how to live my life! I don't need to hear that."

"I would never tell you that, Sweetie. Ooops. I probably shouldn't have called you Sweetie."

She sits back down on the edge of the bed, looking at her hands in her lap. "You … can … call me anything you want. But is this going to morph into something more permanent? I mean this you and me thing."

"I'm not sure Gigi. We just met. What do you want it to morph into?"

"I want the old cliché! A little house somewhere over the rainbow, with a white picket fence, and roses all over the place." She smiles, cocking her head, and does her little simian waltz back and forth in The Hole.

"What's the deal with you? You are holding something back. I may not have known you for very long, but I'm a good judge of people. What are you hiding?" I ask her.

"If I tell you, will you still love me?"

"Who said I'm in love with you now?"

"Some stinkin' blue bird." She gives me a smile that melts my heart. "I'll tell you what I'm holding back, DH. But you have to swear you won't tell anybody about this, except maybe that diary thing you're writing, cause I know you're gonna write this down, and you'd better not let anybody read that until I'm dead! Do you promise?"

"Of course," I agree, and I mean it.

"When I was 12 a friend of my dad's came over, and while nobody was in the house he raped me."

"Oh, Gigi ..."

"I was just a little girl, and this big bruiser dropped by to see my dad, but my dad wasn't there. I wasn't too worried about lettin' him in the house. He was my dad's best friend! But when he sat down beside me on the couch I knew something was up. I was young, but I wasn't stupid." Gigi took her hand and wiped the snot from her nose. "So I started to get up off the couch. I was going to go out the back door and get the heck out of there, but he grabbed my arm and said, 'Where you goin' honey?' That line made me freeze, and the rest is history."

"A family friend! A real friend and not some beer buddy thing?"

"A real friend. When my dad came home and found what he'd done, and it was obvious, he wanted to go after him with a gun. But mom and I talked him out of it. It would have ruined his military career. He might have even gone to jail. That sleaze ball wasn't worth it. We found out later it didn't make any difference, cause he tried to do the same thing to some Mexican girl in San Berdoo, and her brother shot him dead."

"Good grief …"

"My dad did go to the cops about my rape, but the Mexican guy beat the cops to the punch. So … what can I buy you?" That last statement comes out of nowhere.

"Huh?" I'm confused.

"I've got about ten grand in my purse. You want a new car? That VW looks pretty rickety to me."

"Gigi, I don't want any of your money, and if this relationship is going in that direction I'm not sure I …"

"Hold on Mr. Parsons. Ha! That's different. A guy turning down a rich girl!"

"I'm not turning YOU down. I just don't want to base any relationship on money. You can keep the cash, but you can give me YOU."

"You know, I'm not sure if you're playin' me or not. Other guys have played me big time. But if you're not, I know I'm in love with you."

"Gigi …"

"Don't go any further. Don't spoil this. I'd like to think that it's gonna work."

"Me too."

"I'm already too late for that appointment. Guess I'll lose that bartender job."

"Gigi, you don't need the money."

"I know, and now that I've hooked up with you and that goofy crowd you seem to hang with, maybe I won't feel the need to find friends in such nasty places like that any more."

Two Hours Later

Gigi has just left. We had been painting for quite a while when she told me it was time for her to head home. I asked where that was, and she told me the address. She lives on Palm Tree Hill! That figures. Where I almost died at the sorority party with Jack. Apparently she has her own home there, and lives completely by herself. This whole Gigi thing is absolutely mind-boggling.

My feelings for her are so mixed. One minute she can talk like a sailor and be tough as nails, and the next she's as sweet as honey. And she's very, very rich! I mean VERY rich! I know that Frank would slap me right now if he could hear my thoughts. He'd say something like, "Are you out of your mind! Go for this little vixen!" followed by *The Laugh*.

Frank called me about five minutes ago, and wanted to know if I could come to the Castle this evening and see his latest work. Is the Pope Catholic? Of course I would drop everything to do that. Apparently, Maxine and the kids will be there as well. I hope Maxine makes that salsa that she makes.

An Evening at the Reeds

I'm over here in my usual spot on the mattress in the living room of Frank's Castle and, of course, I'm writing in my journal while Frank shuffles stuff around in his studio. I don't really know what he's doing right now. He seems to be going through a deep stack of sketches. He looks like he's looking for something in particular.

"Hey Frank," I holler from my couch in the corner, "am I a part of this party or what? What are you doing in there? Are those sketches?"

"Get your fanny in here, Bud! These are drawings I made about five years ago, but they ain't what I'm looking for."

"What are you looking for?" I'm now standing next to him.

"I'm looking for one drawing I made, of one single concept I came up with the other day. I think it might have gotten mixed up in this pile."

"What's the concept?"

"I'm thinking about designing some furniture. You know, those Bauhaus guys knew how to do it. I think I can pull that off too. I drew a design for a chair the other day — kind of modern looking, but I'm not sure where I'm going with it. I don't have the money or the time to put it together right now, but sometime in the future I'll do this thing. I want you to see the drawing, if I can find it! Where in the world is it?"

I let Frank continue his quest for his holy grail—he's throwing things around like a mad man. I just kind of wander around looking at all the stuff in this place; it's like Disneyland. There goes Jules, giggling, being chased by Mike. They turn around, and now Jules is chasing Mike. They're cute kids.

"Here it is!" Frank exclaims triumphantly.

He places a drawing on the table. To me, it kind of looks like a skeletal version of Captain Kirk's chair on the bridge of the Enterprise. I'm not sure what to make of it.

"What's this thing in the middle?" I ask.

"That's a strap. Like a seatbelt. It's just something I'm working on, but it's not the real reason I asked you over." His voice changes to a whisper as he looks first to the right, and then to the left, making sure we're alone in the room. "Look at this over here."

Frank grabs an odd creation that looks like a clear fiberglass box, with a key inside that must be the key to the box, because there's a padlock on the outside of the box. I don't get it.

"One day I'll tell you all about it, Bud. This is important to me. I just wanted you to see it."

"OK … It sure looks important."

"It's magic."

"I'll take your word for it," I'm intrigued. Frank has the most interesting mind I have ever encountered. It flows like a river, sometimes gushing like a flood, other times slowing to a trickle. But his trickle is more than most others' flood. The mental image makes me laugh.

"What are you laughing at, DH?" he asks.

"Just something I wrote in my journal." I show it to him.

The Laugh—big time, *The Laugh*!

"OK, we're getting into potty jokes now, that means it's time to go into the other room, drink some wine and do a little chit-chatting."

And we do. I go back to my place on the mattress, Frank hits his chair in the corner, and Maxine, God love her, brings in some more salsa. We're all drinking wine. Sometimes I wonder what Maxine thinks of this art stuff, of me coming over here all the time, of Frank and me conversing for hours on end about everything in the world yet nothing at all, of the wine, of … the whatever. Maxine is a mystery to me. I respect her for a number of reasons, mainly because she puts up with Frank. That has to be a full time job. Also—and I almost hate to say this—she reminds me of him in a way. She has the same explosive way of speaking, and some of the same mannerisms. Often when I watch the two working back and forth together, I get them mixed up. I wonder sometimes if Maxine is being like Frank or Frank is being like Maxine. The one thing I'm sure of is that Maxine is a very bright woman, and Frank is lucky to be married to her. Will I ever find my Maxine? Will it be Gigi? Will it be some Muse that transmigrates the molecular structure of her otherworldly body on a regular basis to step through her dimension into mine … Ann? Who exactly is Ann?

And Gigi—what the heck am I going to do with her?

"So, Bud, how'd you and old Gigi get along after I left?" Frank whispers to me when Maxine leaves the room to go to the bathroom.

"I don't know. I'm kind of confused about it."

"Confused? My Aunt Mabel! She's a babe, DH. I hate to admit it, and I'll never own up to it, and you never heard me say this, but"—*The Laugh*—"that little white thing has talent! Have you ever seen a broad so bleached out white like that before?"

I smile. He's right. Gigi's skin is incredibly white, like she never gets out into the sun. And what does that mean? My paranoia is coming into play here. I know it's stupid, but there are so many questions about her, and so few answers.

Frank butts into my train of thought. "You look pretty confused, Bud. What's the problem? This chick is beautiful, and she has talent, and she seems to be glued to you at the hip! Grab that thing."

"There's stuff you don't know about her, Frank. I wish I could tell you—"

"But you'd have to kill me, right?" *The Laugh*.

"No, but I am confused. In everything Gigi and I do, we seem to fit together like soup and sandwich, but I'm uneasy about some things."

"You're daft, Buddy Boy. Go for it!"

Maxine walks back into the room and lies down on the floor in her usual spot.

Frank starts singing his favorite song — the "I've got tears in my ears from lying on my back cryin' over you blues baby..." song — and he ends it with a laugh. It's his way of changing the subject so Maxine doesn't know what we're talking about.

"You like the salsa?" Maxine asks. Her eyes seem to drill into me from across the room.

"You bet," I stutter.

I'm not sure if Maxine caught the subject of our conversation while she was gone, but I guess it doesn't matter much. I don't care if she knows about Gigi and me — whatever Gigi and me really is. It's getting late, so I think I need to leave before my welcome wears out.

"It's kind of late. About time for me to go home." I say.

"We just started drinking!"

"I know, but it's been a long day."

"And night?" He winks at me.

"That too," I smile.

"Okay Bud, if you need some Zs, you go and do what you gotta do. I'll walk you out."

Frank sees me to the door and out to my car. He grabs my shoulders, shakes me, and says, "Call Gigi, you pathetic idiot."

"Not tonight. It's too late," I tell him.

"It's never too late for somebody like Gigi!"

I get into my car, smiling to myself. I know he's right.

"Adios, Frank. I'll keep you posted."

Day 73: The Next Friday

From summer to summer — the nothingness in between. My life is lived in the summer. Fulfilled and enjoyed in the summer. Summer is the season of heat and creativity. When autumn creeps in I think a part of me dies inside, and I'm not sure why. Something from a past life I suppose. Some ancient memory.

I've got Dvořák playing on my little black tape recorder now. How contemporary that word "recorder" sounds. So artificial and cheap for this journal. Why do I feel so guilty when I write such a word?

I see a necessity of the recorder in my life. It gives me sounds of the past. That's important to me I guess, as much as anything is important to me at this point in time.

I breathe paint. I really do. That's all I care about.

I've been thinking much about the condition of being an artist. Does that make sense? The times during my life when I've felt the most fulfilled have been the times that I have spent in total dedication to my work. The times spent with other artists and the color of their worlds, the times spent in my own studio; late nights with paint and melancholy music. Art has been good to me. Art has been food for me.

Can an artist be both an artist and a workingman? A man who works for someone else? Can he teach or administer a school during the daytime and then come home to his studio in the evening? Can he take a shotgun and murder his television set and then be content to disappear upstairs to his own thoughts? Where does an artist draw the line at being contemporary?

I'm surrounded by my paintings. They hang and lean and attack me from every angle. My studio is alive. I long for the times of packing in so many art experiences during the week that by Sunday I'm exhausted, and need hibernation time so I can start all over on Monday.

I've been catching up on some painting. I did a one of Gigi, but I'm not happy with it. The real thing is far better than a painting, and she's so hard to capture. She flits around so fast that I can't really see what she looks like. She has an odd gait to her walk. She pulls her shoulders back and thrusts her head forward like some kind of animal on the prowl. To the normal person I suppose her way of walking would be a bit unnerving, but I find it quite alluring, in the way that the Greek Sirens of old were alluring to men of the sea. Or like a Selkie out of water, and out of her natural skin, washed up on shore for the first time. I've never seen anything like Gigi, but it works for me.

I'm capturing strange moods with my paint. My portraits show not just the likeness of the person, but reveal something deeper. True personality? They have a magic about them. As I write this entry, my recent painting of Christina Rossetti stares downs at me from her permanent home, her canvas on my wall. She neither smiles nor frowns. Perhaps she looks a bit haughty, a bit put out by being where I've placed her. But I give her the option to feel the way she wants, for I have invaded her deepest privacies by accosting her, fondling her, ever so gently with my brush. I'm sure that, whenever she wishes, she could simply disappear, leave the canvas. One day I might wake up to find her gone.

How many people in this current society know who Christina Rossetti is? Her poems are the stuff that makes the world go round, and she's been a huge influence in my poetic life.

Echo

Come to me in the silence of the night;
Come in the speaking silence of a dream;
Come with soft rounded cheeks and eyes bright
As sunlight on a stream;
Come back in tears,
O memory, hope, love of finished years.

O dream how sweet, too sweet. Too bitter sweet,
Whose wakening should have been in Paradise,
Where souls brimful of love abide and meet;
Where thirsting longing eyes
Watch the slow door
That opening, letting in, lets out no more.

Yet come to me in dreams, that I may live
My very life again though cold in death;
Come back to me in dreams, that I may give
Pulse for pulse, breath for breath:
Speak low, lean low,
As long ago, my love, how long ago.

Christina wrote that. What a mind she must have had. A true romantic. I believe she was a nun at one time, maybe in the last part of her life. But she had the Art Spirit in her, or she could never have written something so precious as "Echo." I did see a photo of her once. My first thought was, "What a waste, putting this woman in a nunnery!" She was beautiful. She was the sister of Dante Gabriel Rossetti, so she had to have those Pre-Raphaelite genes in her.

And where is Frank this morning? Where's Gigi? I haven't gotten any calls yet. Of course, Frank doesn't call me all the time. He's a busy guy with a somewhat busy and mysterious personal schedule. Frankly, I don't know what the heck he does most of the time.

I know that he has lots of contacts in the art world, and he does a lot of wheeling and dealing in that venue. He has a lot of shows, and that takes a lot of politicking, so he probably scoots back and forth from LA to New York just to stay in touch with gallery owners and art friends he's made.

He's kind of a mysterious character. Sometimes I'm not sure how to take him. I think a lot of what he puts forth is pure bravado, a show biz front. But at the same time, I realize he's one bright dude. I think I've mentioned before that he knows just about everything about everything there is. He really does, yet another reason for that nose with the large nostrils; some of that gas has to escape. Ha! He'd like what I just wrote.

I don't have a clue what I'm going to do today. I need to have a show some time. A One-Man Show. I don't care where it's held. My back yard, that would be convenient! Having a One-Man Show is to an artist like being a Made Man is to a Mafioso. It's when you make your bones. It's when you become something. It's when you're a part of the *famiglia*. And there is a famiglia of art and artists. It's a closed society, as tight in its own way as the Mafia. Let's face it, only those chosen few who make the grade, and establish a presence and a name, get in to the art world. There are so many hurdles to jump, and so many butts to kiss, and there's a whole lot of just silly stuff that goes on behind the scenes that an artist like Frank has to put up with in order to make it big in this profession. They say that prostitution is the oldest profession in the world, and I guess that might be so. But what is the difference between being an artist and being a prostitute? Both have to sell their souls in order to make money, in order to make it work.

There's also the ego part, and the fame part. Are these driving factors, or what? I don't think it used to be that way. Van Gogh never worried about fame. He just painted pretty pictures. That's all he cared about. But today, I really believe it's all about the lure of cash and the seduction of fame. Frank may have hooked into that emotion, I'm just not sure. He does have a big ego, no doubt about that, but I also remember things he has said to me like, "It's all about the art. It's either the art or it isn't." He's right on that. I don't believe that every artist is born a fabulously skilled technician, but I do believe every TRUE artist is born with the Art Spirit, even if his skills aren't perfect. Most of the well-known artists alive today are passable technicians, but while their works have a certain visual impact, they have no Life—no Soul. Consider Jasper Johns, Pollack, Rauschenberg, Warhol; they all have strong, forceful personalities, but that doesn't mean they have the Art Spirit, nor does it mean they are TRUE artists. It just means that they can put together artsy stuff that will be popular with a certain influential segment of the public. No one will ever convince me that a flat, monochromatic Rauschenberg collage is as beautiful, as wonderfully painted as a Monet. There is no argument under Heaven that can rationalize giving Andy Warhol the same "Master" status as Degas. It just can't be done with logic or even common sense. The reason? Warhol does not have the Art Spirit. He is a product of his times, a fashionable fellow who uses his inner energy to enchant the public into treating him like an art god. The same can be said for all the so-called Minimalist or Hard-Edge artists. It is strictly personality that causes them to rise to the top. Not Art Spirit, or even talent.

Many of those covered by the art magazines of today simply have no Art Spirit. I don't know why they're even in them. This so-called performance art stuff, or "Happenings" that are oh-so-popular right now aren't really art. I know Frank's done some, and it seems to be a current fad, but it has no substance. It's corny theater! I think Robert Rauschenberg was the first to do it. It's too bad he didn't get a wild hair up his fanny and join a monastery before he stumbled upon it. It's just show biz. Primarily young college artists trying to find ways to shock the art world, believing that if they do, they can make some money at it. The art business doesn't seem to have anything to do with the Art Spirit any more, just the business of making money.

I will probably never make it big as an artist for all of these reasons. I believe with all my heart that I have the Art Spirit, but I'm shy when it comes to putting myself forward, more like a Van Gogh than a Rauschenberg. That just doesn't make it today. I'd be eaten alive. Frank can pull this off if he puts his mind to it. He has the moxie and the drive. My phone is ringing.

Five Minutes Later

Gigi, the White Goddess from somewhere out in space, just called. She wants me to come to her house. Holey Moley! I'm gonna do it. I don't know why, but I'm sort of scared. I guess it comes back to all those unanswered questions I've been thinking about. What the heck am I gonna find when I get there? What the heck is she really like when she's "at home," and not out in public? In spite of, or maybe because of all that, I have to see her.

She told me to bring my journal, "because I know it will make you happy if you're writing about everything I show you." But then she added, "don't count on writing all the time, because I have other plans for you."

I'm on my way.

Thirty Minutes Later

I'm sitting in my VW in the driveway of what I think is Gigi's house. I can't believe what I'm looking at. I've never seen a house like this before. It's fabulous! There ought to be massive, teeth-baring guard dogs at a place like this! I'm gonna take a quick minute to describe what I'm looking at before I get the guts to go knock on the door.

The house is all on one level, and stretches a long way to the left and to the right, and I'm assuming to the back, but I can't tell from here. It looks like it was built for someone like Frank Sinatra, kind of early fifties Hollywood. The walls are stucco where they're not glass or metal, and there are pointy steeple-looking things extending from the roof. I can see security lights of all kinds, and cameras in a dozen places. How in the world did a guy like me get invited to a place like this? It's unbelievable.

This is all a bit intimidating. Just as I'm about to turn my car around to leave, the bright royal blue front door starts to open. I guess the security cameras caught me. Good grief! Here come the big ferocious dogs I didn't think I had to worry about. Can you believe this?

I was afraid of this. These are BIG dogs, with big snarling teeth, and they're on my car like sharks on a diving cage! I close my windows as quick as I can. But … wait a minute … the dogs are licking the glass! HA! I slowly roll down my driver's side window, and one of these big pooches sticks his head in and licks my face! What kind of guard dogs are these?

"DH!" Gigi yells from about twenty feet away. "Get outta your car! Come on in." I can see her waving at me with a big smile on her face.

"Is it safe with these guys?" I yell back. The two big dog heads are inside my car licking as much of me as they can get to.

"Ha! They aren't really guard dogs! I don't need guard dogs. These are my family! They're Greyhounds I rescued a while back. They're harmless. All they'll do is put a lot of spit on your car, but I have some people that will wash it off for you while you're inside." She smiles, comes over, puts her face through my window and kisses me.

"Come in, Love. I need to show you around."

Later, on the Patio

I'm sitting in a very plush lounge chair on Gigi's patio behind her house, with a pool the size of Cleveland in front of me. Gigi says I have fifteen minutes to describe what she has just shown me, or she'll throw my journal in the pool, so I'll try to make this brief.

Where do I start? This house is huge! Gigi told me it's 12,000 square feet, with seven bedrooms, each with its own bathroom. Can you believe that? I haven't seen it all yet, but the minute I walked through the front door, I could scarcely believe my eyes. I felt like I was in airport terminal. Just inside the door was a hallway that extended for I don't know how far, but it had to be at least a hundred feet. The floor was white marble, REAL marble, not the fake stuff. Large pots of tree-like plants stood against the walls, which were filled with photos of Gigi and her family.

"Quit messin' around with the plants. We don't have time for that."

She took me down the main hallway that led directly into the living room. I swear, I've never seen anything like it. It was massive, with two stone fireplaces, one at each end of the room. The long wall on the left was glass — sparkling glass like it was polished every day — that showed off the swimming pool and the gardens in her back yard. It was like the living room and the yard ran into each other and became one. I looked up at the ceiling and found that it was all glass, too. The entire ceiling was the skylight! Then a little white poodle dog came from out of nowhere and started nipping at my leg.

"That's Venus. She likes you!" Another reference to outer space? I'm beginning to wonder about this girl.

"I like her too …" I'm not convinced. I try to pet her, but she keeps nipping at my legs and hands. I can tell by her eyes that she doesn't like me at all. I'd rather have the greyhounds.

"I'll put her in her room. Sorry about that, DH," Gigi apologizes.

"She has her own room?"

"She does, but I don't think she appreciates it. It was my sister's idea."

"You have a sister?" So many mysteries. So many questions.

"Yep."

"What's her name?"

"Heidi."

"Gigi and Heidi. Great names."

"But you stay away from Heidi because you're mine!"

"Yeah, right. I don't even know where she lives. Besides, I'm hooked on you Gigi." And I'm not sure why.

"Heidi lives here, DH. But she has some problems."

"What kind of problems?" She lives here?

"I hesitate to tell you …"

"Okay, don't."

"Then you'll be ticked off at me." She strikes a pose to display her indignation—hands on both hips, head turned, with her chin and nose pointing up and away.

"Gigi, as long as you have that puffy nose in front of you, I will never be ticked off at you.

Gigi smiles and turns her nose back to face me. "Heidi is two years younger than me, but she has a drinking problem," she explains. "Just like my mother, who left my father, and now lives in Australia. I think. I'm not sure my mother's even alive any more."

Gigi then relates a very long saga about Heidi's second problem, a chronic sex addiction. She wants to go to bed with any man who smiles at her. Oh boy …

"No more talk about her, Love. I want to show you the rest of my house."

She grabs my arm and takes me on the Grand Tour. The whole time I was thinking, "it's just like a movie star lives here."

First she showed me a combination dining room/ballroom that can hold 300 people! "I've had a lot of winter parties in here!" she beamed. Then, before I could make a comment, she pulled me out of the ballroom, down the hall and into a kitchen big enough to fit my parent's entire house into—with a personal chef who makes all of her meals for her.

"So what's your chef's name?"

"Mary. She came highly recommended from the CIA."

"The CIA?" What am I getting in to?

"Ha! The Culinary Institute of America. No spy, just a really good cook. She's made lunch for us out on the patio."

"Gigi, I don't know what I expected, but it wasn't this!"

"You ain't seen nothin' yet, but that comes later," she giggles. "So, how do you like my house?"

"It's incredible," and that's an understatement. "I've never been in a house like this before."

"Wanta see my bedroom?" She gleams, and gives her short blond hair a shake. Her eyes sparkle, and her smile is brilliant, but it's that puffy nose that reaches out and grabs my eyes.

"Can we wait till later? I think if you show me your bedroom now we'll be there for a while."

"What's wrong with that?" She gives me a pouty look.

"Nothing's wrong with that, but I want to see more of your house and do more stuff, before we go into the heaven-knows-what that your bedroom might be."

"It's the biggest room in the house," she says with a smile. "But we can goof around before we go there if you like. Wanta take a swim?"

"I don't have any swim trunks."

"Ha! You don't need 'em here, Mr. Arteest," she laughs.

How did I end up here? I'm becoming a story out of the National Enquirer! Gigi isn't a movie star, but she lives in a movie star house, and I'm just this nobody, from nowhere, who she claims she has fallen in love with, and has brought me home to play with her. You read about it all the time. How many boyfriends and girlfriends do celebrities go through? I'm hoping Gigi is different. She's rich, and she's tough, and she's raw, and she's crude, but she didn't have a Hollywood upbringing. Did she? She comes from a GI family! That's the part I find strange. We're talkin' military discipline and respect and all that. But it's almost like Gigi is in her own world, divorced of her own family, and of most of reality. I can't figure her out, but I'm going to try. And this sister named Heidi? What's with her? Why is she living here? Does she have a job? Did she get a part of the inheritance? Is she from Mars, too?

Speaking of that, and this is the good part, as I've been walking through Gigi's house, I couldn't help but notice her sci-fi collection! You heard me right, Dear Diary! But it's SOME collection! Not just pictures cut out of TV Guide, but original movie posters and photographs signed by all the latest sci-fi people, and her main emphasis seems to be *Star Trek*.

"Hey, Gigi. I gotta ask you something."

"What's that? But take off your clothes while you ask, cause I want to go for a swim." She takes all of her clothes off to make the point.

"All the *Star Trek* stuff in your house, and all of the posters and photos from sci-fi movies …"

"Pretty cool, huh?" she says. "It's the real me!"

"I knew you were a kook."

"You got something against sci-fi? I thought you liked it too?"

"I love it! I was just kidding."

She comes over, hugs me, and gives me a kiss. Then she starts to unbutton my shirt.

"You know, Love, this is a pretty drab shirt. I don't really like it. Maybe I can buy you some new clothes."

"Gigi, we've talked about that before."

"Nonsense. Can't I buy you a present if I want to? I'm not talking about a fancy car, just some clothes. When's your birthday?"

"Next week."

"You gotta be kidding! What date?"

"The 26th."

"What?" She's jumping with excitement now. "We were born on the same day! My birthday is July 26!"

This is too incredible! "Show me your driver's license!" I demand. She runs naked into the house and comes out two minutes later, tossing her license at me with a big grin.

It's true. We were born on the exact same day, exact same year. I thought she was younger than me, but I guess she just acts that way. I'm glad she does because it suits her, and is part of what makes her who she is.

"Wow!" she says. "How cool is this? What are the odds?"

"About a trillion to one, I'd say."

"So what does this mean? I think it means we're supposed to be together. I mean, this goes beyond karma. This is fate. This is even bigger than fate."

I don't know what to say.

"Don't you have your clothes off yet?" She giggles and grabs the zipper on my Levis. "I'm gonna buy you those shirts! Hang on here for a second. I have to go in the house. I'll be right back. Gotta pee. Get those pants off, I want you in the pool when I get back!"

Off she goes, like a sprite, dashing to the house, her little white butt cheeks flopping alternately in the sprint from the pool to the glass doors.

I take off my clothes, but I feel weird sitting here buck-naked in the back yard. Can anybody see me? I look around and find that Gigi's property lies at the top of Palm Tree Hill, and with her fences and bushes all around, there's no way any one can possibly see us out here. I think I'll jump into the pool though, 'cause it looks pretty refreshing right now. It must be 95 degrees out here. I'm going to set the journal down for a bit.

One hour Later

Shortly after I got into the pool, Gigi came running back out of the house, bursting with excitement and yelling "We're gonna have a party!" before she even got to me.

"What?" I yelled back.

"I just talked to my staff and it's all set! We're gonna have a party tonight! You need to help me pick the guests we're gonna invite." She stepped down into the pool. I was sitting on the first step, and she sat down beside me and put her arm around me.

"You know all these art people, DH, so I'm counting on you to call 'em up and get 'em over here. The cooks will have everything ready for about 8 p.m."

"Kinda short notice, Gigi. I'm not sure I can get anybody to come."

"Tell 'em about the house and the pool and the food, and that we'll have wine that'll never run out! A whole lot better than that nasty Red Mountain all your buddies seem to get off on."

"You don't like my wine?"

"I like everything about you, and everything you do, and every-thing you buy, and everything you drink," she smiled. "But tonight is special and we're going to have never ending champagne, and a dozen other French wines you've probably never even heard of!"

"Oh yeah? I ain't no country bumpkin! Try me!"

"Château Lafitte Rothschild 1948! The year we were born!"

"Now I know this is a dream! I've heard of that. It has to be incredibly expensive."

"It is, but I have about 500 bottles of it in my wine cellar."

"You're talking nearly a thousand dollars per bottle… I think!"

"Yep."

"And you have a wine cellar?" I ask stupidly.

"I do." Gigi grins at me like a little kid. "Come on, let's go see it!" She grabs my hand and begins to pull me out of the pool.

"Like this? Naked?" I squeak.

"Why not?" She barely bats an eye. "My entire staff has seen me naked about a billion times, and you got a pretty good bod. What are you worried about? Besides they won't look anyway. I told them if they do I'd fire 'em and get a new staff."

So off we went, holding hands as we walked up the expansive lawn toward the house. Instead of going over to the big glass doors, we went off to the left, where there was a door, hidden in a bunch of ivy creeper things. It opened magically when Gigi pressed a button on the wall. It reminded me of something out of the movie, *The Secret Garden*, totally hidden and so wonderful. The gardens surround this part of her yard — no, estate, since she must have five acres here. Being in the middle of town like this, and on Palm Tree Hill, the land alone must be worth a fortune. The gardens here rival any in the world. How does she maintain all this? Closer observation revealed at least five groundskeepers busy at work in and around the place.

When the secret door opened, Gigi took my hand again and led me through. After turning on the lighting system, she guided me down a stairway and into the wine cellar. I almost fainted when we got to the bottom of the stairs. It was mind-boggling. We're not talking a little basement, with maybe a hundred bottles of wine, arranged in one or two aisles. We're talking a room occupying half the footprint of her house! Thousands of square feet filled with row after row of shelves, made of what appeared to be mahogany, and filled with racks cradling bottles of wine. Each rack was like a drawer that could be pulled out, and each bottle of wine rested in its own rack.

"Watch this," she giggled. I love it when she giggles.

She walked over to the wall on the right where she opened the door on one of those grey electric panel things about eight feet high and several feet wide. There are dozens of switches. She pushed one of the switches and all of the bright white lights in the cellar changed to a beautiful green. At first I thought they were all one uniform shade of green, but as my eyes adjusted, I realized that just about every hue of green in any artist's imagination was present in that cellar. It was beautiful, like the Emerald City of Oz.

"Now, watch this!" She pushed another button, and I heard the pleasant sound of running water. I hadn't noticed it before, but to my left, and a little bit behind us was a large waterfall. With the push of that button, it now began to display its charm. Not some home made thing with a few rocks and some cement, this creation was in an area designed especially for it. It went all the way to the ceiling of the cellar, filling a space of at least 40 feet in diameter. It had tiny silver lights flickering on and off down in the water. The lights were so small I could barely see them, giving more the suggestion of lights than the real thing. Like something out of — of course — a sci-fi movie!

"One more thing." Gigi pushed another button.

"What the heck is that?" Soft, tropical music accented by bird songs fills the air. "I love it!"

"It's my favorite bit of music by a guy named Martin Denny. It's called The Quiet Village. The music is on a loop, after this one ends, the music from South Pacific comes on."

"This is wonderful, Gigi. I've never seen anything like it. And look at all these wines! You must have hundreds of bottles here."

"Thousands. Each one is very special to me. They all have a story to tell, something to do with my life."

"What do you mean?" I ask.

"I have a rule about buying wine. It has to have something to do with either my personal life, or my interests. Especially sci-fi. You'll notice that a lot of the labels have stars or moons on them."

I wandered through the racks. As a connoisseur of fine Red Mountain, I know nothing about good wine, but I did notice that every bottle had an old date, and that most of them were either French or Californian.

"Gigi, you must have thousands of dollars in wine down here."

"Try millions, Love."

"Where did you get all that money? Did you inherit that much?"

"Yep, and I invested it well, and it continues to pay me back. Wine is a good investment. That Rothschild stuff I can sell anytime for twice what I paid for it. It's in great demand."

"How much do these bottles go for?"

"It depends on which kind. Come here!"

She leads me into one of the aisles. She stops about halfway down and pulls out a rack.

"This is an earlier Rothschild. I paid $27,000 for this one bottle. Want a taste?" She grabs one of the cork screws that are found in every aisle, and starts to open the bottle!

"Gigi! What are you doing!"

"I'm gonna give you some wine." Those big eyes of hers don't even blink.

"But this is expensive stuff!"

"You're worth it." She smiles, and out comes the cork. "Here, guzzle baby, guzzle." She hands me a bottle of wine that could buy me a house. I take a tiny sip, and hand it back to her. I've never tasted anything like it before. I can't even describe it here.

"You didn't taste it, DH, you sipped it! DRINK my wine! There's plenty more where this came from." She grabs the bottle from me and takes a long deep drink, and she giggles again. "Like that!"

So I take the bottle from her and I take a really long swig from it. What can I say, it's good, but at what price? About a thousand dollars a guzzle.

"That's more like it! But don't get too drunk, 'cause we have our birthday party tonight. You gotta make some phone calls."

"So it's a birthday party."

"DH, this is written in the stars!"

"I'm not sure about that, but I do like this wine."

"Then make the calls. You can take a bottle or two or a case or two or three home with you tonight—if you go home." She grins.

"Exactly who do you want me to call?"

"All your art buddies. That pompous jerk, Frank, that Jack thing, and that Manny character. And anybody else you want."

"It's gonna be a small group. I don't know that many people."

"I'll invite some of my people too." She smiles, running her fingers through her short blond hair.

7:30 PM

I called all my friends, all three of them: Frank, Jack, and Manny. I thought about calling Norma, but changed my mind. I don't know who Gigi has invited, but whoever the guests are, they should start arriving soon.

Frank was the most reluctant to come. He told me that he'd have to make excuses at home so Maxine wouldn't throw a fit. From the way he said it, I'm not sure I believe that. But the moment I mentioned the wine cellar and Gigi's expensive wine collection, he agreed to come. Jack is always up for anything, and so is Manny. So all three will be here shortly. I'm predicting Jack will be here first. He'll drive up on his Norton motorcycle, then toodle into the house, maybe sober and maybe not. Manny will come next in that silly little thing he drives. I'm really not sure what the heck it is. Then Frank will make his grand entrance, fashionably late of course, as befitting his style. I hear a motorcycle coming now. Yep, it's Jack.

I'm sitting in a lawn chair out on the front lawn waiting for everyone. I'm afraid that just as I didn't "get it" when I first saw this place, they may not realize that this is Gigi's house. Quite frankly, it just doesn't look like her. She may be all sci-fi on the inside, but the outside of the house is more Beverly Hills. So I wave at Jack as he pulls up and takes his helmet off. After taking one look at the house and the grounds he shakes his head and hollers, "WHOEE! You'd better marry this dame! WHOEE! This is a million dollar pad if I ever saw one!"

"More than that, Jack. Wait till you see the whole thing."

"If you don't marry her I will," he grins.

"And if you come on to her tonight I'll kill you," I grin back.

"So where's the wine?"

A Little Bit Later

Other people I don't know are arriving, and some have arrived already. When they got here they looked at me oddly, and then went into the house as if they'd been here before, without giving me the time of day—except for one girl who turned, looked at me, then walked over to my chair.

Heidi

"You have to be DH," she said, with a knowing smile.

She is drop-dead gorgeous. I know this has to be Heidi, Gigi's sister.

I smile back. "That's me."

"I can see why Gigi wants you. You're an artist right?"

"I am an artist." I'm going to be careful with this one.

"Well, maybe we can talk about art sometime this evening, but I think I want some wine first. Did Gi show you the cellar?"

"It's quite a place." I'm guarded. Very guarded.

"Well, I'm going to go into that wine cellar, and I'm going to pop a cork or two, and get just a little bit high. Then maybe you and I can... talk... a little later, Mr. DH. I like your name."

She smiles and walks over to the Secret Garden where the wine cellar entrance is. I don't know what I was expecting to find with this Heidi chick. I thought she'd look more like Gigi, but she is more voluptuous than her sister. Much more. Actually, she looks a lot like Marilyn Monroe. Stay out of the cellar … stay out of the cellar … stay out of the cellar …

Thank Heaven! Here comes Frank on his motorcycle.

He pulls up like James Dean and sits there for a minute or two before taking off his helmet. When the helmet comes off he shakes his hair out, points at me with that big Frank Reed grin on his face, and shouts, "Bud! What is this place? You livin' in the Louvre or what!" *The Laugh*. He leaves his helmet on the seat of his bike and walks over to me.

"This is some place. I think you found the 'Gorilla Your Dreams'!" *The Laugh* again.

"I'm not sure, Frank. This is happening so quick. It's all just a little surreal for me. There's gotta be something wrong with it."

"Go with the flow and ride with the tide, 'cause I think you got a gold mine here with the White One."

"You know, Frank? That's something I can't figure out. She has this huge pool in the back that will make you loose your dentures when you see it, and she's white as a sheet! What's with that?"

"I don't know Bud, but you'd better keep her. And hey, she ain't bad to look at."

"Come on, I'll show you around. Most of our friends are here now so I don't have to sit out here on the lawn."

"You have friends?" he laughs.

"You and Jack and Manny."

"Jack's here huh?" He frowns. "We gotta tame that sucker, he's a pain in the butt."

"I don't think that's possible, Frank. Jack's a free spirit."

"Well don't you ever tell him this," Frank confides, "but I kind of like him. I think it's more because his head is so completely out of this world, than anything to do with his talent."

"That's okay, I think he'd take that."

"Let's go drink some wine," Frank says, and we head toward the front door.

"You're kidding me, DH! Does Sammy Davis Junior live here? This is so fifties!"

"I picked up on the same thing, only I thought Frank Sinatra would meet me at the door."

"Look at this architecture! It's perfect! I swear, this broad has a lot of cash because this place had to be created by somebody famous."

I'm sure he's right. We go through the front door, and Frank gets a view of the marble hallway leading into the living room. He lets out a laugh, grabbing his belly, and shouts, "This is a friggin' palace! I've been in New York homes, and I've been in Hollywood homes, and this competes with all of them. But what's all this creepy men from Mars stuff?"

"Take a good look at that stuff, Frank. It's all signed by the actors and the producers."

Frank whispers to me, "and it's worth a fortune! Is this chick a celebrity?"

"You know, I'd like to say no, she isn't, but I'm just not sure. She told me a lot of stories about how she came into all this money, but this is a heck of a lot of money for an inheritance."

"Don't you talk to her?" Frank raises an eyebrow while we stand in the middle of Gigi's massive living room. I look up through the glass ceiling and notice a plane flying over, and then I also see the reason why she built that massive skylight. The stars are beginning to come out, and there, right smack dab in the middle of the skylight is the Milky Way. It's beautiful!

"You okay DH?" Frank asks. "You know, ever since that Slim girl died, you just haven't been the same. You've been a little bit loopy for my taste. I don't want to wet nurse you, Bud, but you gotta shake this thing. It's holding you back. Listen to me, Buddy Boy, you got this White Creature Thing from the planet Patootie here, who is fabulously wealthy, and she seems to love you to pieces." He smiles.

"But hey, this ain't a bad thing. She's really cute, and she has a good head on her shoulders, and she's also a very talented artist. Let Slim go. Hook on to this White Thing, DH."

I know he's right about some of this. But the main thing doesn't have anything to do with Slim. I'm just not sure Gigi is the one. And there's the other complication with my Muse, Ann. All of this hasn't made me forget about her.

"Let me show you the rest of the house and then we'll go out back where the party is."

"Looks like a long walk, shouldn't we bring along a couple of canteens and some rations?" *The Laugh.*

About an Hour Later

I showed Frank the entire house except, of course, for the master bedroom, which even I hadn't seen yet. In every room, he just shook his head and mumbled phrases of awe and disbelief. We are out back now, in the area by the pool where the party is being held. It is getting dark, so all of Gigi's dramatic lighting effects are on display. It's like the Fourth of July at ground level. There aren't any "bombs bursting in air," just what seems like millions of those tiny Faerie lights. Where does she get those? Gigi is standing with her sister, Heidi, to the left of me and Frank. Gigi is gorgeous in a white dress that's trying to compete with the color of her skin, but doesn't come close.

"This is a nice party, DH. We all gonna get naked and jump in the pool?" Frank asks, his eyes twinkling mischievously.

"We can if we want. Anything seems to go here."

"I don't want to mess up my 'do," he says, patting his unruly curls with one hand. "Who are all these people anyway? I see Jack over there talking to that blonde that looks kinda like Marilyn Monroe, but she's been dead a few years, so it can't be the real thing. What a tragedy to the universe that was! And that little squirt, Manny, is standing over there by the pool. I don't know who any of these other folks are." He turns to me, "But who cares, this is the best wine I've ever had. It ain't Red Mountain!" *The Laugh.*

"You're drinking a Rothschild something or other at about a hundred bucks a swallow."

"What? This is my kind of party!"

Jack saunters over to us.

"Hey Frank," he says, attempting an air of nonchalance.

"Hey Jack," Frank responds, a bit like a rooster preening at a cockfight.

"The party's good but the wine's nasty," Jack says, staring at the ground as if making eye contact would cause him physical pain.

"You've got to be kidding me!" Frank says, exasperated. "This is the most expensive wine on the planet!"

"It ain't Red Mountain."

"No …" Frank is truly at a loss for words. "And why are we even having this conversation?" He turns away.

Here comes Gigi to the rescue. I think Frank and Jack were headed toward a serious argument.

"Hey guys!" She says brightly. "What are you talking about? You all look so serious." She puts on a cute frown.

"We be talking about nothin', Child." Frank puffs up his chest and grins. I take a step back. Nobody calls Gigi a child and lives to tell about it.

Instead of the expected outburst however, she smiles sweetly and extends her hand "Mr. Reed," she says, "you know I think you're a great artist, because DH thinks you're a great artist, and that's the only reason. So can't we just be friendly with each other? You call me Child one more time and you'll be limping out of here tonight."

Frank laughs loudly. He extends his hand to Gigi and she takes it. They shake hands, both smiling.

"You are the craziest broad I've ever met," Frank says, "but I like you. You have talent, and charm, and that incredible white skin. And DH is mad about you!" Frank beams at me. I'm looking for a hole to hide in.

"You seem to be a talented person too," Gigi's mouth is smiling, showing her teeth. This is like a standoff. "I respect you because DH respects you. But I'll be watching you." The threatening grin is replaced by a narrow-eyed scowl. Frank just laughs, but Gigi tells him, "Don't ever forget this is my house, and I have some burly bouncers here that will take your scrawny butt out in a heartbeat." Gigi smiles — for real this time — and walks away, giving me a wink.

"The White One is some dame. She's gonna eat your head off, Bud!" Frank is not laughing. "She's one hot, hair-triggered broad. You be careful with her. I know she has money but …"

"I believe her about most things," I say. "She's so blunt and honest with every thing she says, like a little girl. But I am careful."

"But is she firing on all four cylinders?" Frank asks.

"I'm not sure. But —"

"Yeah. But if I could touch her skin and kiss her the way you do I'd understand. That's what you were about to say, right?" *The Laugh.*

"That's about it."

"So, forget about her. Who are all these people at this wing-ding? Some of them look familiar."

"I haven't a clue. One guy told me he was a movie producer, but I didn't catch what he said. Ivan … something-or-other."

"Ivan Tors! I gotta talk to him!" Cool, sophisticated Frank has suddenly turned into a schoolgirl at a Beatles concert.

"Calm down Frank, I'm not sure what his name is. I've had about ten glasses of champagne. He could be Ivan The Terrible, for all I know."

"But that's him over there! I think I recognize him. DH, this is big!"

Frank is excited, but I'm not sure. I've never met or seen or heard of anyone named Ivan Tors before. I miss Gigi. I wonder where she is; I don't see her anywhere.

I finally spot her over by the pool, and she's looking right at me. We smile at each other. She's talking to some other guy I've never seen before, but she looks bored. She smiles at me again. I'm beginning to wish this night would just go away. I don't care about the celebrities or the pool or anything else. I just want to be alone with Gigi.

As if she's picking up on my thoughts, she heads over in my direction. She looks a bit worried. Here's where I have to set the journal down again.

Thirty Minutes Later

I will try to relate what just happened. Forgive me if it's a bit risqué, but as I am always honest with my journal, I will write just about everything.

"DH? Are you okay?" Gigi asked me. She had just a little bit of snot coming out of her puffy nose. She sniffed, and then said, "You look bored."

"I'm not bored, Gigi. But I wish I could be with you."

"You mean you want to have your way with me?"

"More than that. Something more …"

"Come with me."

She guided me up the long stretch of lawn, back toward the glass doors. Before we got there though, she veered off to the right and we went behind some bushes. Gigi kissed me and whispered in my ear, "Nobody can see us here."

A Bit Later

This is one heck of a night, no doubt about it. I really don't know what to make of it all. There are about 200 people here, four of whom I know. One of them, Frank, is standing by a tree talking to some guy who looks like he's about 60 years old. Another, Manny, finally got here, wandered into the backyard, saw the pool, and hopped right in without as much as a hello. And Jack… uh oh, where's Jack? There he is. He's over by the door to the wine cellar with a very attractive chick who looks about ten years younger than he.

Jack sees me looking at him and he's waving at me to come over.

Minutes Later

This is one of the strangest encounters of my life. Jack waved me over and introduced me to the brunette he was with. Her name is Janice. She's wearing glasses, but she is a looker. For some reason I've always loved black-haired Jewish girls with glasses—which begs the question, why am I hooked up with Gigi? She's pretty much the opposite of all that.

From what I could gather, Jack and Janice had done what Gigi and I had done, over behind the shrubs, and now Jack needs to make a phone call—probably something about Lisa—and he wants me to keep Janice occupied while he's gone. As he walked away he said to me, "I only hired her for tonight but I'll let you borrow her for a while. You have 30 minutes."

I can't believe it! Jack hired a prostitute!

"Hi. I'm Janice." she smiles.

"I'm DH." What do I do with this?

"Is Jack your friend?" She asks.

"Yep. For a long time," I answer. Then I just have to ask her, "What are you doing in this business?"

"What do you mean?" She looks puzzled.

"You're a prostitute aren't you?" I ask.

"Yes, but I'm also a human being." Her reply has the tone of a challenge.

Good grief, what a clod I am. It's none of my business what Janice does with her life. If she wants to do what it is that she does for fun and profit, so be it.

"What else do you do, Janice?" I ask sheepishly.

"I'm a student at RCC. I'm trying to get a degree in science. Maybe I can get a real job soon."

"How in the world can you get by on—"

"—a hooker's paycheck?" She finishes for me.

"I don't think I was going to put it quite that way," I say, trying to defend myself.

"Temple Beth El, downtown, is loaning me a room until I can

get back on my feet."

I knew it! She's Jewish. "I'm guessing you have at least one kid, huh?" I give her what I think is a sympathetic smile.

"Just one. A little girl named Natalie. It's all I can do to take care of her. My husband was killed in Viet Nam, and I'm just a nothing kind of girl—no skills, no education."

"Don't you have any family?"

"I was born in Arkansas, and Johnny, my husband who was not Jewish, took me away from all that. I got pregnant, and he went off to war and never came back. He died over there somewhere. They never found his body. Now I have this kid, and no job, and I'm ashamed to go back home." Tears form in her eyes as her defensive front begins to crack.

Here we go again. I give her a hug and wipe her tears with a Kleenex I found in my pocket. She smiles a little, and offers to "do something" for me, just because she likes me.

"You're a very nice man," she says. But I decline her offer.

Now Janice is walking away, looking back at me over her shoulder, and Frank is coming this way.

"Who was that?" he asks, his voice booming from about twenty feet away.

"Janice," I reply more quietly as he gets closer.

"DH, I never noticed before, but you're a chick magnet!"

"What?" I'm still thinking about Janice and her situation.

"Every time I see you, you have a gorgeous woman at your side."

"Janice is a prostitute, Frank. I don't even know her. And I've never been a chick magnet in my life. I have no idea what's going on, but this is all coincidence."

"Whatever." *The Laugh*. "But the heck with her, are there any real artists here tonight? This has to be the most boring party I've ever been to. Aren't there any art people we can chit-chat with?"

"Just you, me, and Jack."

"Oh great, back to Jack, huh? That guy's like an ingrown toenail. But he's better than nothing."

I don't know what to do. Frank and Jack seem to hate each other, but Frank is bored over here, and Jack is bored over there, and I have no idea where Manny is now. I don't see him in the pool. Poor Manny. He just doesn't fit in to the art scene. He's a garage band drummer. Not a very reliable profession, I'm afraid, but you never know. In the meantime, he's fun to hang with. He has to be a little uneasy being here tonight, though.

Jack is another story. So, while Frank has apparently gone behind some bushes to relieve himself, I whistle at Jack. He heads over here with a big grin on his face.

"DH, I just met the neatest girl! Her name is Zelda, like in Zelda and F Scott! Man she's cute."

"Cool," I frown. "What about Janice?"

"She took off."

"And Zelda filled the void."

"Did you see her over there? She looks like Ann Margaret!" He is certainly beside himself.

"I didn't see her, Jack, but I think Frank wants to spend some time with us. He's pretty bummed out because there aren't any artists here."

"He considers me an artist?"

"I think so. Don't forget, Frank puts on a big show, but he has the true Art Spirit and he knows you do, too."

"Let me get this straight. He hates me and he loves me at the same time?"

"Pretty much."

Frank returns from the bushes. We'll see what happens next.

"Jack! What's up?" Frank comes shoulder to shoulder with Jack. Jack doesn't move.

"Same old same old."

"So, how are you and Lisa getting along?"

"Not too bad. I'm really sorry about the other night when Lisa came in and found us all makin' that mess," Jack says sheepishly.

"No big deal. She got over it, right?" Frank shifts his stance a bit to face Jack directly. "I gotta ask you, Jack, what makes you tick? You're one solitary man, like an island." It appears that Frank is really trying to make friend points with him.

"Hum …" Jack's face changes, taking on a far away look, "The only things that makes me tick are clay and wax,"

"Okay, you jerk! You've got the Art Spirit!" *The Laugh*.

"What are you talking about?" Jack asks.

"I'm not talking about anything! I'm telling you that you're a real Arteest!"

"Why?" Jack is a man of few words. He steps back from Frank and pulls out a Delicado. He lights it up but doesn't inhale.

"Because of what you just said, and because of that one piece I saw in your apartment the other night. Don't get your hopes up, you ain't anywhere near my league," Frank winks at me, "but that one piece …"

"Which piece?" Jack turns back toward Frank.

"That little clay figure over on your bookshelf," Frank says softly, looking Jack square in the eye, "I liked some of your paintings, but that little figure was true Ort."

"You mean the little white piece?" Jack asks quietly.

"I surely do. That thing has finesse." Frank speaks slowly, moving his arms slowly and with grace.

Jack looks down at the ground and shuffles his feet and—like he doesn't really want to say it—says, "It's kind of a portrait of Lisa before she became what she is today. Back when I loved her."

"Okay …" Frank pauses and looks at me, a bit bemused. I know he wants to crack a joke, but he also knows that if he does this conversation will be over.

I jump in. "I have an idea! You two guys stay right here and try not to hurt each other. I'm going to set something up with Gigi. I'll be right back."

I saw Gigi sipping, no, guzzling wine with a couple of other women over by the waterfall. Did I mention there's another huge waterfall out here that runs into the pool? This ain't no regular rectangular pool painted blue under the water. It's all rocks and boulders and running water and grottoes, like something you'd see at Disneyland. I expect to see the Pirates of the Caribbean come floating out from behind the waterfall.

I went over and asked Gigi if I could take Frank and Jack down into the wine cellar, just to sit there, sip wine and talk.

"Here, Love." She handed me a key ring with several keys on it.

"What's this?" I asked, puzzled.

"I had those made for you. Those are the keys to everything on the property. The gold key is the one that opens the wine cellar."

"Gigi …" I'm speechless.

"You don't ever have to ask me anything about getting into any room or whatever any more. Just do it. Everything here is yours." She smiled her Gigi smile, and her puffy nose did a quick little wiggle. The women she was talking to — I have no idea who they are — all giggled and watched me like they all knew something that I didn't. I must have looked like a fool because I think my mouth was open and my eyes were wide.

"DH, take your little friends down into the cellar and talk all you want. I know that Reed guy is bored. I can read faces pretty well. Maybe if you feed him some wine he'll get looser. I don't like unloose people."

"So we can open a bottle or two down there?" I ask, dumbfounded.

"You can open a hundred bottles if you want. You know where the Rothschild's are, and there are some even more expensive wines down about three rows from the Rothschild's, but they're in a locked room. That little silver key with the green stripe opens that room. Take your buddies in there and have fun. Do you care if I drop in on you later?" Gigi winks.

"My God. Gigi … "

"Do you care?"

"Of course not. If I had my way …"

She cuts me off with a smile. "Be careful there are ladies present."

I take another look at the ladies. I had tuned them out somehow, but is that … ? I recognize one of them now. She's a former First Lady! I mean, as in married to the President of the USA type First Lady! I don't believe this. She sees in my face that I just recognized who she is. She smiles at me, and looks demurely at her glass of wine. This is almost too much for me; I'm just an art student. I kiss Gigi on the cheek and wander back over to Frank and Jack. I hope they haven't killed each other.

Back With Jack and Frank

Jack and Frank are fine. I never thought I'd ever be able to write that, but there they are, laughing and waving their hands in the air as they talk. In many ways these guys are like two peas in a pod. They both have tremendous egos, both are incredibly talented, and they are both highly intelligent. The thing that sets them apart is their social skills. Frank is oozing with wit and charm which he has used skillfully to build his network of contacts. When it comes to charm, Jack has none. He rarely even makes eye contact during a conversation, and when he does, it is with such piercing intensity from his icy blue eyes that you wish he would look elsewhere. Frank loves an audience. Jack is a true loner.

"I hate to break up your private little party, but I think I'm about to make it even better for you." I announce as I return.

"You gonna poison all these freaks?" Frank smiles mischievously. Jack is gazing out into space, lost in his own thoughts the moment the conversation pauses.

"No. I'm going to take you somewhere you've never been before."

"Sounds like *Star Trek*." Jack brightens up, so I guess he was paying attention.

"In a way, you're right my friend. Just follow me."

I guide the boys to the wine cellar door. The sight of the door itself is intriguing, and Frank and Jack have fallen under its spell.

"What the heck is this," Frank asks, "the family crypt?"

"Nope. Hold on to your hat Mr. Reed. You ain't gonna believe this."

I lead Frank and Jack down the stairs into the wine cellar. I go to the electric panel, turn everything on, and wow! Even I got a major surprise. Jack wasn't wrong when he said it sounds like *Star Trek*. I didn't know anything about which button does this and that or whatever, so I pushed them all. The last one set in motion something Gigi hadn't shown me. Something amazing. All the monkeys and the South Pacific music faded away and out of sight, and a whole new scene came on.

It was *Star Trek*! The theme music permeated the entire cellar. Electric blue lights came on, and little Fairy-like things started buzzing around our heads. It must have been some sort of projected image, but it all seemed so real. Suddenly, the voice of Captain Kirk is heard over the music, "… to boldly go where no man has gone before." Then a brilliant white strobe light extravaganza blasts out over the entire cellar.

"DH," Frank yells, his hands over his ears, "how do you turn this off?"

"I don't know. I'm doin' the best I can! Maybe if I push the same switch the opposite direction it'll go off!"

I do, and it does.

"Wow," Jack says, unfazed, "That was tremendously cool!" He takes a seat on the stairs to await the next act.

"It was a friggin' nightmare!" Frank says, rolling his eyes and wiping the sweat from his brow. "Technology is good to a point, but crimeny! This Gigi is a friggin' kook!"

"I like *Star Trek*," Jack says calmly.

"Me too, Frank. Sorry."

"So, did we come down into this crypt for a reason?" Frank asks. He's looking around nervously, preparing for the next surprise.

"We did. Follow me." I give Frank a grin, and lead both of them past the Rothschilds. I walk slow enough for Frank to read and appreciate the labels. Coming to the glassed in room where the really expensive wines are kept, I take out the silver key and usher them through the door.

"What is all this?" Frank's face displays increasing amazement as he realizes what the room contains.

"Look at this wine, DH! Do you recognize these names? Here's a bottle that has to be worth a million bucks." Frank is holding a bottle of wine in both hands, cradling it like a newborn baby. "We ought to be wearing white gloves touching this stuff." He's whispering like he's in church.

Jack has been exploring the nooks and crannies. "Look at this over here guys," he says.

There is yet another door tucked into a corner of the expensive wine room.

"You got a key to this, DH?" Jack asks.

"I don't know. Gigi told me I had a key to everything on the property. I guess I'll have to try them all."

"You mean that White Alien Thing gave you her keys?"

"No, Frank, she gave me my own set of keys, to everything on her property." I answer a bit smugly.

"You gotta be kidding!" Frank and Jack whisper simultaneously.

"Well then, find the key!" Frank can hardly contain his excitement and curiosity. "This is like a treasure hunt!" *The Laugh*.

There are so many keys. I try several of them, until I find one that turns in the lock with a solid click. Just to be dramatic, I look first at Frank then at Jack, then I say, "Maybe we'd better not…" like something out of a Charlie Chan movie.

Before I could get more words out, Frank grabs the keys from me, feigning an evil laugh. "We go into this room or you die, Parsons!" Jack and I both laugh as the door opens with a creak.

There's a light switch inside to the right of the door. I flip it on. It takes us a minute to comprehend what we are seeing. We are in a tunnel about 50 feet long. The tunnel is lined with glass cases. The cases are filled with cigars! What in the world would Gigi want with a cigar collection? But nothing about her ever surprises me anymore.

"No Way!" Frank exclaims. "These are REAL cigars—Cubans, mostly Havanas! There are thousands of them! We're talking Big Bucks here, Bud! I hate to tell you this, but I don't think this girl is telling you the whole story. You told me she had a military dad? Ain't no way this came from his retirement! I was in Korea, my retirement's nowhere near this." *The Laugh*. "This just ain't right."

"I'm beginning to think so, too, Frank, but I can't explain it and I don't know what to do."

"Well, mysteries can be fun. Hang with this White Thing as long as you can, and enjoy every minute!" *The Laugh*. Even Jack nods his approval to Frank's statement.

Jack has opened one of the many glass cases. "Can we smoke one of these?" He asks as he reaches for a cigar.

"According to Gigi, you can smoke and drink as much of anything and everything down here as you want." I reply.

"And I mean it." It's Gigi, her disembodied voice coming from the direction of the stairs.

"You guys have fun down here." She says as she comes into view. "I'm not worried about the stock of supplies. It can all be replaced. Have your little art pow-wow, enjoy the wine, and smoke a cigar or two. It's all on me."

"Miss Gigi, my new friend." Frank smiles and gives her a courtly bow, complete with a kiss on her hand. "What's the deal with all this? You ain't no military brat." He can't resist. He has to confront her.

"Mr. Reed, I am indeed a military brat, and if I wanted, I could show you proof. But I don't want to." She winks at me.

"I never knew anybody on a military dole to come out with this kind of money." Frank drills her with those steely eyes of his.

"I had a couple of other inheritances that are really none of your business, Mr. Reed. You don't want my wine and cigars?" Gigi walks over to a glassed-in cabinet and pulls out four cigars. "These are the most expensive cigars in the world. One for your Mr. Jack, one for you Frank Reed, one for the love of my life, DH, and one for me. Light 'em up boys. When you get through with these, light some more, and put some in your pockets to take home with you. There's plenty more where these came from." She smiles her sweet, crooked little girl smile, and I can tell both Frank and Jack are in serious "melted heart mode" right now. I know I am.

We do exactly as Gigi instructed — we all light up. Now, I don't smoke, but smoking this cigar is an experience. More important than that, watching Gigi smoke a cigar is an experience.

Frank has a big grin on his face, looking almost as if he just swallowed LSD. "Gigi," he says, "you have to be the most incredible and bizarre woman I've ever known."

"You don't know me, Mr. Reed," she answers with a chill in her voice.

"I guess not." Frank shrugs his shoulders and is silent. I think he's finally met his match.

Jack has his eyes closed and is slowly blowing out a stream of smoke. "Man this is good. Thanks, Gigi." Jack is just Jack, paying no attention to Frank, or me, or whatever.

"You guys just do what you want to do down here." Gigi tells us. "Have your way with the wine and the cigars. I might come back and look in on you later. Try that Bordeaux out there on the third shelf with the green and pink label. It cost me more money than you all will ever see in your lifetime!" She turns to me. "DH, Could you step out here for a minute?"

While Frank and Jack are in heaven in the cigar room, Gigi takes me by the hand, and leads me back into the wine cellar.

"Come here. There's another room I want you to see." She whispers as we proceed to wind in and out of all the aisles and corridors of this fabulous basement, eventually ending up at another hidden door. This one is literally hidden; she has to push boxes out of the way to get to it.

"The boxes are empty, they're just a cover." She smiles at me, her eyes piercing my own.

"Now what?" I ask.

"I want to show you something very special to me. But you have to promise you'll never show Frank or Jack or anybody else." Her puffy nose fascinates me. Every time a word comes out of her mouth her nostrils flare just a tiny bit.

"I promise with my life." I tell her, and I mean it. She smiles at me, and opens the little door.

It's dark as we enter the mysterious room, but when Gigi turns on the lights, I am, once again, astonished. "When we get through here, you can go back to your little art party. But I want to share this with you. I've never shared it with any other man, so write that down in your little journal." She kisses my cheek.

The room is a shrine to her war hero father. There are candles burning everywhere; hundreds of candles.

"How do you keep these candles burning like this in this hidden place?" I ask.

"I pay a lady to do it for me. She's so sweet. She lost her husband over there too. She comes every day, twice a day, to make sure the candles are fresh, and they don't burn out, or burn my house down."

"This is a shrine, Gigi." I look around at the dozens of photos of Gigi's dad. He must have been something very special. There's a tear falling from Gigi's left eye.

"Gigi ... I don't know what to say. It would take me days to go through all this."

"You have a key," she says, pointing at my hand.

She is so sweet and so innocent in so many ways, and this is so important to her. This is one of the sweetest moments I've ever experienced.

"Go back to Frank and Jack," she tells me. "I'll be okay. I just wanted to share this with you." Gigi smiles with tears in her eyes and snot in her nose. "Do your art talk thing. I might join in later. I have a lot of boring people out there I need to tend to."

This White Thing, as Frank calls her, is much more than what he imagines her to be. Somehow I have to convince him of that.

"Gigi?" I hesitate to ask her this but I have to get it off my chest.

"Yes, Love?"

"You told me that you had an inheritance from your grandpa who was an artist and all that, but something isn't meshing here. It's obvious that you are fabulously wealthy, and when you were talking to Frank you said you had a couple of inheritances. What's the other one?"

"DH, I'm going to trust you with this, but again you have to swear to me on your life you will never tell a soul."

"Gigi, I would never betray you in any way." I told her, and I meant it with all my heart.

"My other grandfather was a very famous actor, and only a few people know this about me, because I've kept it a secret all my life. I'm going to whisper his name in your ear …"

"You're kidding!"

"Come over here." She leads me to the far side of the room where there is still another door.

Gigi unlocks the door, "You have a key in your set, too. It's the pink one," she says. We walk through, turn on the lights, and I get another surprise. The room is like a vault; it must be fifty feet wide and a hundred feet long. It's filled with memorabilia, souvenirs and photos of her grandfather. Now I see why she has all this money, and why all the celebrities are upstairs.

"But why do you keep this quiet? All those people up there know who you are!"

"Those are the plastic people. I don't care about them. I care about you and Jack and Manny and even that Frank Reed character. You are my real friends. But I'm afraid if even those guys learn who I really am, they'd go all gaga like everybody else does, and it wouldn't be real. I don't want people to love me for my money or who I'm related to."

"I think you're too late on that. When Frank and Jack tasted your wine and smoked your cigars, I think they fell in love."

"Well they can have all the wine and smokes they want, but I'm giving everything to you."

"Gigi, are you sure? I'm just a kid. I'm just an art student with nothing behind him and …"

"I know hearts, and I love yours." She grabs me and kisses me.

Twenty Minutes Later

Gigi went back to her guests, and I rejoined Frank and Jack in the Cigar Room. Frank is seated on a box in one corner of the room, and Jack is sitting on the floor by the door, each puffing on a cigar that neither one of them could ever afford in this lifetime. They are thoroughly immersed in the pleasure of the moment and look like they've been kissed by the La-La Fairy. To top it off, they actually seem to be getting along with each other. I wonder what Maxine would think about Frank at a party like this without her, so I ask him.

"I don't tell Maxine everything," he explains. "We need to have our separate identities. She thinks I'm somewhere else right now. Ha! I'll never tell her about Gigi or this party." He looks a little uneasy, so I leave it at that. Ain't goin' there.

"Say Frank, if you could have any wine in the world right now, what would it be?" I ask, changing the subject.

"Easy answer, Bud—a Spanish wine. I love anything that makes those Spanish girls dance those dances." He moves his arms in the air like a Flamenco dancer.

"I don't know any Spanish wines. You mean to tell me you would pass up all these French wines for a Spanish wine?

"It ain't got nothing to do with the country, or even the price of the wine. It has to do with the romance. You got those beautiful, hairy arm-pitted Spanish women dancing around, sweating and stinking, jiggling that Latin flesh, and they're all drinking Spanish wine. You just can't put a price on that." Frank smiles, lost in his reminiscence.

"Let's go back out there and find some different kinds of wine," Jack suggests.

"Not a bad idea," Frank agrees. "It's her nickel."

I lead the way back out into the wine room where Frank zeros in immediately on a bottle of something or other. I'm clueless, but he's excited!

"DH, do you know that this one single bottle of wine could pay for your parents house about ten times over? I'm going to pop this

sucker open and savor every drop myself. Tell your parents I'm sorry."
He laughs, then says to himself, "Who the heck is this Gigi chick?"

"Forget about it, Frank," says Jack with his customary solemnity.
"Just drink the wine and enjoy the show." I keep my mouth shut.

"But this is unreal. I mean it!" Frank hates being confronted with
a puzzle he cannot solve.

"So?" Jack comes back, "Just enjoy it. You got this multi-million
dollar house with a wine cellar and a cigar room, and all you can
worry about is how Gigi pays her bills?" Jack looks dreamy eyed.
"This sparkling little White Fairy that comes and goes at will …
just let her do what she wants."

But Frank won't let go. "With her money and her looks she could
destroy the whole wide world."

At that moment, Gigi returns.

"You like our wine?" she asks.

"Our wine?" Frank queries.

"Mine and DH's. You like it?"

Frank looks at me with raised eyebrows, then turns back to Gigi
with a look of surrender. "Gigi, you're one heck of a hostess."

"Thanks for sharing all this stuff with us," Jack says smiling shyly.

"I think I like you, Jack."

"By the way," asks Frank, "where the heck is Manny?"

Jack supplies the answer. "He's in the deep end of the pool
with some girl named Janice. She went home once, but then she
came back."

"The prostitute?" I speak before thinking, and Gigi reacts.

"Prostitute! What prostitute! I don't want any prostitutes here
tonight! Where did she come from?" She is mad; really mad.

"I hired her," Jack confesses. He's got guts.

"Jack! Who do you think you are inviting a prostitute to my
house? Just when I think I like you."

"Sorry Gigi, I didn't mean any harm. I really didn't." Jack isn't so
much apologetic as he is confused.

Gigi begins pacing the floor, her peculiar simian stride more pronounced than ever. I have to admit this is a comical scene. Jack is really upset. Frank is sitting on a box puffing a cigar, smiling while waiting for the play to unfold. Gigi is circling the room with a cigar in her hand and looking wild-eyed. I shake my head and a tiny laugh escapes me.

She whirls to face me and yells, "What are you laughing about?"

I just look at her and smile. After a long pause she smiles back looks down at her cigar, then comes over and kisses me on the cheek.

Frank and Jack look away. Sort of.

"As you were, gentlemen," Gigi says. "I'll take care of the prostitute." And she walks briskly away.

"Holy cow!" Frank says, looking at me. "Maybe she really is a military brat!" *The Laugh.*

"She is Frank, believe me. I've seen the proof."

"Wow," Jack says. "I bet she gets my hooker out of here in a heartbeat."

"What were you thinking Jack?" I ask.

"I don't know. I try not to think too much," Jack says, and Frank laughs.

"Jack," Frank looks at him, "I would have done the same thing. If I'd have known in advance all these old fuddy-duddies would be here tonight, and you guys wouldn't be here, I'd have brought a bag lady to this party and drunk wine with her!" *The Laugh.* Jack is smiling now.

"But you are havin' fun. You have to admit that," I say

"Oh yeah! But you won the prize DH," Frank says.

"What prize?"

"That White Gigi Thing. What a prize that is. You won the jackpot with her! She's absolutely gorgeous, she has a head on her shoulders, she's a darned good artist, and, by the way, she's RICH!"

"Still …" I stutter.

"Still what?" Frank yells. "Jack! Go out there and see if there's a psychiatrist in the crowd somewhere!" *The Laugh.* And Jack starts to leave.

"Not really, you numb nut!" Frank yells. "I was just kidding! But this DH guy, my Bud, ain't playin' with a full deck." Frank turns to me. "DH! You're single and young and have the whole world in front of you, and this Gigi Alien Thing comes out of nowhere, and drops smack dab in the middle of your life. What's the matter with you? Slap yourself man!"

"Frank … I just don't know. I think I love her, but I'm also afraid that it won't last. This girl is way out of my league."

"Bud, listen to me. Your league ain't got nothin' to do with it. You ain't even got a league," Frank laughs, "so just go with the flow."

"And ride with the tide," Jack adds.

"Long term scenario, I'm afraid Gigi and I will get married, and then she'll get tired of me and dump me. She's a celebrity!" I throw my hands in a gesture of futility.

"Let her dump you! If you're married you can sue her for half of ALL OF THIS! What are you? Stupid?" Frank laughs *The Laugh*.

"I would never sue her. Even if she dumped me." I look down.

"Then you are stupid," Frank says with a shake of his head. "DH, this whole thing is called the game of life. It's just what happens, and it happens all the time."

"Maybe I'm not so good at playing the game of life," I say morosely.

"You aren't getting suicidal on us are you?" Jack's eyes are big and wild. I think he's really worried about me.

"No, but I think I'm a real dolt sometimes."

"Dolt! What are you talkin' about DH?" Frank says with mock bluster. "I don't hang around with dolts!"

"This all seems like a dream—like a fairy tale. She is so young and so beautiful, and she has her entire life ahead of her, and some guy's gonna come along some day, and he's gonna have big biceps and a six pack ab thing goin' on, and that's gonna be it for me."

"I have to admit, I don't know what she sees in you either," Jack says.

"Jack, you'd make a good counselor!" Frank throws his empty cup at Jack. "But come to think of it, you might be right. DH doesn't have biceps or abs, and he's a poor boy like the rest of us. Look around. Those are movie stars out there! I could swear I saw what's her name … that flying nun chick."

"You mean Sally Field?" I ask. "You gotta be kidding! She's one of my favorite actresses!"

"I'm sure it was her. Maybe we ought to go back out there and see what's going on."

"Good idea." Now I'm excited. Sally Field!

"So," says Frank, with a smirk, "you'd dump old Gigi for Sally, huh?"

"Never in a million years, Frank. Never in a million years," I smile. "But I'd love to have Sally's autograph."

Frank shakes his head in mock despair. "DH, DH, DH … You just don't get it do you, Bud? You don't ask celebrities for their autographs at parties like this! And besides, this is YOUR party! YOU are the main celebrity here tonight! Give it a couple of hours, and old Sally will be asking for YOUR autograph!" *The Laugh.*

At that point we reluctantly leave the wine cellar. I lock it up, and we walk back out into the sort-of real world, where we notice that someone has lit a bonfire on the north lawn. Bob Dylan music is playing, some folks are dancing, and it all looks a bit surreal in the bonfire light.

My mind flashes back to how it must have been in the 30s and 40s in Hollywood during the glory days. There must have been a lot of this going on back then, and it's kind of exciting to be a part of whatever it is that's happening here right now. I'm now noticing that there are a lot of movie stars here that I recognize. I just wonder how long this will last. How long will I be a part of Gigi's life?

"Sit down on the ground and write this in your journal!" Gigi has snuck up behind me, wrapping her arms around my shoulders. "I LOVE YOU. And put it in big capital letters." She's hugging me and it's hard to write.

"Come with me, I have something else I want to show you."

Disneyland. Like I said, this place is Disneyland. Gigi takes my hand and leads me over to the waterfall that feeds the pool.

"Watch this."

There's a short post coming out of the ground next to the waterfall. On the top of the post is a small grey box. Gigi opens the lid of the box and inside is a single button.

"When I push this button the waterfall will stop and we'll have about one minute," she giggles.

"One minute for what?" I ask, always expecting strange answers.

"One minute to walk over those rocks down there," she points, "and go into the grotto behind the waterfall without being drenched."

"You mean this button turns off the waterfall?"

"Watch!" She pushes the button and the water stops falling, then she grabs my hand, and we make a mad dash, hopping from one stone to another.

I think there were about 20 stones leading to a place behind where the waterfall should have been falling, and we got there just in time. The second we stepped foot on the hard ground, the waterfall kicked in again. We are now standing behind the waterfall, in this grotto, as Gigi called it.

"Wait a sec, Hon," she says, walking over to a stone on the left side of the waterfall. I think she pushed another button. A really nice light blue radiating light has comes on and I'm now able to see all around the grotto.

We are in a large cave, and there is a bar and some tables and chairs.

"What kind of music do you want to hear, DH?"

"I don't care. I guess you have just about everything."

"You want classical? Or country, or how 'bout this?" She pushes more buttons and out comes her favorite, Buffalo Springfield. She starts to dance around the cave to *Oh hello, Mr. Soul, I dropped by to ...*

Gigi is all over the place with her dancing. Right now she's on top of a table pulling her shirt off and slinging it around in the air above her.

"Dance with me." She extends her arms and smiles invitingly.

I'm an awkward dancer at best, but I want to be close to her so I go to her. She grabs me tight.

"I want to be as close to you as I can, so we can merge together into one person," she purrs. But I'm not dancing.

"Gigi, they can't see us out there can they?"

"All they see is a blue light behind a waterfall. Kiss me." And I do.

Then she stops abruptly and says, "Recite me a poem."

"Huh?" I say, dumbly.

"Huh?" she repeats and breaks out laughing. "I don't think I've ever heard anyone say that to me before. I hope that isn't my poem. Huh?" She laughs.

"Gigi, I'll recite you a million poems if you want, your statement just surprised me."

"Recite me a poem here on the spot." So I do. Off the top of my head.

> *Hanging on to the future dream*
> *Knowing*
> *That dreams may never come true*
> *A flash in the past and this girl who*
> *Is always beside me is eternally far away.*

That's it. That's my poem. As I end it, I notice Gigi is crying.

"What's the matter?" I ask.

"I don't like that line about dreams never coming true. You are my only dream. If you don't want me, then I will never love anyone again."

"Gigi, I'm not saying I'm going to drop you, and even if I did, you can't make a statement like that."

"DH, there is nothing about those people over there by the pool that I care anything about. Without you in my life, I wouldn't even care about love."

"Where's that strong sci-fi woman who's able to confront Frank Reed and the rest of the world! What's the matter here?"

"I'm sorry," she sobs.

"What's really the matter Gigi?"

"I just can't imagine not having you in my life."

"You are very sweet to say that, but I'm sensing there's more to this."

"When I walked in on you and the boys in the cellar, I heard you telling them about how confused you were about me."

"Oh, sweet little Pixie." I pull her toward me and hold her as tight as I can.

"I'm sorry," she whispers.

"No Gigi, I'm sorry you heard that exchange between Frank and me, but I really am confused. This is all happening so fast, I don't know how to handle it. I keep thinking there's something wrong with this picture."

"What's happening fast?" she asks.

"This whole thing!" I tell her. "I'm a young, poor art student, who's met this celebrity chick, that I should be willing to die for, because she's given me the keys to everything she owns. Every time I look at you, I see how beautiful you are, and I wonder to myself, what in the world am I doing with this Goddess of wealth and beauty? I also wonder how long this is all gonna last."

"Forever. It will last forever." She looks up into my face, tears flowing down her cheeks.

A Bit Later

I've lost all track of time. Gigi and I were in the hidden grotto long enough for her to stop crying, and we just sat staring at each other for a while. I was the one to suggest we go back out to the party, which is beginning to break up. I'm sure I saw Sally Field walk by me — I think — but I didn't have the nerve to say anything to her. I now see some fairly prominent local politicians heading out through the house to get into their fancy cars.

I think I need to take off too. It's been a really long night, and I need to get some sleep, plus I'd like to do some painting tomorrow. I know those paintings will be of Gigi.

Day 74: The Next Afternoon

I got home at about 4 a.m. Gigi wanted me to stay the night with her, but I knew if I did I might never get away. Now I'm kicking myself for telling her no. She looked really hurt when I left. The last thing I want to do is hurt her.

I just now got out of bed, having slept most of the day away. It's already 2 p.m.—I never do that, but I was so tired, and my head was whirling so much … wait a minute …

I had to look. I still have the keys to Gigi's house in my pocket, so I know everything I remember from last night really happened. But I need to do something different today. I shouldn't go back there just yet. I think maybe I might paint a couple of pix of Gigi, and then hit the theater tonight.

I've mentioned the Stage One Theater before, the small, hole-in-the-wall movie place here in Riverside. There isn't really much to it. It's a long narrow room with 60 or 70 seats, a fairly small screen compared to the bigger theaters, a tiny lobby where they sell cokes and popcorn, and that's about it. I think it might be a mom-and-pop thing.

But here's the deal—while the other theaters in town are showing the latest first run movies, the Stage One lands all the foreign films, art films, film noir, and cinema vérité. It's where I saw my first Ingmar Bergman film, *Summer with Monika*! What a flick that was. I was still in high school when I was first introduced to Bergman's *Monika*. She made quite an impression.

The Stage One is not really the place you take your girl on a Friday night, unless your girl is really into art films. It's more of a place you take your mind to, and turn it loose and let it run free. Every movie they show there is riveting; all in black and white. I don't think I've ever seen a color movie there. But they're good flicks. No grandiose special effects, no "realistic" violence with arms being severed, and blood flowing out of some guy's head. No loud explosions and bad music. Just interesting plots and good acting.

Some of the movies today! If someone isn't getting blown away every fifteen seconds it just won't sell! Or if a large building isn't being blown up, or if there isn't a really dramatic car crash, the movie won't be the mega hit that it has to be in order to make the millions of dollars necessary to appease the mega-movie stars and the mega-corporations that do what they do to make the movies. But what does that say about the people who actually pay money to see them? What does that say about a culture that gets off on that infantile garbage?

In all of my experiences with the Stage One Theater, I've never seen one person blown away, or one building destroyed. But I always leave the theater deep in thought about how the film I had just seen relates to my own little world, or how I could adapt my own little world to relate to the film that I have just seen.

Bill Hunter comes to mind. He and I come to the Stage One often. I'm not sure what I want to say about him, but I feel the need to do so. He's a pretty big influence in my life right now, and I don't think I've mentioned him in my journal yet. But I want to light my pipe first.

I sometimes smoke a pipe. It's not that I really want to smoke a pipe, I think it's just because I'm young, and trying to cultivate an image about me that will blow the socks off the world. I'm still not sure what that image is, but I was reading some Jean Paul Sartre the other day—in fact I'm reading two of his books at the same time, *No Exit*, and *Nausea*—and my mind has been spinning. I saw this photo of Sartre on one of the book covers, and he had a pipe in his mouth. I got this wild, childish idea, that if I looked just like him, maybe I could write just like him. Maybe I could even be a famous philosopher someday. But the more I thought about it, the more I realized that being a philosopher is a kind of futile occupation. If you look in the want ads, how many do you find for philosophers? Also, JPS was a kind of smarmy looking character. I don't really want to look like that, and besides, I don't speak French.

What a strange desire. How many young men entertain the

thought of wanting to be like Sartre? How many even know who he is? I can understand wanting to be like other writers who lead more traditional lives, and who write books you can act out in your own living room. I can understand wanting to be like Henry Miller, or Ernest Hemingway, that's good glamour stuff. But Sartre? What a bizarre role model for a guy who should want to be just like all the other guys, who are studying to be mechanics, and insurance salesmen, and agricultural specialists, and medical technicians, and professional TV addicts—all the ordinary occupations, the expected and accepted occupations. Sartre was kind of an ugly sucker, so I doubt that anyone would want to actually look like him. It's more probable that a guy would want to act out the characters in his books, because they're a pretty big fad right now. But if you consider his characters carefully, logic would dictate that it would be a pretty stupid thing to want to be like them, too. They were losers. Pathetic, sick, losers. Hmmm … maybe I'll stop smoking this pipe.

So, into my life walks Bill Hunter, the man who's teaching me that anything and everything I ever wanted to do in or with my life, I can do. Bill's motto is, "There doesn't have to be a norm!" He lives that motto. He walks a path different from just about anyone I've ever known, and he expects everyone else to do the same.

"Anybody," Bill will tell you, "man or woman, can be anything they want to be in this world. They just have to have courage and determination. It takes guts to go against the establishment, but if you don't do it, you'll become a part of it, and if you become a part of it, you'll be just as miserable as they are, for the rest of your life."

Bill is my English professor at RCC. When I first came into his class, I didn't really know what to expect. I'd been fed so much crap by high school counselors, and from older friends, who already had a year or two of college under their belts. The counselors informed me, "You have to toe the line in college. The professors don't give any slack!" My older friends who've been there and done that told me, "The profs are really cool! They let you get away with a lot of stuff you could never get away with in high school."

Bill Hunter is none of the above. He's one of a kind. Everything anyone ever told me about college professors flew out the window the moment I got my first glimpse of this balding, rotund little man, who always wears the same short-sleeved light blue sport shirt, who always has at least one shirt button unbuttoned, who can't for the life of him keep that shirt tucked into his pants because of his pear-shaped belly.

The first day I walked into Bill's class, just a few weeks ago, I saw this unkempt little man standing next to an overhead projector, playing with a transparency sheet, and talking to himself. What a sight. There was that blue shirt hanging out of the right side of his pants. As a new student I had prepared myself for a much larger, far more intimidating man than the one who stood before me that day. I thought to myself, this can't be a college professor! This has to be somebody's disheveled old uncle, or maybe a custodian, or maybe even one of the students. He can't be "The Professor."

But he was. My preconceived image of how he should look was shot. I was really disappointed at first, but as the classroom began to fill up with the new students, I watched as Bill Hunter watched every student who walked through the door. He sized them up one by one, all the while with a crooked little half smile on his lips. I sensed that this guy was a whole lot deeper than I first thought.

On that first day of class, he watched every motion the students made. He studied their faces, their ages, the way they walked, where they chose to sit in the classroom, the way they sat down, the way they crossed their legs, the way they talked. I know he did this because I watched him doing it. And all the while that little smirk was on his face. At first I thought to myself, "Who does this guy think he is? Pompous old fart!" But Bill told me about three weeks later, after I got to know him better, "You can tell more about a student by where he sits on the first day of class, than by anything else he does all year long."

His theory was that the ones who sat in the front rows were there for the wrong reason. They wanted to be noticed by the Prof as being something they really weren't. The ones that sat in the back rows were also there for the wrong reason. In fact, they didn't want to be there at all! They were usually the ones who were being forced to take the class to fulfill some sort of course requirement—the future real estate agents, the med students, and the jocks.

"I teach the ones in the middle rows," he told me, "because those are the ones who want to be here. Those are the average ones who know how to think for themselves and who take something home in their heads when the class is over." Then he added with a smile "The ones who sit in the middle rows next to the windows are usually the ones who end up teaching me."

Back on that first day, I walked into the room, I stared at Bill for a while, then I took one of the chairs from the outside third row, pulling it way out from the rest of the class, all the way over to the window. At that time I didn't know what that made me "be" in the eyes of Bill Hunter, but he did stop playing with the transparency sheet, and he stared right at me. I got just a little worried and I thought to myself, "Maybe this is one of those professors I was warned about, maybe I should put the chair back. So, as quietly and respectfully as possible, I slowly slid the chair back to where I'd found it. To my absolute horror, Bill Hunter, started walking slowly toward me. I was terrified. Suddenly this little man was six foot six and weighed 300 pounds. I thought, "Now I'm gonna get it! I'm a freshman. I just got here, and I screwed up already!

But when Bill got to where I was sitting, he motioned for me to get out of the chair, and when I did he took the chair and slid it back under the window where I had first put it. Then he said to me, "You were right the first time, son. There are far better things to learn out there, beyond that window, than you'll ever learn inside these hallowed halls."

Then Bill turned away from me and did something I've never seen any teacher do before. He returned to the front of the room. The class was quiet. Everyone was watching Bill, waiting for him to do something, or say something like, "Hi. My name is Bill Hunter and I'll be your English professor this semester, blah blah blah …" but it didn't happen. He didn't say a word. When he got to the blackboard he just stood there for what seemed like a very long time, silently staring out at the class with that quirky smile on his lips. Then, without warning, the son of a gun turned away from the class, faced the blackboard, stuck his hand in his pocket, and pulled out a piece of chalk. On the board he wrote, in very large letters, a certain four-letter word that I will not write in my journal.

Then he turned toward the class, walked back to his desk, put his hands on top of the desk, leaned over, and stared at us. Continuing his silence, he eyed everyone in the room, one at a time, that crooked smile playing on his lips all the while.

At the end of about five minutes, Bill very calmly and very softly said, "Class dismissed." And that was it! The first day of class was over! We didn't crack a book! We didn't hear a lecture! Zilch! Five minutes of total silence and then, "Class dismissed." The little man with the crooked smile was finished with us.

You could have heard a pin drop as everyone exited the classroom, the students looking at each other in confusion, whispering comments back and forth as they neared the door.

The prudish women who had been sitting in the back rows, started chattering loudly about how they'd "never come back to this man's class again!" About how they didn't understand what this man had done! How they thought he was too weird for them.

A group of guys in the front row were also upset. I heard one of them say sarcastically, "We paid money for this?"

But I loved it! At that time I wasn't sure exactly why Bill had done what he'd done, but I knew it had to mean something, and I didn't see it as an insult at all. I saw it more as the first page to an exciting new chapter in my life, and I thought, "If the first page is this good, I can't wait to read the rest of the book."

Something inside of me was crying out, "Wow! Bill Hunter isn't just a professor! He's a great big door that somebody left open. I'm gonna run through this guy! I'm gonna find myself in the middle of some sort of magical land, and I'll never go back the other way." I wasn't sure what was going to come next. I wasn't sure where all of this would lead, but I was determined I wasn't going to be "like them." Like the simpletons who left the room chattering like chickens.

I'll never forget how, as I left the class that day, I smiled at Bill and he smiled and winked at me. He said very quietly, "You'll be back, Child, and I expect big things from you." With that, he nodded his head, turned, and walked back into the empty classroom.

I wasn't entirely sure what he meant by that, but I knew I'd be back.

The next day I did come back to Bill's class, but about half the students didn't. The women in the back row didn't come back. The guys in the front row didn't come back. Most of the folks in the middle rows returned, looking a bit wary, but they were there. When we were all settled in, Bill looked up at us and said, "Good! We got rid of the contented ones. The ostriches have run away. Now we can all learn from each other, and we will do just that." He smiled broadly.

So far, I've not heard Bill Hunter say, "Open your books to page this or that." He always says, "Open you minds to page this or that." It's more than just clever of him to say such a thing, he means it.

This semester under the tutelage of Bill Hunter, I'm devouring Sartre, Camus, T. S. Elliot, E E Cummings, Allen Ginsberg, Greg Corso, Jack Kerouac, Lawrence Ferlinghetti, and a dozen other writers, who somewhere along the line in their own lives, had their own Bill Hunter, to stimulate their creativity. I've barely read any of their work before now, but I know Bill is presenting them to me as a gift.

A Bit Later

I must be a prophet. I was going to go to the Stage One, but the plan never got off the ground. I got a phone call from Bill Hunter, and I'm now sitting in The Pit with him and Frank Reed. I arrived first, and while I was waiting for Bill to show, Frank appeared. Five minutes later, Bill came sauntering along with his shirt hanging out, carrying some sort of snack in his hands. I waved at him, and he came over and sat down.

"DH, who's your friend?" Bill nods in a friendly manner at Frank.

"This is Frank Reed."

"The artist," he responds, recognizing the name.

"How do you know me?" Frank's eyes light up as he offers up his hand for a handshake.

"The whole art department is abuzz about you, young man. Have you met OK Harry, our painting teacher?" Bill asks, shaking Frank's hand.

"I have," Frank replies, smiling, but somewhat cool.

"OK thinks you have something really special inside you. He loves your paintings. I have to admit I've seen a few photos of them, and I think you need to be in a museum somewhere. I loved that one of the woman in a chair with all that paint dripping down."

"I sold it already." Frank is little guarded with Bill, since he's meeting him for the first time, but Bill is as sweet as can be. He always is.

"Oil paint, right?" Bill asks.

"Yep."

"Maybe we could set something up with one of my classes. Would it be possible for me to bring one of them over to your studio on a field trip sometime?"

Frank can't resist Bill's charm.

"That would be good, Bill." Frank is sitting up straighter and there's a genuine smile on his face. "You name the time." Frank scribbles his phone number on a piece of paper and gives it to Bill.

"Mr. Reed," Bill says, "I think I'm your biggest fan here at RCC, and I appreciate this."

"No prob," Frank answers warmly, and the two of them take off into a conversation of their own.

When I graduated from high school, I enrolled here at RCC simply because it seemed to be the thing to do. School has always been a kind of game to me. Still is. I hadn't cared too much for high school because I was forced to attend, but I'm enjoying college now, because I don't have to be here if I don't want to be here. I can get a job somewhere if I want, become an electrician or something, but I really like RCC.

I don't recall ever having studied as much as I do now, though. I was perfectly satisfied with C's and B's and maybe a few A's in high school. I got my grades simply by showing up to class on a semi-regular basis and breathing, and faking my way through an exam now and then. But I wasn't a "studier." Never have been, and never really had to be. High school was a breeze.

The Pit is my favorite place at RCC; I pull a lot of time doing homework down here. Day or night, hot or cold, all kinds of weather. Actually the sky looks a bit ominous tonight, but since it seldom rains here in Riverside, I'm not too worried about it. That's one thing I miss about my childhood back in Kansas, and Oklahoma. I miss the rain. I love California, but rain and all the stuff that comes with rain, like thunder and lightning, is rare here, and I miss it.

Back in Ponca City, and Tulsa, I used to watch the billowing grey rain clouds go overhead, and the only time it got scary was when the clouds started turning round and round, and the funnel they formed began to drop down toward the ground. That's when we all ran for our lives, because it meant a tornado was about to hit.

The problem for my little family was that we didn't have a cellar. If a tornado touched down in our neighborhood, we would have been creamed. I remember one time when my mother was in the hospital, and my grandmother, Nana, was watching my brother, Jim, and me. A twister appeared in the sky as we were standing out in the street, getting what was called a fudge-sickle, or something like that, from the ice cream truck that came by at least once a day. Nana grabbed us by the hands, took us back into the house, and the three of us laid down on the hallway floor, covered with mattresses that Nana had pulled from our beds. I was kind of scared, but I also thought it was a great game. I don't know what Jim thought. I am the Peter Pan brother, and Jim has always been the more mature of the two of us. That tornado was a memorable experience for me. I don't really want to go through any of those any more, but I miss a good rousing thunderstorm with lightning and rain and all that.

Bill is talking about beatnik poets and writers. He's very calm about it, unlike Frank. Frank waves his arms around like he's going to take off flying any minute, but Bill just sits there calmly, speaking in that soft voice of his, and hardly ever looking any one in the face. He spends most of his time looking down at the tabletop, but that gesture isn't subservience on his part. He's filled with so much important stuff to say that he has to do it in order to concentrate on what comes out of his mouth next.

"You know," Bill was saying, "Allen Ginsberg is a really fine writer. Kerouac gets all the credit for the beat generation, but Ginsberg has talent, too."

"But Ferlinghetti was the brains behind the whole movement," Frank adds.

"I'm not sure it was a real movement, Frank. May I call you that, Mr. Reed?"

"Uh … sure." Frank gives me a look that asks, *What planet is this guy from?*

"These men are just regular Joes who were writing poetry and taking down notes about their lives. Many of them kept journals, like our friend, DH, here," Bill said, smiling at me. "Those journals eventually became books. Corso is actually a better poet than he is a speaker. I once had the displeasure of seeing him at a live reading. He sounded like he had mush in his mouth while he read. I couldn't understand half of what he said. But I like his poetry."

"*A Coney Island Of The Mind* has to be one of the finest books of poetry ever written," Frank says. "I met Ferlinghetti a couple of summers ago in San Francisco. DH met him too, just a month ago right, Bud?"

"Yep," I said. "I walked up to the City Lights Bookstore in San Francisco, and sitting on the sidewalk by the window were Larry Ferlinghetti and Allen Ginsberg, sipping coffee and shooting the breeze. I didn't know what to do. I was this star-struck kid walking around in a daze. I just threw caution to the wind and went right up to them. I begged them to take a picture with me, and they both nodded to say yes at the same time, and Allen said, 'Cool.' I still have the photo. Larry took a copy of *Coney Island Of The Mind* off the shelf, signed a personal note in it, and handed it to me with a big grin on his face. Corso came by just then and saw what we were doing. He was a wonderful, disheveled kook and I couldn't understand half of what he said, but he grabbed my arm, and signed his name on my right wrist, and said, "There's my autograph. In a couple of days it will be worth just about as much as my sorry butt." What a character. What a wonderful, brilliant character.

"They invited me to sit at the table with them, so I did, and we chitchatted for about two hours. They were very personable, and they wanted to know everything about me.

"Allen seemed to be the most curious about me. When I told him I was born in Winfield, Kansas, he asked me if that was where Dorothy and Toto lived. We all laughed at that even though I'd heard it a hundred times before. Sitting at a table sipping coffee with these guys had put me in a state of shock."

"My goodness, DH!" Bill says, "do you realize the experience you had with these men? I mean do you really realize it?"

"I think I do Bill," I answer back. "I know I do."

Franks butts in. "I don't think DH knows much about nothin' right now, Bill. He's so in loooooooooooove"—he drags the word out—"with this chick he's dating, that he can't even see straight." He grins at my discomfort.

"You have a girl?" Bill inquires.

"I think I do," I reply, not meeting his gaze.

"What do you mean you think you do?" Bill scratches his head and looks up at me, puzzled.

"Well ..." I don't know what to say.

"You either have a girl or you don't, and if you are this hesitant about this girl, I think you'd better wait for the next one." Bill has a frown on his face. I've never seen him like this before. "What's her name?" he asks.

"Gigi."

"Gigi, hmmm. Not a bad name, but not right for you."

"What are you talking about, Bill?" I am truly confused by his behavior.

"I'm not sure, but Gigi doesn't work for me."

"Okay." Now I really don't know what to say.

Frank breaks into the awkward pause. "DH, listen to Uncle Bill. He may be right on this one. I got a strange feeling about this chick too. I know she's beautiful and rich but, it does seem a bit too good to be true."

"I have feelings about it too," I respond defensively, "but I do love her. I think."

"You've got it bad son," Bill says. "That's all the more reason to slow down. Lust and love are two different things."

"It isn't lust Bill. I know some things about Gigi, and I've spent some time with her own memories. She's a whole lot deeper than you guys give her credit."

"DH, I've never met Gigi. Frank have you met her?" Bill asks.

"Oh yeah, we're best friends!" *The Laugh*. Even I have to smile.

Bill continues softly "DH, I just want what's best for you. I don't want your heart to be broken. You have a lot of talent in your writing, and I think that's where your life needs to go, but if you hook up to the wrong woman all of that might be stifled."

"Thanks Bill, but I don't think Gigi would stifle anything about me. She's so supportive of everything I do. She gave me the keys to her house!"

"She's one rich babe Bill, I kid you not!" Frank adds. "But I wouldn't trust DH with the keys to my bike!" *The Laugh.*

I love both of these men. I really do. But I also love Gigi, and that puffy nose of hers tells me that I'm not wrong in doing so.

The billowy clouds I wrote about earlier are starting to drop rain down into The Pit. Luckily we're all sitting under the protected side, but several of the other students are grabbing their books, and heading up the steps like they're running for their lives. This is the first rain we've had all summer, and that, in and of itself, isn't so important, except that it's happening to me, and I can feel it first hand. I can see the trees, even in the dark, and I can sense them gulping down all the water. I love the rain.

While everyone flees the downpour, there is one, lone, mad girl, coming down the steps into the Pit. This chick has got to be soaked to the bone, because she's wearing a short little go-go dress, sandals on her feet, and not much else. It's Gigi! She's seen me sitting here with Frank and Bill, and now she's running toward us, almost falling down, then catching herself on a table.

"Will you look at this!" She greets us from several feet away, grinning from ear to ear. "I know this wise guy," pointing to Frank, "but who's this other guy?" she asks as she reaches our table.

"This is Bill Hunter, my English teacher." Funny, all three of us stand up as she speaks, like the Queen of England just walk in. I smile back at her, and I don't really care what either of these guys thinks.

"Ha! You already speak English DH! What do you need this guy for?" she says with a laugh. Even Bill smiles.

"He needs me, young lady, because I'm going to try to do the impossible. I'm going to form this young man into a writer."

"But he's already a writer, Mr. Hunter." She puts her hands on her hips and cocks her head to one side. "He writes in that little journal every second of ever minute of every day. Except when he's messing around with me, of course," she smiles big, looking just like Peter Pan!

Frank turns his head away and says, "Amen." Bill just sits there, turning almost as white as Gigi.

"Miss Gigi," Bill says, "you are one of the loveliest girls I think I have ever seen, no doubt about it. But I'm going to teach DH how to turn all those journal words into novels. I see something very special in that young man. One day he'll write a best seller."

Bill's last statement floors me! I've never heard him say that before. Frank even raised eyebrows when it came out of Bill's mouth.

"Well," Gigi says, "when he does sell a book, Mr. College Professor, it won't mean anything to me, cause I love him just like he is."

"I don't understand why." I smile and wink at Gigi and change the subject. "So what are you doing here? It's a terrible night to be out." We've pushed our table next to the wall where the rain is missing us by about three feet.

"I missed you." That's all she said, but she had a worried look on her face.

"You missed me? So you drove all the way over here?"

"I want to be with creative people."

"So where are you going to find them?" Bill asks, a twinkle in his eye.

"Right here, you fat old thing." She smiles at Bill and adds, gently, "But I like you cause you look a little like my dad."

"Your dad was a fat, old, diabetic thing, just like me huh?" Bill smiles back at Gigi.

"He wasn't diabetic or he couldn't have fought in the war." Gigi sits down by me and puffs herself up like Shirley Temple.

"Well," Bill's eyes get a little misty. "I have to tell you that I don't care much for war, but I do love those young people over there who are fighting for our freedoms, and giving their lives. Is your dad still over there, Sweet Child?"

"No. He was killed." Tears are, of course, forming in her eyes, but she's still sitting tall and puffed up.

"I'm so sorry, Child. I'm so sorry." Bill reaches for his handkerchief.

Bill is the most sensitive and sympathetic man I know. For all his tough stuff in the classroom, if a person needed him for anything, he'd be there in a heartbeat.

"Mr. Reed once called me 'Child' and I almost decked him. But somehow it's okay coming from you, Hunter." Gigi is crying softly.

"You are so white, Child. Why are you so white?" Bill bunches up his forehead and hugs Gigi tightly over to him.

"And you are so funny, you crazy old man!" Gigi laughs and hugs him back. "I'm white because I'm a friggin' vampire!"

The rain is really pouring down now, and Gigi keeps looking at, me flashing that Gigi grin, like she's getting fed up with me writing in the journal instead of paying attention to the conversation.

Thank heaven we're under the protected part of The Pit. It's dumping buckets now, and I notice that one drop of rain has landed on Gigi's puffy nose, so I reach over and I wipe it off.

Frank is looking at us with mock disgust. "I'm getting out of here. You lovebirds are a distraction to my creativity."

"Me too," Bill says. "I have a class in about five minutes," He draws me aside and quietly says, "But DH, can I tell you something?" He pulls me over away from the table so Frank and Gigi can't hear, and he whispers into my ear, "DH, Gigi is a sweet girl, and I'm going to love her just like I love you, but she isn't the one you've been waiting for. There is another, and you will know her when she comes, but not yet. So slow down." Then he starts slowly climbing up the steps of The Pit in his gentle way. Frank grins at me, blows me a kiss, and follows after him.

Just like that, Frank and Bill are gone, and I'm sitting here alone with Gigi, totally confused.

"Now what?" I ask Gigi.

 She smiles at me "We'll just sit here and cuddle."

"Here in the rain?"

"Rain never hurt a thing."

A Long Night with Gigi and Frank

Gigi took me home with her; there was no way I could talk her out of it. I left my car in the RCC parking lot, and we drove to her house in a new car I hadn't seen before. It was dark, and I couldn't tell what the make or model was. When I asked her she said, "A Jag, of course." Of course.

We parked in her driveway and we were met immediately by a couple of big guys. A house like hers must have a surveillance system to match. As they opened our doors for us, I looked up at the guy who opened mine. He could have crushed me with his right hand, he was that big. I smiled at him, and he gave me a half smile that clearly told me that I'd better mind my p's and q's while I'm here on Gigi's digs.

We walked through the big front doors and there, lined up in the long hallway leading into the living room, was the household staff, just like in the novels about English manor houses. There were about a dozen women and a half-dozen men, all dressed in the traditional black and white maid and butler uniforms. Not one of them made eye contact with either of us as we walked down the hall. I felt like I was in a British movie.

When we got to the living room, a precious little girl, who looked to be about three years old, came running over from where she had been standing in the corner. She announced very loudly but very sweetly, "Mr. Dennis Artist, you are invited to dinner tonight, right here." She looked back and forth from me to Gigi as she spoke. Then she ran back over to where she was when we walked in. Really cute. As soon as the little girl ran off, a butler-suited man brought us glasses filled with what I think was some more of that champagne we had the other night.

Gigi had obviously been planning this moment for some time. She just kept looking at me every ten seconds or so, checking my reaction. All I could do was look back at her with a silly grin on my face.

One of the uniformed young men took me gently by my right arm and led me into the dining room. The long dining table was big enough to seat fifty people, but Gigi whispered in my ear that we were the only two for this night. She put her right hand in my left pocket tugged me over to the table, and sat me down. "You be good, this is going to be the nicest night of your life," she said.

Then the show began. I've seen the old movies with all the pomp and whatever, but this show took the cake. Her head chef, Mary, came in and introduced herself to me, then the waiters started coming out with all kinds of food. Things I'd never seen before. We were served wine, salad, and some sort of oyster thing that had green sauce—like pesto—poured over it, and topped with Parmesan cheese. The whole time, classical music came softly out of invisible speakers in the walls and the ceiling. Beethoven's Ninth Symphony at first, followed by Rimsky-Korsakov, Dvořák, and Bach—all of my favorite pieces. How in the world did she know that?

Then the main course came out. I'm still not sure what it is. Some sort of grilled steak about four inches thick, with potatoes and green beans soaked in olive oil and covered in cream. I think.

My wine glass never goes below half; it's always filled by the stoic waiters, who never make eye contact. But Gigi does. Her eyes remain fixed on mine, never breaking contact. In fact I don't think she ever blinks!

"Well, DH," she coos, "how do you like the food?"

"It's beyond anything I've ever had, Gigi,"

"And the service?"

"Better than any restaurant I've ever been in."

"Most of these guys have been with my family for years. Carl's the headwaiter. He's been around forever. Since I was a little kid."

"I'd like to have seen you back then when you were a little kid,

Gigi."

"I have some photos!" She gleams. "But they're over in my bedroom so it will have to wait too after dinner."

"I can wait." I smile.

"But I can't!" She giggles, gets up, grabs my hand and drags me off in the direction of her bedroom.

Gigi pulls me into a gigantic bedroom big enough to park ten Buicks in, and leads me over to a big, double-doored, cherry wood cupboard. She opens the right-hand door, and I see four, or five shelves, each filled with what looks like scrapbooks.

"Come over here, Love. Sit on the bed with me." She pulls me over and we sit on her enormous bed. This is not a king-sized bed. This is something much bigger, for maybe three kings!

"These are my family albums!" She is transformed by the happy memories of happy days. Her smile is sweeter and that puffy nose of hers is cuter than ever. "Look at this!" she says. And I devour the albums like a little kid in a candy shop.

Two Hours Later

We are back in the dining room. Gigi said she wants to pick out some wine for us to take back to her bedroom.

For the past two hours, this young White Being has given me an introduction to her entire family history. I couldn't believe my eyes. In one of her baby pictures, her famous actor grand father was holding her in his arms on the set of a movie production. He was grinning up at the camera for all he was worth, and the photo clearly showed, that he KNEW he was famous, and this was a photo opportunity that couldn't be passed up. The face of little Gigi there in his arms in that photo was nearly the same then as it is now! She's been cute all her life. She's been Gigi all her life.

"Okay DH," Gigi says calmly, "here's what I want to happen. Write this down in your little book, I have some big plans for tonight." She grins.

"You mean another party?"

"Maybe," she smiles. "But you're gonna love this."

Carl, the head waiter/butler guy, is standing by the kitchen door. Gigi gives him a nod and Carl rings a bell, and… I don't believe it! Frank, Jack, Bill Hunter, Bill Mitchkelly, and even Manny, just walked in, all laughing like a bunch of little schoolgirls!

"Gotcha!" Frank yells, following up with *The Laugh*.

What is this, another birthday party? Gigi is giving me another birthday party! At the moment of that realization, I hear another little bell go tinkle tinkle, and in comes a monster cart with the biggest cake I've ever seen! On top of the cake is a perfect representation of Gigi and me, but we aren't wearing the cliché marriage clothes you see on cakes like this, we're dressed in Army green fatigues. Ha! What a treat. I know this is some sort of tribute to Gigi's dad, but the fact that she's including me in it is priceless. Here come her tears, and I'm really touched. For the first time in my life I'm being honored for being … what? Some woman's love? No, for being a part of her life! She trusts me with her life and with everything about her life. Her family history—you know, she made me promise not to reveal certain things about her and her family, and I have to tell this journal that I never will.

"You guys! What's the deal with this?"

"You're 20! Tonight we're making it official." *The Laugh*, again, and all of the guys start applauding me.

"Man I'm old." I stumble with words but I feel I have to say something.

I turn to Manny. "Where the heck have you been? The last time I heard, you were in Gigi's pool with a prostitute."

Manny looks sheepishly at Gigi. "Gigi, can I tell him what happened or not?"

"Tell him whatever you want kid." She winks at me with her hands on her hips.

"Janice and I were in the pool by the edge, when Gigi came storming in from outta somewhere. She reached down and grabbed Janice's arm, and said something like, 'come with me worthless,' and these other big burley guys came over and helped Janice out of the water, and that's the last I saw of her. I swear, these guys looked like Mafia thugs."

Gigi smiles at him. "Calm down, Manny-Poo," she says. "They're my bodyguards and I use them for what I have to use them for, but I ain't gonna have a prostitute crash my party. I was gentle with her." Gigi looks at me and grins.

"Right," Manny says. "You looked pretty tough to me."

"My bark is bigger than my bite, Manny."

"I think we're all finding that out," Frank adds.

Gigi challenges Frank with an icy stare. "Just what do you mean by that?"

"Hold on," — *The Laugh* — "I just meant you are one formidable woman, Ms. Gigi, whatever the heck your last name is."

"I have no last name to you, Mr. Frank Reed." She stares him down with the same steely stare he's staring her down with.

I'm not sure where this night is going. I don't like the way these two keep at each other, even if it is my birthday. I just want it to end, and I think Gigi is picking up on my vibes 'cause she keeps glancing over at me. And the Janice thing. I don't like the way Jack brought her into all this, and the way that girl got manhandled and thrown out on the street. A sweet, Jewish girl, who's had a run of bad luck, doesn't deserve that kind of treatment. Birthday or not I have to speak up.

"Gigi, was it really necessary for you and your goons to rough up Janice like that? She's had a pretty tough life. All she was doing was trying to feed her kid and get by. Besides, Jack brought her into all this."

"Relax, Love," she answers. "They didn't really rough her up. They put her in a car and drove her across town to her new home in La Sierra. They also brought one of my attorneys with them so they could explain how her new bank account works. I set her up for life. My attorneys are also going to locate her family and fly them out here. We're gonna straighten that whole thing out too.

I'm floored. I look at Frank, and see that he is floored, too. Even Jack is floored.

"I'm sorry, Gigi," I stutter. "I didn't know …"

"You don't have anything to apologize for, DH. You don't know a lot about me—yet. For instance, I never told you that I, and my entire family, are Jewish. I give chunks of cash to that Temple downtown, and there's no way I'd let one of my heritage sisters live like Janice has been living."

"My, oh my, oh my," Frank smiles at Gigi. "You never cease to amaze me, White One."

Gigi changes the subject, putting the focus on Frank. "Frank Reed, I think you're one heck of an artist. I haven't seen any of your work, but I can tell by being around you that you have the Art Spirit."

Frank's face goes pale. "I've got to admit, I'm pretty impressed with you, Little White One," he says, regaining his composure.

"Why do you say that? And don't you ever call me that again, or I'll find your house and kill all your pets." She smiles sweetly.

"You know about the Art Spirit!"

"Whata you think, I'm stupid? The Kunstwollen? No big deal," she says.

"The heck it isn't!" Frank is on fire now. This is his religion they're talking about. "Very few artists know what the Art Spirit is! And here you are, and I'm not even sure what you are yet, but I'm now finding out that you really are an artist!"

"Why Frank, big jerk that you are, you're finally recognizing me?"

"Honey—and don't hit me for saying that—I recognized you a long time ago, but when you mentioned the Art Spirit …"

"Frank, I think I might like you a little more than I did before, but listen to this Mr. Big Guy, DH has ten times the Art Spirit I have. You need to zero in on him."

"Hey, it's his party." Frank says with a grin and a shrug of his shoulders to me.

"It's more than that, big shot. Watch this."

She signals to Carl, the butler, with a nod of her head. He steps out into the long hallway, and returns a few seconds later with two big, stone-faced guards, armed and uniformed, like off a Brinks truck. They march directly over to Gigi and me. My art buddies are standing by the kitchen door, watching with amazed curiosity as the scene unfolds. Apparently they don't know any more than I do. I look at Gigi. She's trying to keep a serious face, but she can't hide her grin. Something very special is about to happen.

One of the guards is carrying a briefcase handcuffed to his left wrist. He holds his right hand near the gun holstered on his hip, and he's looking straight at me. What the heck? Now he's setting the briefcase down on the table, the whole time keeping his eyes on me and his hand near his gun. The other guard is intently watching the boys over by the wall. He too has his hand close to his gun, and he doesn't look too friendly. I don't know what the heck these guys have in that briefcase, but it must be very, very important.

Gigi looks at me, winks, then slowly and dramatically walks over to the guards, stopping briefly to look back at Frank and the other guys. I look at them too, and I see Frank make a face that says, "I don't know what the heck this is all about."

Returning to me, Gigi says. "I wanted to give you a very special gift for your birthday, DH, and I thought long and hard as to what that might be. You know I have a lot of money, and I could fly 'round the world and shop for just about anything on earth, but nothing on earth would be special enough to give to you. So, this is what I came up with." She goes back to the guards at the table. The one on the left—the one without the briefcase attached to his wrist—takes a key from his pocket and hands it to Gigi.

Gigi slowly puts the key into the lock. Both guards elevate their level of vigilance, moving their right hands to the handles of their guns. I feel like if anyone sneezes, these guys will jump into action, and it will be the end of this party. But I take one more look over at the boys, and I see that they aren't about to move a muscle until this is all over. Gigi is clearly in charge here.

Manny's eyes are the size of silver dollars! I stifle the urge to crack a joke or let out a nervous laugh.

One of the guards snaps his fingers, and in walk four men in black suits with bulges under their left arms. They take positions surrounding Gigi — north, south, east, and west. Poor Manny looks close to wetting his pants right now. I look over and see that even Frank is looking a bit edgy. Jack and Bill and Bill are frozen like statues. I'm a bit nervous, too. The four men in black have their right hands tucked into the left side of their unbuttoned suit coats, and they're not just scratching their armpits. What does Gigi have in that little box, the friggin' Hope Diamond?

As Gigi starts walking back to me, all the guards come with her, looking in all directions like Secret Service agents do when they protect the President. When she gets right in front of me she whispers, "Happy birthday, Love." She gives me a smile of such sweet tenderness that I just want to kiss her right here and now, but the looks coming from the guards puts a chill on that impulse.

Very slowly, Gigi hands me the box. As she does so, all of the guards tighten up even more. I'd better be careful here, or they'll shoot me before I get it open.

"Thank you, Pixie. I just don't know what …"

"Shut up and open the box, DH! You don't have to say anything, and be sure you do it slowly, and carefully, because I don't want these guards to take you out before we go back to the bedroom." She winks. "I might let them take out those other guys though." She smiles, looking over at Frank and Manny and the Bills, and I see that none of them are laughing. In fact, my buddies look like a police line-up standing over there. What a goofy picture that would make.

I take the box in my hands. It's bright blue and has a red ribbon around it tied in a bow. I hesitate for a second, glancing up at all the guards. They are intent my every move, and just waiting for a wrong one. Finally, I take the end of the bow and pull it.

The ribbon falls to the floor, and I hesitate again before taking the top off the box. It's kind of like a box a ring would come in, but Gigi wouldn't buy me a ring. It has to be something else. A diamond maybe? No kidding! She could afford to buy the Hope Diamond if she wanted, but that seems kind of schmaltzy for Gigi. She's not that kind of girl. So … okay … here goes. One last look over at the boys. Frank just has to say something. Great …

"Open that thing, DH. Good grief, get on with it!"

All of the guards instantly focus their steely eyes on Frank. They don't pull their guns, but they look like they want to. Frank smiles sheepishly and puts up his hands in a "sorry, guys" gesture.

I carefully open the box.

My eyes fill with tears of joy and disbelief. Gigi has cut a lock of her hair, tied it up in a piece of pink thread, and presented it to me for my birthday. This is the reason for all the armed guards.

"Every part of me," Gigi says softly, "every hair on my head should be as important to you as any diamond in the world. Every hair on your head will be that for me."

Oh boy.

"Thank you so much for this, Gigi. I will treasure it forever. This is the best birthday present I've ever had." I look over at my art friends, and there's not a dry eye among them. Even one of the guards is tearing up.

Leave it to Manny. As the guards take the briefcase and start to walk away, leaving me with the lock of Gigi's hair, he has to be the one that yells out, "You guys are actors! Ha!" In a split second every one of the guards has pulled out a gun and aimed right at him.

"Hey, Manny," Gigi says calmly. "Don't move. Please don't move. They aren't actors. They work for me. The guns are real, and the grimaces on their faces are real, and they'll pump your scrawny hide full of lead in a heartbeat, if I snap my fingers."

"Well then, please don't do that," Manny pleads softly, slowly backing away.

"I won't Manny. You're too much fun to have around." She grins and we all laugh. Manny looks like a little lost sheep, and Frank mutters, "This is one crazy birthday party."

"Okay men," Gigi says, looking at the guards, "hit the trail." And they do.

"Where'd you get those guys?" I ask her.

"I looked long and hard for them, DH. They're all ex-GIs that fought with my father. Three of them used to work for the Police Department, but I made them an offer that was better than what they had."

"Gigi, this really is the best birthday I ever had, even better than when I was eight years old living in Tulsa."

"What happened when you were eight in Tulsa? That sounds like a country western song."

"I'd been sick with something or other, and my family lived in this little housing tract on the outskirts of Tulsa. I vividly remember my mother, and my brother, making some excuse to take me out into the garage. When we got there, they surprised me with a birthday party. You'll never guess what my main present was.

A box of bubble gum with baseball cards in it. I mean a whole box! That was really something to me. We didn't have any money at all back then. Dirt poor. A whole box of bubble gum was really something. I was so sick that I almost passed out after I opened the present and saw what was inside."

"Poor baby," she croons sympathetically.

"The cards were all big name players like Mickey Mantle and Yogi Berra I don't know where the cards are now. I think they got lost in one of our moves."

"Too bad. They may be worth some bucks in a few years," she says.

"So now what?" I ask her, lightening the mood. "Where does the party go from here?"

"I have a plan," she answers with a devilish grin.

"You always do Gigi."

"As we speak, my staff is setting up a big table in the middle of the living room. You and I, and the boys, are gonna go in there and sit down at that table,"—she aims her glittering gaze at Frank—"and we're gonna roast the pants off Mr. Frank over there!"

"You're kidding!"

"Nope! We're gonna hammer him."

"But what's the deal with that, Gigi? I thought you didn't like him."

"Of course I like him! I like anyone you like!"

"But all this wrangling back and forth between you and Frank—it's like the Civil War."

"It's all a game. Frank is playing a game, and so am I. We both know it."

"Does Frank know about the roast?"

"Nope. This is another present for you. I thought about roasting you, but roasting Frank would be much more fun for you.

"So what do we do?" I ask.

"The first thing you do," she says sweetly, "is pull out that lock of my hair, and smell it and kiss it."

"If I'd have known you were giving me this tonight I—"

"You would have bought me the moon, right?" She laughs. "Calm down DH. I have everything I ever want from you. You don't ever have to give me a birthday present—just yourself. Now, are you ready for the Forum?"

"What Forum?" I ask.

"That's what I'm calling Frank's roast, because I know it's going to evolve into something more than that. I'm hoping for some art talk. Don't ever tell him I said this, but he really knows his stuff."

"Ha! You finally figured that out, huh?"

She laughs. "It didn't take long. But don't tell him cause I want to razz him a while. Besides, he loves it."

"Should I be jealous of you two?" I ask, feigning suspicion.

"Never. I respect Frank for who he is, and the potential he has, and maybe who he might become, but if he and I ever got together we'd probably kill each other."

"That's it? No other reason?" Something in my voice or eyes must be showing concern.

"Oh yeah Babe, and the biggest reason of all—YOU are every-thing to me, and no other man on this planet can ever come up to that. Never. I would marry you."

I'm stunned into silence by her last words. "Let's do the forum, my Love!" As she takes my hand to lead me into the living room, I think I hear her say, "The wedding will have to wait."

A Little While Later

I find my name printed on a white card at an empty place at the big round table in the living room. The others are already seated in their assigned places, as indicated by their names on place cards. Each place is also set with an empty wine glass. There is an atmosphere of curious expectation. Bill Hunter is sitting placidly, absorbing the experience. He is one smooth, cool man—an observer who misses nothing.

Jack is being Jack. He's flirting with one of the maids as she passes out little yellow writing pads and pencils to all of us. She's cute, and Jack likes cute. I have a feeling that he might go home with her after this night is over. He'd better be careful, that maid is on Gigi's payroll.

Bill Mitchkelly is the most reserved of the group. I can't really tell how he's reacting to all this. He's being very quiet. I know he didn't like the armed guard thing earlier, but now that we're seated at the table, he seems to be lightening up a bit.

Manny, seated between Bill Hunter and Frank, looks uncomfortable, as if he feels he doesn't belong here. He is shy and unsure of himself, and I kind of feel sorry for him. Manny isn't an artist, he's a musician, which shouldn't make much difference, as far as egos go, but he really is out of his league here with these guys.

"Gentlemen!" Gigi smiles at us all as she tinkles a little silver spoon on the edge of her wine glass. "I've called you all together for one of the most important moments in the history of the universe." She throws a smile at me. "Tonight, besides celebrating the birthday of my precious DH, we are going to do something that has never been done before." She pauses to consider what she just said. "Then again, it may not be important at all," she adds.

I look around at the faces at the table. All eyes are riveted expectantly on Gigi. They seem to have no idea that we're about to roast Frank. This is going to be an interesting experience.

She continues, each of us hanging on her every word, "Tonight, we are going to pay tribute to one of the greatest living artists in the world. This man may or may not make it big in the art world, but he's one of the most talented painters I have ever known. Even though I've never seen his paintings, I know his crazy personality, and that tells me everything." Laughter from the crowd here. "This guy is a jerk from the word go,"—more laughter—"but he has potential, and I really do feel that in my heart." Gigi turns to Frank and gives him a little half bow. "Frank Reed, prepare to meet your fate. We roast you tonight in the cauldron of Fun and Good Will, and if these other guys can't think of anything to tease you with, I'll fill in the blanks." She grins at Frank. More laughter

"Criminy!" Frank grins. He's visibly surprised and, yes, moved. "I thought you were talking about DH."

"He comes later, but this is for you, Mr. Frank Reed."

The Laugh. "So, what brought this on?" Frank asks.

"You can thank DH." She flashes a big grin." He thinks you're some pretty hot stuff, and I think he might be right. So just go with it."

"Don't they usually have wine and food at roasts?" Frank smiles, looking to the rest of us for agreement.

To answer him, she rings another little bell, and here come the waiter type guys, with wine and hors d'oeuvres. They set an assortment of delicacies in the middle of the table, fill all our wine glasses, then walk away.

"Help yourselves. If this ain't enough, we send out for pizza!" We laugh as we begin to sample the offering. "But remember, we aren't here to eat," she continues. "We're here to roast this guy on my left here—this Frank Reed dude that ain't like any other dude I've ever known."

Frank gives Gigi a wary grin and asks, "Why are you doing this, you little white whatever-the-heck you are?"

"You can get away with that tonight Mr. Frank, but don't forget I can call those guards back in here." She grins back at him.

Frank shivers with mock fear. "I'm shaking in my boots!" *The Laugh*.

"You're a mess, Reed," Gigi says, "and that's why I'm taking the first poke at you. I haven't known you very long, but I've known you long enough to know you're a pompous jerk." I glance at Bill Hunter and notice him trying to hide a smile. "But pomposity is what makes the art world work."

I can't believe these words are coming from Gigi. She sounds like a college professor.

"You, Mr. Frank Reed," she continues, "have a level of pomposity I've never seen before, but you are indeed the stuff that makes art — real art — work! I really mean that, Frank." She looks at him with earnest sincerity.

"I respect that, Gigi. You're a real bag of surprises."

"Sorry about the white stuff, kid. Uh oh, I said, 'kid.' Now the claws come out huh?"

"No claws tonight," she says with a smile.

"But what about that white skin? What's the deal?" Frank is genuinely interested.

"Maybe I really am from another planet, Mr. Reed. Maybe my people are really, really white." That's all she'll give him before turning to Manny. "But Manny," she says, "you're going to be the first one to tell us about Frank."

"I don't know." Manny looks startled. "I haven't known him very long. Been to his house a couple of times, I guess. He paints good." He's really uncomfortable being put on the spot like this.

"That ain't much of a roast." Frank gives me a look that says "What's with this kid?"

Jack covers the awkward moment. "I'll roast this jerk," he says, grinning eagerly.

From Frank: *The Laugh*, followed by, "I bet you will!"

"Here it is, Big Frank. You and I have hung around with each other for about a year now, and the one thing I can come up with that's true roast material, is that when you were over at my house the other night, you didn't paint anything on the wall like the rest of us did. Lisa was ticked at everybody but you."

"That's a roast?" Frank asks.

"I can't say anything bad about you, Frank. You're just who you are, and you are always doing what has to be done to make the way for things to go right in your own life."

"What the heck did you just say?" Frank asks and give me another puzzled look.

"You figure it out," Jack replies. "It was a compliment."

"Jack, I'm gonna be honest with you," Frank responds. "You're right, we haven't known each other for very long, but I've noticed your talent. You need to forget pottery and painting and zero in on sculpture. I've never said this before, but Jack … you're right up there as a sculptor with Manzù."

Jack's ice blue eyes are fixed on Frank in stunned silence. Frank's words have touched him deeply. This is supposed to be a roast of Frank, but it's becoming some sort of sharing time. I can see why Gigi called it a Forum. I'm learning that all of these guys think very highly of Frank, his work, and of each other.

Bill Mitchkelly takes his turn. "Frank," he begins, "first of all, this whole Reed roast thing is kind of strange. This is DH's birthday party and not yours—he's the one that we ought to be roasting. Also, I know we've had our differences in the past. You know I think you're a pompous man, we fight all the time about it—it's more a clash of personality than anything—but I do have to admit that you are one fine artist. Your work is far beyond what is being produced in the world of art today. Everything out there is either pure trash, or something that's been done before."

"Why Bill, you sound like me!" Frank is delighted. "Ha! DH, isn't that what you and I talk about all the time?"

"Yes it is, Frank, and I believe Bill is right on. But what I don't understand, is these Performance Art, these 'Happenings' you do.

What's the deal with that?"

"Money!" *The Laugh* "Art is just a business, no different from any other, and the purpose of a business is to make money. Unfortunately the galleries make most of the money, and that's why performance art is so important. If you hang a painting on the wall, the galleries get their 33% when it sells. If it sells. But if you come in and do some sort of performance piece, like sitting buck-naked in a tub of Jello while darning socks—" everybody, even Gigi, laughs at this one—"If you do that, then … Hey, Gigi,"—Frank looks at her and winks—"you might be able to pull that off!" *The Laugh*.

"Watch it, Reed. I'm just beginning to like you, but that can change in a heartbeat."

Frank continues, "If you do a performance art piece in a gallery, it's a one shot deal, and the gallery makes most of the money, because they don't have to hang expensive paintings on the wall and wait for them to sell, which might be never! Lots of times the artists do the performance for free, just to get their name out there. It's as simple as that. Like everything else in life, it's all about the money. With performance art, galleries don't have to insure the paintings and they don't have to pay you the big bucks. It's kind of like in the REAL world," Frank smiles. "If you get a full-time job with an employer, you get all the benefits. But if you're a miserable part-timer, you get zippo, my friend. Performance art is part-timer art. But"—he gets excited and waves his arms in the air—"it opens doors for an artist who needs to have doors opened. It draws attention to the artist and gets people to look at the REAL art he makes. So it's both a bad thing and a good thing."

"Are you going to do any Performance Art, Frank?" asks Bill Hunter.

"I am, but I'm not going to say much about it here. I'm going to try to do something different, something that hasn't been done before. But I ain't kidding myself, I know this stuff isn't real art. It's just show biz, trying to draw attention to a bunch of people who think they're artists, but they really aren't. That's why I'm trying to change the scene a little. There's a tiny bit of validity in Performance Art, but not the way it's being done today. And, quite frankly, now that the first few performances have been done, everything that comes after them is going to be copycat stuff. That's the built in flaw with Performance Art. It's a shock thing. Once somebody invents the shock, everybody that comes after him is just riding on his deal. Hopefully, this is a flash in the pan. If it's still around in a few years, that will mean the art world has become bankrupt of talent and originality. It will also mean that true art has morphed into mere entertainment art. Artists will have become really boring, and really bad, entertainers, and the Art Spirit will be no more."

"I kind of liked the idea of Gigi in the jello," Jack says.

"Manny?" Frank mimes looking for Manny. "There you are! You're a quiet little numb-nut!" He smiles. "What do you think about all this chit chat my friend?"

"I'm not sure. I'm a musician. Some of this doesn't make sense to me."

"That's another thing, Manny. I keep hearing you're a musician, but I've never heard what kind of musician you are. What the heck do you play?" Frank asks. "I've had you over to my house a few times, and I don't know anything about you. You might be an ax murderer for all I know!" *The Laugh.* "You're the quiet type, the guy that lives next door and buries bodies in the basement." *The Laugh* again.

"That's funny Frank. Can I call you that?" Manny looks so… so pathetically simple, still not able to look Frank in the eye. I feel sorry for him.

"You can call me that. I was just kidding you." Frank smiles like he's sorry he hurt Manny.

"I play several instruments, and I write music," Manny says. "I play the drums for a small jazz band here in town. We also go down to the beach and play at some clubs. I play a clarinet … and piano."

In response to that information, Frank bellows, "Gigi, Sweet Goddess of the White Skin, you don't happen to have a piano in this blimp hanger do you?" He winks at her.

"Nobody winks at me but DH, Frank, or those guards will come in here and put you out on the street." Gigi glares at him, and I hope it's all play-acting. "But I do have a Steinway in the music room. I can have it brought in here."

"You have a music room?" Why am I not surprised? "I haven't seen that yet."

"I do, Love. I just forgot to show it to you. I have several rooms I haven't shown you yet. Those are the ones that mean the most to me." Whispering in my ear, she adds "I'll tell you about them later. You have keys to them all, but I want to show them to you first." She kisses me on the cheek.

Gigi rings her little bell again. In seconds, all of the guards are in the room, hands reaching under their jackets, ready for action. "Relax boys," she laughs. "I don't need your guns, I need your muscle to bring the piano in here." They relax, letting their now empty hands drop, but we were all impressed by their quick action. Frank laughs and says, "Don't these guys ever sleep?"

"They sleep in shifts," she replies.

"So you have goons around you 24 hours a day?" Frank asks.

"I do. They follow me everywhere I go in two cars, one in front and one in back."

"Who the heck are you, little White One?" Frank asks, more intrigued than ever. "This just ain't normal."

"I'm from another planet, Frank, remember?"

"I just want to know why she's so white," Bill Hunter says quietly. "She told me she's a vampire, but I don't believe her."

"So that's it, little girl," Frank grins. "You're a story teller!"

I butt in. "Frank, everything Gigi has told all of us is the absolute truth. She's shown me things that are almost impossible for me to believe. But I will guarantee to you that everything out of her mouth is true, except maybe the alien thing, and I'm not so sure about that yet." I wink at her.

"Frank," Gigi says solemnly, "there are some things about my life that I keep very private. I've shown DH almost everything, and he now knows who I am. But some of it I just can't reveal to the rest of you at this time. You have to respect that."

"Sorry Gigi." Frank is apologetic. "I joke around quite a bit, but I also use my head, and lots of things don't make the grade here. But if you need to keep those personal thoughts private, I respect you for that. Everyone in this room has secrets they want to keep." Frank smiles at Gigi and salutes her. It's a good gesture; Gigi seems pleased.

"You want the piano in here, or what?" Gigi asks.

Bill Hunter smiles and says gently, as is his manner, "I would love to hear what this young man, Manny, has to play for us."

"Guys!" Gigi orders her men to bring in the piano.

Every room in Gigi's house is built so that large objects — like pianos — can be moved around at will. Every door is large with ornate, sliding doors. I can't help but think about my little plywood door back at The Hole, the one my grandfather made with his own hands. I feel so small here. But I also feel like I'm the king of the world because of the way Gigi feels about me, and the way she treats me.

And here it comes. The big brutes are wheeling an enormous grand piano into the living room. I wish I had a camera.

"Right there guys," Gigi points. "That's all for now." She smiles and the guys leave.

Frank grins at Manny, who is standing in the corner looking like a lost sheep, "Manny-Poo, I guess you're on."

I'm not expecting much. If Manny's piano playing is anything like his personality, we're in for a long night. I'm a bit concerned how Manny will take it if he blows it.

"Go ahead, Manny," I say, "take your seat. What are you going to play for us?"

Looking down at his feet he replies, "First I'll play some Chopin, then something from Beethoven, then a Brahms piece and then I'll play a concerto that I wrote last night."

Beethoven? Brahms? Chopin? I look around at the faces of the other people here. Frank's expression is a combination of amazement and disbelief — eyes wide and brow creased.

"Chopin?" Frank asks, clearing his throat. "I thought you were a garage band drummer!"

"I've been playing the piano for the last 12 years," Manny says, still looking at his feet.

Then he walks over to the piano and sits down. As he does, a subtle change comes over him. His fingers make contact with the keys and all of his insecurity and self doubt seem to melt away as he becomes one with the instrument. I look around at the others again. Bill Hunter has that beatific look on his face; I know he's expecting good things. Bill Mitchkelly is absentmindedly holding a piece of chalk to his mouth as if it were a cigarette — he quit smoking a while back, but old habits are hard to break. His expression is one of curious anticipation. Jack is holding the hand of the maid. He doesn't usually seem to care much about what's going on around him, but now his attention is sharply focused on Manny.

And Frank — God love him — Frank is all hunched over, staring intensely at Manny as he sits at the piano. Frank's right hand is holding his chin up. He is really taking this performance seriously.

Manny begins to play. Good heavens, Manny begins to play!

One Hour Later

I'm speechless — or wordless as the case may be. I'll try to convey our reactions as we listened to Manny's magnificent performance.

This was a Manny that none of us knew. The quiet, usually shy little fellow enthralled us with his recital consisting of a diverse selection of music. I've never heard such perfection before. His hands moved up and down the keyboard with graceful and mesmerizing dexterity. I'm probably not the best judge of classical music, but as far as I can tell, he never missed a note. It was absolutely beautiful.

His first piece was by Chopin. He announced the title to us, but I can't remember what it was. As he hit the first few notes, Bill

Hunter said, "I knew this lad was something more than he appears to be." Bill Mitchkelly's jaw dropped. All he could do was shake his head and smile. Even Jack! I heard him whisper, "You gotta be kidding!" Frank watched and listened without moving, leaning forward with his chin resting on his hand. He just stared at Manny as he went through his music. Then at the end of Manny's rendition of Beethoven's Ninth, Frank quietly stood up, and began to applaud, declaring, "This Manny of ours is a friggin' genius!" At that, everyone in the room began to applaud.

But it wasn't until Manny performed his own music that everyone really appreciated his talent. He called it, "Concerto For A Mad Artist in D Minor." It was exquisite — haunting. Just before he touched the key on the first note, he turned to Frank and said, "I wrote this for you." Then he immersed himself in his music. Frank melted as Manny played. I saw him wiping his eyes several times. At one point he had to leave the room, but he didn't go very far. It was just a macho thing. He didn't want anyone to see him cry.

When Manny finished playing, everyone stood and clapped loudly. Frank came back into the room and over to Manny. He tried to speak, but the words came out in a stutter, "I'll never call you, 'that Manny-kid again.'" Frank hugged him, and everyone applauded again.

"Manny,"—Gigi had to almost yell to be heard over the applause and exclamations of surprise and appreciation—"I'll still call you what I want! But you've earned my respect. You are one incredible talent."

"Me too, Manny," I said. "I never knew …"

Gigi whispers in my ear, "This is special. Where does Manny live 'cause I'm going to have the goons deliver this piano to him."

"Gigi," I whisper, "this is a really expensive piano!"

"It belonged to someone very special."

"Beethoven?" I ask.

"My grandfather."

"Oh …" The tears welled up in my eyes.

"DH," she said, "I don't even play a piano, and this little Manny guy is really something."

Wiping the tears from my eyes, I turn to Manny and ask him, "Hey Manny, what's your address?"

"My address?"

"Yeah, Gigi's sending out thank you cards."

Manny tells me his address, then Gigi rings that bell of hers. The goons come in, she gives them instructions, and out goes the piano. I know when Manny gets home tonight he's going to find that thing sitting in the middle of his living room. Lucky for him he still lives in his mother's house, it's a lot bigger than The Hole. A big piano like that should fit okay.

"Gigi, I can't believe you're doing this. This was your grandfather's piano. This is the second sweetest thing I've ever seen you do."

"The second?"

"The first was that lock of hair."

"You'd better keep that forever,"

"I will." She kisses me.

Frank's voice rises above all the others. "Who'd a thunk all that could come out of Manny! He's a friggin' artist!"

What is it that makes an artist a great artist? What is it that brings immortality? Is it integrity? Painting your guts out till you come up with your own unique style, and then remaining faithful to that style, regardless of how un-art-worldly-correct it is? I wonder about Frank. Has he even discovered his own true original style yet? I've seen several of his paintings and his sculptures, but he keeps telling me he wants to innovate art — that can't be bad. I'm not sure how he's going to do it, but if anyone can, he can. I do believe that most of his talent lies in his personality. He's a pompous arrogant jerk to most people, but I see it more as confidence. I believe his work proves me right. His reaction to Manny and the piano shows a side of Frank I've rarely seen, and it makes me love him even more.

Wiping his eyes, Frank asks Manny, "Where in the world did you get that talent?"

"My mother plays the piano and she taught me." Manny has retreated into himself again and is once more talking to the floor.

"Hey, Manny," Frank says, "look me in the face!" Manny looks up. "I don't know what you think of me, but I think you're one heck of an artist with that piano thing. You gotta quit looking down at the floor, man. You're a friggin' genius!" Frank hugs him. I can tell Manny is uncomfortable, but he's smiling, and everyone in the room is smiling too.

I realize that is one of the things that makes a great artist. Frank is more than meets the eye. His arrogance is a cover for his compassion for the little ones like Manny. I'm not sure how Frank behaves at home with his wife and kids, he may be a holy terror, but with scenes like this … I've seen him cry a few times, and that speaks volumes to me.

"Let's do a painting!" Jack calls out impulsively. "Gigi, you got any paint and brushes and stuff?"

"Since I met DH, I bought a bunch of stuff, just in case he wanted to come over and paint." She grins.

"You did?" Once again, I am amazed.

"I did." She gives me a big smile "It's all in one of those rooms you haven't been in yet."

"So bring out the paint and we'll all do a group painting!"

"You got a deal Mr. Jack," Gigi agrees. "I'll take DH with me, and we'll bring the stuff out in a flash!" Gigi is being very nice tonight. No sailor talk and smiles all around.

Gigi grabs my hand, and leads me out into a very long hallway, past her bedroom, and into some area of the house where I've never been before—"… to boldly go where no man has gone before," comes immediately to my mind.

Her house is like a labyrinth, but finally, at the end of one hall on the right hand side, we come to a door. This girl would have been great as a host for The Price Is Right! It's all about doors with her. This door is very special, it's all frosted glass, and it's so bright on the other side; I can't wait to see what's inside the room.

"You have a key, Love. It's the one with the painter's palette inscribed in gold on the metal."

"What?" I fish around in my pocket for my keys. Sure enough, there is a perfect golden etching of a painter's palette on one of the keys. I put it in the keyhole, the door opens, and we go inside.

If this doesn't beat all! It's a complete art studio with skylights and glass windows, and a sliding glass door that looks out over Gigi's back lawn, pool area, and her property beyond—I can't imagine what lies out there in the beyond part.

"Gigi, Did this studio belong to your grandfather?"

"No, he had studios in New York and LA. This used to be my own bedroom as I was growing up. Until I graduated from high school, this is where I spent my time. I slept on a bed that was over there in that corner." She points.

"So …" I'm confused, which is my natural state when I'm with Gigi.

"I had some people come in and turn this into a studio for you."

"You're kidding!" I almost wet my pants.

"I'm not kidding. You have the keys, you can come over and paint any time day or night."

I'm beside myself. "Look at that easel! And the sky lights! The pool view out the door! Who couldn't paint in this place!"

"Open that door." Gigi points me to what looks like a closet. I walk over and open the door. It's really dark inside, so I search around for a light switch. I find one and turn it on.

"I don't believe this! It looks like a friggin' art store!"

There are seven or eight aisles of art supplies—paints and canvas, pencils of every kind, chalks and everything.

"Pick out what we need to do the painting with the boys," she prompts.

"You got any butcher paper in this place?"

"Fourth aisle, second shelf. You'll find a ton of it. I knew you'd want it." She smiles and that puffy nose of hers quivers just a bit.

I find the butcher paper just where she says, and I lay a roll of it by the door.

"Pull out everything we'll need, and set it by the door. I'll have the guys take it back to the living room," Gigi says.

Since we're going to do this on butcher paper, I grab some colored pencils, crayons, and watercolors.

"It would be nice to do an oil painting," I say. "But that would be pretty messy, and most of these guys have never done oil before. I don't think Bill Hunter has ever done a painting of any kind before."

"If you want to do oils you can, my Love. We can paint on the back patio; I've got lights out there that look like daylight" she says.

"But oil paints are forever, Pixie. If you spill them they stain real bad."

"That's why I have people to clean up after me." She smiles.

A Bit Later

Gigi's goons brought all of the art supplies out onto the back patio, and my art buddies are now standing around, wondering what to do next. Manny and Bill Hunter look a little befuddled, but Bill Mitchkelly and Jack seem to be quite serious about coming up with a subject. Frank is sitting in a lawn chair under some really nice colored lights, and he appears to already have an idea. I can see his mind work.

"Hey guys," Frank says softly, "this is Gigi's house and her deal, so let's let her come up with the idea for the art work. Gigi, that's one heck of a roll of butcher paper."

"I bought it at the local market. I just went in and asked them if they had some butcher paper, and this is what the guy came out with," she explains.

"And whatever Gigi wants, Gigi gets," Jack adds.

"I asked him where he bought it, and he told me. I had someone make a call, and bought fifty rolls of the stuff."

"Goodness Child," Bill Hunter shook his head, "you have so much money. You really need to watch how you spend it. Do you have someone helping you?"

"You mean financial help?" Gigi pinches Bill softly on the cheek.

"Yes I do," Bill replies.

"I have more attorneys than your college has teachers Mr. Hunter." She kisses him on the forehead. "But thanks for asking. You have to be the sweetest man I've ever known."

Bill blushes and backs away. Jack unrolls the butcher paper. Bill Mitchkelly looks like he's planning a major excursion. He scratches his head, bunches up his brows, then bends over and places his hands on his knees, studying the blank butcher paper. Gigi has rolled out over 50 feet.

"What's it gonna be, your Royal Whiteness?" Frank asks.

"We already did a farm scene," she says. "And DH and I did a sci-fi theme, so that's sacred. Hmmm …"

"How about music?" Manny offers.

"Great idea!" Gigi exclaims. "We can draw musicians and pianos and whatever, throughout all time!"

"You mean portraits of composers?" Jack asks.

"Composers and musicians," Gigi says.

"Do we know what they looked like?" Bill Mitchkelly asks.

"Good point," I say. "Maybe we ought to have a theme without people. Gigi, I know we did the sci-fi thing before, but I'll just bet this group could come up with some really crazy stuff if we do that again."

"I suppose." She kisses me on the forehead. "Sci-fi it is. Something really futuristic." She emphasizes her point by striking her Peter Pan pose.

"Alien women!" Jack says with a Groucho Marx lift of his eyebrows.

"How about those of us who are a bit artistically challenged," Bill Hunter asks. "Can we maybe just write some poetry or dialogue of some sort on the paper?"

"Good idea, Hunter!" Frank says. "This will be a space-themed dialogue of drawings and words. DH, this is Performance Art!" Frank is in his element. "Do you have a movie camera, Bud? We can make some money off this!"

"No, I wish I did. Not for the money, but for how silly we're all gonna look while we do it."

Gigi comes over and whispers in my ear, "I have movie cameras, Love. I own a production studio."

"What?" I whisper back at her. "You do?"

"It was a big part of my inheritance, and another reason I have all this money."

"You are a bag of surprises, Pixie. But if we bring that stuff out, all these guys will know about your secrets. I say no. We just draw."

"I was hoping you'd say that," she said, smiling.

"Were you testing me?" I'm a bit hurt.

"No, I really meant it. If you want me to, I can make a call, and we can either drive into LA and do this in my studio, or I can have a truckload of stuff delivered here in about an hour, with the technicians to run it. I was just hoping you would say exactly what you said, and you did. Exactly. You are perfect my Love. Perfect. Perfect. Perfect." She kisses me on my cheek like a madwoman.

As a personal honor to a man I hold in the highest regard, I ask Bill Hunter to put the first bit of work on the paper, and he does. He writes what we had all mentioned previously, "To go where no man has gone before" in the lower left corner. Jack moves in and begins to draw some comets in white, and yellow, against a black-blue sky. He makes them very large, so it's kind of impressive, taking up three or four feet of the paper. Bill Hunter follows Jack, writing, "Tomorrow and tomorrow and tomorrow creeps into this petty pace from day to day to the last syllable of recorded time…" in a curved arch in front of Jack's drawing. I like that.

Bill Mitchkelly doesn't seem to know what to do. He's done some painting and lithography in his career, but his main thing is clay. He looks a little befuddled, but he walks over to the paper and bends down, studying it deeply, his bushy black and grey eyebrows bunching up with the effort. He picks up a watercolor brush, and dips it into the water bowl that Gigi provided. Putting just a little bit of blue watercolor paint on it, he writes very lightly, "Where no man has gone before." Then he paints the background black. I look at Gigi She's smiling and shaking her head.

"I guess we got a theme," she says, looking back at me.

"Hey, Manny," I shout, "put something on the paper!

"Like what, DH?"

"Anything! This ain't the Louvre! We're just having fun."

"I can't draw," he says timidly.

"You don't have to know how to draw. Do stick figures if you want."

So Manny takes a black crayon and draws two stick figures. One a man and one a woman; you can tell by the body parts which is which.

Gigi laughs and says, "Give me that crayon! No! I want a blue one!"

She takes a blue crayon, and on top of Manny's drawings she draws two more stick type figures, only with a greater detail to them in the … umm … important parts. Even Frank laughs.

Frank then uses a white crayon to draw several five pointed stars on about four feet of the paper, then he draws a couple of white streaks that appear to be comets or something, and adds some yellow outline. I can barely make it out on the white butcher paper. Then he takes up a brush and paints a black, watercolor outline, around the stars, and the comets. Leaving a space around the borders to write, once again, "Where no man has gone before."

Gigi laughs, and shakes her head again. Frank's drawing is lovely, and it is fun to watch him work, especially those elegant hands of his.

Bill Mitchkelly comments, "Frank, that isn't bad. You think you'll ever amount to anything?"

Frank laughs. "You know, Mitchkelly, every time I walk into the ceramics studio you ask me that same question. I'm gonna try to amount to something more than you have!" *The Laugh*.

Bill takes the comment with good nature, cause he's heard Frank's stuff before, but he also picks up a red crayon, and begins to draw on the butcher paper. Just at the point where Frank left off, he draws a bizarre sculptural alien figure seated on a chair. "If we're doing sci-fi we need some aliens," he says. It really is a nice figure.

Jack says, "You want an alien? I'll give you an alien." He draws an even more sophisticated creature that looks like it might have come out of *Star Trek*, then he throws his crayon down and says, "How come there ain't any women here?"

"You want me to scour the streets for some prostitutes, Jack?" Gigi asks sarcastically.

"No, but it would be nice to have some other women here other than you, Gigi. I like you a lot, but you belong to DH," he says as he lights a Delicado.

As if by magic, just as Jack utters those words, the big patio door opens. Gigi's sister, Heidi, and a couple of her girlfriends are here. Gigi's dog, Venus, goes crazy at the arrival of the women, nipping at their heels as they walk toward us.

"Venus!" Gigi yells. "Stop it! Venus!"

Heidi and her friends just laugh, looking a bit surprised at what's going on with all these weird guys hanging around, not to mention the long piece of butcher paper on the ground.

The girls Heidi has brought with her must be models. They are tall—about six feet—and their outfits look like they came from the pages of Vogue magazine. One of them has long bright red hair flowing down her back, the other has short black hair. Both of them are stunning.

Heidi glances at me, winks, and licks her lips. Gigi moves closer to me and takes my arm possessively. She and Venus are both on guard.

"Here to spoil the party?" Gigi asks Heidi.

"Wouldn't think of it," Heidi replies. "Just came in to get a few things, then me and the girls are going to a go-go bar. What are you doing with this paper thing on the ground?" She makes a face like she just smelled something bad.

"We're making a group drawing."

"More of that art nonsense, huh? You ever show these guys your paintings?"

Gigi is suddenly shy and uncomfortable.

"Gigi?" I ask. "You have some paintings?"

"She has about 300 paintings in that studio of hers," Heidi says disdainfully.

"300! What studio?"

"It's another room I was going to show you tonight, DH." Gigi gives me a sheepish look, but shoots daggers at Heidi.

"You told me you love art history, and I know you can draw, but you didn't tell me you have a studio and 300 hundred paintings!"

"Maybe more than that, Love." She gives Heidi another icy glance. "Thanks a lot, Heidi."

"Wow!" Frank says. "This ain't gonna be another one of those Gigi-DH moments where you guys go off and explore another room together, is it? I want to see those paintings too, Gigi. Don't leave me out!"

Gigi looks at Heidi again. Heidi has a self-satisfied smirk on her face. I'm close enough to hear Gigi say, "Mind your Ps and Qs, little sister, 'cause I'll throw you out on your butt, if you're not careful."

"You'd never do that. I'm your sweet sister." She smiles a smile that isn't really real, and Gigi says, "Try me."

Gigi announces to the group, "It's field trip time. Follow me." She turns to Heidi and her friends and says, "Everybody but you."

She rings her bell and two goons come from out of nowhere. She tells them something, and they cross to Heidi and her friends where they stand like statues, blocking them from following us, as

Gigi leads me and the group back into the house and down the hall in the direction of the studio she made for me. As we go, I glance at Heidi. She winks at me, squeezes her right breast, and smiles.

Gigi leads us down the hall and past my studio. We make a right turn down another hall, and there's another door.

"DH, can I borrow your key?"

I'm not sure if she has her key with her, or maybe she's making some sort of point in front of the guys, but I hand her my key ring. She puts a key in the lock and turns it. I'm guessing this is going to be more Disneyland stuff. When she turns on the light, I find out I'm right.

I didn't know she painted, but this is proof positive that she's serious about it. It's almost a carbon copy of the studio she made for me, except it's about 20 feet longer. She has used those 20 feet to stack, in perfect order with little dividers between them, dozens of what I presume are her paintings.

I turn around and look at the rest of the guys. They are as amazed as I am. Even Frank. He has his hand to his chin, and I can tell he is thinking about what he would do with a studio like this.

"Here it is, boys," Gigi exclaims.

"Gigi," Frank says, "this is lovely. And so clean — there isn't a spot of dust anywhere in here!" Frank's own style of art demands neatness and precision. His studio is in his house, but it's like an oasis of order surrounded by the chaos of his lively family.

Finally he blurts out, "Show us your Ort, White One!"

Gigi walks over to the rows of paintings at the end of the room.

"This isn't all my stuff. I also have a warehouse at the back part of the property that has about 250 paintings. But this will give you an idea."

I hear Frank exhale an expression of amazement. The rest of us are speechless with wonder.

Gigi takes us on a magical mystery tour of her work, painting by painting — seascapes, small children, women in 19th century clothing, horses, landscapes. It's all beautiful; every painting done in an Impressionist style that would rival the masters.

Frank speaks first. "You ARE Berthe Morisot, or her reincarnation!"

"I'd have to see some photos of her stuff," Gigi says calmly.

He goes on, "Your work is exquisite. Look at this beach scene. Any one of the Impressionists could have painted this, only this is better!" He is flushed with the pleasure of discovering True Art.

"Thanks, Frank." She smiles shyly and moves closer to me.

"And these are all your paintings?" Bill Mitchkelly asks.

"No. I painted them, but they all belong to DH now." She gives me a loving look I've never seen before. I just shake my head.

Jack says, "DH, you'd better marry this girl, 'cause if you don't I will."

I don't know what to do or what to say. I was becoming a bit uneasy.

Bill Hunter comes to my defense. "Don't pressure him, Jack. DH has to make his own decision about who he wants to marry. I'm sure that we all want him to make the right decision."

"The right decision is to do what you gotta do to be happy, but this kind of money can't hurt," Jack says.

"Hello!" Gigi is waving her hands in the air. "Are you guys forgetting that I'm standing right here?"

"White Honey," Frank says, "they're right. These are DH's best friends, and they're just trying to convince him to take you for his loving wife."

"DH and I already have an agreement on that," she says looking at me serenely. "And if you want this evening to continue, you'll stop this train of thought right now."

There was something about her voice that worked with Frank and the rest of the group. All talk of marriage stopped, and we just milled around for about an hour, looking at Gigi's paintings and going, "Wow!" and "Incredible!" because they really were.

Frank especially was intrigued. "These are beautiful Gigi," he told her. "I had no idea."

"Thanks, Frank."

"No, I mean it. These are exquisite paintings. Why in the world aren't you showing somewhere?"

"Because I don't have to."

I know what she means, but I'm not sure Frank does. She already has all the money and the connections in the world, and most of all, she has zero need for public acclaim to satisfy her ego.

"You've got to be kidding. You've got to be friggin' kidding! Talent like this"—he waves his arms to indicate the impressive body of work—"needs to be shared with the world!"

I think I agree with him on that. These are beautiful paintings, and I think the world would be a better place if they were out where people could see them.

"If you ain't Berthe Morisot, you gotta be related to her," Frank says with wonderment. "You could display in any gallery in the world and make millions."

"I already have millions, Frank. Why should I bother?" Gigi walks over to me, while continuing to speak to Frank. "I have all the money in the world. I paint for fun, and the only valuable thing in my life is this guy right here. If anybody has a problem with that they can leave the party."

End of discussion. Nobody leaves.

"Then let's go back to what we were doing. We have a very large sci-fi drawing to finish."

Our drawing lies as we left it on the imported marble pavement of the patio. Four of the big guards are patiently standing watch, holding the paper down with the toe of one foot each.

After a quick assessment of our work thus far, Gigi says, "Aha, Bill Hunter! The guy who looks like my father, only fatter and diabetic. You need to add something more to this thing."

"My Child," he replies, "I have no idea as to what I can contribute. I am merely an English teacher."

"Then contribute some friggin' English!" Gigi smiles and kisses him on the top of his bald head.

"I'll do my best," he says, blushing.

Bill Hunter picks up a green crayon, stoops down on one knee,

and says, "I can't draw, but I'll write a poem,"
    We all applaud.

> *The winter street is lonely*
> *Devoid of green leaves and shimmering heat*
> *Depressed barren cold*
> *In blues and greys*
> *Wet slick asphalt*
> *Walks hard and uneven beneath moving feet*
> *Headlights*
> *Auto headlights in the rain*
> *Reflect from*
> *Mirrored marionette faces*
> *Dripping*
> *Scurrying*
> *Hastening*
> *To where they must go and do not wish to be*
> *Gutter water pours*
> *Dead leaves flatten on the sidewalk*
> *Sounds have ceased*
> *With too many private thoughts to stop them*
> *A string of smoke escapes*
> *From the pipe of the artist*
> *The only warmth near the winter*
> *Street.*

I lean over his shoulder to read what he's written. "Come here guys, look at this." They all crowd around.

Manny says, "But it isn't winter." That makes Bill smile.

"Mirrored marionette faces ..." Gigi reads the words quietly out loud, questioning their meaning.

"Is that what I wrote?"

"You don't know what you wrote?" she asks.

"I just write whatever comes out of this tired old head of mine,

Sweet Child." Bill says.

Gigi turns to me with tears in her eyes. "I just love this man."

"Bill," she says, "I see your words coming true in the lives of all of us."

"You do, Gigi?" he asks, with concern.

"Don't you see it? Everyone here is a mirrored marionette face. Even me. None of us are what we appear to be. None of us are what we think we are. We're all just puppets looking at ourselves in the mirror of life."

Bill wraps Gigi in a fatherly embrace. "Sweetest Child," he tells her "if you were in my class I would give you an 'A', and if I did have a daughter, I would wish that she would be just like you."

Again, not a dry eye in the place. This has to be the most sentimental group on Earth! Maybe it's the wine, but maybe it's just because all these guys I hang with are artists. Artists are notorious for being sentimental.

Frank had to leave the room again. He puts up such a tough exterior, and then, at the drop of a hat, he falls apart like all the rest of us. It's like a constant storm fighting inside him, and he doesn't know how to handle it.

Back to the butcher paper.

Frank has returned, and he and Bill Hunter have their heads together in conversation. "Hunter," Frank is saying, "that's a darned good poem. It makes me think."

"What does it make you think about, son?" Bill is not asking just to be polite; he really wants to know.

"About life. I love the line about the 'dead leaves flatten on the sidewalk'."

"What do you like about that line?" Bill prompts.

"It's about life. It's about the artists who try to reach for the stars, but never make it. They get flattened on the sidewalk."

"Maybe that won't be you, Frank. You have such a talent, maybe you will soar to the skies."

"I'm gonna give it everything I got, Bill."

"I know you will, Frank, and it's a privilege to know you. I mean that."

"I like you too, Bill," Frank replies. "There aren't a lot of people on this earth with the kind of heart that you have. I hope you never change."

"My, my …" Bill says. "I'm not sure what you mean. I'm just doing what I do."

"Well, keep doing it Bill, 'cause you're making this crazy world a better place!"

Gigi elbows her way in. "I want to draw something," Everyone stands back—for a number of reasons.

"I love your poem Bill, so I'm going to add something to it."

Gigi starts to draw little flowers and things on every line of the poem Bill wrote.

She draws a street with sidewalks next to it, and makes it look like rain is falling. Then she draws two faces, like marionettes looking at each other, very strange, I guess the *mirrored marionette faces* line is what she's getting at. Then she jumps over and draws some leaves that look like they've been flattened, and she puts some little teardrop water things on them.

Her drawing reminds me of the drawings Cezanne did of his son. They are so delicate—so wonderful. What's this she's drawing now? Ha, it's me, smoking my pipe! I guess that's a part of the poem too. Thanks Bill!

Frank picks up a pink crayon. "Everybody move over! I don't want you all to get the wrong idea, but this ain't real Ort!" *The Laugh.* "This is for Gigi."

He begins to draw a single outline drawing of what I know must be Gigi, because he puts her in that simian pose. When he's finished he tears the drawing from the end of the butcher paper and hands it to me."

"Frank … this is beautiful. Thank you. It looks just like her," I stutter.

"I've been wanting to give you a painting or some drawings for a long time, and since this is close to your birthday, it's the best I can do for now. To be honest, Bud, I've been thinking about doing your portrait for a while." Then he grins wickedly, and adds, "You've got a personality I'd like to bring out."

"So will I be dripping all over with bright primary colors?"

"Maybe, maybe not. I never know what's gonna come out of this head of mine." *The Laugh.*

"I think it's a pretty smart head," Gigi chimes in.

"Thank you, Gigi, but I'll bet you could paint a portrait of DH, too."

"I already have," she says, giving me a penetrating look.

"What?" Yet another surprise.

"I've drawn and painted dozens of portraits of you, Love," she gives me a hug.

"Can I see them?"

"Of course. They all belong to you," she grins. "They're in that building I told you about at the back of the property. I'll take you out there if you'd like."

"We'd all like to see those portraits," Frank says.

"I might bring one of them back with me, but nobody goes into that building but DH."

She takes my hand and starts to lead me across the lawn, away from the party, and toward some vague place back in the distant dark. She turns back to the guys and says, "Bye-bye! Back soon. Keep working!" And off we go.

As we crossed the lawn, "the building," as Gigi calls it, loomed large on the dark horizon, and grew even larger as we neared it. It's becoming very dark outside, and all I can make out is something that looks like an overgrown Quonset hut. It appears to be painted pure white, and it's glowing from the outdoor lighting installed around it. You can't really see it much, until you get over the hill that divides the pool area from the back area that Gigi tells me is all done up in vegetable gardens. I couldn't see the gardens in the dark, but as we get closer to the storage building, I couldn't help but think of those Mormon Temples that get all lit up at night. That's the impression this building gave as we approached it. It is massive, done in a 1950s style similar to the house.

"It was built by a French architect," Gigi tells me. "I saw a picture in a book about Bauhaus buildings. I couldn't get a German architect, so I hired a French guy to come over here, and build this for me. It has two levels."

"All that for a storage building?" I ask.

"You'll see." She smiled as we walked through the door.

And my oh my … this isn't just a storage building, it's an art gallery. The walls are filled exclusively with portraits: her father, grandfathers, mother, grandmothers, and other relatives unidentifiable to me. And ME! There are dozens of paintings and drawings of me in this place!

In the middle of the lower level, is a fountain with colored lights under the water, and a Greek statue of Aphrodite standing in the center.

"I brought that back from Greece. It was in the basement of a museum. I convinced the museum officials that it would have a better home with me."

"You've got to be kidding." I say that a lot around Gigi. "This is a national treasure. They would never let it out of the country."

"Oh yes they would, for five million dollars." She hugs me and kisses me on the cheek. "So, go around and look at my paintings, DH. These are the ones no one has ever seen. You're the first."

"Gigi, you have so many surprises. Is there anything else you can throw at me?"

"You're not happy?"

"I'm ecstatic! But I feel like I'm on a roller coaster. So much—"

"Can't you just enjoy the moment?" she asks, and I can see her getting all mopey again.

"Please don't cry."

"I can't help it." She tries to hold back the tears. "I want you to be happy."

"I'm happier than I've ever been, Pixie. But this takes some getting used to. I live in this little room I call, The Hole, remember?

And you have —"

"I have nothing." She looks down at her toes.

"What?"

"I have nothing. WE have all of this. You and me. I'm going to speak with my attorneys and have them put everything in my name and your name together."

"Gigi! Are you sure you want to do that?"

"There is no question or hesitation." She smiles through her tears.

"I don't know what to say."

"Then don't say anything. Just look at my paintings and give me your honest opinion. I painted this one of you the first night I met you." She points to one of the paintings. "I fell in love with you while I was painting it. I remembered your eyes. I couldn't get them out of my mind."

We walk over to the painting. Again, the Impressionist style that looks like Monet or Degas could have painted it. It is stunning.

Suddenly, we hear the door to the gallery open, and close. We turn our heads and find Frank standing there with a big grin on his face.

The Laugh. "You caught me!"

Gigi comes unglued. "What do you think you are doing in here!" She rushes to a panel on the wall and pushes a button. In seconds, one of her goons comes in with his gun drawn. He grabs Frank, pulls his arms around his back, and puts cuffs on him.

A few seconds later about ten other guards, new ones I haven't seen before, come in and surround Frank, guns drawn. He still has a huge grin on his face!

"Holy cow, Gigi, it's me. It ain't John Dillinger."

"Back away boys!" Gigi is still angry but I can tell she's trying to regain her composure. "But if he moves one bit, shoot the jerk!"

I can tell now by the tone of her voice that everything is okay. But I do hope Frank doesn't do anything to change that.

"What are you trying to do?" Gigi has taken her stance right in front of Frank, hands on her hips, spraying spit in his face with every word. "Who do you think you are, Reed?" Then she lets out a stream of language that would make a sailor blush — I've purposely spared my journal of the choicest words, and there are some good ones.

Frank losses the grin and looks at her penetratingly.

"I'll tell you what, you little White Demon," he says as he nudges one of the goons aside. "You have a talent that the whole world needs to know about, and you can have these bastards shoot me if you want, but I'm going to look at these paintings, and I'm going to talk you into exhibiting them somewhere on planet Earth! So, what's it gonna be? Shoot me, or let me walk over there and look at that painting of DH? Tell these Italian goombahs to unhand me, or I'll beat their butts black and blue."

Gigi stood there for a moment. Then she looked at me, winked, and whispered in my ear, "He thinks he's something, doesn't he?"

"That he does. But he really is, you know," I whispered back.

She whispered again, "I know, but he's such a pompous turd." She kisses me on the cheek. That's all Frank needs.

"You kids gonna make whoopee on the frigigin' floor, or are you gonna tell these wise guys to let me go so I can see some Ort!" *The Laugh.*

I think Frank is the bravest man I've ever known. He has a dozen handguns aimed at his head, and a dozen big burly dudes, with bad frowns, staring him down. I think they all want to shoot his butt, but he keeps making jokes.

"Is there a helicopter overhead, Gigi?" I ask. "What's that sound?"

"They came with that button I pushed. There are three helicopters overhead. Two are my guys, and the third belongs to the police."

"Ha!" Frank cries out, followed by *The Laugh.* "I haven't had this kind of reception since —"

"Let him go. Let the idiot loose," Gigi orders. "And get those choppers out of here!"

The goons hustle to take the handcuffs off Frank. One guy is using a walkie-talkie to call off the choppers, and there they go. Adios amigo, and they're out of here. As quick as they appeared, so they vanish.

"Get your butt over here, Reed," Gigi yells. "No one has ever come in here except for DH, and you spoiled the whole thing, you insufferable jerk!" Gigi slaps him hard on the face.

"Ouch," he says as he rubs his reddening cheek. "Sorry." Frank is grinning again. "But art is art." He dismisses Gigi with a shrug of his shoulders and walks over to examine the paintings on the wall.

"You're one lucky you know what," Gigi tells his back. "If you'd have been anybody else I would have had my guys kill you dead and bury you under the back lawn."

"I knew you wouldn't," he said absently.

"You don't know zip." She glares at him.

"I'm an artist, and you're an artist, and we both exist for one purpose." Frank turns around and looks at her. "It has nothing to do with money, but it has everything to do with money. I make art for money and for love. You don't need the money, so you just make it for the love. But you respect me because I have that magical Art Spirit inside, and I respect you because you do too. It's as simple as that. Basic physics 101. Except I ain't so friggin' white!" Frank puts his hands on his hips in that Peter Pan pose that comes much more naturally to Gigi, blatantly mocking her.

The two of them are squared off like boxers in an arena. I resist the urge to play referee.

"What are you anyway," she yells, "friggin' Irish?"

"No," Frank yells back. "I'm friggin' Norwegian!"

The spit is flying back and forth.

"And you can do what you wanta do—call your friggin' goombahs back in here and shoot me dead—but I'm gonna light a pipe, and I'm gonna stroll over there and look at that painting of the guy in the army suit. I think that's one of the most beautiful Impressionist portraits I've ever seen!"

Once again, tears form in Gigi's eyes. She whimpers, "That's my dad," then lowers herself to the floor, crying. Frank kneels beside her. He takes hold of her like he did me that day back when, and rocks her in his arms. I can see tears streaming from his eyes as he murmurs, "That's alright little girl, that's alright."

Gigi sits up and wipes that sweet puffy nose of hers. "I'm sorry for being a turd, Frank. You're a nice man. Let's just forget about it. Help me up, I'll show you the gallery."

Frank helps Gigi up, and she begins to give us a tour of her gallery. Her paintings are indeed beautiful. They definitely remind me of Berthe Morisot, but they have more color to them.

Frank is smiling. Not the previous impish grin, but a real smile of genuine pleasure. "Gigi," he says, "you're like Helen of Troy. You have the face that launched a thousand ships, but you're also the Trojan Horse. You have so many secrets inside."

"I have no secrets, Frank," she replies. "I put everything out in my paintings, just as I suppose you do."

"But I don't," he says, shaking his head and looking at me. "I try to reveal as little as possible in my paintings."

"And why's that?" Gigi asks.

"Because some things are meant to be kept private." A shadow crosses his face as he looks away from us.

"Goodness gracious. The great Frank Reed frowning and look-ing all dismayed?" But she says it gently, placing her hand on his shoulder in a gesture of sympathy.

Frank looks directly into her eyes and says, quite suddenly, "You guys have fun. Guess I'll go back to the party and paint on that butcher paper now."

"What?" His abrupt change catches me by surprise.

"I thought you wanted to see my paintings?" Gigi says, baffled by his sudden change of mood.

"Maybe some other time, but thanks Gigi." He shakes her hand. Gigi and I look at each other.

"You're a good kid, Gigi," he says "Do something with this talent of yours." Then he just smiles and leaves.

"What the heck was that all about?" Gigi says.

"I don't know, but I need to find out. He's my friend."

"Follow him, DH. We can come back here any time. You need

to take care of Frank."

I follow him out the door as quickly as I can. He is striding rapidly down the grassy slope to the pool, so I holler, "Hey Frank! Wait for me!" He stops, turns toward me, and sits down on the ground.

"That grass is wet," I say.

"I don't give a rat's patoot."

"Are you okay? This isn't the Frank Reed I know."

"Maybe it's the Frank Reed nobody knows."

"What's wrong Frank?" I ask him.

"Nothing, Bud." He pauses as if to reconsider. "Everything."

"What's the deal? I've never seen you like this before."

"I don't know, DH. It's all just coming down on me right now. I don't want to talk about it. I'll work it out."

"But you helped me."

"It ain't the same, Bud, it ain't the same." Frank buries his face in his hands, shaking his head.

I'm afraid to come near him. I want to touch his shoulder, but I know I shouldn't even try. He gets up and walks back to the patio. I know something is wrong, but if he doesn't want to talk to me, there's not much I can do.

I look back over my shoulder and here comes Gigi, strutting across the lawn like she owns the world. I guess she sort of does, even more than Frank, 'cause she has all the money in the world.

"So, where's Frank?" she asks.

"He's over there on the patio."

"He's a real jerk, but he's growin' on me. I think he has some personal problems though."

"What do you mean?" I ask.

"Just the way he acts and the way he says things."

"You might be right, Gigi. He was a mess just a minute ago."

"He's married, right?" she asks.

"Yep. To a really beautiful woman named Maxine."

"Should I be jealous?" Gigi looks down at me while I'm still sitting on the ground.

"No. Frank will never leave Maxine. Besides, she doesn't even know that I exist."

"That's good." Gigi takes my hand and pulls me up to her.

As I'm getting up, we hear Jack's voice coming from the patio. "Hey, DH, Gigi, let's finish this thing! Are you out there somewhere?"

So Gigi and I suck it up and walk over to the patio where the butcher paper still lies waiting to receive further manifestations of our collective creative genius. All of the guys are there, too.

When Manny asks in that innocent voice of his, "Where you been?" I want to answer him with "I'm not sure where I've been."

Gigi answers for us. "We've been in my gallery." Manny just nods and takes what she says as gospel.

"Where's Frank?" Gigi asks, looking around for him.

"I don't know," I say, taking in the scene on the patio for myself. "Say Jack, where's Frank?"

"Haven't seen him," he says.

I walk to the front of the house to see if Frank's bike is there, and it isn't. Gigi is with me, looking concerned.

"Was he ticked at something I said?" she asks.

"I don't think so. Something else was bothering him."

"I don't want you to leave me, but I think this is important, DH. Go find Frank." Gigi smiles and kisses me, and I decide she's right.

I get into my VW. I don't have a clue where to go, but I have to pee, so I decide to stop at The Hole first, then I'll track him down as best as I can. He might be at the college.

Back at the Hole

I pull up into my driveway, and there's Frank, sitting on his bike smoking his pipe.

"How long would you have waited if I hadn't come home tonight?" I ask, smiling.

"I knew you would." He doesn't smile back.

"Why's that?" I ask.

"It's simple. You've made whoopee with Gigi a whole lot of times, but we've been Buds for a lot longer than that."

I have to grin, because Frank is right.

"What's goin' on, Frank?"

"You got any wine?"

"Is the Pope Catholic?"

"Then go in and grab a couple of glasses and a jug, and bring it out here. I want to watch the night sky."

I go into The Hole, grab some cups, and an unopened gallon of Red Mountain. I bring it back out to Frank, who is still sitting on his bike.

I put the jug of wine down on the ground in front of him with the cups.

"Hang on!" I say.

I go back into the garage, relieve myself in my tiny bathroom, and grab some folding lawn chairs. Outside again, I tell Frank to get off the bike and chitchat with me—with a smile, of course. Frank smiles back and gets off his bike. We sit in the lawn chairs and I pour wine into our cups.

"Did I foul up the party?" Frank asks, gazing into his wine, his brow doing a furrow thing.

"I doubt it," I smile. "I think the party is going on even as we speak." I take a sip from my mug.

"So, this Gigi chick and you are a hot item, getting even hotter, huh?" Frank asks.

"I think so. But I'm more worried about you than I am about that."

"You knew I'd be here didn't you, Bud." Frank is gazing into his wine again.

"Actually, I came here to pee." We both laugh. "But then I would have gone to your house, and then to RCC. I would have found you eventually."

"Let me get this straight, DH." Frank looks at me seriously, his sharp eyes probing mine. "You left that really cool party, and all that wine, and that White Goddess of yours, and came looking for me?"

"I did."

"Why the heck did you do that? What a friggin' putz you are."
He smiles. I can see tears forming in his eyes.

"Because I'm psychic."

"Psychic!" What in the world does that mean?" He does the brow
thing again.

"I ain't stupid, Frank. I know there's something wrong in your
life. Something isn't right."

"Guess you are psychic." Frank takes a deep swallow of wine.
"I wish I could tell you about it—I really do—but I can't."

"So why did you come here to my place?"

"I don't know. Just to look up at the stars or something. This is
the one quiet place I have in my life that I can come to."

"Are you having marriage problems?"

"No comment. But that's not what I mean. I'm talking about my
own head—my own thoughts. I've got all this garbage running
around up here." Frank points to his head. "I have all of these ideas
and I'm becoming a friggin' mess. I'm not who I want to be."

"Who do you want to be, Frank?"

"I'm not really sure, but I know I don't like who I am right now."
He sips his wine again.

"Look up at those stars, DH! Those are the same stars that Van
Gogh and Cezanne looked up at. Friggin' Picasso looks up on the
same stars over there in Spain or France or wherever he is!" I know
Frank is drunk. Not just with wine but with the Art Spirit.

"Man," he says, "I feel really bad about taking you away from the
White Thing."

"It was the White Thing that ordered me to go after you, Frank.
She was worried about you."

"You gotta be kidding! Gigi told you to leave that multi-million
dollar sanctuary and come after me?"

"She did." Just as I utter those two words, I see a red Jaguar flying
up the driveway in a cloud of dust.

With a honk of the horn Gigi pulls up, gets out of her car, and
runs over to us. She kisses me on the cheek, then she takes Frank's

hand and asks, "Is everything okay?" And she means it.

"Gigi," Frank says. "What are you doing here?" His eyes are getting misty again.

"I was worried about you!" She is intense.

Frank shakes his head. He turns to me and says, "What is it with this chick? Is she the best, or what?"

I just smile.

"Frank Friggin' Reed, you just ruined my party!" Gigi says, standing up straight and putting her hands on her hips.

"All I did was leave." *The Laugh*, but a bit off the usual *Laugh*.

"It's how you left." Gigi's eyes are on fire. "When you left it was like dominoes. DH left, then Jack, then Manny, then the two Bills, and that was it. The party was over."

"What about the butcher paper!" Leave it to Frank to worry about the art.

"My goons are taking care of that." She stands there with her hands on her hips, her head held high, and that puffy nose twitching. I start to laugh.

"What are you laughing at?" Gigi asks with mock indignation.

"I've noticed that twice now you've referred to your body guards as goons. That's one of the names I call them in my journal."

Gigi smiles. "Guess you're rubbing off on me."

"Get the White One a chair, Bud. We can all look at the stars together," Frank says.

I go back into the garage and get another folding chair and bring it out, opening it up for Gigi.

"Look up at those stars!" Frank leans back and extends his arms as if to encompass the sky. "Don't you get it? Those stars up there are what it's all about."

Gigi and I look at each other quizzically.

"What do you mean, Frank?" I ask.

"Romance happens at night, DH. All of the poetry and all of the art in the world has always been about romance, and the effects of the moon and the stars. Look at the beautiful planet Venus up there on the right—the Goddess of love. Astronomers didn't name her that by accident! She rules the night, and lovers come out under this sky every single night, and they kiss, and they make love, and they make googly eyes at each other, and it's been going on for centuries. If I had to make a choice, if a gun was being held to my head"—he smiles at Gigi, who is smiling too—"and some gallery owner told me that I had to pick one of three choices: seascapes, portraits and the night sky, I'd pick the night sky."

"Why's that?" Gigi asks. "I mean, besides the romance stuff." She puts her hand on my lap and smiles at me.

"Art is all about romance, Gigi," Frank says. "That's the sum total of everything to do with it. Why does a poet write of love? Unless you're E.E. Cummings, writing about bells, and throats, and cats, you're gonna be writing about love!" *The Laugh*—and I'm glad to hear it.

"Frank," Gigi says, "I've never seen one of your paintings, but I'll bet they're electric"

"I'm not sure what you mean by 'electric', White One, but they're real good." He looks thoughtful for a moment. "I kind of like that electric stuff. I'll have to remember that."

"I mean, I'll bet they have a lot of emotion in them. Your personal emotion has to come out in your work. You saw my stuff. DH is all over the place in my work! He's my emotion."

"That is the greatest mystery in the universe!" *The Laugh*. "What on Earth do you see in this guy!"

Gigi smiles. "I know you're kidding now, Mr. Great Friggin' Arteest, because I know you love 'this guy' too."

"That I do, Goddess," Frank says as he winks at me. "But I swear, I don't know why."

"It's the Brotherhood, Frank," Gigi answers. "The PRB." Gigi looks directly into Frank's eyes. "Artists have a Brotherhood in every era."

"The Pre-Raphaelite Brotherhood! Have we talked about them before?" Frank asks. He is surprised and looks at me.

"I think DH has mentioned them in his little journal. But the point I'm trying to make is, study those guys!" Gigi is on a roll now. "Rossetti and Burne-Jones and Millais, and all the others! Their wives and models and girlfriends—Jane Morris, Liz Siddal, to name just two—were passed around from guy to guy, and nobody seemed to give a hoot!"

"Come on, Gigi, this ain't gonna be some feminist thing is it?" Frank says, rolling his eyes.

"No Mr. R!" she responds. "In fact, I'm going to surprise you here because I'm on your side!"

"Whoop-di-doo!" Frank laughs out.

"It was the times they lived in, and the way they did their thing." Her face is alight with excitement. "I'm not the feminist you think I am. I don't give a rip 'bout politics. I just like art."

"Ort," Frank corrects.

"Ort," Gigi smiles back.

"DH, if you don't marry this White Thing, I will."

"No chance, Frank, I want him." She points at me.

"Frank," she says, "you're one impressive jerk. No doubt you're gonna do something big with your art, and I hope you do, but DH has something about him that you don't have."

"And that is?" Frank does the brow thing.

"Innocence," she says, looking at me with those big blue eyes. I squirm in my seat like it's on fire.

"Gigi," Frank says, "you're a piece of work."

"I'm just me, the White One."

"No kidding, White One, I don't think I've ever met anyone who could parry my thrusts like you do."

Gigi moves closer to me and places her cheek next to mine. "Mr. Frank Reed, paint this."

Frank says, "I just might do that." Then he laughs and continues with, "Maybe I ought to go, so you kids can go play in The Hole."

"You sound just like Bill Hunter," Gigi teases.

Frank responds with, "Good grief," and a roll of his eyes.

"What's that all about?" Gigi frowns. "Hunter's a special guy."

"Hunter's an ace, Gigi. I love him too, don't get your knickers in a twist."

"I don't wear knickers."

Frank looks at me with a sly grin and says, "That's probably more information than I need, but I'm enjoying my thoughts right now."

"You're a mess, Reed," Gigi says, shaking her head.

"I told you he was a mess, Gigi. But he's a real good artist."

Gigi asks Frank, "So when do I get to see your paintings?"

"Anytime, White One."

She accepts the invitation as given. "How 'bout now?"

"Now?"

"Why not? You've been depressed all night. You can show us your paintings and that will perk you up. Besides, you screwed up my party and you owe me."

"Can't do it kid," Frank says. There is a bit of regret in his voice. "It's way too late and the wife's at home. I don't think she'd appreciate us barging in like that. I think I'd better just leave and let you kids get some sleep — or whatever."

"You don't have to go, Frank," I say. "You can hang around and we can draw for a while. I've got a lot of wine."

"Naw, I think I'll head for home and get some sleep." He gets up and walks toward his motorcycle. As he gets on he adds, "But why don't you guys come over tomorrow afternoon? I'll bring out some stuff. Maxine will be at work."

"Whatta you think, Gigi?" I ask, smiling at her.

"I'd love too! Can I sleep here tonight, DH? Then we can go to Frank's tomorrow?"

"Sleep?" Frank rolls his eyes, starts the engine on his bike, and heads down the driveway.

Day 75: The Next Day

I think it's about one o'clock in the afternoon. Gigi and I are standing in Frank's studio at his Castle. He has surprised us by turning this casual visit into a real affair. He had met us outside when we arrived and ushered us into his studio with a grand flourish. There was bread, cheese, wine, and a bowl of cherries laid out on his worktable. Gigi snagged those up right away. Frank took my arm and guided me to the end of the table, where there was a small stand, like a lectern.

"Put that stupid journal right there," he said, indicating the stand. "I'm tired of watching you juggle that thing around and write in it at the same time. I'll bet half of what you write isn't even legible."

**Filled in Latter Because Frank
Wouldn't Let Me Write**

"You're right. I can't read half of what I write."

"So," Frank said, "here we all are, now what do you want to see? It's pretty much all around you."

We look around. There's the bronze head Frank made, a few paintings, some sculpted pieces.

"Most of my work is stored in a gallery or two," he said, looking as big headed as he can.

Gigi is looking at the bronze head. "Wow! That's lovely."

"That's got quite a story behind it, doesn't it, DH?"

"It surely does," I replied, smiling at the memory.

"Long story short," Frank explained, "I tried to cast it at RCC, and the mold fell apart on me, so I came home. I made another wax impression the next day, took it to a private foundry, and had some professionals cast it. It is a nice piece."

"Nice, ain't the word for it, Frank," I said. "It's stunning."

"I heard you mention Manzù the other night," Gigi said. "I went to the library and looked him up. You're stuff kind of looks like his."

"I think when an artist does a realistic sculpture, it doesn't matter what era he's living in or what continent he's living on. The head either looks like the girl or it doesn't," Frank said. "Michelangelo once said, 'Man passes; only art is immortal.' I believe that."

"But this really is lovely. Do you have a photo of this girl?"

"No photos," Frank said stoically.

"That's his Muse," I said, expanding on Frank's reticence.

"Speaking of Muses," Frank said brightly, "I haven't heard you mention yours lately DH." Then he looked at Gigi and frowned. "Oops. Maybe I shouldn't have said that."

"What are we talking about, boys?" she asked.

"It's a long story Gigi." Frank waved his hands trying to dismiss what he just said, but he knew he was too late.

"I'd like to hear it," demanded Gigi, her eyes filled with questions.

I start to explain. "For a long time, everywhere I went I kept seeing this same girl, and she made the same gestures and—"

"Do I need to worry about this?" she pouts.

"Take it from me Gigi," said Frank, "you ain't got anything to worry about. This is some sort of make-believe girl that comes out of some other dimension. What's her name again, Bud?"

"Ann is the name I heard her say."

"So," Gigi said, looking none too happy, "is this a lover?"

"No Gigi," I told her quickly. "I don't know what the heck she is, but I haven't seen her since I started going around with you."

"Sounds like a stalker to me."

"No, I don't think so. I know this is going to sound weird, but I don't think she's real at all. I think she just 'appears' now and then … and …"

"And?" Gigi looks frosted.

"I don't know if you believe in this stuff or not, but I think she's … I think she's my daughter."

Gigi and Frank responded simultaneously, first with stunned silence, then, "I didn't know you had a daughter."

"I don't. In this life."

"What the heck are you talkin' about, Bud?"

"The last dream I had of her, just before I met Gigi, she called herself Annie. Then she smiled at me, and called me something that I didn't get, but I'll swear it sounded like 'Daddy'. I woke up feeling terrible, and all that day, I had these strange memories popping in and out of my head of this young girl, Annie. I knew she was my daughter. I can't explain it."

"You're a friggin' mystic, DH," Frank said.

"Or a friggin' kook," Gigi added.

"I'm not a kook. I've had dreams like this all my life. Guess it's just an active imagination." Just as I said that, a drip of mustard came out of the corner of Gigi's mouth and dripped on Frank's table.

"Ooops. Sorry about that," Gigi said, wiping the mustard from her lip and chin.

Frank looked at me, eyes wide. "DH! Did you see that?"

"I did." I think both Frank and I were both as white as Gigi at that moment.

"What's the matter with you guys?" She looked confused.

"It's a part of the story, Gigi."

"Well, tell me! You guys look like you've seen a ghost."

"In every appearance, or apparition, or dream, or whatever the heck of Annie, the one consistent sign that proved to me it was her was a drip of something coming out of her mouth."

Gigi looked down at the fresh mustard stain on her napkin. She touched her finger to her lip, looked at me, and then at Frank. I looked at Frank, and he looked at me. Then Frank looked at Gigi, and Gigi looked back at me — and then we all cracked up. It really was funny, like a scene from a Charlie Chan movie.

"Well, maybe I'm your Muse!" laughed Gigi. "But hey, no kidding, I believe in that past life stuff. I've had a few dreams myself."

"Good grief," said Frank, rolling his eyes. "I thought we were here to look at Ort."

"Seriously, Frank," said Gigi, rolling her eyes in response, "don't you believe in reincarnation and past lives?"

"I believe in the Carnation building in LA. We had lunch

there once. Remember, DH?"

"So you don't believe in reincarnation?" she persisted.

"I think once around is bad enough."

Gigi continued, "How do you explain child prodigies? Someone like Mozart, who gets up one day as a little kid, and starts writing music? Or Picasso?"

"Or," I added, "How do you explain somebody like you, Frank?"

"Red Mountain!" *The Laugh*. And we all laughed at that.

He got serious. "I'm not sure I can explain me. I've been fiddling around with drawing since I was a boy, but something just hit me one day, and I knew this is what I needed to be doing. Not that I necessarily *wanted* to do it, but that I *had* to do it. I started painting and doing pots and sculptures. It felt really, really good."

"So, tell me about the little painting leaning up over there on the other table?" Gigi asked.

"It's a twenties girl. Like a Flapper," Frank explains. "At least, that's what OK Harry said when he saw it."

"Is that a corset around her belly?" Gigi asked.

"Okay, here we go. Here's my story on this painting." Frank smiled, so I knew this was going to be good.

"This is a painting of Isadora Duncan, just before she took that fateful drive in her open limo, when the wind blew her scarf into the car wheel, and it got caught up, and choked her to death.

"I was experimenting with color contrast, and the juxtaposition of the color of the figure to the color and shapes in the background. See the bright yellow strip at the top?" Frank gets up and walks over to the painting. "I put some white in the yellow, and then moved some of it down to give this kind of erratic halo behind the head."

"You dripped some there in the corner," Gigi remarked.

"I did. It was an accident, but I liked it and left it. I think that, often, GOOD art is an accident. An artist can plan and sketch and do whatever he or she wants, but in the end, the masterpieces are always the accidents."

"I love those greens," I said.

"I did something strange with those. I mixed just a little bit of dried clay into them, just to see what it would do. I think it turned out really good. It gave it some texture."

"So what about the yellow corset?"

"Originally the lady was nude, but the pale flesh didn't mix with the background colors, so I added the green Flapper hat, the fur, and the jacket, and then I put the corset down there to cover her private parts."

"Well," I said, "I'm kind of an upstart at this art stuff, but you know what I think is the most powerful thing about this little painting?"

"What?"

"Two things really. The contrast between the pinks and the greens, and that exquisite face. If you isolate that face and bring it forward it would make a great portrait of whoever this is, in and of itself. And I know it isn't Isadora Duncan," I paused for a second as recognition set in. "This is your mother isn't it?"

Frank looked at me with an expression I had never seen on him before. "You ARE psychic DH," he whispered, as if the surprise of my statement had knocked the breath out of him. "I've never told anybody that before. Maxine doesn't even know it." He looked back at the little painting.

"Frank," I said quietly, "this is a beautiful painting, and it's just more evidence that you are great artist even before the critics see it."

Gigi added, "No kidding, Frank. This is beautiful."

"Frank shook his head and turned to Gigi. "What YOU do is beautiful. That Impressionist touch of yours is the finest thing I've ever seen. My Ort isn't beautiful—it's timely. That's all it is. I'm trying to paint paintings that are just a little bit ahead of all the other Joe Blow painters out there. I know I have the Art Spirit and all that crap we've already talked about, but I'm also in it for the money. Unless I come up with some new gimmick, I'll retire to the poor house like everybody else." *The Laugh.*

"I don't know if this painting is a new gimmick" Gigi said, "but it's lovely, and I don't think I've seen anything like it before."

"Too bad you missed my show at the Mission Inn. I had more there like this."

"I wasn't invited."

"I didn't know you then. DH had that Norma girl stalking him back then."

"She's a bore," Gigi said.

"She's history," I said. "There's only one woman in my life now, and that's you, Pixie."

"Pixie?" *The Laugh.*

"Don't even go there, Reed. That name is sacred."

Frank looked serious. "Let me guess, your dad called you that didn't he?"

"Now who's the friggin' psychic?" She's misting up again.

"I'm sorry Gigi." Frank put his hand on her shoulder. "I didn't mean anything by it."

"I know you didn't. I'm just touchy about my family stuff."

"Here. Maybe this will make you feel better." Frank handed her a little bronze figure of a reclining nude woman. "Take this home with you. I made it out of the leavings from the bronze head."

"Why, it's beautiful! Thank you so much." She gave Frank a kiss on the cheek.

"The kiss makes it worth it, White One." Frank smiled and then looked at me. "Don't get jealous, Bud. I ain't tryin' to move in on your chick."

"Better not. I'd hate to have to kill you."

"Heck no!" he cried. "Don't do that! Think of what the world would lose." *The Laugh.* Then we all laughed.

"Hey," Frank said, "you know they've got a lot of Impressionist paintings over at LACMA. We ought to drive over there and check 'em out. You'd love it Gigi. I'm sure they have a Morisot in the main gallery."

"Name the time, name the date."

Frank looked at his watch. "It's only two o'clock. We can be there in an hour!"

"DH?" Gigi looked at me.

"Okay by me. Can we take the Jag?"

Gigi smiled. "No prob."

"Ridin' in style!" Frank grinned. "Let's hit the road!"

At the LA County Museum of Art

I love LA, and I love this museum. I've been here about a bazillion times; some of those times with Frank. The last time I was here I was with that girl at the Soutine exhibit, when I wore the borrowed suit with the baggy pants. But today I'm wearing my Levis and a blue work shirt. They fit me to a T, so I can relax and have fun.

The museum is open later than usual because of some outdoor festival they have going on, with lots of little kids running around getting their faces painted, and eating hot dogs. I love the hot dogs here.

Frank, Gigi and I are strolling through the halls of the museum, heading toward the Impressionist works, but Gigi gets sidetracked by a huge painting of a mountain and lake by Thomas Moran.

"Wow! Look at that."

"I can paint like that," I boast.

"My butt!" Gigi protests. "That's the most beautiful thing I've ever seen."

"It's pretty grand," Frank agrees.

"Just look at that! What color and light."

"The neat thing about these 19th century landscape artists is that they truly captured nature," Frank said. "I'm not surprised that you're so excited about this painting. In a way it's similar to the Impressionists movement, only on this side of the pond."

"It's so lovely." Gigi is enthralled.

"But you gotta see the French Impressionist stuff, Gigi." Frank is excited, and he's moving us down the hall to the room housing the Impressionist collection. There's a huge Monet water lily painting on one of the walls. I never realized that Monet painted such large paintings.

"Look at that thing!" Frank yells, drawing the attention of the guard. "Isn't that a piece o' work! Man oh man; nobody paints like that any more. That's the one thing about Impressionism. It's the movement that ended it all. All of the artists with true finesse went out with that era."

"Then came Picasso, and Braque, and Calder, and Motherwell and the whole Modernist bunch," I add wistfully.

"They blew the whole thing out of the water," Frank continues. "Not a bad thing, just a different thing. But I have to admit, it just ain't the same."

"Look at this Degas!" Gigi is delighted. "Look at this thing!"

"It's beautiful," I agree — it really is. "But I don't see any Morisot paintings here."

"I could have sworn they had one here," Frank says, looking around. "I don't get it. She ought to be as prominent as all the other Impressionists. Her work is incredible, and, Miss Gigi, your style is so close to hers that it's almost scary. My favorite Morisot painting is simply called, "Tea." It reminds me of one of the paintings I saw in your gallery — a woman with red hair and a blue dress seated at a table. I'm guessing she was your mother." Frank has a sheepish look, like a little boy caught doing something he shouldn't.

"She is my mother. It's from a photo I have of her," Gigi says softly.

"Well, you gotta see this Morisot painting. I swear, if the girl in that photo had your short blond hair, she'd be a ringer for you!"

"Really?"

"Really."

"Holy cow!" I cry.

"What is it, Love?"

"Look over there," I point. "I don't know why he's in here, but it's a Soutine." I take Gigi's hand and pull her over to show her what I consider to be an incredible painting.

"It's one of the ones that was in the exhibit that Frank and I saw. The museum must have bought it!"

Gigi quietly examines the painting.

"Wow." Her response is hushed, almost reverent.

"It's a bell boy," I explain.

Frank breaks the reverent mood with, "Just like you, Immortal White One!" *The Laugh.* "You and that stinkin' bell of yours. Hey, Bud, I guess we're out of Gigi's bell range!" *The Laugh,* again. "We're safe for now!"

But Gigi reaches into her purse, pulls out her little silver bell, and rings it three times. From every direction, here come the goons. Frank is thunderstruck.

"You've got to be kidding me. How did you pull that off?" he asks Gigi.

"Where I go," she says with a smirk, "the goons go." She turns and winks at me and I wink back.

Now the skinny little museum guards are running over here with their walkie-talkies, looking like they want a fight. I can tell by the expression on the face of one of the guards, that he doesn't really know what to do about this.

"What's going on here?" a scrawny little guard yells out.

Minutes later, a team of LAPD guys arrive. Apparently some sort of a silent alarm was set off—probably by one of the guards—and the cops are in full battle gear, looking for trouble.

"Gigi?" I query. I glance at Frank. He has his hands in the air.

"Hold on." Gigi approaches the police officer that seems to be in charge. She whispers something into his ear, and pulls out what looks to be her driver's license. Just like that, the cop salutes her, and the whole thing is over. The museum guard comes over and apologizes directly to Gigi, and all of the guards leave the room, shutting the doors behind them. Gigi and Frank and I have the room to ourselves. I look at Frank; he looks baffled.

"Gigi?" His manner is quite—for him—subdued. "I know I've asked you this before, but who are you?"

"None of your business, Mr. Reed," she answers. "Let's just enjoy the paintings."

"It's your call," Frank says, looking at me and shaking his head.

"Look at this Soutine!" I try to get us back on track. "Look at the color! All reds and blues, with just a little black." Now that the guards are gone I reach up and touch it gently. Wow.

"I have to admit," Gigi says, "I've never seen anything like it. It really is powerful."

"Powerful!" Frank comes alive. "This guy once knocked a hole through a wall in his house to get the right kind of light just to paint a friggin' dead chicken. That's powerful. Talk about the Art Spirit—Soutine and Van Gogh have to be tied for the lead in that department."

"I kind of like the hands," Gigi says.

I agree. "I think they're great, too. My favorite Soutine portrait is the one of Maria Lani. I love her hands. And that distant look in her eyes."

"I'm going to have to buy a book on this Soutine guy," Gigi says.

"I have the book I bought at the exhibit. You can look through it sometime."

"Didn't you show me that one night?" Gigi asks. "I think I wrote something in it?"

"Yes. But we got side tracked before you got into it." I smile at the memory.

Gigi whispers into my ear, "Can we get sidetracked somewhere in this museum?"

I whisper back, "I think we'd be arrested if we got caught."

"I'll pay the bail."

Like a teacher calling distracted students back to attention, Frank demands, "What are you two chitchatting about?"

"I was just asking DH if there was some place in this museum we can go so we can make whoopee." Gigi takes her characteristic pose—feet apart, hands on hips, and a twinkle in her eye.

Frank starts to say something, then looks at me, and says, "Just don't get caught." To Gigi, he adds, "You could probably buy this museum, and then you could whoopee anywhere you want."

"I know I could. But I don't like all of the art in here, just some of it."

I want to get Frank back on track to take advantage of his vast knowledge of art history and technique. "You guys can jibber and jabber all you want, but I'm not through with this Soutine. Look at those blues. Frank, is that Pthalo?"

"I think it is," he answers, "but you have to realize that the paint colors and names were a bit different back then. Some of the names we use today didn't exist in the 1800s, and the early 1900s. In fact, I'm convinced that that's why their paintings are superior to the paintings today. They mixed their own paint, and it just looks different from the artificial junk on the market today. I'm not sure about Pthalo though. My favorite painting by Soutine from that exhibit was *The Praying Man*—bright red background, with a mottled yellow and red face."

"I remember that one."

"I would like to have seen that show," Gigi says. "I feel like I really missed something."

"It was impressive," I tell her. "When we get back to The Hole I'll show you that book again. I want to buy some more books on Soutine."

"Don't get too hooked on him, DH," Frank cautions. "Remember what we talked about before. You gotta find your own style. Maybe Gigi can help you with that."

"How can I do that?" she asks.

"Come on, White One, art is all about romance, remember? All you have to do, is do what you do with him, and his style will follow."

"Frank, are my eyes deceiving me, or is that Bill Mitchkelly coming through the door over there?"

"I think it might be. I thought we had this place to ourselves," he says, then yells "Mitch!" Sure enough, Bill turns around and comes toward us.

"What the heck are you doing here?" Frank asks.

"I have an art class with me," he says. "What a surprise! I really wanted to come in and see these paintings, but I saw the door closed. The guard said that a private party was in here, but he thought it would be okay if I came in and asked their permission. Wow, Frank, you have more pull than I ever dreamed."

"It ain't me," Frank confesses. "Gigi got us this ticket."

"What a coincidence seeing you here, Bill." I shake his hand.

"Billy boy!" Gigi pipes in, grabbing his hand in both of hers. "Is this synchronicity or what?"

"Nice to see you, Gigi," Bill says. "You are truly a lovely thing, and you know what? I kept thinking about it, and I realize that you remind me of that model, Twiggy. I think it's your nose and that lower lip."

"Yeah, I've been stopped on the street. People think I'm her. But she's a Brit, and I don't have the accent."

"There is a strong resemblance," Frank says. "Look at those eyes!"

Suddenly, she grasps my arm tightly with both hands. "DH, I'm not feeling too good."

"Gigi?"

"My stomach hurts, and I feel like I'm gonna pass out."

"How long has it been since you've eaten?" I ask her.

"I don't know."

"Maybe you need one of those hot dogs they're making outside," Frank suggests.

"I don't think I could handle one of those."

"I think we'd better go back home, Frank," I say, looking at him.

"I don't want to spoil the party," Gigi says, "but I really I think I'm about to pass out." She leans into me and does just that.

Thirty Minutes Later

We're in the Jag on our way back to Riverside. Frank is driving. When Gigi passed out Bill Mitchkelly went out to get help. He came back with one of Gigi's big burly dudes who immediately sized up the situation and got on his walkie-talkie to call for an ambulance. I told him to hang loose for a minute because Gigi was coming back to life. I was shaking with anxiety and fear for her.

Gigi opened her eyes, but still looked distant. "Where have I been?" she said weakly.

"You passed out, Pixie," I said.

Frank spoke up, his voice tense with concern, "Get this girl some water."

The guard spoke again into his walkie-talkie, and within a minute another of Gigi's men was there with a cup of water, and some wet paper towels.

She took a sip of water and looked around, but I could tell she was still in a daze.

"Gigi," I said, hiding my fear as best I could, "should we call for an ambulance?"

"What for? I don't need that. I have you." She smiled up at me as I cradled her in my arms.

By that time, the room had filled with guards. The goons had taken up position in a circle around Gigi and me, hands in their armpits, watching in all directions. The museum guards stationed themselves in a larger circle around the perimeter of the room. One of the museum guards said, "I think we need to get an ambulance for this little lady." He spoke gently and with real concern. Then he walked over to us, through the ring of Gigi's personal guards and said to me, "This is one very special person, sir."

"Gigi," I said, "The guard thinks you need to go to the hospital."

"He's very sweet," she said. "But I'll be okay. Maybe I could use one of those hot dogs."

One of Gigi's goons snapped his fingers and yelled out, "Hot dog!" The order was echoed down the line, and in a minute a hot dog appeared. It was transferred to one of the goons, who then presented it to Gigi.

After taking a couple of bites, she said to me, "I think you need to get me back home, Love."

Back to Real Time

As I said, Gigi and I are in the back seat of her Jag, her head in my lap, and Frank is driving. What was meant to be a joyful afternoon at LACMA, has turned into a nightmare. She's shivering like a wet fawn. Every once in a while she looks up at me and smiles, and I just melt. I don't know what to do for her. I'm hoping this isn't anything serious. Maybe she just needs to get some sleep and some better food. We've been keeping some pretty late night hours, and eating a lot of junk, and drinking a lot of wine.

Frank glances at us in the rear view mirror. "Is she okay?"

"I'm not sure, Frank. I don't like this."

"I don't like it either," he says. "Somethin' ain't right. "We need to take her to the hospital in Riverside."

"I don't know if she'll agree to that." It's a moot point, because Gigi has passed out again. "She's out cold Frank. Take us to the hospital as quick as you can."

"On our way, Bud. Hang on."

Three Hours Later in the Emergency Room

I'm sitting in the emergency room at the hospital. Frank and I have been here for quite some time. We had to have some guys bring a gurney out to the car, put Gigi on it, and wheel her in. She was still unconscious.

I think Frank's even more worried about her than I am. He's pacing the floor and sweating.

"I don't like this, Bud," he says. "Where are those doctors!"

"I don't know. They've had her in there for a long time."

"Too long!" Just as he says that, out comes the doc.

She introduces herself. "I'm Doctor Visitor. Which one of you is DH?" Her expression is one of professional gravitas meant to convey neither hope nor despair, but only competence and concern.

"I am."

"Your friend, Gigi, is going to be okay for now," the doc says. "But I need to tell you, that after all of the tests we have done, we have determined that she has lymphoma, a form of cancer."

My God … My God. I had to sit down.

Frank utters an anguished "No!" as he comes over and puts his arm around me.

I feel as if all of the air has been sucked from my lungs. "No. Please …"

"I'm sorry, DH," the doc says, letting more compassion come through. "You have to be brave with this. You have to help her. This doesn't mean she's going to die. We can treat this thing."

"Where is she?" I'm afraid I yelled at the doctor. "Where's Gigi?"

That's when I stormed through the doors, looking for her, and knocking things over. The doctor was hot on my trail, but before I could get too far, I was tackled by one of Gigi's goons. I went down hard on the floor, hitting my head and drawing blood.

"Sorry sir," the goon said, sopping up my blood with his coat sleeve, "but Miss Gigi can't see you like this." I looked up at him, and I knew he was right. The goon and I were both tearing up.

"I'm sorry, Bud." Frank said as he came over and gently pulled me away from the goon.

"But I have to see her," I said.

The doctor, out of breath, said, "You can take her home, DH. This isn't a death sentence. We've given her some medication, and we are scheduling more tests and treatments. Hopefully we'll catch it in time."

"I'm sorry. I didn't mean to hurt your hospital. I'm afraid I knocked a few things over." I feel like an idiot.

"It's okay," Dr. Visitor says. "I'm just glad this gentleman was able to stop you before you found Gigi." She looks up at the massive goon who tackled me, who is trying to look tough through the tears in his eyes. "It's no good for her to see you like this. You need to build her up."

"Did you tell her about the cancer?" I ask.

"She knows."

I don't know what to say.

"She's going to be coming through that door over there in about five minutes. What I recommend is that you take her home and give her all the love you can, and feed her good food. We're going to get her back in here in a couple of days for treatment. We've already started the preliminaries."

"I'll do whatever you want me to do." I hear my reply as if it were spoken by someone else. This news is too enormous for it to have gotten inside of me yet. Frank, standing next to me, is white as a sheet.

Gigi arrives in a wheelchair propelled by an orderly. I begin to panic, but the doctor assures me that the chair is only a formality.

"Liability, and all that," she says

Frank got to her before I did. He squeezed her shoulders gently, saying, "You're gonna be okay, White One. DH and I ain't gonna let anything happen to you." Frank's cheeks are wet with tears.

"Thanks, Frank. I know that."

By then I'm right beside her.

"You know," Frank says, "I kind of think of you as a little sister. I think anybody would if they got a look at that face of yours. I know you are strong and independent, but a person can't help but want to protect and watch over you. If you weren't paying your goons to do that I know I would — if I had the money!" *The Laugh.* A very feeble one.

With that, the mood lightened a bit. Gigi brightened up and kissed Frank on the cheek. Then she whispered in my ear, "I'm damaged goods, DH. Do you still love me?"

I didn't have the words to answer her, so I picked her up in my arms and carried her out of the hospital. Frank drove us back to Gigi's house, the goons in their cars ahead of and behind us. They had radioed ahead, so when we pulled up at the house, there was a hospital gurney waiting on the driveway. Gigi must have had one stashed in one of the many rooms in her house.

"I don't need that damned bed thing," Gigi protested.

When we get out of the car, I tell the goons to wheel the bed back to where they got it, and I take Gigi's arm and walk her into the house.

"It ain't like I'm sick, Love." She smiles at me. "I can walk now.

I'm not going to pass out again. They gave me a shot of something at the hospital and I feel great."

"Are you sure?" I ask.

"I'm sure. I just need a drink."

"But the Doc said that might not be good for you."

"I don't think a glass of wine would hurt anything," she says. "I wish I had some of that nasty Red Mountain you guys drink."

One of the goons approached me, and said with a commanding tone, "Keys." I knew exactly what he meant, and I didn't argue with him. I gave him the keys to The Hole—it's a lot closer than any market—and he left to complete his errand.

"I think it would be nice to just sit out by the pool, chitchat with you guys, and drink some really bad wine," Gigi says. "It's getting dark, and it's going to be a lovely evening."

"No party. But I may have the chef do up some grilled steaks."

"That would be nice," Frank says, echoing my thoughts. It's been a while since we last ate.

"Would you like to invite your wife over, Frank?" Gigi asks. She has been wanting to meet Maxine since she first learned of her.

"I don't think so this time," he says evasively.

Gigi probes for more. "She still doesn't know about me does she?"

"Gigi, this place"—he spreads his arms to indicate the house and grounds—"is like a sanctuary to me. Kind of like Bud's Hole. I can come here and just be who I am, and not have to answer for anything. It isn't that I don't love Maxine, because that isn't true. I do, and I will never leave her. But I need this island of serenity once in a while, Sweet And Precious White One."

"I get it," she says, "but I would like to meet Maxine sometime."

"You'd like her," I say.

"Yeah," Frank agrees warmly, "you'd like her."

So we leave it at that.

Mary, the chef, is then summoned to come out to grill the steaks. It really is a beautiful evening for this. The sky is getting darker and darker, and all of the stars are coming out. I can smell the orange blossoms on Gigi's trees nearby and—here comes Bill Mitchkelly!

"Are you alright Gigi?" He is focused solely on Gigi, oblivious to Frank and me. "I would have called, but I don't have your number. I did call Bill Hunter from the museum, though."

"Thank you, Mitchkelly. I'm good," she says warmly.

"Boy, that scared me at the museum," he says, shaking his head at the memory.

"Scared me too," Gigi says. "But I'm okay."

"Maybe you have hypoglycemia," Mitchkelly suggests.

"No. Cancer," she says matter-of-factly.

"What!" Bill's eyes go wide.

"I've got cancer. But the Doc's going to work on me in a couple of days, and all will be well."

"I'm sorry." His expression shows that his words are genuine. "At least you have DH to watch over you. He'll make sure you get everything you need." He gives Gigi's shoulder a gentle squeeze.

She looks at me and gives me a smile that makes my heart stop. "I know that," she says.

I've got one of those Catholic holy cards at home with St. Therese, The Little Flower. The picture was taken just before she died. Gigi has that same smile on her face and look in her eyes.

Those doe-eyes grow even bigger, so I take her in my arms and kiss her. I don't care who's watching.

"So, DH," Frank asks, "you gonna marry this girl or what?"

"I am," I declare, as I smile into Gigi's eyes.

Gigi starts to cry. She says she has to take a pee, but I know she just said that to hide the fact that she's crying. She heads off into the house.

"Not exactly the reaction I expected," Frank says.

"I'm worried about her," I say. "I know she's tough, but I also know she's worried about the cancer thing."

"Who wouldn't be?" Mitchkelly adds.

"I don't know what to do," I say.

"You can't do anything," Frank says, almost sternly. "You just have to give her all of the support you can."

And here comes Bill Hunter, almost at a run, blue shirt hanging out on one side. The ever-present smile is on his face, but his eyes show deep concern.

"What is this," exclaims Frank, "Grand Central Station?"

"Bill!" I call out in greeting. One of the goons is leading him over, but not in handcuffs. The goons love Bill.

"Just in time for the barbecue," Frank says, adding sarcastically, "So much for no party."

"Where is the child?" Bill asks. He is as close to agitated as I've ever seen him. "Where is the child?" He's trying to tuck his shirt in and talk at the same time.

"She's in the house, pottying," I tell him.

"Is she okay? Mitchkelly told me she was sick."

"She's sick, Bill." Nobody dares talk over me now. "She has cancer." I feel tears welling up in my eyes, and I see them in Bill's eyes and in everyone else's.

"Oh, DH ... oh, DH." He hugs me, and Frank has to get up and walk away. Mitchkelly buries his face in his hands.

Just then Gigi comes back out.

"Hunter! Ha!" She runs forward nearly knocking him over, and plants a big kiss on his nose. "I'm so glad to see you!"

"Oh Child," Bill's face is wet with tears. "Are you okay?"

"I'm okay, Hunter." She smiles and locks eyes with him in a steady gaze. "I'm real okay!"

Bill Hunter draws her back to him and holds her and says, "No you're not, Child. No you're not." And Gigi crumbles into his arms, sobbing.

"Bill, can you take her inside and talk with her? Please." Bill can offer the kind of fatherly comfort that I am not equipped for.

Bill leads Gigi back into the house.

"You know," Bill Mitchkelly says, "we need to think positive. Modern medicine has lots of good things about it. There may be a cure for this."

Frank has recovered himself and joins our conversation. "Yeah DH. I heard about a vegetarian restaurant and health food store that just opened up here in Riverside. It has all kinds of pills and stuff. Some of that might be good for Gigi."

"I'll try anything," I say. "Anything."

A shadow flickers across Frank's face. "You know Bud, you've gone through this thing before with—"

"—with Slim," I mutter as the memory comes back to me.

"You gotta steel yourself for whatever happens, Bud."

"Yes, DH," Bill Mitchkelly says. "We're hoping for the best, but ..."

I refuse to accept the alternatives. "Let's just do that guys. Let's just hope for the best."

Gigi and Bill Hunter return to the patio. One of the goons had come back about fifteen minutes ago with two jugs of Red Mountain from The Hole, so I have a glass of wine sitting here waiting for Gigi.

Frank greets her with, "Oh White One, the Red Mountain has arrived!" *The Laugh*.

Gigi responds with gusto, "Good!"

She takes Bill Hunter by the hand, leading him to sit in a lawn chair. She pours him a glass of wine, but he waves it off.

"I can't drink wine, Sweetie, I'm afraid I'm allergic to alcohol."

She offers it to Mitchkelly, who also declines. "I don't drink much, Gigi," he says. "Diabetic."

"Man," Gigi says, "both Bills are diabetic." She winks at me and says, "Remind me not to name our kids Bill." Then she takes a big gulp of Red Mountain.

She walks to the edge of the pool and stands there, looking into it. "Want to swim?" I ask.

"Thinkin' 'bout taking the long swim," she says.

"The long swim?" I think I know what she means.

"To China," she says.

I know exactly what she means. "Night of the Iguana!"

She turns to look at me. "You've seen it?"

"It's my favorite movie!"

"You're kidding. Mine too!"

"But if you want to take the same long swim that Burton tried to do in that movie, you'd better think twice," I say, earnestly. The long swim that Burton's character attempted was a suicidal swim out into the sea.

"Why?" she asks.

"Because the minute you jump into that pool, I'll be there to pull you out."

At that, she dives into the pool, clothes and all. Frank and the Bills come running, but I'm first into the water. Then I remember I can't swim!

But Gigi surfaces and takes hold of me to steady me as my feet find the bottom. Thankfully, we are in the shallow end. "Just wanted to see if you meant it," she said.

Frank and the Bills look relieved. Frank's shoes were off, and he'd thrown his wallet on the ground, and he was ready to dive in.

"Thanks guys," Gigi says, "but it's steak time. DH and I will be with you in a minute."

She swims to the side of the pool, pushes a button, and the pool lights go off.

Day 96: Three Weeks Later

Gigi died Sunday. The cancer was much worse than Dr. Visitor had thought. All the time we were hanging together, and carrying on, it was eating her alive from the inside. Apparently it had been doing that for quite some time. Chemo did nothing for her, except to make her sick to her stomach, and all her hair fall out. When she finally had to go into the hospital on Friday night, I was there with her, and I stayed with her till Sunday. She looked terrible Sunday afternoon when I woke up beside her, but she held on to me as tight as she could, and I would not have let her go for all the money in the world.

I sat with her like that into the evening, just watching her breathe and returning the slight pressure of her hand in mine. From time to time, she would open her eyes to look into mine, giving me a sweet smile as they closed again. Eventually, her eyes no longer opened, her breathing slowed, and her feeble grip relaxed. I pushed the button to summon the nurse, who then called in the doctor. They tried to gently pull me away from her, but I couldn't let go. Gigi died there in my arms. She died. She just died.

Gigi was lowered into the ground about an hour ago. Heidi, her only remaining family, was there, of course. She held onto my arm and stood by me like she really did miss her sister.

Frank, Manny, and the two Bills are still here at the cemetery. Jack is here, and he even brought Lisa. It's a sad time for everyone, but it's the most terrible moment of my life.

All of Gigi's goons were here for the main service, too, just standing on the sidelines, looking as despondent as I feel right now. One of them approached me and took my hand saying, "I'm Charles, Mr. DH, and life has changed in a big way for me today." The big guy started to cry. I hugged him and told him, "It's changed for me too, Charles."

There were dozens of people at the very private, unpublicized service. Many, I had never seen before, and some I had, on TV shows and in movies. No other relatives besides Heidi. I had asked Gigi once about her mother, and she told me she was an alcoholic living somewhere in Arizona. She had left her father for another man, and it didn't turn out so well for her.

I'm sitting on a bench under a big tree, writing in my journal. A man has just sat down next to me and put his hand on my shoulder.

"Gigi told me all about you, DH," he says. "You must be quite a guy for her to love you like she said she did." Rock Hudson smiled at me, and shook my hand. He hugged me hard, and then walked away.

Frank now occupies the space beside me on the bench.

"I've been sitting over there in Harvey, watching you, Bud. I just can't take it. I know you're dying inside, so I came over. I had to."

"Dying inside, and dying for real, are two different things," I tell him, looking at him through bleary eyes. "I wish I was dead right now."

"I know, Bud. But you have to face the real world." He looks at me knowingly. "This isn't the first time you've gone through this."

"Gigi is different from Slim, Frank. Slim was a moment in time. Gigi and I had some history going."

Frank smiled at the memory. "That you did." He paused again in reflection. "Man, we all loved her. What a sweet girl. And what a great talent! Gone from this world."

Bill Hunter has joined us. He has on a light blue sport coat, but his shirt is hanging out in front as usual, which makes me smile even though I feel like crying. I guess I'm cried out now any way. Frank and I make room for him on the bench. He sits next to me and puts his arm around me.

"Sweet DH," he says. "Oh my friend, that precious child has passed over." Tears are streaming down his face.

I hug him to me. "Bill, you are so special. Gigi loved you very much." That's all I can say.

Then Manny, Jack, and Bill Mitchkelly arrive. I think they all want to hug me at the same time, but I wave them off.

"You okay?" Bill Mitchkelly asks.

"No, I'm not okay." My eyes fill with tears. "I'm thinking about taking a swim."

"Not the Long Swim!" Manny surprises me.

"What do you know about the long swim?"

"It's from my favorite movie, *The Night of The Iguana*."

"You've got to be kidding." Yet another reference to the somewhat obscure film.

"I love Burton," Manny says.

"I didn't know that."

"What the heck is the long swim?" Frank asks.

"Suicide," Manny says calmly.

"My butt, DH!" Frank cries out. "You ain't gonna kill yourself cause I won't let you!"

Frank and Jack grab me, and together they drag me over to Harvey, and force me into the back seat. Frank gets in and drives me back to The Hole.

Twenty Minutes Later

"I wasn't really going to kill myself!" I yell as they drag me out of Harvey and take me inside.

"Not until we turned our backs," Frank declares. He has one hand on my left arm, and Jack is holding the right.

They bring me inside and sit me down on my bed. I must look like a lunatic; I'm squirming around like a frightened animal.

"Let me go!"

Just then, Manny and the two Bills arrive.

Bill Hunter addresses me in soothing tones. "DH," he says, "you have to get over this. That's what Gigi wants."

I know he means it. "I wanted to marry her," I say.

He sits down on the bed beside me and hugs me hard. "I know that, Sweet Child, but she's gone now. She wouldn't want you to be acting like this."

"I'm sorry, Bill. Grief is a terrible thing." I throw my arms up in an expression of surrender and they let me go.

"She's in a better place now," Frank says. I'm not sure what he means by that, but somehow I believe him.

"We can't just go off and leave him now," Manny says. "He really might take that long swim."

"There ain't no water here, Manny," Jack says.

"It don't take water to kill yourself."

"Guys," I say, "I'm not going to kill myself. I just want some time alone."

"That's what they all say before they shoot themselves in the head," Manny says.

"I don't even own a gun. Search the place." And Manny begins to do just that.

"I just want to go to sleep for a long time and think about Gigi."

"You guys all need to go," Frank says. "I'll stay with him for a bit." His face says he means it, so everyone leaves.

Minutes later I'm sitting here on my bed, and Frank is in the chair by my plywood desk.

"Listen Bud," — Frank is serious — "I know this is the worst thing you've ever gone through. It's killing me." He wipes a tear from his eye. "The White One is gone, but I know darned well she wouldn't want you to mope around like this."

"I'm not moping, Frank. I'm mourning. I just can't take it any longer."

"Baloney, DH! Write her a poem or something, but get this out of your system."

"I wrote a poem on Sunday."

Frank goes quiet, looking at anything but me.

"About fifteen minutes before Gigi died," I tell him. "I wrote a poem."

Frank looks at me again with tears in his eyes. "You remember what you wrote?"

"It's in my wallet." I pull out my wallet, and the piece of paper that is Gigi's poem falls to the floor. I just stare at it. Frank reaches down and picks it up.

"Can I read it?"

"You're gonna have to," I say, "because I can't."

Frank begins to read:

> *I don't want anybody else's poetry coming through.*
> *No dead guys or tired old college profs.*
> *This is the real stuff.*
> *The purest of the pure and even beyond that.*
> *The guts of life and the beauty*
> *The tenderness and the torture of the nothing*
> *That everything will become*
> *if my*
> *sweet*
> *white*
> *Gigi dies.*

"Hang on a minute Bud." Frank turns his back on me. He seems to be looking at some point beyond the door. "I can't take this," he continues, his voice quivering. "You must be going through hell." He pauses, gathering his thoughts. "You know," he says, "there's something wrong with this picture." He's looking directly at me now, his eyes intently focused. "Gigi was so damned young, and every one of us, you and the Bills and Jack and me, we should have gone before her." Frank shakes his head again.

"If only," I say.

"If only, my butt!" Frank gets up and fills a mug with Red Mountain.

"If only this sweet, white, pure, innocent one had lived," he says as he sits beside me on the bed. "She was a gift. What a talent! Such a sweet spirit." He sips more wine.

I hear a car driving up.

"Now what?" asks Frank, annoyed at the interruption.

"I don't know, I'll check."

A bright blue BMW is sitting in the front driveway. The door opens slowly, a leg slides out, and then the rest of the body, in one of the shortest skirts I've ever seen.

It's Heidi, the last person I want to see.

"It's Gigi's sister, Heidi," I announce to Frank.

"That Monroe chick?" The tone of his response carries feelings that match mine.

"The same."

"Want me to leave?" he asks.

"Not on your life! I don't want her in The Hole." I know that sets Frank up for a comeback joke, but I trust he's in no mood for frivolity right now.

"DH," Heidi calls to me. I go out to meet her halfway.

"Hey, Heidi."

"I just had to check on you," she says, a mask of concern on her face. "I think that's what Gigi would have wanted."

"You think so?" I'm not convinced.

She shakes her head. "Oh DH. I know you saw Gigi and me fight a few times, but it was all girlie sister stuff. We loved each other in our own way."

"That's not the impression I got, Heidi." I hear Frank come out the door. He's standing by the breezeway calmly lighting his pipe. I can smell the Latakia.

"You just didn't know us when we were growing up together. The whole house was always in an uproar because of what our family was—Hollywood people and other celebrities coming and going all the time."

"Gigi didn't like you, Heidi," I tell her straight up.

"No, she didn't like me. But she loved me as a sister. I know I wasn't the perfect sister to her. I was always the 'loose one' as my dad used to call me."

I look at her straight in the eyes. "Heidi, you and Gigi were light years apart. You got involved in all the fame and the glamour that surrounded your family. You lived your life like a celebrity. Gigi did art."

"Ort," I hear loudly from behind me. Heidi throws a stabbing look at Frank.

Ignoring him, I continue. "Gigi cussed like a sailor, and she could drink me under the table, but she had the heart of an innocent child. I don't know how she kept that innocent heart living in the midst of a family like yours, but she did. It had to be your dad's genes running through her. I don't know where you got your genes Heidi, but you ain't Gigi by a long shot."

"Well." She makes a harrumphing noise through her nose, and walks back to her car.

She pauses to glare at me as she gets in. "All I can say, Mr. Artist, is that if Gigi left you anything in her will, I will contest it!" She gets into her car and peels out of my driveway, leaving a huge dust cloud behind. Frank starts applauding.

"What a witch,"— *The Laugh*—"but DH, you're a champ. Gigi's up there in heaven looking down on you right now, and she's gotta be sending you big time love for what you just did!"

"Heidi's a tramp," I say. "Gigi was tough, and danced to her own tune, but there's a difference." My jaw is clenched and I know I'm frowning.

"Indeed there is." He smiles and shakes my hand. "Indeed there is. But DH, that was good. Really, really good."

"So," I say, "let's go back in and have some wine."

"That's a good idea. I want to ask you about Gigi's will. This might be a promising thing for you."

He takes a puff of his pipe. "You know what's in the will?" he asks.

"I helped her write it," I say as we go back in.

"Oh yeah?"

"Oh yeah."

Back inside Frank refills his mug from the jug of Red Mountain. I pour one for myself. He sits down in his usual spot—my desk chair. Leaning back and looking regal as he always does, he says, "So tell me about Gigi's will, Bud. This has to be a good story." He smiles, hands behind his head, feet up on my bed, looking forward to the story

I begin. "The week before Gigi died, she came here. She was

in a very serious mood. I thought she was just worried about her cancer, but it wasn't that."

Frank smiles. "Ah, the will."

"As I walked her from her Jag to The Hole, I noticed that she had gotten even whiter, if that's possible. Her face was thinner, and she wobbled just a little as she walked toward the breezeway."

At that point, I open my journal and read from the pages I wrote on the day of Gigi's last visit:

> *"You okay, Pixie?" I asked her. She just hugged me tight as we went inside, saying something like, "Not to worry."*

Frank shakes his head, muttering, "I can't believe this girl. She has to be the strongest person I've ever known."

I continue to read:

> *We came in here and sat on the bed next to each other. "You want a glass of wine?" I asked her.*

> *"No, I don't think it will set well with me." She looked up and gave me a brief, wistful smile.*

> *"That's okay," I said. I looked down at her frail frame sitting next to me. "You look like a potato chip."*

> *She grinned. "I feel kind of like that."*

> *"Are you okay?" I asked.*

> *"No, Love,"—she looked away—"I'm not okay. I had another test today, and they told me the cancer is doing a blitzkrieg in my body, and I don't have much time left." But she wasn't crying.*

> *"Gigi,"—my heart was pounding and my head was spinning—"they gotta be wrong. What about the chemo?"*

> *"DH, look at me in my eyes. It's too late for the chemo. I'm dying. One doctor told me I have less than a month, and I believe him, and that's why—"*

> *"No Gigi!" I cried. "No!"*

"—that's why I came over here. I need to talk to you about my will."

My mind rebelled at what she was saying and my body was reduced to a blubbering mess.

She continued. "I'm writing a will. My attorneys are on it right now, and I want to leave you everything I have."

As my tears started to fall, Gigi, this frail little potato chip, White Thing, hugged me to her. I was afraid she'd break something, like a rib or two, so I pushed her back a bit and said, "I don't want to be in your will, Gigi. Nothing you have is worth anything to me. The only inheritance I want are my memories of you and me."

"But DH," she pleaded. "Please."

"No Gigi. If I get any money out of your death I would never be able to spend it. Never."

"Then what am I going to do with all my money? I don't have any family left, except for Heidi, and she won't get a penny."

"Do you have a charity?"

"Not really."

"Then I have an idea." I smile, and I whisper in her ear. She starts to laugh.

"You're a genius, Love! Won't that just grab Heidi by the wig!" It was so good to hear her talk that way, even though I had a tear that was ready to fall.

"Don't cry, DH." Gigi pulled me even closer to her. "Everybody has to die. It's just my time."

But I didn't want it to be her time, I thought as I held her. She's too young to die and there are so many others out there who are just filling up space.

"So?" Frank's voice has brought me back to real time.

"So, what?" It takes me a minute to pull myself from my memories.

"Who gets all her money, you dolt?"

"I'll never tell anyone. It's our little secret."

"You're good, DH. You're very, very good." Frank is grinning, enjoying the bit of drama.

"But Gigi said she was going to leave me one thing, and there was nothing I could do to stop her. At that point, seeing how frail she was, and feeling how she was shaking, I couldn't turn her down."

Frank is sitting up and leaning forward on the edge of his seat. "What did she leave you?" he asks, almost whispering.

"Do you swear on a stack of bibles you won't tell anyone about this?"

"Yeah!" His eyes are wide.

"Because the reading of the will isn't until next week."

"I won't tell a living soul, Bud, I swear!"

I leaned in close to Frank, and I whispered in his ear.

"What? A friggin' toenail! The White One has millions, and you get her toenail?"

"I told her to clip off a toenail, and leave it to me in her will. I know it will drive Heidi crazy."

"So there's an ulterior motive." Frank wipes his brow in a gesture of exaggerated relief.

"A bit. But also, I want some of her here, with me."

"DH, you have ALL of her with you, Bud. I can even feel her presence in this room right now. She has to be here. This is one heck of a love story, Bud."

After a pause to reign in his emotions, Frank gathers his thoughts and continues. "Remember that king of England who gave up his throne for that American woman, Wallis Simpson? That little tale ain't got nothin' on this. She was one ugly broad. What was the matter with that guy? You had a reason to abdicate your throne! Gigi was—she IS—gorgeous. Beautiful and talented and with a heart of gold. I watched her with Bill Hunter. It was like he was a sort of substitute father figure for her, but she was sincere with him. She loved that old coot."

"And he loved her," I add.

Frank nods in agreement. "I know. Is he a sweet guy or what?"

"I think he's the sweetest man I've ever met. He came to see me after Gigi died. He didn't really say anything, just hemmed and hawed and stared down at his shoes for a while. He was really broken up. He had something special going with Gigi, like you say, some sort of daughter thing. But he came here, and he sat at the end of the bed for about ten minutes in total silence. Then he just said, 'I'm going to miss her.' We hugged and that was it. He took off."

"Hunter's a good guy," Frank says. "I think he's a revolutionary of sorts."

"What do you mean by that?"

"I mean the guy is way ahead of his time. He's a good teacher, and that poem he wrote on the butcher paper at Gigi's place that night reminded me of Corso, or Ginsberg, or even Kerouac."

"I thought the same thing. Kind of incoherent, but kind of brilliant too!" We both laugh.

"But I think his true place really is in the classroom," Frank continues. "If anyone should be teaching young folks how to 'do English' it should be Hunter. But the way he seemed to love Gigi, that was pretty sweet."

"Yes it was."

"Other than yourself DH, and maybe me a close second, I think Bill Hunter felt her death the most. That's a sign of a good guy."

"So now what, Frank? Where do we go from here?"

"I ain't worried about me, DH. Where do YOU go from here? That's the question. Are you okay?"

"I think so. But …"

"But what, Bud?"

"Frank,"—I'm not sure I have the words for this—"I think I've only loved three girls in my short life and they're all dead."

"Hold on, DH. That's just the way things are. You hardly knew Slim. Gigi must be one of the other two, and let me guess"—he puffs himself up and puts on his best Frank Reed face—"The Muse! That Annie-Ann thing!"

"She's not a thing, Frank. I still believe her to be my daughter."

"From another life. Riiiiiiight! Well, maybe now that Gigi is gone, God rest her soul, maybe now you can concentrate on your Muse, and figure out what's going on with all that."

"I don't know …"

"I guess that's kind of the statement of the year, DH. We don't know much about anything do we? We don't know where little Gigi went when she left us. I mean not really. We don't know what to do without her. We don't know who this Muse is that keeps popping up all over the place, including your dreams. We don't know if she's your daughter, or some babe that's out there stalking you, or if your imagination is creating things in your dream state."

"It is confusing. I'm not worried about Gigi. I think Bill Hunter is right; Gigi's in a better place. She's probably charming every one up there in Heaven right now."

"No doubt," agrees Frank.

"But you're right about my Muse. She could be anything or anyone."

"What if she really is a stalker, DH?"

"But I haven't seen her in a long time."

"Well duh! That's because you've been spending every waking moment with Gigi!"

I try to dismiss the topic with a wave of my hand. "Anyway, it's a moot point. If the Muse isn't my daughter from another time and another life, I'm not interested. Gigi is my one and only love."

"DH, DH, DH. You're only 19—excuse me, 20! If you think you're through with women at that young age, I got a bridge in Brooklyn to sell you."

"Well, at least let me get through my mourning stage."

"Take all the time you want, Pardner. Maybe this Muse person won't ever appear again."

"Maybe not," I say, not knowing if I want her to or not.

"So, Frank, what now?"

"What do you mean?"

"I mean, I don't want to stay here all day, and all evening by myself.

I'm afraid I'll drink myself to death."

"So let's do something!"

"I don't know what to do."

"Well, let's see. Maxine and the kids are at home, so it wouldn't be a good idea to go there right now. Why don't we call old Jack and see if he's free?"

"You think Lisa will ever let us back in their apartment?"

"But if Lisa ain't home …," Frank says with a wink.

"I'll call Jack."

Thirty Minutes Later

I called Jack. He is home, and Lisa is not. In fact, she is out of town for three days at some sort of meeting, and we have the place to ourselves. Frank and I are sitting on the couch, and Jack is putting a Donovan album on the stereo. I have no idea what we'll be doing here tonight. We haven't even discussed it. But I don't care as long as I'm with these guys. After the death of Gigi, I don't want to be alone.

As the soft, upbeat strains of "Jennifer, Juniper" begin to float from the speakers, Frank says to Jack, "What do you want to do? This is your pad, you make the choices." The tone of Frank's question to Jack sounds almost—do I dare say it?—friendly.

"I do have an idea."

"And?" Frank asks.

"We can't paint on the walls any more, cause when Lisa gets back she'll know we did, and I'll get killed."

"You're too young to die, Jack," Frank says sympathetically.

"Why don't we drink some wine and write a poem together," Jack says. "I have some paper, and I'll write it all down as we go. Frank, you can create the first line, then DH, then me. At the end of the night after we've consumed a couple of gallons of wine, we can read it all back and see how silly it is."

"You know," says Frank, "in a perverted kind of way, I like the idea." *The Laugh.*

I agree enthusiastically.

"So, Frank, speak the first line and I'll write it down."

"Okay, here it comes …" and Frank belches loudly.

"How can I write that?" Jack protests, but he writes the word "BELCH" in capital letters.

"I was hoping you would be more serious than that,".

"Alright," says Frank, giving in. "How about 'It is the best of times and it is the worst of times'?"

"Your turn, DH."

"The best because of the wine, and the worst because Gigi isn't here to do this with us."

The room goes silent, even Donovan.

Frank is the first to recover. "That kind of put a damper on the party."

"I'm sorry."

"I've got a better idea," Frank says, brightening. "Let's do a drawing of DH's Muse!"

"Very funny," I say.

"I'm not trying to be funny, I think it's a great idea. We've got three artists in the same room together, and we all have these amazing talents."

"And these big egos," Jack adds.

"But listen! This could be fun! Jack, don't you have a roll of paper around here somewhere?"

Frank has taken charge. "Go get it. We can divide it into three parts like a triptych, and we can each do our individual impressions of what DH's Muse MUST look like."

"Sounds good to me," Jack says, and he's off to the bedroom for the canvas.

"I'm not sure," I say, turning to Frank.

"Bud, this is therapy! Just get into it and go with the flow."

Jack comes back with a stretched canvas about eight feet long and five feet high.

"GAWD!" Frank exclaims. "You weren't kidding!"

"This is an odd size," I say.

"I stretched it myself today. I was gonna do a painting of the Goddess, Diana, on it."

"This is going to be better, Jack!" Frank is already up, grabbing a piece of charcoal from one of several that Jack has brought from the other room.

"Wait!" says Jack. He goes back to the other room, and comes out in a minute or two with an assortment of colored pencils and crayons. I love crayons.

Jack leans the canvas up against the wall near the kitchen.

"Just don't get any stuff on the wall!" Frank cautions.

"Lisa won't be back for two more days, thank the good Lord above!" Jack puts on an exaggerated display expressing his genuine relief.

"So," declares Frank, "Damn the torpedoes and full steam ahead!" He begins to draw lines on the canvas. "Okay guys. There are four boxes here, and you'll notice that the last box is a little bigger than the other three. I'll work in the first box, just because I'm me." He looks around and makes a mocking bow. "DH will work in the second box. Jack in the third. And this fourth box,"—he points to it—"that's the one we all work in together. We'll take the most outstanding parts of each one of our individual drawings, and we'll make them into a whole, and that's what DH's Muse looks like, whether she friggin' likes it or not!" *The Laugh.*

Leave it to Frank. A brilliant idea! This should be a fun night without Lisa prowling around.

He makes a formal gesture of handing me a piece of charcoal. "DH, since this is your Muse, you get to draw the first lines."

"This is such a large canvas I think we can all work at the same time," I suggest.

"Okay. Gentlemen, start your engines!"

With that, we each focus on our assigned portion of the canvas to bring forth an image of my Muse, Annie. I'm calling her that now, as I'm convinced that she is my own daughter, and that I've actually seen her in dreams. Tonight, I will try to accurately record how she appears to me.

Frank is sketching with charcoal. His mastery of technique and skill with all artistic media is evident in his deft handling of the humble black stick. It is an effort to pull my attention from the elegant dance of his hand across the canvas to work on my own rendering.

Jack's activity on the other side of me is a wild contrast to Frank's disciplined movement. He is attacking the canvas with an assortment of colored pencils, pausing at intervals to take a gulp of wine from the mug nearby. In spite of the apparent chaos, an intriguing figure is beginning to emerge. Abruptly, he puts down the pencils and heads for the kitchen.

"I'm going to make us a big pot of something to eat." Frank and I continue with our work.

There's a sense of freedom here tonight. With Lisa gone, we can do whatever we want. We are being very careful that we don't spill things, or get charcoal on the walls though. Gigi would have loved this. I can only hope that she's up there somewhere, watching the whole evening unfold. I know she is.

Jack calls from the kitchen, "DH! Would you come in here and chop up some mushrooms?"

"We ain't got all night!" I shout back to him. "I want to finish my portrait."

"We DO have all night," Jack yells back. "And tomorrow night too, if we want it."

This is turning into a kind of artist's camp out. I'm still feeling pretty beat emotionally after Gigi, but I think the energy of Frank and Jack will carry me through the evening.

Without losing focus on his drawing, Frank yells toward the kitchen. "Jack, I can only stay for about three hours or so, then I have to go home to the nest."

"I can have the spaghetti done in thirty minutes!"

Frank complains, "Him and his spaghetti. Is that all he knows how to cook?" But he's smiling, so that's a good thing.

"But it's gonna be really good spaghetti," I assure him.

"Yeah, but priorities," he says, exasperated. "Be quick about it. We got a whole lot of drawing to do."

In the Kitchen With Jack

While I chop mushrooms, I have a chance to talk to Jack about his shacking up with Lisa. Actually he was the one to bring it up. He's not a happy camper.

"Well, why do you stay with her?"

"I'm not sure."

"But there must be something to your relationship, or you wouldn't keep living with her."

"There was a physical attraction at first," he explained, "but now that I'm getting to know her better, I'm not sure I want to be with her much longer. Her physical stuff doesn't match her emotional stuff."

He's right. "I've seen that in action," I agree.

"She can be a holy terror, DH. I'm not sure how to handle it. She flies off the handle all the time. She slaps me and calls me every name in the book."

"Sounds like you need to take a hike, Jack. You can't live like that."

"She wants to marry me!"

"Don't go there, Buddy! That would be a big mistake. It's like Frank told me earlier, back at The Hole. He said 'DH, you're only nineteen!' You're a little older, but it's the same for you, Jack."

"I know, but right now I'm in no position to leave her. This is her apartment. I don't have a very good job, and I doubt that I could support myself."

"That's a tough thing. But you need to get something going so you don't have to put up with this for the rest of your life."

"No way, Jose! She's a gorgeous woman, but her fiery red hair matches that atomic temper of hers."

"Well, just protect your butt. There are millions of women out there." I smiled at him. My mushrooms were all cut up, so I told him, "The rest of the spaghetti is your deal. I gotta get back and see what Frank's been doing."

"Heaven only knows."

"Hey," I said, "I notice you and Frank are getting along pretty good these days."

"Yeah, just like long lost brothers."

I laughed. "Well, maybe not that good."

"I think old Frank is starting to appreciate me for my talents. I've always admired his. He has that pompous thing going on, but I finally realized that that isn't who he really is on the inside. He has to fake that arrogance in order to climb to the top of the art ladder. You and me DH, we ain't never gonna make it up there 'cause we don't do that. It suits Frank, though, and I respect him for it."

"So maybe we can help him get up there," I mused.

"I doubt it. Frank's kind of a one-man show in his own self, and in his own career. Besides I don't know anybody in the kind of circle he runs with."

"Neither do I. Guess I'll go back to work on the portrait now."

Jack turns his attention back to his pots. "The pasta will be ready soon."

Jack is in his element in the kitchen. To him, everything is art, even spaghetti. So I left him to go back to the canvas where Frank is working. For Frank, any and all art is serious business, even when we're just having fun. Frank had drawn a portrait in charcoal of what he thinks Annie looks like, and I swear, it looks like Da Vinci had drawn the thing!

I'm looking over Frank's shoulder as he applies the final touches.

"You're back." He's still concentrating. "You'd better get your rear in gear and finish your portrait, Bud, 'cause in just a minute we're gonna have to stop and eat that spaghetti."

"You don't like spaghetti?" I ask.

"I love it! But like I told you, there's a time and a place for everything. This is the time to do Ort!"

"You're right. But I can't control Jack, and I don't want to hurt his feelings."

"I know. You know, I'm just beginning to kind of like that guy, but I still have some issues with him. He's so unfocused with life. He starts something and he never finishes it. And that crazy Irish girl of his, that Lisa chick, needs to hit the road. She's a mess."

"We were just talking about that in the kitchen," I say. "Unfortunately, since this is her apartment, it's Jack that would have to hit the road."

"Ha! So he's turned his own relationship into a plate of personal spaghetti!"

Jack finally emerges from the kitchen. "The spaghetti is ready," he announces with an air of formality.

Frank and I give each other looks that convey the agreement that the easiest thing to do is to play along with Jack. With that, we put down our charcoal and allow him to usher us into the dining room, which he does with a flourish befitting the maître d' of a five-star restaurant. What we find in there is in accordance with the character Jack is playing.

The table is set perfectly, like an illustration from Emily Post, with what appears to be Lisa's best china and table linen. Two serving bowls—one for sauce, and one for pasta—sit atop the heavy lace tablecloth. A single candle burns in a candlestick placed between the bowls. Jack is trying to maintain his maître d' mask, but there is a twinkle in his eye as he watches Frank and me take in the scene.

Back in the Livingroom

The spaghetti was really good, even Frank liked it. But it's gone now. We're full as ticks, and we really need to finish the portraits before Frank has to leave.

I step back to see if my efforts with a brown crayon have given Annie's eyes the look that I remember from my dreams. "I wish you didn't have to leave so early, Frank."

"That's the way it is when you're married, Bud. And Jack, you might think of that before you jump off a cliff with Lisa."

"I'm not gonna jump off a cliff," Jack says. "I think I'm gonna leave her."

"Oh?" Frank and I both pause in our work to look at Jack.

"I'm kind of tired of the way she treats me. She doesn't even like art."

"What doesn't she like about it?" Frank asks.

"She says it's a useless pursuit."

"Ha! She's right! There aren't too many who make it to the top, Jack, and all the ones down there at the bottom have only two choices, stop painting or teach school."

"Is it a rule that bad artists always end up teaching school, Frank?" I ask.

"No. It has nothing to do with their skills, it has to do with their guts!" *The Laugh* "The artists who make it to the top give up everything in life. They do whatever it takes to get there. Period. End of friggin' story."

After a moment of reflection, Jack says, "Kind of a sad way of looking at it, Frank."

"Sad? My fanny! It's just the way it is. You either pull out all the stops and claw your way to the top, or you sit back and teach high school art, and knit doilies."

Frank is right. Look at Bill Mitchkelly. He's one of the most talented artists I know, but he just doesn't have the personality to do what has to be done — that is, step on people — to get to the top. He's a good man.

Bill Hunter is a good man, too. One of the most talented poets in the world, but he, too, doesn't have the kind of drive that Frank is talking about.

It takes an extra something — an extra callousness and the sacrifice of nearly everything else in your life — to make it happen. I think Frank has that. Honestly, sometimes it scares me. Sometimes I wonder about Frank's character, but I know he's just doing what he needs to do to be what he wants to be.

Frank moves in to look over my shoulder. "What are you drawing?

"This is Annie the way she appeared to me in a dream one night."

"I don't know about you and this Annie chick, DH. Just what kind of dreams are you having about her?" His tone is teasing, but he really wants to understand what's happening.

"I don't know if I can explain this or not, but I'll try." I close my eyes and describe the scene as I recall it. "She looks like she is about fifteen years old. She's wearing a plaid dress that comes down to her knees, and nothing more. She has a really beautiful face, but it is a serious face. She's standing on the edge of a cliff over looking the ocean. Below the cliffs are giant rocks. The surf is crashing against them. I can hear the roar and feel the vibrations as the waves pound the shore. Annie's arms are raised, her hands lifted to the sky. She is speaking. I can't make out the words, but the dark clouds above her seem to be responding to what she is saying." I open my eyes and return to the so-called real world.

"Okay," says Jack. "This is weird, but I like it."

Frank probes me for more. "So, what makes you think the clouds were obeying her?"

"Frank, I swear to you, whenever Annie waved her arms and said something to the sky, the clouds rumbled and shot out bolts of lightning. The lighting struck the ground all around her, but never came close to her body. I remember thinking in my dream, 'Are you doing all this, Sweetie?' And it was then that she looked directly into my eyes, smiled, and said, 'Join me, Daddy.' She reached a hand out to me, and I tried to say something back to her, but I couldn't form the words. I didn't know what to say. Then I woke up."

Frank looks at me, his face displaying wonder and incredulity. "Good grief, DH! That sounds more like a nightmare than a dream. I've seen movies like that!" He tries to laugh, but it doesn't quite come out.

"It wasn't a nightmare, Frank. It was a very moving dream. As powerful as she seemed standing there in that terrible storm, I could feel so much tenderness coming out of her. I mean, I really felt it! It was as if I was physically present on that cliff with her."

Jack appears to have become lost in my story. His face has grown slack, his lower jaw drooping. Suddenly, he blinks and shuts his mouth as if he has just woken up. "Wow!" he says. "That's better than any ghost story I ever heard!"

Frank, however, is firmly grounded in the "real" world. "DH, I'm not sure how to interpret your dreams, but I am sure of one thing, that I know how to paint! So let's tackle this canvas and see what comes up.

An Hour Later

We're each finished with our individual renderings, and now it's time to critique them and to extract from each drawing the most accurate features. I'm not sure how, but I think this will work. The image of the girl I have come to know as Annie has come into my mind a number of times in the last few months. In these images, the details of her appearance have been consistent, so I feel confident that I really can draw her likeness.

None of us have been watching the others work, so now we are going to step back about six feet and survey the result.

We are speechless as we absorb the impact of the three portraits side by side. If we just leave it as it is, we have one heck of a triptych. All three renditions are great. Each one is different, reflecting the style and character of each artist, but collectively they present a true picture of Annie as I know her. I have no idea what to do now.

Frank turns to me and breaks the silence. "You're the guy in the driver's seat. Whatta ya think? Can you pick out some features that might be your little Muse, Annie?"

"Yes I can, but look at this thing! It's incredible!"

Frank has created one of the most beautiful charcoal drawings I've ever seen. Jack has melded his colored pencil doodles into the form of a woman, complete with paisley clothes and a face that looks hauntingly like Gigi. My crayon drawing is the best rendering of Annie I've done yet, and yes, I included the drip from the corner of her mouth.

"I don't know where to start," I pause as I mentally dissect each image. "Frank, your drawing is beautiful, and although it doesn't look exactly like Annie it certainly captures her spirit. There is one feature that is perfect though, and that is the hair. It looks exactly like hers.

In every vision I have ever had of Annie she has appeared with a ponytail of light brown hair with red highlights. Frank has accented the charcoal with sanguine and terra conté to capture it perfectly.

I turn my attention to Jack's portion of the canvas. "That's quite a portrait, Jack. It looks like it should be made into a record album cover. Maybe The Beatles would buy it."

"Hey thanks!" He grins, pleased with my response.

I continue my assessment. "It certainly shows the playful side of Annie. It's pretty abstract, but the thing that tells me it's Annie, are the eyes. It's uncanny, really. She has very large hazel eyes that always seem to be holding a smile of some kind, and you nailed that, Jack."

While I spoke, Frank studied the drawings intently, comparing each one to the others. "Holy cow, DH. I can see in your drawing exactly what you're talking about. The hair I've drawn, and the eyes Jack has drawn are identical to the hair and eyes you've drawn." He looks at me, and then at Jack. *The Laugh.* "Is this *Twilight Zone* stuff, or what?"

He's right. They match up perfectly.

"Let's do this!" Frank says, sounding like a coach sending his players onto the field.

So we all start to work on the empty section that will contain the true portrait of Annie. It's a bit difficult to fit three working artists into a space only big enough for one, so we decide to take turns. Frank goes first, I go second, and Jack goes third. Frank is precise in every move he makes on the canvas, but he works slowly and steps back often to survey his progress. Jack works like a madman. Fortunately, he has only the eyes to paint, and he is being a little more careful with this part of the work.

Just as Frank is about to add a brush stroke to her lips, I find my voice. "Stop! Don't add one more mark! It's her!"

Frank looks at me. "Huh?"

"We're done. That's Annie."

We all step back to the opposite side of the room to look at our masterpiece. Jack is looking particularly thoughtful.

"What is it, Jack?" I ask.

"That's the new waitress at the Royal Scot!"

Frank laughs. "You've got to be kidding!" In a spooky voice he adds, "The plot thickens."

Jack is insistent." I swear it! She was hired the same day as Gigi's funeral. I know, 'cause I was so depressed that night I went there to get some coffee and do some drawing. She was the one that waited on me. She's really cute! I asked her what her name was, and she just smiled. Wouldn't tell me."

I can feel my hair prickling on the back of my neck. "Are you lying to me Jack?"

"No way," he protests. "She told me it was her first day on the job."

I pull my car keys from my pocket as I head toward the door. "I gotta go."

Frank is close behind me. "Where the heck are you goin'?" he asks.

"To the Royal Scot!"

"Bud, it's almost midnight! Who's to say she'll be working the late shift?"

I turn to face him. "It doesn't matter. If she isn't there, I can at least find out what her name is from one of the other waitresses."

"Don't forget, Norma still works there."

"I know that. I'll take my chances."

"You're a friggin' lunatic, DH," Frank says, looking me straight in the eye. "But you ain't goin' alone. I'm going with you."

"You still think I'll take the long swim?"

"I ain't gonna take that chance."

"Me neither!" says Jack. "I'm coming too."

"Oh, for cryin' out loud."

So we all pile into my VW and head on over to the Royal Scot. Frank is at the wheel, because my mind is traveling at light speed and I don't trust my own driving. When I asked him to drive he rolled his eyes and said with a laugh, "There is a God."

I have no idea what we'll find when we get there, but this is something that has to be done. The worst possibility is that Norma will be there—no telling what kind of a scene that might create—but I have to take the chance. I have to find out if Annie is real or if, as Frank says, some girl is stalking me.

That just might be the case. I go to the Royal Scot all the time, and if the stalker girl wanted to, she could get a job there to be near me. But that just doesn't make sense. Why the heck would any woman want to stalk me? But why all the appearances of all the girls that look like Annie? Why all the girls with that drip hanging from their lips?

I remember talking to Manny about this. He believes in reincarnation, other dimensions, and stuff like that. He told me that he thought Annie really is my daughter, and that she's just sending me signs through these other girls who look like her, and all those drip things off their lips are a part of it. I remember laughing at what he said, but now I'm seriously wondering if he might be right.

"Maybe Annie feels sorry for you because Gigi died and she's trying to set you up with somebody," Jack offers on our way to the Royal Scot.

I told Jack before we left The Hole earlier that day that I had started seeing Annie before I even met Gigi

"If Annie's on the other side, like up in Heaven, she may have anticipated that, and planned this whole thing out before you met Gigi," Jack explains.

"How in the heck can you come up with a word like 'anticipated' after drinking all that Red Mountain?" Frank asks Jack. "I just want to go home and go to bed. Maxine's gonna be ticked."

"Are you and Maxine fighting?" Jack asks.

"No comment," Frank replies. "But it ain't her fault, it's mine."

At the Royal Scot

Here we sit, in my favorite booth in the corner by the door by the big window. I love sitting here because I can watch what's going on both inside and on the outside. I'm a real people watcher. There's nothing more fascinating than the human species in all its varied forms and fashions.

So far, no Annie, but there are some real characters in here. One regular customer who never sits at a table, he always sits at the bar and orders only coffee. He's a dead ringer for Carl Sandburg, the poet, so that's what I call him, Carl. Carl has some really strange and unbelievable stories to tell. I think he's primarily just a bum off the street who comes in here to get warm. The waitresses give him coffee, he sits there on that bar stool, and he talks and talks, telling all his stories. He's over there right now, talking very loudly and waving his arms in the air, kind of like Frank does. He's telling a tall tale to a new waitress I've never seen before. She has red hair, and I think he called her Crystal.

"I rode with Pancho Villa. Down in Mexico when things were really bad." He drones on. "Billy The Kid was with me, too! He and I were best friends. I remember the day I heard Pat Garrett gunned down my friend, Billy. I was lost … just lost. I wanted to go out and hunt that lawman down, damn him!" Carl slumps over his coffee and looks distraught. Crystal puts her hand on his shoulder and her eyes show her sympathy for this pathetic man.

Then she looks up. Her eyes catch mine and she sees me watching her, so she grabs some menus and brings them over.

"Hi, I'm Crystal. You guys need menus?"

"Since it's so late, can we just sit here and sip coffee?" I ask. I smile at her and add, "I'm a big tipper."

Crystal returns the smile. "It's a slow night with a lot of kooks coming 'round. You can sit here as long as you want. I'll bring you that coffee."

"Crystal? You're new here aren't you?"

"Yep, three days ago."

"I haven't been here in a few days, but it seems like the Royal Scot has hired a lot of new waitresses."

"Just me," she says. "Oh, and that one other new girl."

"What's her name?"

"I'm not sure. Ann or Annie I think."

"No!"—this is getting to be too much for Frank—"You gotta be kidding me!"

Crystal looks alarmed at Frank's outburst, like she's going to call security.

"Don't mind him," I assure her. "He's the resident drama queen. Can I talk to you alone for a minute?"

Crystal gives Frank a dubious look, but shrugs her shoulders and says, "It's almost one a.m. and this place is deserted. You can probably talk to me for a long time. Follow me."

Crystal takes me back into the employee's bathroom, the same one that Norma and I have used before. She shuts the door behind us, and turns the lock.

She turns to face me. "Got somethin' to say?"

"Uh, yeah"—this is really awkward for me—"Does Norma still work here?"

"No," she replies. "There's no Norma working here. But waitresses come and waitresses go. You know?"

"That's good."

"Why? Did you have something going with this Norma?"

"Yeah, sort of … ."

"There ain't no 'sort of' with waitresses, honey. What's your name?"

"DH."

"Well, DH, I like that. It's so British to have initials for a name, and I love the Beatles."

She starts singing—"I want to hold your hand, yeahhhh"—and grabs my hand to pull me into a dance.

"I'm part British, but mostly Irish and some Norwegian, and a little Scots, oh yeah, some Italian and some Russian." I tell her as I undo the tangle she has drawn me into.

"Scots? You're kidding, I'm Scots!"

"What's your name?" I ask her.

"Crystal MacPherson."

"MacPherson? Really? That's one of my ancestral family names! The Parsons part of my ancestry goes back to the MacPherson Clan. My family's roots have been traced back to the 1100s, or so."

"So, you're part MacPherson. I'll be!" She steps back and puts a hand up to her mouth as she examines me in the light of this new knowledge.

Apparently, she is satisfied with what she sees, as she steps back to me, gives me a big hug, and kisses me on the cheek. She smells good.

"You smell good. What are you wearing?"

"Just Noxzema. That's all I ever wear."

"Noxema … nice scent." I clear my throat awkwardly.

"Uh … yeah"—she releases her hug and steps back a bit—"but you wanted to talk to me about something."

"I do, but I'm not sure how."

"Just tell me," she says with gentle encouragement.

The whole story of Annie comes pouring out—all the apparitions, and the dreams, and the questions—but when I'm done talking, Crystal appears to be unaffected.

"I haven't really met her yet, but the Annie who works here is about thirty years old," she tells me. "She can't be your Annie." She smiles, and when she does, I notice her teeth are very white.

"You aren't a smoker, are you, Crystal."

"Never have been. Why do you say that?"

"Because you have the whitest teeth I've ever seen."

"Just my genes, nothing more than that." And she flashes her brilliant teeth at me.

I bring my hand up to my chin, study her face again, and smile as I ask her, "What do you do? I mean, besides this job, what else do you do?"

"I study art at RCC."

"Now I know you're puttin' me on."

"Why?"

"Because my entire world seems to be revolving around art right now. It's a long story, so don't even ask."

She looks at me like a cat playing with a mouse. "So, why is that?" she says.

"I told you not to ask."

"MacPherson's never do what they're told," she replies.

"When do you get off work? You could come out and meet my friends, they're all artists. Then maybe we can all hang together for awhile."

"With your friends?"

"It all depends on how this night goes"

"You caught me at just the right time. My vacation began yesterday."

"Yesterday?"

"That's when your Annie chick came to work. By hiring her it gave all the other waitresses several hours off. I now have three days that I can do anything I want." She smiles. "I came in today because another girl was sick and the boss begged me."

Back at the Table

Together, we return to the table where I introduce Crystal to Frank and Jack.

Frank stands up and shakes her hand, trying to make up for the bad impression he made at first. "Pleased to meet you," he says with his trademark charm.

Jack's greeting is a brief, "Hi."

"I think Crystal and I are going out for the evening. We have a lot of things to discuss."

Frank leans over and whispers in my ear, "DH, you're back in the chips. But you still have to take me back to my bike at Jack's place. Sorry."

"You guys all came together?" Crystal asks.

"Yeah, we came over in my VW. I guess I'll have to take them back to Jack's, then you and I can go back to my place.

"But what about little Miss Annie?" Frank asks.

I give him a sharp look. "False alarm," I tell him.

"What?" Jack tries to look innocent.

"The new waitress is at least thirty years old. Good eye, Jack."

I am disappointed by our trip to the Royal Scot, but maybe it wasn't entirely wasted. I did find a distant cousin of sorts that I didn't know I had, and she's an artist. If all of this stuff about Annie working things from the other side is true, Crystal just might be some sort of connection to it all. The coincidences and synchronicity are simply too much to ignore.

Back at Jack's Apartment

We got back to Jack's place quickly. Frank and Jack rode with me in my VW, and Crystal followed in her Dodge pickup. When everyone was out of the vehicles, I asked Crystal to come in for just a minute to see the drawings we guys had made. She smiled as she took my hand, and we all walked in together.

Upon entering the apartment, Crystal pauses, sniffing the air. "Hey, spaghetti!" She follows her nose to the kitchen and points to Jack's pot of leftovers on the stove. "That smells good!" That's when I notice the tattoo on her left arm. It's a complicated design that looks vaguely familiar.

"What's that tattoo on your arm?"

She gives me an odd, half knowing, half mischievous smile. "You don't like tattoos?"

"I'm just curious. I've never seen one like it."

Crystal steps to my side so I can see the design right side up. She pulls her Royal Scot sleeve up a bit higher, and I recognize the crest of the MacPherson clan. I know it well because I've painted it. The motto, Touch Not The Cat But A Glove, is written below the crest. I've never really understood what that means, and Crystal has added to the puzzle by including a question mark and the letter *D* below the motto.

I point to the mysterious addition. "What does this mean?"

"I had a dream once that I would meet a man who was also of the Clan MacPherson, and that his name would begin with the letter *D*."

"So that's why you've been so friendly tonight."

She cups my face in her hands and fixes me with a deep, penetrating gaze, then she pulls me to her and kisses me.

"That's why," she smiles. "But right now I gotta pee."

I lead her out of the kitchen toward the hallway and to the bathroom, passing by the big canvas in the living room.

She pauses to examine the multiple portraits. "Wow, that's good! I love it! Who is it?"

"It's a long story; you'd better pee first." I smile and direct her to the door at the end of the hall.

A couple of minutes later we return to the living room where Frank and Jack are waiting for us. Frank is grinning and Jack is playing with a piece of sculptor's wax, both are looking at us like they think they know what just happened. Even though we are innocent—for now—I manage to add to their amusement by looking guilty in spite of having done nothing.

We all gather in front of the drawing. After a few moments Crystal says, "Frank did the first one, DH did the second one, Jack did the third one, and then you all worked together on the last one." She turns to us with a smug smile.

"Huh," says Frank, "are you a friggin' psychic too? You're right on," I think he's getting used to this sort of thing. Jack is not. He simply stands there, stupefied.

"My mother was fae, and so am I."

"What the heck does that mean?" asks Jack.

"*Fae* in Scotland is also called the second sight," she explains. "It's what we call being psychic here in America,"

This piques Frank's interest. "Are you from Scotland?" he asks. "I have some Scottish background I'd like to know more about."

"What's your last name?" she asks him.

"Reed."

"I've never heard a Scottish name like that before," she says.

"My father was Norwegian, my mother was Scots. I have no idea why my father's name is Reed. It doesn't sound Norwegian. Maybe, he had some skeletons in his closet that I don't know about, but I do have a slew of relatives in Norway," he explains.

"That's cool," She moves away from the group—apparently not interested in discussing Frank's genealogy—and begins to explore the rest of the living room as Jack continues on the topic of Frank's family history.

"I thought you were Canadian."

"You dodo head, Jack," says Frank, shaking his head.

Crystal wanders back into the kitchen where she dips a fork into the pot for a taste of Jack's cold spaghetti. Returning to the living room, she asks, "So who the heck is this girl you guys are all preoccupied with?"

There is a drop of spaghetti sauce clinging to Crystal's lip, ready to drip.

My heart skips a beat.

"Not again!" cries Frank. "This has to be a sign of something!"

"It's friggin' spooky," Jack adds.

Poor Crystal! She stands stock still and wide-eyed, startled by our reaction to her.

"Did I do something wrong?" she asks.

I draw her close to reassure her. "No, Dear. It's all part of the long story."

I smell the scent of her Noxzema, but I'm still thinking about Gigi, and the times we had, and the guilt starts up. I know it shouldn't be this way, but it is.

Crystal sees the conflict in my eyes. "Are you okay?" she asks.

This is going to take more time and privacy than we have here at Jack's place. "Can you and I go back to The Hole?"

"I beg your pardon?" she says, showing confusion at my response.

"It's where I live," I explain shyly. "When you see it you might not want to ever see me again."

"Let's go."

Thirty Minutes Later

We are back at my home in The Hole. I'm sitting on my bed, and Crystal MacPherson, the red headed waitress whom I have known for only a few hours, is standing in front of my plywood desk with her back toward me. She is asking me questions and talking about art.

She turns to me, smiling with delight and holding up a book for me to see. "I have this same book on Manzù!"

"You know him?" I ask.

"Oh yeah. When I was at UCLA I did some sculpture classes, and he was all the rage."

"You went to UCLA?" I guess I'm sort of stunned. "What are you doing taking classes at RCC?"

"I did go to UCLA," she explains. "I have an MFA in art from there. I majored in art history with a minor in painting. I'm taking classes at RCC because I don't have my own studio space, and I need a place to do art. Plus it's a fun place to hang out."

Another one! Another woman who does art. What is this, Synchronicity? Coincidence? Chance? Fate? All I can say is, "So, you paint?"

"I do." She smiles and looks around the tiny room. "You do too, don't you?"

She sits on the bed beside me holding the Manzù book in her hands. She opens it to a photo of a sculpture in bronze. The subject is a girl seated in a chair—the same one Jack is trying to copy.

"Isn't this an incredible work?" she says. "And what a beautiful girl. How would you like to be able to do something like that?"

Suddenly, my mind is filled with doubt and hesitation. Could Crystal be ... ? That comment about a seated, nude girl ....

"It is beautiful," I say, careful to give no inflection to the comment.

She continues, lost in her admiration of the image. "Her skin is perfect, and her face looks so real. It looks like she could get up out of that chair and walk across the room."

"That would be interesting," I agree, cautiously.

She sighs, "Just gorgeous."

I have to find out. "Crystal, can I ask you a personal question?"

"You aren't by any chance … I mean you talk about how pretty the Manzù girl is and …"

"Ha! You think I'm a lesbian!"

"Well … no … I was just …"

Crystal begins to laugh. She throws me on my back on the bed and says, "Let's just see."

Four a.m.

I'm on the bed with my back propped up against the wall and my legs stretched out in front of me. Crystal is lying next to me. We talked for a little while earlier, but then she fell asleep. I didn't know what to do, so I got up and sat in the chair at my desk until I got sleepy and decided to lie down next to her. It's a small bed, but there was room and she was out like a light — she still is. I tried to sleep, but I was much too aware of the pretty woman next to me, so I sat up. I've been sitting like this for a while now. I think she's waking up.

Her eyes show concern as she looks up at me. "DH, are you okay?"

I compose my face into what I hope is a reassuring smile. "Why shouldn't I be?"

"It's so early." Her voice is a sleepy whisper.

I lie to her and say, "I'm just getting up to go to the bathroom."

I stand up and decide, what the heck, I'll go relieve myself for real, and, since it's a clear night, I'll go out in the back yard and do it under the stars.

"Hang on, DH. I need to go, too."

She rises up and sits on the edge of the bed for a moment, wiping her eyes.

"I think I was asleep."

"You were."

"So did you have your way with me while I was out?"

"What do you mean?"

She casts a sly grin at me. "You know what I mean,"

"Uh … no."

"DH, do you like this bed?"

Where did that come from? "What do you mean, Crystal?"

"It's so small."

"It is a bit small," I smile at her as I head to the door. "But I really do need to go. I'll be right back."

"Me too!"

Together, we walk outside into my parent's enormous back yard. A patio paves the space between the house and the lawn where several large shade trees grace the mown grass. Beyond the border of ragged eucalyptus, a rugged hillside drops down into empty fields; about ten acres, in all

I guide Crystal out to the edge of the hillside.

"I come out here in the middle of the night because I don't want to disturb my parents in the main house," I explain. "My little bathroom doesn't work very well."

"What do you do, aim over the side of the hill?"

"Yep."

"That may easy for you, but if I try that I'll fall over the side and roll down to the bottom."

But she goes over to the edge of the drop off and does her thing anyway. Meanwhile, I turn my back and walk several feet away to do what I need to do.

"There's a full moon tonight, DH." Her voice is soft, but distinct in the still, predawn air.

The moonlight is bright over pastures and the hillside beyond the shadow of the trees. Even though the source is the cold moon, not the warm sun, and I can feel it shining down on us.

"It's quite a sight, isn't it?" I say.

"It's so romantic; the moon and the warm night air."

I am suddenly struck by the absurdity of the situation. There is Crystal, squatting behind a bush, and here am I, standing behind a tree. We are each doing as nature demands, out in nature, while casually commenting on the beauty and romance of the night.

"That moon is so big I think I can almost touch it." Her voice comes from the shadows with a dreamy tone.

"I can see your face clearly out here tonight," I say.

"You're peeking," she laughs.

"I can't help it, I finished first."

Crystal emerges from the shadows buttoning her pants. "Your parents aren't home are they?" she asks as she walks toward me.

"No, they've gone on a camping trip for about a week."

"Just didn't want them to peek out the window and see us piddling in their yard." She smiles and kisses me on the nose. "You seem a little distant at times, DH. Is it because of the Annie chick, or is it Gigi? I heard Frank talking about her at Jack's."

"Maybe a little of both, Crystal."

She averts her eyes as she considers her next words. "You know, you have to let that stuff go or you'll never be happy."

"That's what Frank told me."

"He's right," she says. "The whole world is going around, and things just happen. We can choose to be destroyed by them, or we can get over them and find new adventures and new loves."

"I know, Crystal. But sometimes I don't understand all this. What the heck is it that brings two people together and makes them fall in love, and then kills them off?"

"Just life, DH. Love has become cheap. People use the word 'love' like they use the word 'spinach'. It doesn't mean much any more, especially when you're young. Young people think they're in love when they're really just feeling their oats for the first time."

"I know all that. I also know that the love I had for Gigi was not a lust thing, it wasn't even a married thing. It was more like a brother-sister thing. I knew she wasn't the girl I'm really holding out for. There at the very end, I told Gigi I was going to marry her, but I only said that because I knew she was dying. I knew I never would marry her. I hope she'll forgive me for that."

"I'm sure she already has, DH. Just remember, you are still very young, and you are bound to meet many girls over the next few years. You will probably fall in love with them all simply because that's what the young do. But that's okay; experimentation is a big part of growing into maturity. The Gods must have built that into us I guess, else why is it such a big part of everyone?"

"You might be right."

"Can we sit down and watch the moon?" she asks.

"You'll get twigs and dirt and grass all over that Royal Scot uniform."

"I'm willing to live dangerously." She laughs and sits down on the ground.

The scene is nearly perfect, lacking only one thing. "Hang on, I'll be right back!"

"Where are you going?"

I hurry back to The Hole where I grab two cups and a new gallon jug of Red Mountain, and hustle back to Crystal as quick as I can.

"My hero!" she cries.

I pour wine for both of us, and sit down next to her on the dirt.

"I don't know about this. If I get a snake crawling up my pants I'm gonna be ticked at you. This is your idea."

She giggles, and then says something in a language that I don't recognize.

"What did you just say?" I check my cup and see that most of the wine is still there, so I'm not drunk.

"I just told you in Gaelic that I love being with you."

"You know Gaelic?" I ask.

"I speak it fluently." The moonlight glints off her white teeth as she puts on a boastful smile. "There are two languages of Scotland. One is the ancient Gaelic, which not many speak any more. The other is just common Scots talk, and some Americans think even that is hard to understand.

"Like what?" I'm fascinated.

"Like the phrase, 'bothy ballad'. A bothy is a hut in the Highlands that hikers, shepherds, fishermen, or who ever can use for shelter at night or in bad weather. The larger farms and estates had a building kind of like a barrack that was used to house the unmarried men who did the labor. Those were called bothies, too. During long nights, or in bad weather, the men would make up songs to entertain themselves. Those became known as bothy ballads."

"What did they sing about?"

"It was usually something very bawdy and naughty—you know how a bunch of men on their own can be." She starts to squirm, and then suddenly gets to her feet, shaking first one leg, then the other. "And right now, a typical Scots would say, 'I have a beastie crawling into me arse,' which I do!" I laugh as she reaches down the back of her pants to get rid of whatever it is.

"Wait till you get one!"

I laugh again as she continues her dance.

"Wheesht! Be quiet," she scolds.

"I'm not sweet enough to draw them in like you, Crystal."

"Ah, but you're sweet enough to tell me that."

"So, are you first or second generation Scots? You do have a slight accent." It's actually gotten stronger since she started explaining the language. "Did you get that from your parents?"

"Well, DH," she says, drawing the accent even thicker, "Ye kin be surprised tae learn 'at Ah wis born in Auld Reekie." Her face shows amusement at my blank stare. "Ye haven't a scooby whit that means hae ye!"

"A what?"

"A scooby. A clue. You haven't a clue," she explains, dropping back on the dialect. " And Auld Reekie is slang for Edinburgh.

"Back in the day, the air was filled with smoke. Everyone burned wood or coal at home for heating and cooking, and there were hundreds of factories that burned coal day in and day out. The place reeked of smoke. It was terrible, but there was nothing anyone could do at the time. It's just the way it was."

"What's you're birth date?" I ask, mostly just to say something, but I am a little curious.

"27 July, 1948."

Her answer raises the hair on the back of my neck, and I sit up straight.

"Hae ye got a beastie up yer crease, Hon?"

"I was born on July 26, 1948!" I tell her. I don't tell her that Gigi was born on the same day.

"Wow," she says seriously, "we're both Leos." Then she looks straight into my eyes and says, "Tha gaol agam ort."

"Same to you," I reply. I have no idea what she said.

"It means I love you."

I stand up, holding my hand down to her. "Get up. We're going to take a walk."

"But it's dark, and I don't have shoes on."

"You won't need them. I want to show you something."

I lead Crystal back to the patio and over to a blue lounge chair by the barbecue.

"You see that chair? Every time my parents have a barbecue, that's where the guest of honor sits. My dad is an aerospace engineer. He's working on something he calls 'The Shuttle Thing' that will take astronauts up into space one of these days."

Crystal's eyes grow wide. "You mean he's an astronomer?"

"No, he's an engineer. He designs things."

"Groovy!" That word sounds funny, as her Scots accent has gotten stronger with her excitement.

"My Dad is always bringing these aerospace guys home with him, and we sit out here and eat barbecued steaks. I haven't got a clue as to who some of them are, but I think a lot of them are really important. One guy named Carl has an odd way of talking. He's an astrophysicist and he tends to, draw out his words when he speaks, but he has great hair and a good sense of humor, I call him Uncle Carl. And, there are several air force guys and astronauts that are in training to go up in that shuttle thing, and they've all sat in that chair. But the point I'm trying to make is—"

"DH," Crystal butts in, "can we have a barbecue, and can I sit in that lounge chair?"

"You mean right now?"

"Why not? I know it's late, but your parents aren't home. I have some days off—"

"I don't have anything to barbecue," I protest.

"Can't you invite one of your friends and have them pick up some meat on the way over over?"

"Crystal, it's late … uh, early … and you have rocks clinging to your butt."

"Well, brush them off, and then go call somebody."

I know Jack is home, but Lisa is there, so he probably couldn't get away. Frank is home, and I think Maxine is there, so that probably wouldn't work, either, and rightly so. Who else can I call?

"Crystal, it's like five a.m.," I point out, while slowly brushing the rocks off her fanny.

"I don't wear a watch." She smiles and seats herself in the lounge chair that all my father's friends have sat in.

Troubling thoughts come into my head so quickly that I can hardly keep up with them. How long has Gigi been gone? When was her funeral? When did I meet Crystal? And even though Annie the waitress is over thirty, I'd still like to meet her, just to be certain. I have to figure this out.

"Well," says Crystal from her position on the lounge chair, "are you gonna call somebody?" She's stretched out now, her long legs slightly open, her large eyes sparkling in the moonlight. What was that word she used? Fae? As in faerie?

"I'm not sure who to call at this early hour. I've been running over some names in my head and—"

"Call them anyway. We can do a barbecue breakfast."

"Don't you have any friends?" I ask her.

"They bore me; they aren't artists. And some of them are guys that I would not want to be here."

I frown at her. "I don't want them here, either," I say.

"Not that kind of guy," she laughs. "They aren't romantic experiences. They're slugs that work at the Royal Scot, and wear pencil protectors in their pockets."

"Okay, I'll make a deal with you. I'll try to get two guys over here and you get two girls. If you can do that, we can do the breakfast thing."

"You're on. But all I can come up with are waitresses. That's my world right now."

"Good enough for me."

"You'd better not hit on any of them!"

"Why would I do that? My life is too confusing right now without getting involved with something like that."

"You're a mess," she teases. I kiss the top of her head, and she says, "I'm hungry. Are you committed to this barbecue or not?"

"I'm gonna try, but it's still early. I'm not sure who I can get on the phone."

"Me neither," she says. "Let's make it a game—I challenge you to get two of your friends over here, and I'll try to get two of mine. And somebody has to bring the meat." Lapsing back into heavy Scots she adds, "Noo gang aheid an' gie it a gang. That's 'go ahead and give it a go' for you."

So I wrack my brain again. No way on God's green earth will I get Frank out of bed. Jack and Lisa, same story. If I call Manny, it will wake his mother—who is gorgeous, I might add. I don't know what the Bills are doing. It's just so darned early.

"Crystal, can't we wait another hour or two? Everyone I can think of is still in bed."

"Where's your phone," she asks, heading through the door to the breezeway.

"In the kitchen."

"I'll make the first call. I don't care if I wake somebody." She takes my hand and pulls me through the breezeway and into the kitchen.

I point her to the phone on the wall and she dials up a number. I just watch.

"Did I get you out of bed?" she asks somebody on the other end of the line. "That's good. You have the day off right? Listen, my boyfriend and I"—she turns and winks at me—"are having a barbecue breakfast at his house and I wondered if you might like to come on over. … Great! I need one other girl. You got somebody in mind?"

After a minute or two of girl talk, giggling, and giving directions to my house, Crystal says, "Bring her." She hangs up the phone and turns to me. "It's your turn."

"You mean you have two girls coming over at this early hour?"

"They both work the night shift. It ain't so bad for either one of them." She kisses me on the nose.

"They're both waitresses at the Scot?"

"Yes, Karen hasn't been there long, about six months or so. You're gonna like her. She's very pretty but kind of rough around the edges. Got some sort of odd last name like it's Portuguese or something, but she's a regular American. Karen told me that your precious Annie is also available and she's going to bring her."

Even though I've been told she's the wrong Annie, my heart skips a beat.

"You're kidding!" I'm afraid I'm just a little excited.

She gives me a concerned look. "I'm not kidding. Karen and Annie will be here in about twenty minutes. So it's your turn."

I don't know who to call! Bill Mitchkelly is probably still in bed with his wife. Hmm, Bill Hunter? What the heck, I gotta do something.

I dial Bill Hunter's number and hold my breath. I don't know much about his private life, and I don't want to offend him.

"Hello?" His bright and cheery answer comes on the second ring.

"Bill?" I ask cautiously.

"This is DH isn't it?" I can hear his smile through the line. "I was just thinking about you."

"Yes, it is. I'm sorry if I woke you up."

"You didn't. I've been up for at least two hours. I'm going sailing today." Bill owns a sailboat that he keeps down at Oceanside. I've been out on it with him many times, fishing for bonito.

"Is everything okay, DH? Are you alright? Because I can come over there right this minute if—"

"Bill, I do want you to come over right this minute, but not because I'm not all right. I'm having a barbecue breakfast, and I would love it if you could be here."

"I'd be delighted! I'm not sailing till later this afternoon, so this will help pass the day. Is there anything I can bring?"

"Actually, if you could stop at the store and pick up the steaks, and maybe some beans or something, that would be great. It'll save me a trip. I'll pay you when you get here. I have plenty of charcoal and lighter fluid."

"I'm on my way. Did you invite Frank?"

"No, I thought he'd be in bed, and Maxine would get mad if I called."

"I remember Frank once saying that Maxine goes to work very early, so he might be able to make it. Wait about an hour and call him. It would be nice to have him there. I like that young man."

"You call him, Bill. I don't have the nerve."

"Okay, I'll see what I can do." The smile comes across again, and I hang up the phone.

Crystal looks at me expectantly. "So this guy is coming over?" she asks.

"Yep, he is."

"What's he like?"

"He's an English professor at RCC."

"Old? Young?"

"In between. No, scratch that. Bill Hunter is ageless. You just have to get to know him."

"Is he bringing anyone with him?"

"There might be a chance that Frank will be able to make it."

Crystal's brow wrinkles as she tries to match the name with her memory.

"Oh, that guy." The tone of her voice expresses reservation. "Guess I never really heard his name, but I don't know if I like him. He's a bit much for me."

"That's what they all say. Give him a chance, he grows on a person."

"We'll see. I'm a pretty good judge of character, but I can be wrong. I guess we ought to tidy up a bit, huh?"

"Probably a good idea."

"I have a change of clothes out in my car, do you care if I take a shower in your parents house?"

"Not a bad idea. I'm going to need one too. You can go first while I get some dishes and things together."

She looks at me with a glint of mischief in her eyes. "You're a shy guy, aren't you, DH."

"Why do you say that?

"Because you have a perfect opportunity to take a shower with a beautiful redhead and you're not going to take it." She smiles as she heads toward the bathroom. "Could you go out to my car and get the clothes off the back seat. Just bring them on into me; I'll leave the door open."

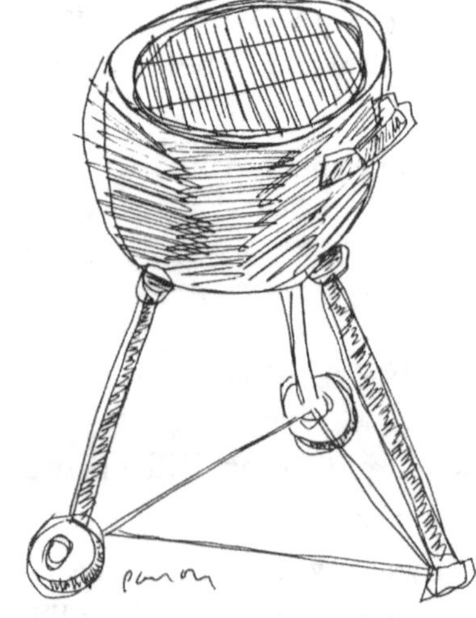

Day 97: My Muse Becomes Real?

We ended up showering together, and now we are back in The Hole, frantically dressing before our friends arrive. I'm watching her as she struggles to put her uniform back on. I couldn't find the clothes she said were in her car. Apparently she forgot to bring them.

Crystal is so different from Gigi. She seems to be just a regular girl with no pretensions and nothing to hide. No secrets. No famous people in her background. Just a waitress trying to make it on her own. A little rough around the edges, but I guess that comes with the waitress territory. I don't know anything about her except her Scottish ancestry. I wonder if she's ever been married. Does she have some snot-nosed little daughter waiting to be picked up at the babysitter? I doubt that, since she has these vacation days she plans on spending with me. It may get me into trouble, but I have to ask, "Have you been married before?"

"I'm married now," she answers matter-of-factly as she buttons up her shirt.

"I'm married to a doctor here in town, but we split up several months ago. I'm living on my own now."

"Okay."

She finishes with her buttons and turns all of her attention back to me. "Does that bother you?"

"I, uh … I don't know. I guess not. You have the right to dump your husband."

"It's complicated. The guy was sleeping with at least three other women, but he has all the cash now, and I'm trying to get some of it." She's straightening out her shirt when I notice two little bumps on her chest.

"Why are you smiling?"

"Because you've got a couple of things poking out there."

"I'm sorry. I also forgot to put on a bra when I got ready for work."

She has turned her back to me, and is attempting to put her pants on. The left leg is on up to her knee, and she is standing on that foot, trying to get the other foot into the right leg. She turns her head to look at me over her shoulder, loses her balance, and ends up on the floor.

"Are you okay?" I ask.

"No," she pouts, "I'm not okay." Then we both start laughing. She looks ridiculous sitting on the floor with her Royal Scot pants tangled around her legs. I reach down and give her a hand up.

She looks down at her clothes with disgust. "DH, I don't want to meet your friends in this stupid uniform. It's not who I really am. Besides, it smells like hamburgers and French fries."

"I might have something you can wear. It won't be fancy, but it's clean and it should fit."

"Anything is better than this."

I shuffle through the few items of suitable clothing that I have in the little closet. "A ha! Here's a pair of Levi shorts. I cut them off myself when I went to Laguna a few weeks ago."

Crystal eyes them doubtfully. "They're too big."

"We can make them work," I tell her.

"How?"

I pull my belt off and hand it to her. "Strap 'em up!" I tell her.

Still not convinced, she puts them on. "Good grief! These are really short! I'm going to be hanging out in the back!" She twists her body around in an effort to see behind her.

"Don't worry, I'll stand behind you all morning." Just then I hear a car pulling up in front.

Crystal looks ready to panic. "Someone's here already!"

"Hang on!" I tell her. I reach back into the closet, pull out a white t-shirt with a Beach Boys picture on it, and toss it to her.

"Put this on, quick. I'll see who just drove up."

Crystal catches the shirt, saying, "Stall them just for a minute. I'll be right there."

I rush out to find Frank sitting on his motorcycle. He takes off his helmet and gives me a sly grin. "Don't tell me. That Crystal chick is still here, huh?" He asks.

"She is," I reply, a bit shyly.

"Hunter called me. I have to drive to Costa Mesa today, so he was lucky to catch me."

"I hope you can stay for breakfast." I shake Frank's hand. He gets off his bike, hugs me, and looks me full in the face.

"You okay?" His eyes drill deep into mine like he means business.

"I'm okay."

"This Crystal babe might just be the ticket for you, Bud. She is gorgeous!"

"I'm not sure yet, Frank. There are so many unanswered questions."

Frank puts his hand on my shoulders, looks me in the eyes, and says, "The only unanswered question you have to worry about, is where the heck is my breakfast!" *The Laugh*.

Just as Frank laughs *The Laugh* that he laughs, Bill Hunter arrives, driving up very slowly. There is another car behind him that I haven't seen before. Must be Crystal's friends.

Frank and I watch in fascination as Bill Hunter pulls his car over to the side of the driveway like a snail on drugs, backing up, pulling forward, backing up again, pulling forward again.

"What's the deal with that?" Frank says, shaking his head. "He drives like an old man! Is that a Rambler?" Frank continues to watch with amusement as Bill gets the job done—a perfect example of parallel parking behind my dad's pickup.

The car behind him is a VW like mine, only bright red. I brace myself to jump out of the way as it comes to an abrupt halt beside us.

The driver's side doors open, and a leg emerges simultaneously from each car. The Rambler leg is short and clad in rumpled and baggy khakis; the VW leg is long, slim, and tightly encased in dark blue denim.

The rest of Bill follows his leg. As he walks toward Frank and me, that sweet smile of his lights up his face and just kind of melts my heart. Turning to me, Frank says, "Is this guy a saint, or what?"

Bill greets Frank first, using both hands to warmly grasp the one offered. "Frank, so nice to see you, my friend." Releasing Frank, he turns to me. He pulls me into a hug and asks, "DH, how are you Child?" With his hands still on my shoulders, he pushes me back to arm's length. Looking into my eyes, he says, "Are you really okay?"

"I'm fine, Bill," I say, returning his gaze. "I really am just fine." Another quick hug, a pat on the shoulder, and it's down to business.

Bill starts back toward the Rambler. "I have a lot of food here in my car."

I hear a loud, vocal, "Whoop!" come from the direction of the VW with the long leg. I turn to see what's going on, and discover two figures standing by the car. One of them — the owner of the leg — is a woman who appears to be about forty. She is dressed in a kind of Western outfit, complete with fringes and boots; the hat is in her hand. I'm assuming that's where the "Whoop" came from.

The other figure is much younger, more girl than woman, and — hang on here, this has to be Annie, or whatever her name is. I have to get closer. Oh my!

"You DH?" the cowgirl yells as the two girls walk toward me.

"That's me." I extend my hand for a handshake, but the cowgirl pushes it away and hugs me like a bear. I think she sprained one of my ribs. I can hear Frank laughing — just wait 'til it's his turn.

She pulls me in again, and while I am caught in her grip, I am able to get a good look at the other girl who is standing about five feet away. This has to be Annie, the one Jack told me about. My vision narrows and I see only her. She seems very shy and uncertain of why she is here. Her chestnut colored hair is pulled back in a ponytail. Her hazel eyes are large, and her mouth is … and the freckles on her nose are … . She is the image of my Muse, Annie! She notices my scrutiny and begins to blush, so I look away. Cowgirl lets me go.

Frank's voice brings my attention back to the here and now. "Hunter! You got the meat?"

Bill, who has been watching me closely, turns to Frank and says, "I have a cooler full of the best steaks in Riverside."

Frank reaches for the ice chest. "Then let's get this show on the road, Mr. Hunter!" he says with a grin.

While Bill and Frank head through the breezeway to the patio, Karen, Annie, and I get the rest of the food and barbecue out of the trunk. As we follow Frank and Bill, I notice that Karen is watching Frank with great interest. She's a big woman, at least six feet tall, with biceps that could curl a hundred pounds, and fists that could drive nails without a hammer. I'd hate to leave her a bad tip.

On the Patio

We are all on the patio now. Crystal finished dressing and came out to meet everyone there. She greeted her coworkers with hugs, and now she and Karen are conversing. Frank and Bill are standing by the grill. Frank appears to have taken over and is now lighting the charcoal while Bill watches. I can't tell what anyone is saying because everyone is talking at once—everyone, that is, except Annie. Although she is standing near Crystal and Karen, she is separated from them and the others in shy solitude. She seems content to merely observe.

The scene has taken on a sense of unreality. It's almost like watching the opening credits of an old movie. Each member of the company here shines with his or her own unique light. Gigi, while gone from this world is still present in my heart and mind. Then there is Frank, the wonderful artist whom I hope one day will be famous; Hunter, the English professor who has become like a second father to me; Crystal, the redheaded waitress goddess; Karen, the beautiful, gregarious cow woman, and the quiet, enigmatic Annie Creature, now seated on a lawn chair on the other side of the patio, sort of in this world but not of it.

I have to talk to this Royal Scot Annie. She has to be the key to everything in my life at this time. My need propels me across the patio.

"Is your name Annie?"

"Yes," she answered softly. The rest of the party fades away as she focuses her steady hazel gaze on me.

"You work at the Royal Scot with Crystal and Karen?"

"Just for the summer. I'm working my way through college."

She looks so much like the Muse Annie I've seen in my dreams and visions, but I know she can't be her, because if she was my daughter in a past life, how—

"Do you have any children?" she says, interrupting my thoughts.

I have to take a long breath. Why would she ask that just as I was thinking about my daughter, Annie?

I can feel beads of sweat forming on my forehead, but I smile as I answer. "Not in this life. Do you?" I know she's older than me. Crystal told me she's around thirty.

Annie continues to smile, but averts her eyes as she tells me, "I'm not married. I have no children."

The touch of a hand on my shoulder breaks the spell. I turn around, and there's Bill Hunter.

"I think Frank is doing a wonderful job with the grill. The coals should be ready soon." He turns to address Annie, and a small crease of concentration appears on his forehead between his smiling eyes. "Do I know you young lady?"

"I don't think so, sir," she says.

"You look so familiar to me," Bill says, still puzzled.

Frank calls from across the patio, "She looks familiar to me too!" He pauses as recognition sets in. "Hey Bill, did you see that triptych drawing DH and Jack and I did?"

"No."

"Remind me to show it to you some time." Frank winks at me while counting heads to put steaks on the grill.

Crystal joins us. "Hey kids!" she says, smiling. Turning to face Annie, she continues, "Annie, right?"

"Yes, Annie," Annie confirms.

"We've always had different shifts. I thought your name was Annie, but I wasn't sure."

"Well then ..." Crystal lets the thought drift away. Turning to me she says, "Can I tear you away from this for a minute?"

She takes my arm and pulls me behind the house. Away from

the others she asks, "Is this the Annie of your dreams?"

"No. It can't be. I mean, I don't think. She has some similar features but I don't think it's the same Annie, and she seems so frightened."

"A wall flower? And she doesn't have any boobs!"

I'm about to tell Crystal that her comment was kind of offensive, but just then we hear Frank call out, "Gonna be steak in about two minutes!"

"Creepers!" she says to me, "That guy is annoying."

"Hey, Crystal, this party was your idea." I'm beginning to get a little annoyed with her.

"I know," she admits, a touch of penitence in her voice.

"We need to go back to the patio," I tell her, as Cowgirl Karen appears from around the corner of the house.

"Howdy, you guys! Did I break in on something?"

"No," Crystal replies, affecting a smile.

"No," I agree, a bit relieved that she had interrupted us.

"If you guys are doing' somethin', let me know, and I'll just vamoose outta here." Karen smiles. She has a lovely smile.

Then, as if a gremlin has taken possession of my mouth I ask her, "Why are you so darned tall?"

Karen just laughs — she also has a lovely laugh — and tells us, "My parents are both over six feet. They were both basketball players." Then, looking right at me she adds, "And no, I aint gay! I like men." She winks at me and continues. "Most folks think because a girl's tall and plays basketball and likes livestock, she has to be gay, and I'm tellin' you that ain't the truth!"

Where have I seen her before? She looks so familiar to me.

"I didn't think you're gay, Karen, and that wouldn't bother me anyway." I protest. "You're a very lovely woman."

She returns my smile and says, "And you're a very lovely man." She winks at me again.

Crystal has been looking increasingly miffed

throughout this exchange. Karen turns to her and says, "Hold on to your saddle horn, honey. I ain't after your man. Just tryin' to make friends here. I kind of feel like I'm a bit out of place with all these intellectuals, and artists, and that sweet little professor back there on the patio. Ain't he somethin'?"

"You're not out of place," I tell her. "Everyone here is totally different. In fact, the waitresses outnumber the intellectuals."

Laughing, Karen asks, "So, who's the guy with the goofy hair?"

"That would be Frank Reed, honey," Crystal tells her. "I haven't figured him out yet, but DH swears to me he's okay."

"He's kinda cute." The look she gives him is one she might give a prize bull.

"He's married," I tell her.

"Well darn. But it's kind of cute the way he's over there trying to barbecue and be all manly and the like, and he don't really know what he's doin'. Then he goes over and sits in that lounge chair and starts yappin' an' wavin' his hands like he's throwin' ropes on doggies, and then he laughs really strange, and get's up again to put the steaks on, then back to the lounge and back to the steaks. It's like following a bouncing ball."

"Karen," I say, "it would take the combined intellect of several hundred rocket scientists, mathematicians, art historians, and cowgirls to figure out what Frank is all about. All I can tell you is that he's one heck of an artist, and he has perhaps the most brilliant mind of anyone I have ever met. Of course I'm only 20 and I haven't met that many yet."

"Honey, you are cute as button. Come over here!" Before I know it, she's locked me into another hug. Releasing the hug, but keeping one arm around my shoulders, she turns to face Crystal. "Crystal, honey, you'd better hang on to his reigns tight, or some filly's gonna come along and steal him away from you."

She winks playfully at Crystal, but Crystal looks kind of … mad? No — confused, I guess. I don't think she feels threatened by her, but Karen does make a person feel like they've just been passed over by a Texas tornado.

"Karen, where are you from?" I ask.

She grins and replies, "Texas! Is there any other state?" Her grin looks familiar.

"Well, you kids go back to your messin' around and whatnot. I'm gonna see how that beef's doin' over yonder. Ta-ta."

Crystal reacts with a momentary shudder. "Ugh. She's one hot tamale." She looks at me speculatively. "Surely you're not attracted to her, are you?"

"I don't think so, Crystal. She scares me just a little."

"Ha! Just a little?" Crystal laughs.

"She's like an Amazon," I add, "misplaced in an alternate time."

Shaking her head, Crystal says, "Maybe we ought to get back to the barbecue."

"We probably should," I agree as I look into her eyes. I have so many questions, but I keep them to myself for now. Placing my hands on her shoulders, I turn her around and guide her out in front of me.

"Let's go! You lead the way." She was right; those short shorts are way too short.

Back on the Patio

Frank is seated in the blue lounge chair, and Bill appears to have taken over as master steak cooker. Karen is sitting on a folding chair next to Frank, looking at him with googly eyes. Little Annie is sitting way over in the corner of the patio next to the door, as if she's planning her escape. She is so cute; she could be any man's daughter. It seems that it's just coincidence that she looks like mine.

Bill is smiling as he turns the steaks. They look like they are almost ready to eat, but he doesn't seem to care if any of them are rare or medium or well done.

"This is one glorious morning!" Frank says. "After I eat that big piece of meat Billie-boy is cooking over there, I'm going to take a drive over to Costa Mesa."

"Oh, yeah. What's that all about, anyway?" I ask.

"Can't give any details yet, but I'm gonna rent a condo or something, and spend most of my cash on a studio. I need to get closer to the art scene. Riverside is a dead end, DH. Art is happening in two places in America right now, LA. and New York. LA and New York are in competition with each other, and I swear that one day soon, the young LA artists are going to be recognized for who they are. Then some fat old turd will write a book about us!" *The Laugh*.

Karen, still making google eyes at Frank breaks in. "You're married, aren't you, Mr. Reed."

Frank, puzzled, looks at her and says, "I am."

"That's too bad, Mr. Reed." With a heavy sigh, Karen gets up and goes into the house.

Hey, wait a minute! This is my house. I don't want all these people roaming around in my parent's bedroom or whatever. Karen the cowgirl could be a freak, or a robber, or who knows what! I can't let her go through the place unattended, so I follow behind her. I look back at Crystal and she nods her okay. As I move quietly through the breezeway door, I see Karen slipping up the steps into the kitchen. I try to stay far enough behind her so she doesn't know I'm there. She creeps into the kitchen, and I come up the steps. She's on the phone. I stand and listen.

"Mom? Are you okay? You didn't look like you were feeling so hot last night. … I'm sorry. … Huh? It's me! Karen, I'm your daughter, Mom … sweet Lord …" Karen's voice is filled with pain. She drops the phone as she buries her face in her hands.

I cross the kitchen and pick up the phone and hand it to her. Tears are streaming from her eyes. I tell her softly, "Talk to your mom, Karen."

"Mom is beyond talking to. She doesn't even know who I am any more.

"I'm so sorry." I hold her gently as she breaks down sobbing.

Her weeping subsides and she steps away from me, trying to smile as she wipes the tears from her face. "I have to go. I have to make sure Mom doesn't walk off some place by herself. She's done it before. Thanks DH; you're a nice guy. If Crystal ever dumps you, give me a call." She turns to leave.

She pauses as I put my hand on her shoulder. "Wait a minute, Karen. What's wrong with your mom?"

"She's only fifty-five, but she's got some sort of disease that makes a person lose their memory. She don't have a clue about much of anything any more. It used to be better than this, but just last month she forgot who I was, and now she's getting angry at the smallest things."

"I'm so sorry." I truly am.

"It's okay DH." She smiles at me through her tears. "I think you're about as nice as that old professor guy out there."

"I don't think any one is as nice as Bill," I say. I look up at her — geez, she's tall — and say, "Well, keep in touch, Karen."

She looks down at me, cocking her head a little to one side like she's considering something. She turns and looks out the window for a second. Turning back to me, she says. "This is for bein' nice to me." She comes down to where my face is and gives me a kiss. With a smile she adds, "Don't tell Crystal I did that."

I smile back. "I won't."

In a heartbeat Karen is out the door, into her car, and down the driveway with a cloud of dust.

Oh no! I just remembered that Annie came with Karen. Now Annie is stranded here without a ride and the poor thing doesn't even know it. She'll be worried when I tell her.

Then I hear Frank calling to me from the patio, "Hey Bud! I think Hunter has those steaks pretty darned dead by now. They're gonna be like rubber!" *The Laugh*.

Back outside Crystal catches me first, asking, "Was she trying to steal something?"

"No, she made a call to her mother. Apparently her mother has some sort of illness that has affected her memory. She doesn't even know who Karen is anymore."

"Oh no," Crystal sighs. "That's so sad. I feel so sorry for her."

We go back to where Frank is sitting in the blue lounge chair, and we sit beside him on some metal chairs my grandfather had made.

I survey the group again. What an odd bunch of ducks. But where's Annie? I look everywhere. Where is she? I get up and walk all around the yard and don't see her anywhere, so I decide to get my pipe from where I left it in The Hole, and there on my bed sits Annie. She's reading my journal!

"Annie?"

Startled, she closes my journal and looks up at me, a combination of guilt and fear showing in her face.

"It's okay, Sweetie," I assure her. "You can read my stuff."

"I'm so sorry." She puts the journal down. "I was looking for the bathroom and I wandered into here."

She looks so sweet and innocent, and for some reason I want to bundle her up in my arms.

"Mr. Parsons, I'm so sorry. When I came in here I saw all these wonderful art books. I picked that black one up thinking it was—"

"It's okay." I repeat, smiling at her. "I started keeping a journal a couple of years ago. I let everybody read it." Then I just have to ask her, "Sweetie, are you okay?" I sit down beside her on the bed.

"I'm okay—I guess. I just feel out of place here."

"Ha! That's what another waitress said to me." I put my arm around her and hug her, telling her, "Like I told Karen, everybody here is an odd duck, but the waitresses outnumber the rest of us."

Annie smiles at that. Then she looks up at me and says, "I don't like being a waitress."

"Then why are you doing it?"

She sits up straight, determined and resolute. "Because I'm trying to make a point."

"What point?"

The words begin to spill out of her like water from broken dam. "For the longest time, I've felt that I am out of place here. By 'out of place' I mean I feel like I don't belong in this time, or even on this world. I have memories and dreams all the time about living a life hundreds of years ago, but I'm scared." She pauses to catch her breath. Suddenly, she stands up, and her expression turns to that of a frightened rabbit. Backing toward the door, she continues, "I'm so sorry I've violated your personal space. I didn't mean to. I'm just confused. I gotta go now." She turns and bolts toward the door.

"Sweetie!" I'm not sure why I keep calling her that, but it seems right somehow. She looks so young and vulnerable in spite of what Crystal told me of her age, and I still can't get the daughter-thing out of my mind.

She stops and I gently take her by the arm, pull her away from the door, and sit her back down on the bed.

"Sweetie," I begin, searching for the right words, "I don't know who the heck you are, but I do know you're very special to me." Then more to myself than to her I say, "I wish I could be honest with you."

"I have to have honesty right now," she responds in desparation..

She bolts for the door again. Once more I catch her and pull her back to the bed. As I turn her toward me, I see that her face is streaked with tears.

"What gives you the right to talk to me like this?" she sobs.

I've never seen anyone cry like this before. "Annie, I'm … you … I think you're my kid!"

I expect to hear some protest, but Annie doesn't say a word. Instead, the sobs stop and she looks into my eyes for an infinitely long minute, staring deeply. She starts to cry again, softly now as if from relief or release.

I put my arms around her, drawing her close to me. I feel such a connection to this girl; such love for Annie.

"My parents were killed in an automobile accident five years ago, but they weren't very nice to me while they were alive. They adopted me when I was a baby, and as I grew older they treated me like a servant. I don't know who my real parents are. My adopted parents left me some money in their will, so I really don't have to be a waitress. I can live very comfortably for the rest of my life." She looks at me again, studying my features this time. A small crease of concentration and puzzlement appears on her brow. "I don't know what's going on now," she continues, "but I do recognize you, Mr. Parsons. I feel like I've known you before, but I can't—"

"This is a bizarre world, with so much that can't be explained. I'm not sure what to say to you, really, but please stop calling me Mr. Parsons. You're ten years older than me!"

"Why do you say that?" She looks bewildered.

"Well, Crystal told me that you were about thirty."

Her face lights up with the first smile I have ever seen her produce. "I'm only nineteen! Why would Crystal tell you that?"

Annie giggles, then becomes serious again. "Do you believe in reincarnation?" The question surprises and puzzles me.

"What do you mean?"

"I had a dream once," she begins with hesitation. "There was a little cottage—somewhere in Massachusetts, I think—and I saw what I believe to be my real mother, or maybe grandmother, in some past incarnation. She was so beautiful with her black hair, and her sweet countenance. Then I felt a lot of pain, and I can't describe it really, and I think I turned it off at that point. But I remember a garden—"

"A garden!" I try to control myself. "I've had a similar dream!"

"You have?" Annie's eyes grow wide with excitement.

"There was a cute little cottage surrounded by woods, and there was a large garden in the back filled with vegetables and flowers. Lots of flowers. And there was a ring of trees. It was lovely, but when I tried to focus in on it during my dream, I woke up."

"Thirteen trees?" she asks tentatively.

"Yes! How did you know?"

"I think we had the same dream." She looks alarmed. "How can this be?"

"I can't imagine how it's possible that we could have an identical dream. I always thought dreams were stress release mechanisms for personal memories, or something like that. How can we have the exact same memory? In fact, I'm not even sure it's a memory. I've never been to a place like that. Let me look at you, Sweetie." I have to work to keep my voice calm. "Something is happening here and"—There's a hesitant knock at the door.

"Hey!" It's Frank. "The steaks are done," he says softly through the door.

"Come in, Frank." I know he's curious as a cat out there.

"I'm not interrupting anything, am I?" he says, opening the door just a crack. He looks at Annie, really seeing her for the first time, and turns white. "Dang! You look like our drawing! No way!" He looks like he's seen a ghost.

"What drawing is that?" Annie asks.

"We'll be out in a minute, Frank." I smile at him, and he turns away apologetically, like a puppy with his tail tucked between his legs, peering back through the door crack three times before we lose him.

"Annie, Sweetie …" I begin.

I relate the whole story, telling her about my Muse, about the dreams I've had of my daughter, and about nearly everything except the one final detail. I didn't tell her about the drip on the lip.

"But, how can you be my father, if we're the same age?" she asks.

"It must be that reincarnation stuff."

To my surprise and relief, Annie seems to be taking this seriously. Locking me with her gaze, she says, "So, what do we do now?"

"I don't have a clue," I reply. "We're the same age, yet I could be your father. Ha! Figure that out Einstein."

"That's cute, Daddy." Her words prick something inside me and my eyes feel the sudden sting of tears.

"Are you okay?" she asks.

"Yes." I wipe my eyes. "I don't know why I'm doing this."

"It has to be something in the past DH." She looks at the floor. "I'm sorry, but I don't feel comfortable calling you DH. I feel like I should be calling you Daddy." Tears drop from her eyes.

My journal is so filled with people crying. Frank cries, the Bills cry, I cry, now here's Annie crying. I sometimes think the theme of my life must be nothing more than a great big sob story.

I hug her as tight as I can. "Annie, I have no idea what's going on here, but I know that I love you, and it feels more like the love a father would have for a daughter, and I'm just a kid, and I know this is weird, and I know I'm rambling, but this is the strangest moment I have ever experienced in my life. I don't know what to do with it."

Annie pulls even closer to me. The tears are falling from her eyes onto my lap. I feel like I'm playing a part in a movie at the Stage One Theater, or a character in some sort of Gothic romance novel, but I'm not. It's real life.

"I love you, Daddy," she says.

"I love you too, Cupcake." Where did that come from? Cupcake! I've never called anyone that before.

Can this be true? Can Annie be my reincarnated daughter? But what does that mean? Why would that be? How is that possible?

"Annie, I'm as boggled as you are, but for some reason I do know that you and I will be bonded together forever. Let's give it some time. We'll go back out to the patio and see what's going on, and let the festivities out there bring us back to reality. Maybe it'll all clear up on it's own."

Just then, Crystal opens the door. She gives us each in turn a long, inquisitive look. "Are you two going to eat some steak?"

Frank appears behind her. Putting a hand on her shoulder, he says gently, "Crystal, honey, this ain't a love affair, this is a daddy thing. Come with me and I'll fill you in on some stuff."

As Frank leads Crystal away, Annie looks up at me. Her eyes fill with tears again and, I swear, she looks younger now than when I first came in here! She looks like she's about 15 years old. I pick a t-shirt up off the floor and wipe her tears.

"Okay." She wipes the snot off her nose, and I take her hand in mine. I pull her up, and we go back out to the patio.

Frank is in the corner talking to Crystal, but I can't tell what he's saying. His arms are moving wildly, and Crystal is listening intently. Bill Hunter comes over to greet us. Smiling, he says, "DH—" He pauses as he looks at Annie. A flicker of puzzlement crosses his face, then his smile returns, broader than ever. "This child looks just like you, DH!" I turn to look at Annie. I'd not noticed it before, and Annie's eyes grow wide as she sees it, too.

"Daddy?" The word is barely audible, but Bill Hunter hears it.

"DH? This little one can't be your daughter, you're only twenty."

"It's a long story, Bill."

"She must be your daughter from a past life," Bill says. He may be kidding, but I'm not.

"I think so, Bill."

He studies me closely. "You're serious."

"Yes I am." I look at Annie. Seeing my determination reflected in her face—like father like daughter—I smile.

"But how is this possible?" Bill asks.

"He told you. It's a long story," she says with a smile that makes my heart melt.

Once again Frank comes to the rescue. "Come here Bill. I got one whopper of a tale to tell you. DH, get those steaks off the grill before they turn to ash!" *The Laugh*. Frank is loving this whole experience.

I see Crystal at the other end of the patio. I'm not sure what she's thinking, but she doesn't look happy. Here she comes.

"DH, can I talk to you for a minute?"

Crystal holds a big plate for me to load with the meat. Rather than look me directly in the eye, she examines the fragrant offering in her hands. "Frank told me about you and Annie. I just want you to know I understand and I don't feel threatened by her."

I smile and hug her to me with my free arm. "Thank you, Crystal. I don't understand what's really going on, but whatever it is, I have to ride it out."

She finally looks up at me. "I know you do. Just don't forget about me in the process."

I have no idea how to respond to her, so I just smile.

After a short pause, she says brightly, "Let's eat, I'm starved."

She sets the platter of steaks on the long table which is now filled with potato salad, beans, and who knows what. Bill has gone all out with this party. I yell over to him, "Nice job, Bill. Good grief! You must have bought an entire cow."

"It's on me, my friend," he replies with a twinkle in his eye.

"No," I protest, "I'll pay you for all this!"

"No DH. This celebration is for you." He does look like some sort of saint. "You've just lost the sweet little child, Gigi, that we all grew to love, and now you have this other child, Annie, on your hands. Frank told me the story of Annie and I believe him."

I look at Bill fondly and ask, "How is it that you always know exactly the right thing to say, at exactly the right moment, Bill?"

He smiles his crooked smile and I notice that his shirt is hanging out as he answers, "It's all about caring."

The whole gang is lining up, filling plates with steaks and beans and potato salad—a crazy menu for a breakfast. Frank, of course, is at the head of the line waving his arms and laughing. Annie hangs back, apart from the others. I catch her eye and motion her toward the table. As she steps forward to take a plate, she looks back at me as if I am the only thing holding her in this reality.

Just behind me, Crystal is concentrating on stacking her plate with two large hunks of steak, a heap of potato salad, and a pile of beans. There's nothing wrong with her appetite!

Ten Minutes Later

Our plates are full, and there is a lull in the conversation as we settle down to eat our fill. I glance over at Annie, and give her a reassuring smile when she looks back at me. I'm a little concerned about how she's dealing with this new relationship. I continue to watch her as she conveys a spoonful of beans to her mouth. In that moment, the rest of the world recedes from my awareness as a drop of the bean sauce escapes from the corner of her mouth, drips slowly down her precious lip, and lands on her shirt.

"Ooops!" she says, looking back at me with embarrassment.

Frank's face has gone pale and his eyes wide as if he has seen a ghost. He looks at me and shrugs his shoulders, but says nothing. To my right, Bill sits frozen with his fork halfway to his open mouth, his eyes like giant saucers. Frank apparently told him everything. Even Crystal has gone motionless and on alert. I go to Annie and wipe the sauce off her shirt. Then I take her by the arm and lead her back into The Hole.

"I love you Sweetie," I say, once we are there. Then I pull her to me as close as I can, and she melts into me.

There's a light knock on the door, followed by Frank's voice. "Hey Bud." He's smiling as he enters, but then he issues me a stern order. "I want you to step out for a few minutes. I want to talk to Annie." Annie and I exchange looks—her look is apprehensive and I try to make mine reassuring. I've learned to trust Frank, so I know he means to do something good here. I exit the room, leaving Frank inside, alone with Annie.

Ten Minutes Later

Crystal and I are seated next to each other when Frank and Annie return to the patio. They are both smiling, in fact, Annie is almost laughing. Crystal watches them closely while chewing absentmindedly on her steak.

I turn to speak to her. Her insecurity is painfully obvious, so I try to reassure her. "Crystal, I truly believe that Annie is my daughter from a past life, and there is absolutely nothing romantic happening here."

She glances away and says, "She's younger than me, and prettier too, DH. I'm afraid that with her around, I don't stand a chance with you."

I stand up and take her hand. "Come with me."

I lead her back into the house, down the hall, and into the

bathroom. Positioning Crystal in front of the mirror, I tell her, "Look at yourself. Look at your face!"

"It's just a plain Jane face, DH."

I persist. "You are very beautiful, Crystal. You need to lighten up. There is no sexual attraction between Annie and me. I truly believe she's my kid."

"So, what do we do, adopt her?"

"No. We have patience with her. Annie was already adopted once, and she lost those parents in a car crash."

"Wow. No wonder she's the way she is."

"She's a nineteen year old kid with some terrible heart aches. I think you and I might be able to help her. Just be her friend. You work with her at the Royal Scot. You could be a big influence in her life."

"I really thought she was … like … thirty, or something."

"She's only nineteen."

"I see that now. I don't know where I got the idea that she's older." In a lighter tone, she says, "So, how do we adopt a kid our own age?"

"I have no idea." Shaking my head, I add, "This thing is strange. I can't explain it."

Crystal hugs me to her and says, "I know, Hon. But I believe you. I really do." She pauses to consider for a moment, then says, "There's something kind of familiar about that little girl. I think she may be fae."

"Like you?" I ask.

"Like both of us."

"I'm not fae!"

"Oh yes you are, DH, as fae as fae can be," she sings, her Scots accent thickening. "And she is probably remembering past lives she has spent in connection with you."

"Lives? Like plural?"

"I think so," she says, seriously. Then a playful smile dances across her face. "It is quite possible that she really is, or has been your daughter, so be careful what you do with her."

"Good grief, that would be incest!"

"Just kidding," she says. "But this is going to make my job at the Royal Scot a bit more interesting, taking care of your kid."

Minutes later

When Crystal and I return to the patio, we find Frank holding court. He is giving a discourse on one of his favorite topics, Picasso. "…so this guy has a chateau in Aix-en-Provence, a villa on the Côte d'Azure, and a wife less than half his age"— *The Laugh*—"and all the money in the world! Don't get me wrong, I love the guy's work—heck, he invented cubism—but he hasn't done anything really original since World War Two. He just hangs out in his villa and churns out that ceramic arts and crafts stuff."

"But he's making a lot of money," Bill Hunter says.

"He sure is! But money ain't everything!" Frank retorts. "I mean, I want to make a lot of money too, but—"

I break in before he can go off again. "Tell them about the Art Spirit, Frank."

"The Kunstwollen!" He grins at me and winks. "You got it, Bud! Nobody outside the art world knows what that is."

"Is that German?" Bill asks.

"It is," Frank explains. "It literally translates as, 'Art Spirit,' but the concept is much more than that. It conveys the whole attitude of being an artist. You either have it or you don't. It's the act of living and breathing, of putting everything that you are into your work. We're not talking about the old ladies that gather in the shopping mall or the local bank to show off their flower paintings. We're talking about getting up in the morning and drinking oil paint instead of coffee, then all day long eating canvas and thinking about nothing else beyond the next groundbreaking show you're gonna have. That's the Art Spirit!"

Pleased with himself, Frank takes his plate full of steak and seats himself in the blue lounge chair, claiming it as if it is a throne and he has divine right. Around a mouthful of steak, he commands,

"DH, you tell 'em about Soutine!"

Before I can begin, Annie pipes up. "He's an artist. He painted the most intriguing landscape paintings ever." She smiles at me, pleased with herself. She seems to be gaining confidence. Crystal looks bemused. Frank raises his eyebrows.

Bill Hunter asks, "How do you know about such things, young one?"

"I saw an exhibit of his work in LA not too long ago." She pauses and looks straight at me before she continues. "I liked it so much that I saw it twice."

My head spins as I grasp the significance of her last statement. Annie could have been the Muse girl at LACMA. If that's true, she could have been all of the Muse sightings; I just didn't know who she was then! I can tell by the big grin on his face that Frank is thinking the same thing.

Crystal's voice breaks through the buzzing in my brain. "Frank told me about you seeing your Muse at LACMA. This is getting spooky. I didn't believe him at first, but it's starting to make sense. DH, this kid is your daughter. She has to be."

"I know, but what do I do about it? About her?"

There's the sound of a car pulling up out in front. Taking Annie by the hand, I go through the breezeway and out to the driveway. Crystal follows along. I'm surprised to find two cars out front; one is Jack's, and the other belongs to Karen. She's back.

Jack gets out first. "What's goin' on?" he asks.

"We're having a breakfast barbecue. I wanted to invite you, but I was afraid Lisa would be upset."

"No prob. Who's here?"

"Not too many. Frank, and Bill Hunter, Crystal, and Karen, over there in her car, and me, and Annie."

"Is this your new squeeze?" Jack asks, giving Annie an odd look.

"No, Jack."

Before I can explain, Annie blurts out, "I'm his daughter."

Jack looks at me, then at Annie, then at me again. "What the … ?"

"It's hard to explain," Annie and I say at the same time. We look at each other and smile.

Jack takes a closer, careful look at Annie. "Wait a minute," he says slowly. "This is your Muse." He is beaming now with wonder and excitement. "No way! You found her! Look at those eyes—I'd know them anywhere."

In spite of her likeness to the portrait, Jack is suspicious. "Nuh-uh!" Moving closer to Annie, he shakes his finger at her menacingly and tells her, "Look, little Missy, this is my friend, and if you're scammin' him you're gonna pay." He raises his right arm and flexes his bicep.

"No scam, Jack," I tell him. "This is a long story, too long to tell right now, but Annie is the genuine article."

Still skeptical, he asks, "Annie who? What's your full name?"

Annie is not intimidated. She stands up straight and boldly declares, "I was adopted. My adopted parents' name was Cunningham, but they told me my real name is Annie Katie MacPherson."

Her last statement sends another shock wave through my brain. Crystal, who is now standing next to me, looks stunned as well.

"Annie …" I can hardly speak.

She looks at me with worried eyes and says, "Daddy?"

We're all looking at her like she's some sort of angelic being that dropped in from another dimension.

"Annie, MacPherson is my family name, too."

Annie throws herself at me and grips me in a fierce hug. When she looks at me again, her face is wet with tears and she is shivering like a wet puppy. "It's true! You are my daddy!" Then, as she melts into me again, she says, "Ta gra agam ort, Daddy," and my world is suspended in that moment.

Standing near us, Crystal has heard the whole exchange. "What did you say, Annie?" Her eyes are wide with amazement.

"I said 'I love you'."

"In perfect Gaelic, Annie. Where did you learn that?"

"I've known it since I was born." Her expression turns suddenly from blissful to anxious. "Did I say something wrong?"

Frank and Bill have come out to see what is going on. Seeing

Annie's distress, Bill steps over to her and places his arm protectively around her shoulder. Looking at all of us he says, "Why are you all tormenting this little one?" Frowning, he draws her near to him. "Leave her alone. Can't you see that she's hurting?"

Frank leans close to Bill and quietly tells him, "It's ok, Bill. They need to work this out. Trust me, this is bigger than life." Frank leads Bill back through the breezeway to the patio.

Karen, who has been watching everything while leaning on her car, puts her long lanky frame into motion and approaches Annie and me.

"Annie, honey, are you okay?" she asks.

Annie turns and smiles at the sound of her friend's soft Texas drawl. "I'm fine, Karen."

"I got all the way home and I realized I'd left you behind!" Karen laughs. "Ain't that somethin'?"

"I didn't know you'd gone," Annie says.

"We've had a busy morning, Karen," I add.

"Well, is the food all gone?" Karen says as she starts for the breezeway. "I think I need something to pick me up a bit."

"There's plenty left," I tell her.

Stopping at the door, she turns back to us. "You kids gonna join the party?" she asks.

Jack answers, "Sure, honey," and walks her way. Karen holds the door open for him and gives him a long, appraising look as she follows him through. Crystal, Annie, and I look at each other, shake our heads, and smile.

On the Patio

I make an effort to get some conversation going. "So, Frank, you're off to Costa Mesa soon, huh?"

"Yeah. But I'm in no hurry. This lounge chair feels mighty good!" He leans his head back and his eyes half close in relaxation. So much for conversation.

Jack speaks up next. "You got any wine?"

Leave it to Jack! "Dumb question, Jack, I always have wine."

"It ain't no party without wine," he says.

"It was never meant to be a party," I tell him, "just a breakfast, but I have three gallons of Red Mountain in The Hole. Bill brought those."

"God surely loves that old guy!" Jack smiles at Bill. "I'll go get it, then the breakfast can become a party."

Jack is back in a minute and sets two gallons of Red Mountain on the long table. He fills one of the Styrofoam coffee cups with wine, and then returns to his chair next to Frank.

Karen lets out a whoop. "Yee-haw, Red Mountain! My favorite." She fills her own cup and drinks it down in one swallow, pours a second, then pulls up a chair by others and sits down.

Crystal leans close so the others can't hear. "I think this was a bad idea."

"Whatta ya mean?"

"Well, now that the wine has come out, and this is officially a party, we may never get rid of these guys." She smiles at me sardonically.

"Maybe we can turn it into something productive," I suggest.

"What do you mean?"

"Maybe we can do a group poem or a group drawing."

"That might be fun, I guess"—she pauses to consider the possibilities—"if you promise to take me somewhere every so often and kiss me.

I answer her with a smile on my face and a twinkle in my eye.

From the other side of me, Annie says with mock disapproval, "Are you forgetting that I'm still here?" She tries to frown, but she can't hide the smile.

Crystal laughs. "Get used to it kid."

I make my proposal. "Hey Frank! If I bring out some paper and some stuff to draw with, will you stay long enough to do a group thing?"

"Sure, but I might need a cup or two of that nasty red juice from that gallon jug over there. Costa Mesa can wait."

I take Crystal with me to the garage to get some art supplies.

Inside, she stops to take a long look around. "This is a cool garage," she says.

"Yeah, it has a lot of room. I keep my canvases up there in the rafters, and my paints, charcoal and whatever over there on those shelves."

"What's this?" she asks.

"Just a stool."

"Is this where you sit your naked models to paint them?"

"Sometimes." I look at her. "Would you like to be one of them?"

"I'd be honored!" She pulls the white t-shirt over her head and sits on the stool, positioning herself in what she must consider an artistic pose.

"Not now Crystal! We have a bunch of people out there, and some of them might walk in on us."

"DH?"

"What?"

"Would you go get me a cup of that Red Mountain and bring it back?"

"Okay, but put your shirt back on while I'm gone."

I go back to the patio and fill one of the large drinking cups with wine. Frank stops me as I head back to the garage.

"DH, just how much do you know about Crystal?"

"Quite a bit, actually."

"Is she a good thing, Bud? I want you to be careful. I'm really gettin' sick of these dames dyin' on you. There's gotta be some weird reason for that."

"Crystal's pretty healthy, Frank. I don't think she's gonna die on me."

"Well, don't take too long in there. Get the paper and charcoal out here pretty soon." He leans over and whispers in my ear, "I'm getting tired of talking English Lit with Bill over there. Rescue me! Please!"

I laugh and tell him, "I'll be back in ten minutes."

I get back to the garage and find that Crystal has pulled off her pants and is sitting on the stool totally naked. Good grief!

She smiles at me as I hand her the wine. "Well, what do you think?"

"Do you want my honest answer?"

"Of course."

"I think you need to put your clothes back on."

She laughs and downs about half of her wine. With a shake of her head she says, "Okay, party pooper, we'll do it your way." But she's not happy.

Crystal puts her clothes on, and I guide her back to the patio.

Everyone has a sheet of the white construction paper I brought out, along with various pencils, pens, crayons, et cetera. Conversation has all but stopped as my guests concentrate on filling the sheets laid out on the concrete, like so many kindergartners at arts-and-crafts time.

I'm surprised that Frank has stayed this long, but he's really having a blast. Right now he's working on a crayon portrait of Karen, who is sort of posing for him while trying to do her own drawing, a portrait of somebody else. Hang on—it looks like me! She looks up and winks at me. Great, that's all I need.

Jack is working on one of the most exquisite drawings I have ever seen. It looks like Botticelli's Birth of Venus, but with a contemporary twist.

Bill is writing poetry and embellishing it with little doodle drawings. He is actually cute! Being like this, out of his own classroom, he's like a little kid, only with a brain the size of Texas. I love the guy.

Even Annie is fully engaged in the activity. She is using crayons to create a lovely garden scene. I move closer to get a better look. It's the garden we have both seen in our dreams! Standing behind her to watch her work I can see that she's a natural born artist. Now she's starting to write words on her paper. I can't read what they say. Hang on—she's writing the words, *I am a Witch. I am a Witch. I am a Witch.* What the heck does that mean?

Becoming aware of my presence, she looks up over her shoulder at me. For a moment, I feel as if someone else is looking at me through her eyes. Just then somebody grabs my collar and pulls me back from the drawing. It's Karen.

"Everybody's talking about this Hole thing, and it seems like I'm the only one that ain't seen it, Cowboy." She smiles roguishly. "I want a tour."

Reluctantly, I break myself away from Annie's drawing. I don't really want to, but I also don't want Karen to have hurt feelings, so I pull myself away and motion for Karen to follow as I head toward the breezeway. We enter the garage and I usher her through and into the Hole.

As she straightens up and looks around her, her face lights up. "Art books! "I don't know much about art but I love color. I love paintings with reds and blues and yellows."

"I love color, too" I tell her, and I really do. Think red, yellow, and blue balloons, like Wonder Bread. I love primary colors.

"I'm gonna sit down on this here bed. You can stand there if you want, Cowboy, but you're gonna answer up to me for somethin'."

"What's that?"

"What on God's green Earth are you writing? You've always got that black book in your hand, scribbling away like a little kid in a coloring book."

Whew! Is that all she wants to know? "I started a journal a while back, and I can't seem to quit. Everybody teases me about it. Even Frank."

"Well don't let them tease you, DH. One day you might write a book and be famous."

"You're the second person to tell me that."

"So this art stuff." Karen reaches over to the desk. "What the heck is this?" She picks up my Soutine book. The one Gigi signed. The sacred one.

"There was an exhibit of his work at the LA Museum. I went to see it." I choke on the memories.

She starts flipping through the pages.

"Next to Frank, he's become my favorite artist," I tell her.

Karen starts to mime some of the paintings.

She pulls her hair back, positions her hands in her lap, and moves her mouth down to the left side. "'The Farm Girl'," she says.

She turns the pages to the portrait of Mari Lani. After studying it for a moment, she crosses her arms in front of her chest, half closes her eyes, and cocks her head to the right.

"You could be a stand up comic, Karen."

Flipping through a few more pages, she stops again. "Oh, here's my favorite." Lying back on the bed, she opens her mouth and rolls her eyes upward. "Moo," she says. "'Side of beef'."

I laugh. She really is very funny.

"So, DH," she says, sitting up, "if you were to describe me, in your capacity as an artist or a poet, what would you say?"

What would I say? I'm thinking of Veronica Lake here, only six inches taller.

"Go stand over in front of the closet, and I'll write my evaluation of you—a kind of word portrait."

She obediently goes to the closet, but instead of standing there as I asked, she peeks in. "Whatta you got in here?" Opening the door wider, she exclaims, "Holy cow, DH! You need a maid!"

"The messy closet is a part of who I am," I tell her. Now shut the door and turn around." She really is an Amazon!

She smiles at me with mock innocence and asks, "Now what? Do I just stand here?"

"Yes, you just stand there. I'll describe you in my journal, and then I'll let you read it.

Karen had told me earlier how tall she is. I think she said 6'4". She's thin as a rail, her legs are longer than any woman's legs should be, and she has on a really short skirt.

Her style is Texas cowgirl, and her frame is long, lean, and tall. And her face! She has a face that could launch the proverbial thousand ships. Her nose is long and elegant, her lips are straight out of Hollywood, and her eyes are large and wide open; kind and sweet. The whole package is topped by a waterfall of long, richly blonde hair flowing down her back. Botticelli's Venus has nothing on her. A bit intimidating, really.

I ask her to turn around.

"Are you still writing about me, or are you just gawking?" she asks.

"Both. Now shut up while I write. I'll let you read it when I'm done."

"Okay." She turns slowly, throwing me a wink over her shoulder.

I study her backside for a moment before deciding that I really don't have time for this right now. We really need to get back outside.

Sensing my stillness, Karen turns back to face me. "What's the matter? You're not writing."

"Nothing," I say as I close my journal and stand up. "We need to get back out to the party. I am the host, you know."

"You know, DH," she says, "after I left this little hoedown earlier and went back to my place, the first thing I did was get on one of my horses and ride for about an hour. That's when I remembered I'd left Annie here. I hopped in my car and came back without even changing my clothes, so I'm really sweaty and I think I might stink purty bad. Maybe I ought to go out and grab that little girl and get outta here."

"Nonsense," I tell her. "You smell just fine to me. And I doubt that Annie is ready to go just yet."

Standing next to me, Karen has to look down to meet my eyes. "You're short," she says, as if she has just now noticed.

"I guess I am. I'm only 5'10"."

Then she asks me, "How 'bout you and Crystal? How deep does that go?"

I tell her truthfully, "Karen, I'm only twenty, nothing is deep for me yet."

"Then what's keepin' me and you from hookin' up right here and now? Or will somebody walk in on us?"

"Oh boy," I mutter under my breath.

"Did I say something wrong?"

"No." I smile at her as I continue, "But Frank or Jack might come popping through that door any minute, or maybe even Crystal or Annie. That wouldn't be good."

She continues to press. "Are you in love with Crystal? I mean, for sure?"

"I'm not sure, Karen." Then I change the subject the way she did a minute ago. "You're tall."

At that moment there is a light tapping on the door, followed by a timid voice. "Daddy?"

"That's my daughter! Karen, go sit on the bed and look at some books." She looks at me like I'm crazy, but does as I asked.

"Trust me, I'll explain this all later."

I open the door and a warmth fills my chest when I see her. "Annie, Sweetie! Come in. I was just showing Karen some art books."

"Hi, Karen," Annie says.

"Is everything okay?" I ask her.

"I just missed you. Feeling out of place again." She glances shyly at Karen.

Karen smiles and says, "I think I'll go back out and eat another steak." I think she understands that I need to be alone with Annie.

"Talk to Frank about this," I whisper to her on her way out.

"Annie? Are you okay? What's the matter?"

"I don't know, I had this crazy thought," she says. "Maybe I'm not your daughter!" Tears are welling up in her eyes. "Maybe I was your lover in a past life! There! I've said it."

I hug her close, and bring her over to the bed where we sit side by side.

Suddenly, she grabs my face and kisses me — not like a daughter, but like a lover!

"Annie!" I pull away from her and stand up.

"I'm sorry!" She gets up and bolts for the door, but I catch her.

Bringing her close to me, I look into her eyes. "I'm as confused about all of this as you are. You know, if reincarnation is a fact, then we could have been all of the above. I could have been your father, your lover, and even your brother at different times throughout eternity."

"I'm so embarrassed." She cuddles closer to me. "But in this time"—she looks back up into my face—"in this time we're both young, and I've never met any other boy as wonderful as you."

"Don't you think we ought to give this some time?" I ask her. "Let it play out a bit."

"I can only go with my heart, and right now my heart is very confused," she says. "But I'll be good."

"I can't imagine you not being good." I smile at her and she smiles back. Then I say, "Let's go back out and see what's happening."

Annie and I walk back out to the patio. Everyone turns to look at us, but we ignore the attention. Jack is still working on his Venus drawing, and Frank is standing over him, moving his hand around and giving him suggestions I know Jack won't take. Bill Hunter is cleaning up the mess, putting all the paper plates in the trash and wrapping up the leftovers. Is this guy for real or what? Karen and Crystal are across the grass where the back yard drops off into the field behind. I'm wondering if Crystal is remembering what we did there when she turns to me and winks.

I feel a touch on my right shoulder. It's Frank.

"Hey Bud, can I talk to you for a minute? Somewhere a bit more private."

"Sure, let's go into The Hole" So here I am again, with Frank this time. He is sitting in his chair and I'm sitting on the bed.

"What's up?" I ask, as we both sip at our Styrofoam flavored wine. I've never seen him so subdued.

"This Costa Mesa thing … I gotta get out of Riverside. I'm not gonna go anywhere in the art world if I stay here, and I think UC Irvine might be interested in me for a teaching job, or at least some lectures."

"So, you're gonna move away huh?" I ask, not wanting to hear his answer.

"I'm gonna have to. If I stay here I'll just be spinning my artistic wheels. If I move to Costa Mesa, I can rent some studio space and be a little closer to the LA scene. Plus, the Irvine gig could give me a boost with the artsy-fartsy intellectual group."

"Well …" I begin with my usual stutter, "… to be honest, I hate the idea, but I also understand. But …"

"Hey Bud, it ain't that far to Costa Mesa! We can still visit!"

"I doubt I'll hear that motorcycle roar up in my driveway very often."

"I'll be pretty busy," he says, sensing my melancholy. "But my house will always be open to you. We're always gonna be buddies. No matter where you go, or where I go, we'll always keep in touch." He smiles again.

"I hope so, Frank." I smile back. "So is this it? Are you moving out right now?"

"No. I have some stuff to take care of first. Selling the house and all that, plus a few other loose ends. It'll be a good month before we move. I'm thinkin' November. I'm sure we'll have some more barbecues before I leave."

"Well, I'll sure miss you being around all the time."

Frank stands up and puts his hands on my shoulders. Looking me in the eye, he asks, "You gonna be okay? I mean really okay? I'm talkin' about everything. You've had some pretty major stuff hitting you from all angles here lately."

"Yeah, I'll be okay. I've got this Crystal thing going on, I guess, and then there's Annie. I don't know what the heck to do about her, but just the activity of worrying about it will keep me occupied and okay."

He shakes his head. "I still don't get this Annie thing, Bud, but it has to be real. There are too many coincidences, and too much synchronicity. There's no way on Earth that she ain't that Muse we drew!" *The Laugh.*

It's so good to hear him laugh. I wonder how many more times I'll hear that before he moves away.

"Hey! I'm not finished with my Ort out there on the patio! Whatta ya say we get back out there?"

"I'm game." I smile back at him, and we head for the door. As we leave The Hole, I make sure that Frank doesn't see me wiping still one more tear from my eye. These past few months have, indeed, been the roughest ride of my young life. It's got to get better.

On the Patio Again

This little breakfast barbecue idea that Crystal and I came up with has turned into an all day affair, but everybody is having a ball, so that's ok. Even Annie is drawing up a storm. I'm impressed with what she's doing. Her art seems to be primarily about the past. She's drawn the circle of the thirteen trees next to the old cottage from our dream, as well as some other stuff I can't figure out—looks like little fairies flying around a bunch of flowers.

Sweet Mr. Bill Hunter. I'm really surprised that he's stayed so long, but he seems to be enjoying himself as much, if not more than everyone else. He has several pieces of construction paper he's scribbled poems and little doodle things on. To be honest, it all looks pretty darned good. I even heard Frank tell him, "Man oh man, Hunter! You ought to frame those and have your own show!"

Karen keeps looking at me, and I keep looking back. I really don't know what to do with her. I'm just a kid. I don't want to make commitments with any girl or woman right now, but I also don't like doing what I've been doing over the past few months. I know I need to grow up, but I'm not sure I can just yet, 'cause I AM just a kid. I have some decisions to make with my life, especially now that I know Frank is leaving town. I also need to find that something that I know is out there somewhere, whatever it is.

Jack is on the far corner of the patio trying to make a kite out of the white construction paper.

Without looking up, he yells, "DH, you got any rags and string?"

"I do," I call back. My grandfather leaves some of his tools and things in the garage, and I know there's a large ball of strong string in one of his toolboxes. "I'll be right back"

I find the string in the garage, then I head into The Hole where I have a ton of old shirts I can tear up for rags. With the stuff in hand I race back out to the party. By now everyone is gathered around Jack and his kite. Look at that! It's his Venus drawing! He's taken his Venus drawing, and he's formed it into a kind of rough kite shape. How neat is that!

"I'm gonna need some scissors, DH." Jack says.

"Got 'em right here. I knew you'd need them."

Jack starts to snip and cut at the large piece of paper with the naked Venus. He slices up my old T-shirts, glues and binds everything all together, then he goes to the edge of the drop-off overlooking the field, where he gathers a few sticks that have fallen off the trees. In a few minutes he brings to completion one of the most beautiful kites I've ever seen.

"Nice," says Crystal, delightedly.

Jack looks pretty proud right now.

"Think it'll fly?" asks Frank.

"No," says Jack, "I KNOW it will fly."

Jack attaches an end from the ball of string to the kite. Turning to face us, he says, "Who wants to run with this baby?"

"I will!" It's Annie, clapping her hands and hopping with eagerness, just like a little girl. That's my kid. I guess. I think.

"You'll have to take it down to the field over there," I say, "so you have some running space."

"How do we get down there?" Jack asks.

"There's a path over here. Come on guys! Bring your wine."

We all head over to the west end of the gully. Frank, Crystal, and I stay at the top of the hill and watch while Jack, carrying his kite and beaming like a six year old kid, leads the others down the path to the field below.

Jack hands the kite to Annie and she looks up at me with a smile on her face. I nod to say, "Go ahead, Sweetie." She turns away, holding the kite like a person should hold a kite to launch it.

Frank yells out, "Go Little Muse!"

She grins at him, and calls back, "Okay, Uncle Frank!" then she takes off across the field, running for all she's worth, sending

Jack's kite up into the sky.

"That's my friggin' niece!" Frank yells out, and he really means it.

Look at that, it's working! There it is, the naked Goddess of Love looking down on all of us from her place up there in Heaven, soaring like a bird in the sky, the long string of rags floating gracefully behind. I look at Annie's face, lit up with the morning sun, and she looks just like a little angel. A little Angelic Being that knows nothing more than innocence.

Frank, shielding his eyes from the sun watches the kite rise. "Holy moly, look at that thing fly!"

Jack beams with pleasure at his achievement. "Hot dang!" he exclaims as he lights up a Delicado.

"I am astounded," Bill says quietly. "I honestly never thought Jack would ever get it off the ground."

"Give Jack a few glasses of wine, and he can get a hippo off the ground," Frank laughs.

"Excuse me," I say. "Annie is the one that actually got the kite off the ground."

Crystal slips her arm around my waist while we watch the kite. "It's beautiful," she says. "And look at our … little girl. Aren't we proud?"

I'm a little disturbed by the tone she used for that last statement. "Are you being sarcastic?" I ask.

"No, I just don't know what to do about her. Do we send her to college with little brown lunch bags or what?"

I give her a look of disapproval combined with doubt. "You are being sarcastic."

"How else can I be?" she asks, stepping away from me. "Look at her over there!"

I look, and I see Annie laughing and running as if she hasn't a care in the world.

"She's a kid," Crystal continues. "I've been thinking this over, DH. Something's wrong with this picture. Annie may not be who she's pretending to be. Can't you hire a PI or somebody to check her out?"

"Why would she be scamming me?" I ask. "I'm just a kid, I have nothing to be scammed. Besides, what about all the coincidences?"

"I don't know, but until this resolves itself I think I'm outta here." She just walks away, my doubts turning to disappointment as I watch her go.

Frank, who has seen the whole exchange, gives me a concerned look. I shake my head, smile, and give him an OK sign, so he turns back to watch Annie run with the kite. But he keeps glancing back at me.

I'm feeling beat, so I sit down on the ground. Frank comes over and sits beside me." Is Crystal ticked at something?" he asks.

"Just the Annie thing." I say, looking at nothing.

The Laugh. "Well then, forget her!"

Startled, I turn to look at Frank. He's exactly right. I've been walking on eggshells with Crystal, and it isn't my fault. I've tried to be as honest with her as possible, but she just doesn't understand. I'm not sure I do either. But I do know that patience is one of the key fundamentals of a good relationship, and if she's that quick to give up, it ain't never gonna work.

Frank smiles and says to me in a confidential tone, "You know something Bud? Karen over there has the hots for you."

"I know, Frank, but I'm kinda getting tired of 'the hots' thing."

"DH, I've told you this before: you're young! Do you know how many women there are out there?"

"I just want one."

"Trust me my friend, you'll get more than just one." *The Laugh*.

From the field below we hear Annie cry out as if in pain. We run to the edge of the drop off, but she is nowhere to be seen. I run down the steep slope, and out into the field. The kite is floating up there in the sky but it's loose and flying away. Annie is lying in the dirt about a hundred feet away.

I'm the first to reach her, followed by Frank, then Jack.

"Sweetie!" I fall down beside her and scoop her up in my arms, cradling her. "Are you okay?"

"I stepped in a hole. I think I sprained my ankle."

There is blood running freely from a wound on her elbow. Karen, just arriving at the scene, takes one look. "That's a nasty cut, little Sweetie," she says.

My attention is suddenly drawn to Karen. I'm the only one who ever calls Annie, Sweetie. Crystal, who apparently came back when she heard the commotion, overhears. I can tell by the look on her face that she also understands.

I refocus on Annie. "Frank, can you help me get her back up to the house? I can't carry her all the way up that hill."

Frank lifts Annie in his arms, and carries her all the way back to the path that leads up the hill. Then he gently helps her climb onto his back where she rides piggyback fashion up to the top. He carries her that way along the upper path to the patio, in through the breezeway door, and into the house.

"You got some gauze and tape here some place?" he asks as he carries her into the bathroom. "I need some antiseptic! You got mercurochrome?"

I find what he needs in the hall closet where we keep that kind of stuff. In short order, Annie's arm is cleaned and bandaged, and her ankle is wrapped."

I look at Frank with wonder in my eyes. He just looks back and says, "Korea."

I never could have carried Annie up that hill, and then I wouldn't have known what to do with her when I got her up here.

"One of these days when you get a chance, Frank, you're going to have to tell me all about the Korea thing."

"Not likely," he says grimly. "I don't want my every word to be in that little journal of yours."

"I'm okay," Annie says. "Thank you, Uncle Frank.

I take her in my arms and hold her as tight as I can.

"You're breaking my ribs."

I let up on the pressure, but I kiss her on the forehead and tell her. "You gave me quite a scare little girl."

She looks into my eyes, and says in a voice no one else can hear, "As your daughter, or your lover?"

I don't know how to respond. She is so cute, and such a precious thing to my heart. Where are we? What's going on?

I simply smile at her as she hugs me closer and says, "I don't care if you do break my ribs."

"So, Frank asks, "is the party over?"

"No way, Cowboy!" Karen cries out. "It ain't over till the fat lady sings, and since we ain't got no fat ladies here, it may go on all night!"

I notice now that everyone else has joined us, either in the bathroom, or just outside in the hall.

"Come on guys." Frank says, rolling his eyes. "Give 'em some room here! More wine barkeep!" He yells over to Bill, who takes off down the hall.

"Just kidding, Bill!" Frank calls after him, but it's too late. Bill is back in no time, with a jug of Red Mountain and a stack of styrofoam cups.

"I hope you don't care, DH. I went into The Hole and got this gallon of wine. You have five more gallons in there that I brought earlier. I took the liberty of putting them under your bed."

"It's okay, thanks Bill." Wow, five more gallons. To the others I say, "Wine, any one?" All the hands go up.

"Maybe we ought to go back to the patio, while we can still walk," Jack says.

"There'd be more room," agrees Karen, laughing.

I look at Annie. "Sweetie, if I hold you up, can you hobble out to the patio, or do you want me to take you to the hospital?"

"No hospital, DH." It's the first time she's called me by that name. "Let everybody else go back out, and you stay here with me for just a little bit."

I look up at everybody and say, "It's kind of crowded in here."

Frank takes charge. "Let's go!" he says, and they all march out to the patio.

"I didn't want to say anything in front of them, but I have to pee." Annie grimaces as she tries to get up off the floor.

"Here, let me help you up."

I step outside the door where I wait until I hear her call out, "I'm done." I go back in, take her arm, and help her walk out of the bathroom and down the hall. I can tell it hurts when she puts weight on her ankle.

"This is hurting you, Annie."

"It isn't that bad." She stops and looks at me. "You're hurting, too," she says.

"What are you talking about?"

"You're thinking about Gigi, aren't you?"

"What? How do you know about Gigi?"

"Jack told me."

"That figures," I mutter.

"Don't be mad. Mostly he was bragging about how great his friendship is with you. He didn't tell me much about her, only enough to realize that Gigi must have been something very special."

"You can never know …" I pause to get the knot out of my throat. "You can never know how special she was to me."

"Could it be possible that you, me, and Gigi, are related in some fashion?" She looks up at me with those huge innocent eyes. "Crystal never was right for you. I had a bad feeling about her."

"What do you mean?" I look at her cute little face and sweet little lips that do look a bit like Gigi's "Twiggy" mouth.

"Frank told me a couple of things," she says.

"Is this a friggin' conspiracy?" I stop in my tracks, and turn my back on this precious little girl, who seems to have more answers to life than I do. But as soon as I realize what I've done, I turn back to her. Annie is leaning against the wall, crying.

"I'm sorry, Sweetie!" I take her in my arms. "Talk to me, Annie." I feel terrible.

Through the tears she relates, "Frank told me that he'd never seen anything like the love you and Gigi had for each other, and it made me think, maybe Gigi is related to this whole picture. I don't think Crystal is. I just don't have that sense from her, even if her name is MacPherson. But I do feel a connection to Gigi, and I think you need to check it out."

There was something in the way she said that last "check it out" that made me smile at her and say, "If you aren't my daughter, you're still the cutest little thing on earth." I hugged her.

Annie and I walk out through the breezeway door—well, I walk, Annie limps. Everyone is back on the floor working on the art thing, but they all look up at us as we come through the door.

"What are we going to do with this thing when it's done?" Frank asks.

"Burn it!" Jack yells, his voice and demeanor evoking images of a pagan bonfire. I can tell he's had a lot of wine.

"No," Bill says calmly. "I think if we're able to somehow put all these pieces together into one large piece and frame it under glass ..."

I turn to Frank, who is looking thoughtfully at all the pieces.

"But I'm not finished," Annie says, as she breaks away from me. She hobbles over to the table, finds a fresh piece of construction paper, and lays it on the floor. She looks up at me, and I'm afraid of what she's going to draw. Then she winks, just like Gigi used to wink at me, and she looks at Frank. Then her smile turns to puzzlement as she picks out a blue crayon. Everyone goes quiet.

Annie looks up at me one more time, and begins to draw a portrait of a woman I've never seen before. She mixes crayon colors together, giving the woman dark, blackish-reddish hair, and a face that looks just like Annie's, sort of, only more mature.

"I think it might be my mother. Her name is Mary."

"You mean your adopted mother, Annie?" Karen asks. "She's very pretty."

"No," says Annie, matter-of-factly, "my real mother who was tried for witchcraft hundreds of years ago."

That statement prompts mutterings of skepticism from the group. I'm convinced that every person here now thinks Annie is a kook. I don't. As I examine the drawing more closely, I get a cold chill up my spine. I, too, feel connected to Mary.

I look down at Annie at the same time she looks up into my eyes. She says simply, "One day you will know who she is, Daddy."

There is total silence from the crowd. Everyone is looking at everyone else, puzzled by her words. But I trust Annie, and I believe what she has just said.

"Past life, Sweetie?"

"Past life ..." she looks around at the faces, "... but forever."

Once again, we have one of those Charlie Chan moments when all of the characters have been brought into the room, and the mystery unfolds. Everyone here is totally silent. All eyes are on Annie. I'm sure some of them are wishing a psychiatrist would come along and take us both away.

Bill Hunter, breaking the awkward silence, says "Annie, Sweetness, this is a beautiful drawing. The woman looks a lot like you except …" Pausing for a moment, he continues, "… except this lovely woman was tried for witchcraft in Massachusetts some time before the Salem witch trials, wasn't she?"

What! Why would he say that?

Annie stands up, runs to me, and hugs me as tight as she can.

"I'm sorry, Annie," Bill says.

"It's okay Bill," I tell him.

"Hunter has to be Fae." Crystal whispers in my ear. I wonder why she is still here.

But where did Bill get that strange information?

Frank looks over Annie's shoulder to give her drawing of Mary a closer look.

"Annie, this is better than anything DH can do." *The Laugh.*

Everyone laughs with him, bringing the party back to a level of sustainability. I think people were about to leave, but everyone is slowly gravitating back to the task at hand. Bill is quoting the poet, Theodore Roethke. That's a good sign.

"Wait a minute." Bill adjusts his glasses and picks up a green crayon. He squats down beside Annie and writes something in the margins of her drawing. Turning to her, he says, "This is for you, Child." Once again, my eyes fill with tears. That's what he always called Gigi. He's even called me that a time or two.

Annie whispers in my ear, "That's what he called Gigi."

"How in the world did you know that?" I ask. "You must be fae, Annie."

She hugs me. Her hair smells so sweet. I've heard stories about Catholic saints who smelled like roses whenever they walked by. That's what Annie's hair smells like.

"Breck," she says, smiling up at me.

"What?"

"You were smelling my hair. I use Breck." She grins.

"Never tell me you aren't a saint, little girl."

"I never will. But I'm far beyond being mere fae, and so are you, Daddy."

I take her at her word; it's really all I can do. There is something inside of me that screams out for me to pay close attention to everything she tells me. Yet, what good is it? I still have so many questions. How does Annie know all of this bizarre stuff she knows? Where does it come from? I've never heard anything like it before. Witches and witch trials? A lady named Mary? Reincarnation and being related to an other-dimensional daughter I never knew I had? And what about all my other Muse sightings, like at RCC for instance? My head is spinning.

I am suddenly inspired. "Annie, I have to paint you!"

"I know that. You will spend the rest of your life painting me."

"Because you're my Muse?"

"No." She looks at me, her face just inches from mine, her eyes almost on fire. "Because it has to be."

That's it for me. I'm thoroughly spooked now. I turn to all the participants in our little art thing, and I tell them, "We have to wrap it up. My parents are on their way home," I lie.

Frank comes over and whispers in my ear, "That's a lie. You want to be alone with Annie. You two need to do some serious chitchatting."

"You can read me like a book."

"Of course I can," Frank says. "If you want, I'll clear these guys out and I'll call you mañana. I can still make the Costa Mesa thing this afternoon."

"Frank …" I pause, just for a moment. "Thank you, Frank. I—"

"Leave it!" Frank says, and starts shooing everybody out. Within fifteen minutes, Annie and I are alone on the patio.

"Now," says Annie, standing in front of me. "We are totally alone."

"Yes, we are." I smile nervously at her as she tries to balance on her taped up ankle.

"Here." I take her arm and lead her over to the famous lounge chair. I sit her down, and pull up a chair beside her.

"This is Frank's seat isn't it?" she asks.

"A lot of famous people have sat in that seat kid, but I'd trade 'em all for you right now."

"Frank told me that Carl Sagan sits here. Is that true?"

"I'm not sure. My dad has a lot of aerospace guys over here, and one of them is a Carl. I know that for fact."

"Does he have big hair, and talk kind of funny?"

"Yeah."

"That's Sagan!"

"And that means what?"

"He's quite a man," she says. "I've read several articles by him."

"Are you an astronomy buff?"

"I study the universe."

"Well then, how long can you stay here with me? It's still pretty early. It would be neat if you could watch the night sky with me." The image of Crystal pops into my head.

"Crystal won't be coming back," Annie says, as if reading my mind.

"I'm fae, remember?" She half-smiles.

"You must be."

"Help me up, Daddy," she says with sudden resolution. "Take me into the garage and paint me."

"Now?"

"Why not? Everybody's gone, and we're here alone. I'll hang around and you can paint me. When it gets dark, you can show me the night sky like you did with Crystal."

"Why do you think I showed Crystal the night sky?" How does she know all this stuff?

"It's okay," she assures me. "Her night sky and my night sky are going to be different. Now, take me into the garage and paint me."

Standing, I take hold of Annie's hand and pull her up out of Carl Sagan's chair. For just a moment, as our eyes meet, an intensity of something I can never describe in words, is passed between us. I have to break it off.

With my left hand I awkwardly pick up a jug of Red Mountain.

Taking Annie's arm in my right hand, I lead her into the garage.

Annie surveys the scene as she settles onto a high stool. "This is where you do your painting?"

"It is," I answer, knowing full well that she probably already knows that, and more.

Sensing my apprehension, she tries to reassure me. "Relax, Daddy. Right now I'm just another model."

"But you aren't!" I protest. "You said it yourself earlier—you're either my daughter, or my lover from a past life, or several past lives!"

"What difference does it make?" She gets off the stool and comes over to me. She puts her arms around me and hugs me like a little girl. "But treat me like a daughter tonight, Daddy. It's important. One day it will all make sense."

So many conflicting thoughts. I am convinced of one thing, though; Annie is more than the sum total of all the parts of whatever is real for me right now, so I listen to her.

The garage/studio is suddenly suffused with a golden light. I look out the window and see the glow of the sunset. It's stunning.

I take Annie's hand and head for the door. "Come on!"

"Aren't you going to paint me?"

"You have to see this first!"

I lead her out to the patio and across the yard, where we sit on the ground overlooking the gully and the field beyond—carefully avoiding the spot that Crystal and I had shared.

We watch the sky as it turns all kinds of colors before going into total darkness.

Annie leans against me contentedly and slips her arm through mine. "Look, Daddy! How beautiful is that!" I put my arm around her shoulder and pull her closer to me.

We watch in silence as the sun and the sky put on their show. After about fifteen minutes, it's pitch black out here, except for all the stars, constellations, and galaxies glowing up there in deep space the way they're supposed to.

"Did you and Crystal come out here to experience this?" Annie asks.

I can't lie to her. "I came out here once with Crystal. We sat right over there." I point to the spot about ten feet away. "But this is different."

"What's different about it?" She's still staring up at the sky.

"I didn't have a clue who you were then. I didn't know you were my Muse, my daughter, and my whoever. Crystal was a diversion; someone who —"

"Shut up, Daddy." She smiles up at me. "I don't care who Crystal was to you. I just care that it's over between you and her, and now we can do what we were meant to do."

I look into her big brown eyes. I can see the freckles on her nose, and the moon sparkles on her teeth.

"You know," she says, "it's a full moon tonight."

I thought it was full when Crystal and I were out here, but now as I look out over the field, I see that I was wrong.

"Look down there, Annie. It's the kite!"

There it is, gleaming in the light of the moon. I can almost see the outline of Jack's Venus, glowing on the front of the kite.

"How lovely it is," Annie whispers. "The moon is so wonderful." Giggling, she turns to me and asks, "Can you bring your little tape recorder out here and play some music?"

"You're wish is my command."

I go back to The Hole and find the recorder and a very long extension cord. I throw a bunch of tapes onto a shirt, using the shirt like a sack to bring the whole works outside.

As I'm setting everything down and placing a tape in the recorder — I don't even know what the tape is yet — I look over at Annie, who's standing there bathed in the light of the full moon and I think that I've never seen a lovelier sight.

Crystal was lovely standing over there, a few feet from where Annie is now, but there's something different about Annie. There is no innocence in Crystal. Annie is the personification of innocence. I still haven't made up my mind about who or what she really is yet. She comes across more as a young girl, unlike Crystal, who is definitely a WOMAN, with capital letters; but it isn't just that Annie is a young and innocent girl. She holds some deep mystery inside her — way beyond anything this world has ever known — and somehow her mystery is connected to me.

The tape begins to play. It's The Doors:

> *Come on baby light my fire*
> *Try to set the night on FYE-ER!*

The night is on fire as I watch Annie do a slow, rhythmic dance in front of the moon hanging just above the edge of the gulley. I don't want to say a word. I just want to watch her sway back and forth to the music. She turns to me, and motions for me to come over and dance with her.

"I can't dance," I protest.

"You don't have to, Daddy. Mother and I will do the work."

What?

Eleven PM

Annie danced for a while as I sat on the ground watching her. I just couldn't bring myself to get that close to her. She had a glow about her that made me think that if I did, I might not survive the experience. The moon bounced back and forth and up and down as Annie moved to the music. The tape broke, yet Annie continued her dance, and all of Creation danced with her. I was spellbound.

Then something brought me out of it; the sound of a car out front.

"Daddy?" Annie's face is close to mine, almost touching. "There's someone here," she whispers, and I feel the breath of her words on my cheek.

"I think somebody just pulled up out front," I tell her, trying to collect my thoughts.

"Want me to go with you?" she asks, smiling.

"No. You'd better stay here." I kiss her cheek, then rush through the breezeway. Frank is sitting on his bike in the middle of the driveway.

"Frank! What a surprise!"

"I didn't know if you'd be up or not," he says, still sitting on his bike. "But I figured I'd take the chance. If you weren't up, I figured I'd just sit here and watch the stars or something."

"Where you been?" I ask.

"Costa Mesa. I think I've got a permanent thing goin' on there. Irvine wants me." Has he been gone that long? I've lost all track of time.

"Well, get off the bike and come on in." He does so, and we walk toward the breezeway as Annie is stepping out.

"Your daughter is still here?" asks Frank, giving me an odd look.

"Can we talk in front of her, or do we have to talk in art code?" Frank asks with a smile.

"Anything you say to me you can say to her."

"I figured that." Frank seems burdened as we walk toward the door where Annie is standing. We all go through and out to the patio where Frank flops his frame in the blue lounge chair. He puts his arms and hands behind his head and stares up at the stars.

Finally, Frank begins to speak. "I know I have to move away from Riverside, and I know I'm gonna move, but I don't want leave you all."

"You gotta do what you gotta do," I tell him. I'm sitting right by him, with Annie next to me.

"It's a big decision, Bud." It's obvious he's now having mixed feelings about it.

"Maxine's on board, and the kids are too young to care. I know it's the best thing to do, but I still can't help having second thoughts."

It's my turn to push him forward. "Frank Reed, as much as I'd like to keep you here in town, I know this is the best move for your career. You need to go for it."

Frank turns to Annie. He begins to speak with uncharacteristic hesitation, "Annie, I need to ask you this. Who are you? I once asked another girl that same question."

"You mean, Gigi?" She smiles at Frank and he looks at me, raising his eyebrow.

"Don't be surprised at anything she says, Frank."

"I'm just me." She looks away. "But that's not the real truth. I don't really know who I fully am yet." She shakes her ponytail, looks at me, then at Frank.

Frank smiles at her. "Hey kid, we don't give a hoot. Just be your sweet, beautiful self."

"I do know that I have a history about me," she says.

Frank laughs. "You mean like Attila the Hun crossing the Alps with his elephants? That kind of history?"

"Maybe even better than that, Mr. Frank Reed." There's a gleam in her eye that I've never seen before, and suddenly she no longer looks like a child and—

Wow! I don't know if this is a coincidence or not, but all of a sudden, dark clouds are massing in the sky overhead, and it looks like we're in for some bad weather. Thunder begins to roar, with waves of sheet lightning rolling all about the Heavens. It's beautiful.

"What the … !" Frank says. "Maybe we ought to go inside! Looks like a storm is brewing."

"No," Annie whispers, "not a storm. Just a little gift."

"Man oh man! That's purty stuff." Frank is out of his seat now, looking up at the sky. "A gift, huh? Who's it from?"

Annie stands up and walks to the edge of the patio. Raising her arms up high, she says softly, "From Mother."

The second she said that, all of the clouds seemed to evaporate, the thunder stopped, and the moon appeared larger on the horizon.

Mother? Whose mother? Annie didn't do that did she? How could she do that? She couldn't possibly, but …

"Keep talking, Frank," Annie says.

Frank looks at me and shakes his head. He pulls out his pipe, fills it with Latakia, and lights it up. He doesn't even blink at what just happened with the clouds and the lightning. He takes one long look at Annie, who still has her back turned to us staring up at the sky. Then he glances at me with a bit of puzzlement on his face, shakes his head again, walks over to his lounge chair, takes a seat, and starts talking as if nothing had happened.

"So, I made it to Irvine, and I made it to Costa Mesa. I have to admit, it's all positive stuff. I guess I need to make the move."

I continue to watch the sky, just in case there is more in store. "I have to admit," I say, turning to Frank, "I hate it that you're going." I pause to look at Annie, who is now on her way back to her chair.

"Irvine's a really pretty campus," Frank says, looking up at the sky. "Have you guys ever been there?"

Annie and I both say, "No," at the exact same time, and then look at each other. Frank looks at us, cocking his head back and forth

"This is getting spooky! What's the deal with you two?" *The Laugh.* "You're like a couple of magical puppets or something."

Annie and I look at each other and smile, then Annie smiles at Frank, and says to him, "History, Mr. Reed, history. The past the present and the future. All anyone will be able to do is just run and hide."

I haven't a clue what she means by that, but she said it with such a straight face that even I am a bit uneasy.

"You are one weird chick." Frank shifts in his seat, giving me a sidelong look, and asks her, "What planet are you from?"

I smile, because I think he asked Gigi the same question.

Annie answers without a smile, "If I were to tell you I created the universe, what would you think?"

Frank looks at me again, shifts in his seat again, and mutters, "I wouldn't be surprised. After Gigi, nothing will ever surprise me again."

I clear my throat and say, "So, Frank, when are you going to move away from all of us?" trying to move the conversation back to the mundane.

"It looks like November."

"So why aren't you smiling?" I ask him.

"Other things. Other complications."

"Your Muse?" I ask. He looks at me with surprise.

"There you go again, Kreskin. But I ain't gonna go there with you, Bud." He looks down at his hands.

"So we're both going to be going wherever it is that we're going!" He smiles. "By the way, what's your major going to be at Cal State?"

"I'm torn between art and philosophy."

"That's a no win decision," laughs Frank. "Two dead ends."

I defend myself. "I took some existentialist philosophy classes at RCC this year, and I kind of liked them."

"No!" Frank rises up off the famous blue chair. Pointing at me, he exclaims, "Don't do that! Existentialism is a waste of time! Do the art thing. Art may be a waste of time too, but at least you can turn out some pretty pictures to look at. You might even experiment a bit with sculpture."

"I've thought about that. I've done a lot of pottery, and a lot of painting, but not much sculpture."

Annie smiles and shakes her head.

"Is there a problem with that?" I ask her.

"No. That's exactly what you're going to do. You'll get your art degree, and you'll even be an art teacher for a while."

I've read stories about the Oracle of Delphi, in Greece, the woman who used to sit on a stool over a large hole in the ground, sucking up smoke and gases, delivering prophecies to kings and warriors of the age. I swear, Annie looks just like that.

Then she rolls her eyes up and tells Frank, "You're going to have a lovely studio in Costa Mesa, but it will not be permanent for you."

Ignoring him she turns to me saying, "You will be a philosophy major for a while, but in mid term you'll switch to art. Jack will be there with you."

Returning to normality—whatever that is—Annie looks at Frank, and smiles.

"You think I'm a kook," she tells him.

"Not a one hundred percent kook, just maybe about a 30 percent kook. No, make that 20 percent, cause I trust DH's judgment."

Annie walks away from us, off the patio, and over to the edge of the drop off.

"DH?" Frank whispers to me.

"Yes?"

"I hate to tell you this but this Annie chick is one—"

"One strange thing," I suggest, "and getting stranger by the second."

"You got it!" A muffled laugh. "But don't get me wrong, I like her. There's something different 'bout her, that even Gigi didn't have."

"Mystery!" he says. "Pure mystery. Just listen to her talk! Gigi had unanswered questions, but no mystery. She was right up front about everything. Annie's some sort of creature that's never been discovered on Earth before. The things she says and does defy logic and the laws of physics." Shaking his head, he continues, "But at the same time she makes some sort of sense. I'm not sure about all the future prophecy stuff, but this chick is wired different from you and me."

Annie comes back toward us with a far away look in her eyes and she says to both of us, "Come with me."

She turns around and walks back toward the drop off. Frank and I look at each other like a couple of bug eyed crazy zombies, but we get up out of our chairs and follow her, as she leads us slowly over to the edge of the drop off, and she doesn't even look back at us when she says, "Watch over there on the right."

We do as we are told. As she finishes speaking those words, tiny lights begin to rise from the field below, glowing and flying in random patterns.

"What the heck is that?" Frank whispers.

Frank stands motionless as he watches the silent, glittering dance below us.

Hundreds of tiny, lit-up insects are flying over the field below, with a few coming up to hover around our heads. It's incredible! I didn't think fireflies existed in Southern California. Beautiful! Like Christmas in July.

"Annie? DH?" Frank is truly mystified. Turning to me, he says, "This can't be happening! I've never seen a firefly here before.

Smiling enigmatically, Annie suggests, "Maybe they're Faeries. Is it not a magical summer's night?"

I'm still looking for a logical explanation. "Annie, how is this happening? Is this a migratory thing? Do fireflies migrate like butterflies and hummingbirds?"

"It's all the romance of the summer coming to its end," she says. As she smiles at me, I see a gleaming sparkle come from one eye. A reflection of the moon? A spark that flies out into the night.

"You know a lot about this stuff don't you, Annie?" Frank asks, pointedly. "Maybe you ought to be a science teacher."

"I'm going to be who I am." She pauses, as if to listen to another voice. When she continues, it is with the confidence of new knowledge. "I am always who I am. My existence now is only a name."

"Okay," Frank says. "This is getting a bit too mystic for me." His expression is one of perplexed resignation.

Ignoring Frank, I say, "It's a beautiful night, Annie, and you have made it even more beautiful for us."

"You think I did this?" Her look is penetrating.

"I know you did," I answer.

"Even more beautiful than the nights you spent out here with Crystal?"

"She's history, Annie."

"You're wrong," she says, looking away. "I'm history. Crystal lives only in the present time. I live in all of time."

"I believe that," I tell her.

"You can say that again," Frank adds.

She continues as if we had said nothing. "One day you will both forget all about me. Just as the fireflies go away and you won't think of them any more, you won't remember me. Your memories will fade."

I look around again and notice that the fireflies are gone. Frank is doing the same thing.

"How did you do that, Annie?" Frank asks almost in a whisper.

"Do what?" she asks.

"You have some sort of magic in you. Fireflies don't happen here in California, but tonight they did. Then, when you said they would go away, they went away." Frank isn't smiling.

"Once Nature is in full swing, it does what it wishes. It needs no help."

"Annie, you're a whole different person from who they think you are down at the Royal Scot."

"I'm not a waitress, Frank. I'm not that at all."

"That you aren't, Doll. That you aren't."

Frank clears his throat and changes the subject. "Well guys, I guess I'll head out of here for the night. Annie, uh, thanks for the light show." He bows to her. "You are one strange chick, but I think you might be the most beautiful girl I've ever met. Have I said that before? DH is a lucky man."

Frank drinks up the last of his wine and heads for the breezeway door. "You don't have to see me out." Smiling, he adds, "You kids have some serious fun tonight."

And Frank is gone. Just like that. I feel bad in a way, because I think Annie and I scared him off. I know he still has some questions about decisions he needs to make in his own life that he wanted to talk about. And something else he's not willing to talk about.

For now, I have my own hands full with a young girl who just might be my daughter, my wife, and my lover, all rolled into one, and, possibly, some sort of witch out of the past, who can command fireflies and storms at her will. I look over at Annie, just standing there, like she's communicating with all of nature, and everything else up there in the night sky.

Frank is right, she is the most beautiful woman on this planet. We joked about Gigi being from another planet, but I'm beginning to seriously wonder about Annie. Carl, that friend of my father's, who sometime sits in what has now become Frank's lounge chair, used to talk about life on other planets all the time. He told me once that there are millions of planets out there in the universe that, quite possibly, could be teeming with life—even human life just like on this planet. He mentioned star systems that are very close to Earth. One is only 4.5 light years away. He asked me, 'Don't you feel it, inside of you that, as a young man, you might one day experience First Contact, with Beings from other worlds? A light year is less than an inch in outer space!'"

So, is it too far-fetched to wonder if Annie might be one of those Beings Carl spoke about? Or perhaps I should wonder if my daughter might be just a little insane. That would force the greater question: how sane am I for believing in her?

Annie's focus returns to this world. "Daddy," she says, "I love your friend, Frank. He's very kind to me. I'm sorry he had to leave so soon."

"He's got a lot of stuff he's dealing with," I tell her. "Even I don't know what half of it is."

"Yes he does."

"Sweetie, do you know what's going on in Frank's mind?"

"I do, but I will only tell you this: you will see him once more after this night, then you will not see him again for many years."

"What?"

"He's going to move to Costa Mesa, then you will be out of touch with him for a while."

"I don't want that to happen."

"It has to happen, for both of you. He has to do what he has to do, and you have to do what you have to do. But don't worry, Father. You will see him again."

I know Annie is telling me the truth. She seems to have a way of knowing what's going to happen before it happens. I'll be headed off to Cal State Fullerton in a few weeks. I'll get involved in my degree work, and I won't have time to party like we've been doing this summer. I won't be able to do much socializing when I hit the books.

Meanwhile, Frank will be doing his thing. He'll rent a studio space and create wonderful works of art, and try to claw his way to the top of the art food chain. He'll probably give lectures at UC Irvine, or something like that. They may even hire him on as a teacher. Who knows? Time will be a precious commodity for both of us, so Annie is, no doubt, correct in this prophecy. Still, it makes me sad. What a great friend he has been to me. What good times we've had just hanging together.

"Don't be so sad, Daddy." Annie's smile lifts my spirits. "You and Frank will both be okay. Remember that the concept of time does not really exist at all. Without your watches and your clocks, there would be no time. Only life."

"Annie, can I ask you a question?"

"Yes."

"When I first met you, you were a helpless little girl who clung to me like I was your father. Now, all of a sudden, you are an incredibly out-going, all wise, almost magical creature of eternal time. What happened? When did it happen? How did it happen?"

"I remembered another dream," she said gravely.

"You mean one of those witch dreams?"

"Yes. It was a very quick moving experience that took me back through time and through dozens of different lives that I have led."

"Wow." I don't know what else to say.

"I can't begin to tell you all the details, but it was incredibly vivid—really more like a journey through a blueprint of my own Spirit. I was accompanied all along the way by a woman who I knew to be my mother. She held my hand for the entire journey."

"Your mother?"

"Mary."

"You mean the witch?"

"I do. It was she. My mother. But witch is not the word she used in my dream, she called herself something else."

"How does this all work?" I shake my head in confusion and walk away from her.

"It has to do with time," she explains patiently. "Mother's very words to me were, 'We all began together. We all began IT together and we will all end IT together.' That's when I woke up. In fact, I awoke with a start, and I rose up in bed staring out into the room, wondering what had just happened. From that moment on,

I was changed."

"What did Mary mean?" My head is spinning from the revelation.

"Not now, Daddy. I love you Daddy." She pulls my face over to hers and kisses me on my cheek. "One day you will have your own dream."

Planning Frank's Going Away Party

Annie spent the night. She's lying in my bed with the covers over her head. I slept on the hard tiled concrete floor. She has one skinny leg hanging out from under the sheets. I reach down and tickle her behind her knee.

"Daddy?" She's half asleep.

"Good morning." I smile down at her.

She rubs her eyes and smiles back at me. "You been staring at me long?"

"Not long enough," I tell her. "I could stare at you forever."

She yawns and says, "You already have." She closes her eyes again.

I can't help thinking Frank might be right about her. She is much too pretty to be from Earth.

"Daddy?" She opens her eyes, fully awake now.

"Yes Dear?"

"Let's give Frank a going away party."

This is it. This is what Annie warned me about—the last time I will see Frank for years.

"I'm not sure … Frank has a pretty full plate right now." I want to put off something as final as a going away party.

Annie props herself up on her elbows. She wipes the sleep from her eyes and looks at me seriously. "You just don't want to do it because you know it's the last time you'll see Frank for a while."

"You're right. I guess it all has to happen the way it has to happen. What's your idea?"

"Your parents are coming home soon?" she asks.

"Two more days," I tell her.

"Then we have to do it quickly. I want to do another barbecue and have everyone here."

"It's kind of short notice," I tell her. "I'm not sure I can get every-body here." What is this, a repeat of the last party?

"Everyone will be free tomorrow evening," she says knowingly

"Everyone?" I ask.

"Everyone. And this party will have a special twist."

"What twist?"

"I want it to be a total art party. We'll eat barbecued hamburgers and we'll make art — a big plaster sculpture. We might even build a bonfire."

"That sounds fun," I say. "Sort of like the raku parties at RCC!"

"Exactly," she grins. "Don't you think Frank would like that kind of a send off?"

"He'll love it!" I'm catching her enthusiasm. "I'll go in and make the calls right now."

"Yes, you will, Daddy." She smiles at me, pleased with her idea, and pleased that I like it.

The Last Day, or the First?

Annie was right. Everyone I called was willing and able to come to the party to see Frank off on his new adventure. The hardest one to get here was Frank! He had a commitment in Costa Mesa—something about looking for studio space. I didn't tell him we were having a party for him, I just said I needed to talk to him about something important, and he said he'd be here in a flash.

Annie and I are sitting on the ground outside the breezeway by the driveway. We went to the store earlier and brought back a ton of food and wine. Now everything is ready for the big surprise. I had told the invitees that it was to be a surprise, and that they should be here a half-hour before Frank. Annie and I are sitting here like mugwumps, waiting for the first to arrive. It's Karen.

I see those long legs spill out of her car, followed by her pretty head. She gives us a hearty greeting before slamming the car door

"Howdy, DH! Hey, Annie Bell, L'il Pardner!" She saunters over to us and continues, "Got another spot on the dirt where I can sit my butt?" she says, with a wink at me. I look at Annie. She doesn't seem too happy at seeing her.

Since Gigi died, and Crystal took off, Karen is really the only person who bothers Annie, and to be honest, I don't know what to do about it. I am attracted to Karen—a little—and I love Annie, but frankly, both of them scare the heck out of me.

"Like my outfit?" Karen smiles as she sits down on the concrete slab next to me.

"Very nice," I say. She has on another very short skirt that she is no doubt wearing because she wants people to notice her legs. Her top is a cowgirl type shirt, with the buttons, the embroidery, and all the whatever.

"Look at this," she says proudly. She turns so I can see the back of the shirt. It's decorated with bead work in the form of horses and Indians. A bit over the top.

"That's really … lovely."

"So, Karen, you're a cowgirl, huh?" Annie asks, oh so sweetly.

"You got it honey."

"Do you have any cows?" Annie asks, all wide-eyed innocence.

"I live on a ranch with my parents. We have about a thousand head."

"You do any roping and branding?"

"I do it all honey."

"How do you find time to be a waitress at the Royal Scot?" I ask.

"I don't any more," she says with a grin. "I quit that job. I didn't need it in the first place. My Daddy has a lot of cash and he hated me working there."

"So he told you to quit?" I ask her.

"Nope, I just got the vibes from him that he didn't like me being there."

"You're pretty close to your dad, then?" Annie asks solemnly, dropping the sweet innocent act.

Karen turns to her and asks very gently, "Aren't you close to your dad?"

Annie turns to me, a stricken look on her face.

"I have to go the bathroom." Annie gets up. "I'll be right back." I think she had tears in her eyes.

Karen watches with concern as Annie disappears into the house. "Man oh man, DH. That is the strangest kid I think I've ever met. Is she okay?"

"It's a long story, Karen. I'll tell you about it some time." I turn to face her, and say in a brighter voice, "You do look good in that outfit."

She smiles and sings:

> *If you had an outfit,*
> *you could be a cowboy too.*

I grin. "The Smothers Brothers! I saw them do that skit on TV."

She laughs in agreement. "I love that show." Then she reaches over and takes my hand. "What's the deal with you and this little girl?" she asks.

I take a deep breath, and I begin to try to explain, "Karen, I'm not sure what this is all about. The only thing I know for certain is that Annie is, indeed, my daughter, and she has these dreams ...”

"She dreamed about you?"

"A little, but mostly it's about the past and the future. I can't explain it all to you right now, but I'll tell you this, she isn't crazy. She's as sharp as a tack. And you should have seen what she did the other night when Frank was here!"

"What did she do?"

"Somehow, Annie caused fireflies to fly out of the field behind the house. Frank and I watched them swarm all over the place."

"There ain't no fireflies in this part of California!" she declares. "We have 'em in some parts of Texas, but not in California."

"I know that. That's what got our attention."

Just then another car drives up. It's Bill Mitchkelly! I haven't seen him in so long. I stand up to greet him as he steps out of his car. He's dressed in blue work shirt, Levis, and cowboy boots.

"Mitch," I say, grasping his hand, "thanks for coming."

"Wouldn't have missed this for the world, DH," he responds warmly.

"Yee-haw, look at them boots! Gotta be Tony Lama." Karen is advancing toward us.

Bill looks at her quizzically, but smiles and responds, "Yes they are. I bought them about two weeks ago."

"Best boots in the world!" Karen grins. "That's what I wear. Got a dozen pair at home."

Mitch, a bit bemused, turns to me and asks, "Who is this friend of yours?"

"Sorry Bill. This is Karen." Turning to Karen, I complete the introduction. "Karen, this is Bill Mitchkelly, the ceramics and sculpture teacher at RCC."

"Howdy!" She puts on a big grin, reaches out her hand, and grabs Bill's hand hard. At that moment, Jack pulls up on his Norton motorcycle. As he gets off his bike, he looks a bit like Yul Brynner — mainly because he's almost bald. He stands there for a minute while he pulls one of his Mexican cigarettes out of his shirt and sticks it in his mouth. Bill and Karen and I are watching him, because it's such an entertaining scene.

Karen breaks the spell, nudging me and whispering, "That guy's all for show, Pardner."

Annie comes out of the breezeway and joins us just as other cars start pulling up. Bill Hunter, Manny, and—who the heck is this? Manny's brought his mother with him!

"DH!" Manny yells as he gets out of the car. "You remember my mother, Hester, don't you?"

How can I forget her? Manny's mother is gorgeous. Whenever I go over to their house, if she's there, all I can do is stare at her. I remember one time when Manny and I walked into his living room, and his mother was asleep on the couch. She had on a pink negligee and one of her breasts had fallen out and was totally exposed. Manny pulled me out of the room pretty quick, but I'll never forget that.

"Hi, DH." Manny's mother extends her hand to me. "Manny told me about this party for your friend and I thought it would be fun." She gives me a warm smile.

"Thanks." Hester looks down at Annie, grasps her hand and shakes it.

"So …" I stutter, "the party is going to be on the patio out back. When everybody gets here we'll do the art thing. The important thing is that we have to surprise Frank."

"Like that's gonna happen," Jack says. "When he drives up he'll see all these cars."

There's the sound of another motorcycle coming up the drive.

"That's gotta be Frank!" I yell. "He's early. Quick, back to the patio!"

Everybody scurries from the front to the back, just in the nick of time. I stand by the breezeway door waiting for Frank to pull up. I don't have to wait long.

But it isn't Frank; it's a different motorcycle! This one is black and gold and has an eagle painted on the side. It pulls up right in front of me, and some guy gets off and takes off his helmet. It's not a guy. It's a woman! A woman I've never seen before. She walks over to me, stretches out her hand and says, "I'm Lonesome."

I blink at her and say, "I'm sorry. Can I help you?"

"My name is Lonesome," she says, smiling. "I'm Hester's friend."

"Manny's mom." I recover my poise. "So, you're here for the surprise party!"

"Guess you're already surprised to see me." She smiles broadly, revealing wet, glistening teeth that seem to sparkle with their own inner light. In fact, her entire rosy face seems lit by that inner glow. Very pretty.

"I'm gonna leave my jacket out here on my bike," she says. "Will it be okay here?"

"I'm sure it will." I smile at her as she takes off her black leather jacket, revealing her tattooed arms.

"Thanks. This one on my left arm is Navy Blue Anchor. I just got out of the service about two months ago. This one on my right is a Pink Rose. That was one of my nicknames as a child."

"Interesting," I say. "Where did you grow up?"

"About two thousand miles from here."

I take a closer look at this biker woman. She really is lovely, like something out of a Degas or Renoir painting — large — make that muscular — with sun-streaked blonde hair cut to a sensible length and combed straight back on her rather Scandinavian head. Steel blue to hazel eyes, and t-shirt filled with well-proportioned breasts complete the picture. She is stunning in a big sort of way. But I like big.

"You starin' at me?" Her expression turns the question into a challenge.

"Well, get a good eyeful, 'cause I'm pretty interesting. Now where's the party Mr. Writer?" She starts to walk toward the breezeway door, then through it, like she knows where she's going.

Then I hear another engine coming up the drive. This one has to be Frank!

It is.

I'm the only one standing out here to greet him now; everyone else is in the back. He pulls up next to me, and hops off his bike.

"You runnin' a used car lot here?" he says as he takes off his helmet.

"No," I reply. Then I tell him a lie, "My parents got back last night and they're having a party out back."

"Can we sneak some food from 'em before we adjourn to The Hole?"

"I think so."

"Or do you want to talk first?" He looks concerned. "Is everything okay with you? Is Annie okay?"

"Annie's okay. I'm okay. Let's go out back and get some burgers, then we can talk about that stuff."

"I could use a burger, Bud." He grins.

We walk through the breezeway, out the back door, and onto the patio. Frank's face lights up as he is greeted with a chorus of "Happy Birthday Frank!"

"You jerks!" he yells back. "It's not my birthday!"

"Yeah it is," Jack says. "You're being born again in Costa Mesa!"

"So this is a sending off party huh? Where's my friggin' gold watch!" *The Laugh.*

"We had to do something, Frank." I look at him, and he comes over and hugs me tight.

"Aw, shucks," he says, tears welling up in his eyes. "You aren't making this very easy for me." He gives me another big hug and everybody applauds.

"Annie prepared all of this Frank. We've got food and wine to last for a week. And another pretty cool surprise for you, too, I might add."

"What's that? Naked go-go dancers?" *The Laugh.*

"Better than that," Annie says. Just as she says that, another engine is heard in the front. Only this is a big engine. Loud, like a freight train.

"What the heck is that? I'll be right back." I head for the driveway to see what's happening.

"Take Frank with you," Annie says. I look at her quizzically, but she brushes it off with a wave of her hand.

"Come on, Frank," I say. He looks first at me, then at Annie, and he slowly follows me through the breezeway door out to the front yard. Our puzzlement grows when we see what is there. A very large truck is parked in the middle of the driveway, and some big hairy dude is standing there with a clipboard in his hands.

"You DH Parsons?" he asks.

"Yep. That's me."

"I got some stuff here ordered by your wife, Ann." Frank cocks his head to one side and grins at me.

"Where do you want me to put it?" the truck driver says.

"I … I … I'm not sure." What's Annie done?

"Whatta you got?" Frank butts in for me.

The driver looks down at his clipboard. "I got 500 pounds of plaster, 50 short rebars, a half dozen 6 foot rebars, some wooden poles and stakes, a bunch of acrylic paint, and about a hundred brushes." He looks up from his list. "Where do you want it?"

Frank starts laughing, and that's when Annie comes out the door and takes control.

"You're gonna have to offload it here and then dolly it to the back," she declares with authority. "Wheel it through the breezeway and pile it on the grass at the edge of the patio." She says it like a drill sergeant.

The guy spits out some tobacco juice and grins at her. "Yes, Ma'am!" he says, executing a mock salute.

Another guy gets out of the truck cab, and the two burly men begin to hike all that stuff back through the breezeway, setting it down on the lawn next to the patio. Of course, all of my friends are looking on with wide-eyes, especially Bill Hunter, who has already taken up his position as master burger barbecuer.

"Don't be mad at me," I say into Frank's ear. "This was Annie's idea."

"Let me guess," he says, "We're gonna do a plaster sculpture. I'm just guessing now."

Annie looks up at him and says, "Is that okay?"

"Honey, anything you say or do is okay with me." *The Laugh*. He leans down to kiss her on her cheek, and a large spark jumps back from her.

Whoa!" he says, startled by the sting. "You must be wearin' wool socks, little girl, 'cause that was some static jolt!"

Annie smiles back at him and says playfully, "I'm not wearing socks, Frank."

Frank pats me on the back, and says, "This is going to be some send off party." The warm smile he gives me turns thoughtful as he watches Annie move away to check on the progress of the food.

Manny wanders over and joins us. "You goin' somewhere Frank?" Manny is always the last to catch on to what's happening around him.

"Costa Mesa. Got a condo and a studio there, and I'm going to try to sell some Ort!" *The Laugh*.

Just then Annie grabs our attention. "Everything is ready, and it's getting dark. We can all converse while we eat, so dig in."

Everybody lines up, grabs a paper plate, and fills it to overflowing.

Frank takes his seat on the blue lounge chair. Annie and I sit to the left of him. Everybody else sits pretty much across from us. Bill Hunter is tending the fire for the burgers.

"I'll cook some more as needs be," he says, smiling.

Bill Mitchkelly is concentrating on his own burger, chewing with great gusto.

The two uninvited standouts, Hester, and Lonesome, the biker chick friend that Hester invited, seem to be mixing in well. Both have full plates and smiles on their faces.

Frank stands up and raises his glass of wine. "This is nice guys! This is really nice. Thanks." Then he sits back down again.

The food is consumed, the wine flows, and everyone starts to mill around. The burgers are gone, and there's a butt-load of plaster on the lawn.

Jack gets busy passing out the tools of the trade. He's more of a doer than a director, but he's giving it an effort. Everybody's getting into the project except for Hester. Realizing that this may all be new to her, I move to her side and extend an invitation to join in the activity.

"Wanta get your fingers wet?" I say.

She gives me long, appraising look. "An interesting proposition," she says, finally.

I clear my throat. "Have you done any art before?" I ask her.

"I birthed Manny."

"You're right about that. That boy is a work of art. What a piano player."

"I was sorry to hear about Gigi," Hester said. "I never got to thank her for that piano she gave Manny. We put it in the living room, right where you stood that day when you watched me sleeping on the couch."

I gulped. "I'm, uh, sorry, Hester. That was an accident. We walked in, and there you were."

"No need to apologize, DH. I'm not offended." She smiled. "You're welcome to come over any time.

Returning her smile, I quickly excused myself and headed back to the party.

I take a seat by Frank, and Bill Hunter brings me a plate filled with burgers and beans.

"Thanks Bill, but I think it's time to get serious about the plaster sculpture. I can eat later." Turning to Frank, I tell him, "I'm taking this show back from Jack, and giving it to you, Frank. This is your shindig, and you need to direct it. What do you want to create, Master Reed?"

His answer surprises me. "Not just me! I don't want this to be my sculpture. I want us all to make a grand masterpiece of someone we loved very much, and miss dearly: Gigi." The crowd applauds—everyone but Hester and Lonesome, who never met Gigi.

"Let's take this party over to the edge of the grass by the gully," he says. "I don't want to mess up your parents lawn. Jack, bring some of those bags of plaster!" *The Laugh!*

Jack, who is the strongest guy I've ever known, grabs the tops of two, one hundred pound bags — one in each hand — and drags them across the lawn to the dirt under the trees bordering the gully.

"DH," he yells, "you got some water hoses and buckets?"

Of course I do. I am totally prepared for this operation, thanks to Annie.

Anticipating that the physical exertions will result in renewed appetites, Bill Hunter chimes in, "I'll prepare some more burgers!"

Annie has already joined the hoses together so that they will be long enough, and Jack pulls the end to the outer edge of the yard. I carry over several empty buckets, and we're good to go.

"We need to build an armature," Frank says, taking full control. "Where's that rebar?"

"Over here," Jack responds.

"Man," Frank says with concern, "we need a welding torch for this stuff. You can't glue rebar."

"I didn't think of that," Annie says.

"It's okay, Little One, we'll make it work." Then Frank yells to Manny, "Turn on the water!" which he does. Frank turns to me and says, "I need a shovel, some tape, and a lot of old newspapers."

"Got it." I hurry to the garage where I find my grandfather's shovel and a roll of duct tape. I bring them out, then head into the house to pick up a pile of newspapers that has been stacking up for several weeks.

"Thanks," Frank says, as I hand him the pile.

He then begins to build his armature. He hammers some long rebars into the ground to anchor it. Then he begins to add structure and shape by taping shorter pieces of rebar to the long ones. He's all over the growing framework, hustling and laboring like a demon. Off to the side, Jack has dug a big hole and filled it with water, mixing it all around inside to make a large batch of mud. Now Frank is wrinkling up pieces of newspaper, and telling everybody to just stand back while he puts it all together.

The Laugh, followed by Frank's booming voice, "It doesn't have to look pretty, it just has to hold the mud and plaster while we pile it on."

We all just stand back and watch. Pretty soon, Frank has a crude looking armature of mud and iron standing under the moonlit sky. It reminds me of pictures I've seen of the Wicker Man effigies the ancient Druids used in their sacrifice rituals. Kinda scary looking for now, but that will change before the night is through.

Frank steps back to examine his work. "Give it about thirty minutes to set up," he says, "then we'll carefully apply the plaster." There is a big grin on his face when he turns to face the group.

Meanwhile, Jack is already mixing plaster and water in the buckets.

"Hang on Jack!" Frank calls to him. "We can't put that on till the mud sets up just a little."

Jack has more plaster on his arms than in the bucket. He looks at Frank and says, "Okay, I'll make a little sculpture out of this, so it doesn't go to waste. Let me know when you're ready."

Bill Hunter is cooking more burgers. Karen and Mitchkelly are waving pieces of cardboard at the sculpture to fan speed up the setting process. Manny is standing by the water spigot waiting for instructions, and Annie is talking quietly with Frank. And then there's Hester and Lonesome.

My eyes catch Hester's, and I can sense some tension there. I look at Lonesome, and see that she is smiling. She sees me looking, gets up out of her chair, and walks to the breezeway door. She signals me with her finger to follow her.

When I join her in the breezeway, she turns to me. "So, what's all this plaster business?" she asks. It's so dark in the breezeway that I can hardly make her out. "You got some place we can go so we can see each others faces?"

"It all depends," I tell her. "We can go to The Hole, that's my room in the garage."

"The Hole? Sounds promising." She looks at me with a crooked smile that I can barely see.

I feel uneasy with Lonesome. I'm not sure that I want to take her into The Hole. It would be rude if I don't, but I'm picking up vibes from her that tell me to be careful.

I just don't get it. Every time I turn around I have a woman who seems to be interested in me. I don't think it's my imagination. Is it just because I'm young that I feel this way? It doesn't make sense. I'm not that attractive. I'm not seeking the attention. In fact I go out of my way most of the time to avoid it. I suppose it could just be the times we live in — the free love, free everything else, Hippie generation that's going on. Everybody seems to be just a little bit loony. Everybody wants to experiment with things they should probably just leave well enough alone. I don't get it.

"The problem with The Hole," I tell Lonesome, "is that for some reason, every time I go in there with a girl, somebody comes and knocks at the door."

"How many girls are we talking about?" Lonesome teases.

"That's a long story, Lonesome." I try to smile back at her.

"Forget The Hole," she says. "Ain't you got a front porch on this house?"

"We don't have too long, Lonesome. There is a party going on out back, but follow me, maybe we can sit a spell."

I lead her out the front door of the breezeway, to the right, and over to the front porch. I turn on the porch light so we can see each other, but she tells me to turn it off. We take a seat in the little white wooden porch swing that my grandfather made for my mother.

"Nice swing," she says smiling and taking my hand.

"My grandfather made it," I explain, filling the awkward silence. "It is kind of nice to be away from the noise, huh?"

"Yeah," she agrees.

We sit for about five minutes, just rocking back and forth, saying nothing. Finally, I turn to her and ask, "So, Lonesome, how long you been ridin' a bike?"

She smiles and replies, "My daddy put me on a bike when I was 9 months old. He toodled around with me on his lap, going circles in a field till I was dizzy. I started screamin' like crazy, but

I was really happy."

"Did your dad name you 'Lonesome'?"

"No, I have a real name. The first letter is 'S,' but I like 'Lonesome' better.

After a few more minutes of silence, I ask, "Why are you holding my hand?"

"I don't know." She drops my hand. "I wasn't thinking."

She starts to get up, but I grab her arm. "Not so fast, Duke!"

"You like John Wayne?" She looks at me with new interest.

"I do."

"He's my hero! Why did you call me that?"

"Because you remind me of him," I tell her.

"What? I got boobs!" She looks at me like she's checking for signs of insanity.

"I know that. But you also have the Duke's walk."

"Huh?"

"When you walked from your bike over to the breezeway door when I first met you, the way you walked reminded me of John Wayne." I smile at her.

"You mean like I got a carrot up my butt?" she said, smiling.

"Yep."

She takes my hand again and we sit in silence for a moment, each of us lost in our own thoughts, swinging slow … and low … sweet chariot.

Lonesome is the first to break the silence. "You really like this Annie girl, don't you?"

"It's a long story, and we only have a few minutes before we put the plaster on that sculpture."

"But she's your girl, huh?"

"Not really … well … maybe."

"What are you talking about, biker boy?"

"I'm not a biker—I don't have an outfit."

Lonesome pulls her Harley Davidson biker shirt off over her head, and pulls it down over mine. "You're a biker now, but I'll need that back before we go back to the party. I don't think the boys out yonder would get much done if I walked back there like this." She smiles. "Now tell me about Annie."

I see two very large, pale pink breasts staring at me, and I notice for the first time that Lonesome also has a rather full-figured belly that seems quite lovely to me right now. I try to concentrate as I explain. "Annie has these dreams, and in these dreams she seems to have some sort of connection with past lives and whatever."

I hesitate, and Lonesome breaks in. "I've heard about that past life stuff before, that ain't so hard to believe. We gotta go somewhere after we die, and we gotta do something when we get there. Maybe we come back and forth all the time." She seems really interested and open to the idea.

"Well," I continue, "Annie seems to make contact with her mother, who lived a life as a witch several hundred years ago, and according to Annie—" I pause, looking at Lonesome who's sitting on the edge of the swing. Even though she seems intrigued by what I'm saying, but I am hesitant to continue. "Annie's mother's name is Mary, and it seems that Annie, Mary, and I, and who knows who else, were all part of a family in a past life, or two, or three, going back to the beginning of time, and … oh yeah … it's quite possible that Annie has also been both my daughter, and my lover, at various times throughout the centuries."

There. I've told her everything. I sit back in the swing and look out at the two giant pine trees silhouetted against the night sky. I swear, I can see a firefly drifting among the boughs.

Lonesome turns toward me, her eyes wide with excitement. "DH, this little girl is a psychic!"

"A psychic?" Oh boy, here we go again.

"You have to listen to her! She may be on to something."

"Lonesome, I'm not sure John Wayne believed in psychics. It isn't exactly what I'd call a cowboy thing or a biker thing, is it?"

"That don't matter. I had an aunt once that was psychic," she explains. "She belonged to the Spiritualist church, and those people did psychic readings all the time. I swear to you, they were almost always right on. Annie sounds like the real deal to me."

Lonesome drops her eyes, suddenly subdued.

"What's the matter, Lonesome?"

"Is Annie is your lover?"

"Lonesome, I'm just a 20 year old kid. I'm not even sure what a real lover is yet, and quite frankly, I haven't got a clue about much of anything in this world, let alone how the future will play out. Can I be honest with you?"

"I'm like a priest," she says, looking at me again.

"This has been the strangest year I've ever experienced in my life. I went for years without ever getting a date, not one single date, except for this one girl named Charlotte, who had a mustache. All of a sudden, all these girls and older women are coming on to me, and I just don't get it. I'm not asking for any of it! But Annie is different. She's very special to me. Our relationship seems to be more like father-daughter this time around." I smile. "And now I've got Hester coming on to me, for cryin' out loud."

She grins. "Hester told me about you seeing her boob."

I sigh and roll my eyes. "There's also Karen, a real cowgirl, who keeps flashing herself at me."

Again, a moment passes in silence, then, "DH, are you turned off by my tattoos? Some guy once told me that my tattoos make me look like a trailer broad"—she places a hand on my cheek— "but

I ain't that kinda woman, DH."

"I'm not sure I know what a trailer broad is."

"They have lots of noisy babies, lots of dirty dogs, and tattoos."

"I think your tatts are lovely," I tell her.

"I think my daddy would like you."

"Is your daddy a biker too?" I ask.

"He loves bikes. He owns five different Harley franchises here in Southern California."

This woman is full if surprises. "If you feel self conscious about your tattoos, have them removed. I bet your dad would give you the money for it."

"It ain't the money, it's the time. I've been so busy doing workin' for Daddy that I haven't had the time to do anything else," she says.

"Well, don't worry about it. I think your tatts look just fine." I smile at her. "You're a biker chick. You look the part. Leave your tatts alone, don't remove them!"

She pulls me over and kisses me on the cheek. "It would be real easy for me to fall for a biker boy like you."

That statement makes me squirm a little.

"I know," she smiles, "we've got to go back and help finish the sculpture of your Gigi. But can you tell me one thing?"

"What's that?"

"Can you see anything within me that has any redeeming quality?" Her expression is like a puppy waiting for approval.

"Are you serious?"

"Let me rephrase that." She looks away briefly, then asks with greater boldness, "Are you attracted to me in any way?"

"Yes ... very." That's all I could think to say.

Lonesome smiles at me, pulls her biker shirt off over my head and puts it back on, and says, "That works for now."

Back at the Sculpture Party

The place is buzzing with activity. Frank is, of course, running around barking out orders. I'm just watching the show for now, eating one of Bill H's hamburgers. Bill Mitchkelly sees me and is headed this way.

"You know, DH," he says quietly, "If I had listened to Frank during his bronze casting that day, it would have come out okay. He tried to tell me I had the formula wrong for the investment, but I wouldn't listen. Looking back on the whole thing, I now think he was right. I feel terrible about it. I'm going to have to apologize to him for that."

"You don't have to apologize to Frank for anything," I tell him. "He doesn't hold grudges like normal people. He lives in his own sphere of existence. Besides, Frank and you are getting along pretty good right now—don't mess it up."

"You're probably right."

"DH!" Frank is waving me over.

He's starting to apply the plaster that Jack must have worked up while I was in the swing with Lonesome.

"Where you been? Start wrapping some of that tape around the exposed parts of the armature so the plaster sticks to it. Work from the top down so I can follow you."

I do as Frank instructs, working fast because the plaster sets up very quickly. I'm not too worried about it, though. If we lose one batch, we have a whole lot more where that came from.

"Annie!" I call. "Help me with this please." She comes over and works twice as fast as me. I keep looking at Frank to see how he's progressing. He's working pretty fast, but he's also very busy being Frank, meaning he's making every inch of what he's doing as perfect as he can. Everyone else in the party is just standing around supervising. They can't really do much because there's only so much room around the armature.

Frank is putting on the first rough coat of plaster. I can already see what he's attempting to do. It's wonderful. If I'm not mistaken,

Frank is going to create a moment out of time: a perfect replica of Gigi in that simian stance of hers.

"We'll let this first coat set for about thirty minutes, then I'll work on the details." Frank looks at me, and grins. "You know what I'm doing don't you?"

I smile back. "I do. What a great idea. That was the real her."

"Anyone want a burger?" Bill Hunter calls out from the patio. I'd forgotten about him.

"No Bill!" I yell back. "But keep the flies off 'em, cause I bet we'll all want one after this sculpture is finished." He smiles his sweet smile and salutes me with his spatula.

Now we're all just milling around for a while, hemming and hawing, and looking up at the stars. I stand at the edge of the drop-off, and look out over the field, hoping to see some fireflies, but none appear. That's a shame. There's no moon, and fireflies would look lovely.

"Hey biker-dude." It's Lonesome.

"Hey." I'm genuinely pleased to see her.

"It's dark tonight." she says, taking my hand. I look around to see where Annie is.

"Don't worry, Honey. Annie's over with that professor cleaning up the table, and it's way too dark for anyone to see us clear over here."

"It's even too dark for me to see your face."

"Good, then you can't see my tatts."

"Lonesome."

"Just joking."

"How old are you, Lonesome?" I ask her point blank.

"Are you sure you want to know?"

"I am."

"I'm thirty-one."

Great. I knew she was older than me, but I didn't think she was out of her twenties.

"Does that scare you?" she asks.

I pause for just a moment, and I ask myself the same question:

does it scare me? And a little voice in my mind whispers, "Time does not exist."

"No, Lonesome," I tell her. "I'm not scared by that. You are exactly who you are and that's just fine."

Lonesome pulls me over and hugs me. She puts her face next to mine and rubs her cheek there for a little bit.

"I really think we should go back and finish the sculpture now, Lonesome."

"I know."

"But maybe after everyone's gone, you can hang around here for a while?"

"What about Annie?" she asks.

"Annie won't be here tonight. She mentioned earlier that she needed to leave before the party ends, but she didn't tell me why. You know, I don't really know much about her. I don't even know where she lives."

There is a flurry of renewed activity as Frank yells out, "The first coat is dry! Hey Bud, where the heck are you? Jack, you got the next batch of plaster ready?"

"I'm working on it," Jack yells back. "Almost done"

"We'd better go," I say.

"I reckon so."

Lonesome and I walk back to the party.

"Okay guys," Frank says, "this is going to take some time. Jack, make sure you mix up small batches of the plaster because it dries fast. Just keep feeding me those small portions as I work my way around this thing. DH, are you here?

"Right here."

"I want you to stand right next to me, and make sure I'm getting this right. I want it to be the exact image of Gigi. If I miss one subtle nuance, you tell me quick, so I can correct it immediately before this stuff sets up on me."

Frank is being the Frank that makes him the greatest artist I have ever known. It's all business now. He's making Ort; that's what he does. That's what his blood is made of—oil paint, and plaster, and clay, and bronze. I read a book not too long ago, about the lives of some of the Impressionist artists. Believe me, they had complicated lives, but Frank out-romances all of them. Those men and women were perhaps the greatest artists throughout all of history, but nearly every one of them got discouraged several times in their lives, and left their artwork.

Not so with Frank. Even if he gets discouraged, he is constantly working. He would never leave his work. Frank literally stands out from all the others, even the great masters. If I could compare him to anyone—and he wouldn't like this comparison—I would compare him to Picasso, simply because he is so incredibly prolific and focused on what he does, 24 hours a day, seven days a week.

"I've decided to put the final coat on from the bottom up," he says. Frank's hands are working like crazy and his concentration is intense. "I want to save that exquisite face for the last—"

"—especially the puffy nose." I finish the sentence with him. He looks at me, I look at him, then *The Laugh*.

Mitchkelly comes over and stands by me. "Look at that man work. He's an animal," he says into my ear.

"He's a master," I respond.

"I think you're right, DH. I think one day we are all going to remember these times, and be very glad we knew this man."

"I'm already glad," I say, looking at Mitchkelly fondly, "to have known all of you." He smiles back at me and nods his head.

Even Bill Hunter is intrigued. He's standing behind Frank's left shoulder, staring at him like a little kid.

He speaks hesitantly. "Frank? I don't want to bother you … so if you're bothered let me know … I was wondering …"

"I'm not bothered, Bill." Frank keeps on working. "I don't know how the heck you would be capable of bothering anybody." He smiles at Bill, briefly raising his eyes from his work.

Frank stops working and gives his full attention to Bill. "What is it?"

"It's a little poem I wrote the day Gigi died. I thought it would be a nice gesture in her memory to place it inside her sculpture."

Frank looks me, then back to Bill. "It'll have to be quick, but can I read it first?" Bill hands him the poem and steps back. Frank unfolds it and rushes over to the patio where there's enough light to read.

As he reads through it, I see his body kind of slump a little, then he turns to Jack. "Hold the plaster for a bit, Jack." And Frank walks into the breezeway.

"I'll be right back," I tell Lonesome. I cross the patio and enter the breezeway where I find Frank sitting on the couch. Even though it's dark, I can tell he's crying. He doesn't say a word as he hands me the poem Bill Hunter wrote. I take the poem into The Hole, and turn on the light so I can read it:

Little Child
Sweet little one with the face of
A baby
And the heart of an angel
I will miss you so much
Little precious White One
I will miss you
And
All will miss you
For you were so much a part of
Us
I cry tears for you now
But one day I hope to see you
Again
I love you
We all love you
Here is a kiss for
Your little nose

It isn't Shakespeare, but the simple little poem hits me like it did Frank. I bury my face in my hands and just sit there on the edge of my bed crying. Frank walks in.

"That Hunter …" he says. "It ain't the best poem I've ever read, but he's got the heart of a saint. When that guy dies, the world is gonna friggin' collapse."

"So what do you do with this?" I hand him the poem. "You've already got your first coat of plaster on. You can't put it inside now."

Frank sniffs. "Bud, I'll make a hole somewhere, even if I have to take a sledgehammer to it, but this poem is going in that sculpture." He grips my arm, pulls me up, and pushes me toward the door. "Find a hammer, Bud."

I find a hammer, and Frank and I walk back out to the party. It's obvious from their expressions that everyone is wondering what's going on.

Frank walks up to the sculpture, takes the hammer, and whacks a hole in the middle of the chest. "This is where it belongs, DH," he says, looking at me. "It belongs in her heart."

Karen's voice rises above the gasps of astonishment, "What is he doing?"

Hester stands up exclaiming, "This guy is crazy! He just did all that work on that thing and now he's breaking it apart."

Then Frank turns to face the group and speaks calmly. "Everybody, come over to the patio for a minute." And they all do. "I want you to hear something, then after I read this, I'm going to drop this little piece of paper into that hole I've made where Gigi's heart is." Tears were running down his face. "Then I'm going to seal it all back up and finish her sculpture. For those of you who knew Gigi, you'll understand what's going on here. For those of you who never knew her, I'm sorry for you."

With tears in his eyes, Frank reads Bill's poem aloud. It really isn't the best poem in the world, but it came from Bill's heart, and it reflects how we all feel about Gigi.

When Frank is finished reading, there isn't a dry eye anywhere.

Even those who never knew Gigi are crying. With that, Frank carefully folds up the poem and hands it to me.

"You might want to kiss this."

I do, then I hand it back to Frank. He takes it over and pushes it into the plaster hole where Gigi's heart is. I feel an arm wrap around me.

"You must have really loved this kid. I'm so sorry," Lonesome says gently.

I appreciate her being there, but I just can't talk right now so I just touch her arm and nod.

Frank has the hole sealed up in just a few minutes, and Jack has brought over a fresh tub of plaster. Without missing a beat, Frank is applying the final coat of plaster that will make it look just like Gigi.

Lonesome says, "I lost a boyfriend once. He was killed over seas."

I turned to her and said, "I'm sorry Lonesome."

"I grieved over him for months. Finally my daddy came up to me, took me by the shoulders, and told me it was time to move on." Then she looked at me and said earnestly, "I knew that what my daddy told me was true. It's time for you to move on too, DH. All of you. Gigi's gone Home." She smiled sadly.

I looked at Lonesome. How can a woman who looks so tough on the outside be so gentle on the inside?

Frank is now applying plaster to Gigi's legs. "DH, are you payin' attention?"

"I am, Frank." I position myself to look over his shoulder.

"What the heck did her calves look like? I can't remember."

"Can I give it a try?" I ask.

"Do 'em." Frank says quickly.

I remember Gigi's legs as if they were drawn indelibly in my mind. I can see them to this day. She wasn't too tall, but she had very long and slender legs that were smooth, without a bump or a blemish, and as white as white could be. Plaster is, indeed, the perfect medium for this sculpture.

I fill my hands with plaster, and begin to mold Gigi's right leg.

Then I move over to the left, and back and forth, until I get to where it looks just like her.

Frank is now looking over my shoulder. "Now I remember!" he laughs. "Maybe I ought to let you do the rest of this, Bud. You've touched her with your hands and I haven't. That's important."

I turn to look at Frank. I nod and smile, even though I feel a bit apprehensive. I know he can do a better job than I can. Jack adds his agreement, "DH! She was your girlfriend! You need to do this!"

"I'm not sure I can." My hands are shaking.

"You can Bud." Frank smiles. "You can." He kisses me on the back of my head and gives me a little shove toward the plaster.

So, ignoring my surrounding and focusing only on Gigi, I tell Jack to keep the plaster coming, dip my hand into the bucket, and get back to work.

An hour later I'm all the way up to Gigi's neck. I pause and look at Frank. He's been standing next to me the whole time, watching every move I made. I could tell he was judging what I was doing, and I could also tell he wanted to get back into this with every fiber of his being.

"Frank, I'd like you to do her face."

"You're doing a great job, DH! It's exquisite!"

"But you can do it better," I tell him. "I want this to be perfect. You know what Gigi looks like."

"I do." He looks at me like he's ready to tear up again. He reaches down and pulls me up, hugs me, then yells to Jack, "Keep those buckets coming!" He gets right down to work.

I know that something has just happened in this one little moment in time that has sealed my friendship with Frank even more strongly. No matter what may come, no matter where we each may go, Frank and I will always be close.

"More plaster!" Frank calls to Jack. "Not much, just a little!"

He's working on Gigi's face now, but I am looking at the way he's smoothed her body. It's amazing; Manzù couldn't have done a better job. It's slick as marble. He's doing something with plaster that just can't be done.

"My gosh," says Lonesome, speaking in hushed, almost reverent tones. "Look at that! It's beautiful."

I notice that no one is talking in a regular voice. Everyone is whispering, like we're all in church. I look up at the night sky, and I think, we are in church. We're in the largest cathedral on this planet, and I think that even the Art Gods must be watching us this night, smiling down upon the occasion. Gigi was their child too.

Lonesome watches, spellbound as Frank continues to work. "DH, this guy is a master. I don't have a clue what made Gigi tick, but I'm betting that plaster thing is exactly what she looked like. I can almost sense her being here."

I look at her and smile. "Maybe you're psychic too, Lonesome."

"More than you know, Biker Boy, but look at how cute Gigi was. She was adorable!

"Cute?" I whisper.

"Cute." We are standing in the shadows, but I can feel Lonesome's smile.

"She was incredibly cute! She looks like she was about fourteen."

"She was very youthful," I tell her.

"She reminds me of that Degas sculpture, 'The Little Dancer.'"

Her words give me a jolt. Here's another woman of apparently random acquaintance who knows art!

"You know Degas?"

"I love Degas. I love the Impressionists," she says. "My Daddy owns a few Monet's. They're just smaller ones, but I grew up looking at them. And," she adds, "he owns some Berthe Morisot stuff. Have you ever heard of her? She isn't very well known."

I'm panting like an excited puppy. "You've got to be kidding. I love Berthe Morisot!"

"No way! Daddy has lots of little drawings by her and … hmmm … I think five or six of her paintings."

I almost faint.

"You okay, DH?"

"I'm okay," I reply.

"You like Morisot?" she asks.

"I love her! I love the Impressionist period. I'm just amazed that your father collects art of that quality. It must have cost him a fortune!"

"Daddy has a fortune. Selling Harleys is good money, honey." She kisses me on the cheek, then adds, "If I tell daddy I've fallen in love with you, I bet he'd give you a Morisot drawing, or two."

I am stunned.

"Lonesome," I say as softly as I can, "you are an enigma wrapped up in a dilemma. Or is it the other way around?"

"Huh?"

"You have to be the most desirable woman in the world." I smile at her, even though I know she can't see it.

"Are you smiling when you say that?" she asks.

"I'm smiling. But I am astonished that you are who you are. That you know about art. That your biker dad collects art. I mean, this changes my whole perspective on life."

"Forget your perspective on life." She pulls me to her in the darkness. "I'd kiss you right if I thought I could get away with it, but I know one of these guys would see it, probably Annie, or Karen the, cowboy."

"Karen's been really quiet tonight."

"Yeah, she has something going on with Hester over there."

"That's okay," she says. "I can kick both their butts and throw 'em out of here if you want."

"Don't do that, Lonesome," I whisper. "I don't want to spoil the party. They'll leave on their own when the time is right." But her offer is tempting.

"Okay Babe, you want it, you got it. I'll be nice."

Then Frank calls out, "It's done, Bud! Where do you keep disappearing to?"

"I'm over here! Just staying out of your way, watching the magic."

I hurry over for a closer look.

"Whatta ya think, Bud?" Frank stands back from his work, putting his hands on his hips, kind of like Gigi used to do. "She's your squeeze? Did I do her justice?"

It really is her. He even got the puffy nose right.

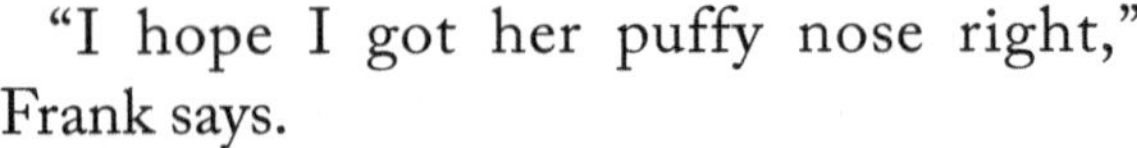

"I hope I got her puffy nose right," Frank says.

"It's perfect." I tell him. "It's perfect." I hug Frank and tell him, "If you were a woman, I'd kiss you right now."

"If you were a woman, you'd be the ugliest woman on earth!" *The Laugh*.

Everyone is gathered around the finished sculpture, talking quietly. From the edge of the group, I hear Karen say a little loudly and to no one in particular, "There's nothin' here for me." She heads toward the breezeway, and a few second later, Hester follows. A few more minutes and I hear a car engine start. The sound fades as the car heads down the driveway to the street. Lonesome hears it too.

"Dogs," she whispers in my ear. "It's not so much that they're jealous of you and me, and Annie, or whatever, I'm just really ticked that they didn't get into the mood of this moment. They didn't appreciate the art you and Frank have created here."

The sculpture is Gigi to perfection. Total perfection.

Bill Mitchkelly comes over, grasps Frank's hand and shakes it, saying, "Frank Reed, this is one of the finest things I've ever seen. I'm betting the college would buy it from you for the permanent collection."

Frank laughs and says, "Forget about it! This belongs to DH. He did half the work anyway." He turns his back to Mitchkelly. The friendship between those two is still, for some reason, an awkward one.

Then Bill Hunter steps up and says, "You boys need to grow up." Frank and Mitchkelly both look at him blankly.

Bill continues, "I've noticed for a long time that the two of you are at odds with each other, and it just isn't right. Life is too short for this kind of nonsense." He grabs the right hand of each of them, and forcefully brings them together.

"I feel like I'm in the third grade!" Frank wails in mock agony. "Hunter, you're that stinkin', short, black haired teacher creature, that used to make me clean the chalk boards all the time!" *The Laugh.*

Shaking Frank's hand, Mitchkelly says, "Frank, I really do think the world of you, and I'm not jealous in any way. You are the most amazing talent I think I've ever met."

"Well then … gee …" Frank shakes his head and hugs Mitchkelly. "All in a days work."

Frank may be on stage right now, doing what it is that he does, but he is sincere. Everything he says and does comes straight from his heart, just dressed up a little for the audience. I watch the show, knowing that this is the last time I will see Frank for maybe years.

Frank turns to me now. "Well Bud, there's your Gigi."

"Thank you my friend." I can hardly talk.

"So …" He looks at his watch and says, "Would you look at the time! It's late, I gotta get outta here. Hey Hunter, you got a burger I can take with me?"

"I'll make you a to-go box Frank," Bill answers.

Then Frank addresses the group, "Okay kids, I gotta go. I have to be at UCI mañana, but it's been one sweet birthday party, ain't nothin' ever gonna top this night!"

They all gather around to shake Frank's hand and give him hugs. I can tell by the long faces that nobody wants him to drive away tonight. We all know what that means.

He releases himself from his friends and starts to move away. "Guess I'll see you all soon."

Frank walks slowly to the breezeway. Opening the door, he looks back to me and says, "Hey Bud! See me outta here, okay?"

As I move to join him, I think that next to the death of Gigi, this is the most traumatic moment in my life. Annie, who has been strangely silent tonight, told me that this is the last time I'll see Frank, for who knows how long, so it is a kind of death thing really—the ceasing of an important chapter in our lives. Frank is making the long walk.

Where the heck is Annie, anyway?

When I get to the door Frank smiles at me, winks and says, "It ain't over Bud. Friendship is never over. Come on, see me out."

We go out to the driveway where Frank's bike is waiting. Frank stands next to it and places his hand on the seat. He has his back turned to me, and he's just standing there, motionless. Then he tells me, "This is as hard for me as it is for you, DH." His voice is shaky. "I have so many complications in my life right now, I'm not sure I can deal with them all."

I put my hand on his shoulder.

"You just don't know." Then he turns around and looks me straight in the face and says, "You've been like an anchor for me, DH. You've been the one place I could go to, and just disappear, where nobody knows me, and even my family has no idea where I'm at, or what I'm doing."

His eyes are wet and close to spilling over. I don't want him to be embarrassed, so I say, "Frank, you need to go out into the world and kick some serious art butt! Please just go and do it!"

Frank grabs me and he holds me almost tight enough to break my ribs. He releases me, puts on his helmet, gets on his bike, and starts it up. He heads down the drive to the street without looking back. He's gone.

I sit down on the ground where I was standing in the driveway. Behind me, the breezeway door opens and closes. I hear footsteps, then Lonesome sits down beside me. She puts her arm around my shoulder and hugs me close to her.

I quickly wipe my eyes. "You must think I'm a real wimp, tearing up all the time."

"No." She hugs me closer. "I think you're one of the best human beings on this planet, and I think I'm in love with you."

That doesn't help much. I've heard it before, and it never played out.

"Listen, Sweetie," Lonesome says, "this party is over. We need to get these people out of here, then you and I are going to go into that Hole of yours. We're going to lay on your bed, and I'm gonna just hold you all night long."

I look at her and say, "I'm a twenty year old kid. I guess emotions come with the package."

"I'll teach you how to fix that, Biker Boy." She smiles.

"You just might."

"No might about it."

We both stand up and turn to go back to the patio.

Have you seen Annie?" I ask her.

As if by magic, the breezeway door opens and Annie comes out.

"I thought you'd left the party already, without saying goodbye," I tell her.

"I wouldn't do that, Daddy. But I am leaving now."

"I'm afraid your ride already split without you."

"I know. I saw her leave."

"I can run you home, just let me get my keys."

"That won't be necessary, Daddy, I found another way." Annie smiled, looking up into the deep space of the night sky.

"We were just about to break up the party, Annie," Lonesome said. "I guess everybody will be leaving now."

"I'm glad you will be staying with my father, Lonesome. I believe he needs a friend tonight."

Lonesome looks surprised by her statement.

"How did you know I was going to stay here, Annie?"

Annie just smiled, then turned to me, and said, "Daddy, I am going to hug you, then it is time for me to go. Someday we will find each other again."

"That's an odd thing to say, Annie, what are you talkin' about?"

"I must return now. There is much to do. But I will always watch over you, Daddy."

Lonesome asks, "Annie, "there is something very special about you, isn't there?"

Annie smiles at her, "Yes there is, Lonesome."

I look at Lonesome as she looks at me, and when we turn back to look at Annie, she's gone. I mean completely gone. Vanished into nowhere …

For some reason I feel just a little dizzy …

Lonesome links her left arm through my right arm and pulls me to her, saying, "You've had a lot to drink, Biker Boy. I'm gonna drag you into The Hole, set you down on the bed, then I'm gonna very politely chase every one of your friends away."

"If you want to get the folks on their way that's fine, but I want to stay out here for a minute or two."

"I understand." She smiles, and walks back to the party.

The clouds have gone. I look up into the heavens and I wonder what's going to happen now. Will I ever see Frank again? What is my life going to be like from here forward? What degrees will I earn? What kind of job will I get? With the departure of Frank, I feel that more than just a chapter of my life has ended, it's like an entire book is over and I need to start another.

Something else is bothering me as well, even more than Frank's leaving. Something seems to be missing from my life, and I can't put my finger on it. It's like a precious jewel was once in my possession, then all of a sudden, it's no longer there. Like for a while, I was the richest man on Earth, and in a flash, everything was taken from me. Before today I was at least capable of feeling myself to be a whole person, but now I feel incomplete. Something is missing. What is this new emotion I'm experiencing? Where did it come from?

I look up at the stars. It is such a beautiful night. The air is crisp, and cleaner than I've seen it in years. Every single star is glittering at peak performance—I can gaze out for millions of light years in every direction. What is out there? What is really out there? I truly believe there must be billions of worlds in this universe, that are homes to billions of civilizations, and every time I look up there, I feel as if a gigantic outer space magnet was locked onto my body, and my spirit, as if to forcibly pull me off this planet, and transport me at speeds beyond the speed of light to … to where? I don't have any idea. But somehow I know that what is out there, is related to whatever it is that is incomplete within my very soul.

Lonesome is coming back out—that Scandinavian Goddess who appeared into my life from out of nowhere just as Annie disappeared into nowhere. To be honest, I'm not sure if Lonesome is real, or if she is some gentle, pink mist—a sweet bouquet of someone destined for my future.

"They'll all be leaving soon," she tells me. "But the strangest thing is going on back there."

"What's that?"

"There are fireflies everywhere!"

"Fireflies!"

I grab Lonesome's hand and we both run back through the breezeway and into the back yard. All of the gang is over by the edge of the drop off, speechless in wonder at the spectacle around them. There are thousands of fireflies floating around all over the place, weaving in and out of the crowd, lighting up in the trees. Annie?

"Can you believe this?" Jack exclaims with delight.

"Yes, I sure can."

We hear a loud rumble of thunder. Looking up into the sky, we see three gigantic shooting stars speeding through space directly over us from west to east.

Lonesome whispers to me, "What in the world can this all mean?"

"I'm not sure it has anything to do with this world, Lonesome."

Then out of nowhere I hear a young, innocent voice crying out one word, "Daddy."

"Did you hear that, Lonesome?"

"Hear what?"

"A little girl calling for her Daddy."

"There aren't any kids here, DH."

"I wouldn't bet on that."

"It's been a crazy night, DH. Maybe in the morning all this will make sense."

"I kind of doubt that, Lonesome. How do you make sense out of something that doesn't seem to even exist? I'm not sure of anything any more. I'm not even sure if you really exist … or if you're the vision of a woman I haven't met yet, that will one day mean everything to me."

Lonesome links her arm through mine. Drawing me closer, she speaks softly into my ear, "Come inside with me now, DH. If you're willing, I'm not afraid to explore the possibilities."

Notes About the Illustrations

The portrait on the cover is an original oil on canvas painted by the author, DH Parsons. The line drawings found throughout the text were also done by him.

The images found on pages 78, 153, and 228 are modified from photographs taken circa 1968. The photo on page 78 is DH working as described on that page.

Original oil paintings by DH were used to derive the images found on pages 63, 73, and 165. Richard Burton, as the Reverend T. Lawrence Shannon, in *The Night of the Iguana* is on page 63. DH's good friend, "Jack," is on page 83, and the portrait on page 182 is the poet, Christina Rossetti.

The illustration on page 311 was originally produced using classic stone lithography.

The small, lumpy bronze figures described on page 102 are pictured in the photograph on that page.

The paisley tie at the bottom of page 65 is the actual paisley tie described in the text. A scanner was used to produce an image, then the image was manipulated using Adobe®Photoshop® and Illustrator®. The tie itself continues to hang in the artist's closet.

The photograph on page 423 was taken and annotated by DH's father, Wayne, around 1963, shortly after the purchase of the house. The porch where the swing will be in 1968 can be clearly seen, as can the garage which will come to house The Hole and DH's studio, and the breezeway door leading to the backyard and patio.

Editing, cover design, and interior design were done by
Susan Bingaman, Bliss-Parsons Institute.

Please visit
www.dhparsons.com
to see more from DH Parsons.